AF269988

OUR TRAGIC LEGACY

Disclaimer:

The purpose of this novel is to expose the abuse that happens in elite sports. Therefore, this book is very heavy and contains graphic depictions of suicide, child abuse, drug abuse and rape. Please read with discretion.

AUTHOR'S NOTE

While this book is based on real things that happen in sports, some aspects are not true, such as the Sine Luni. It is in the novel for plot reasons and dramatic effect. Please keep in mind that while this content is based off of real research, it is still a work of fiction.

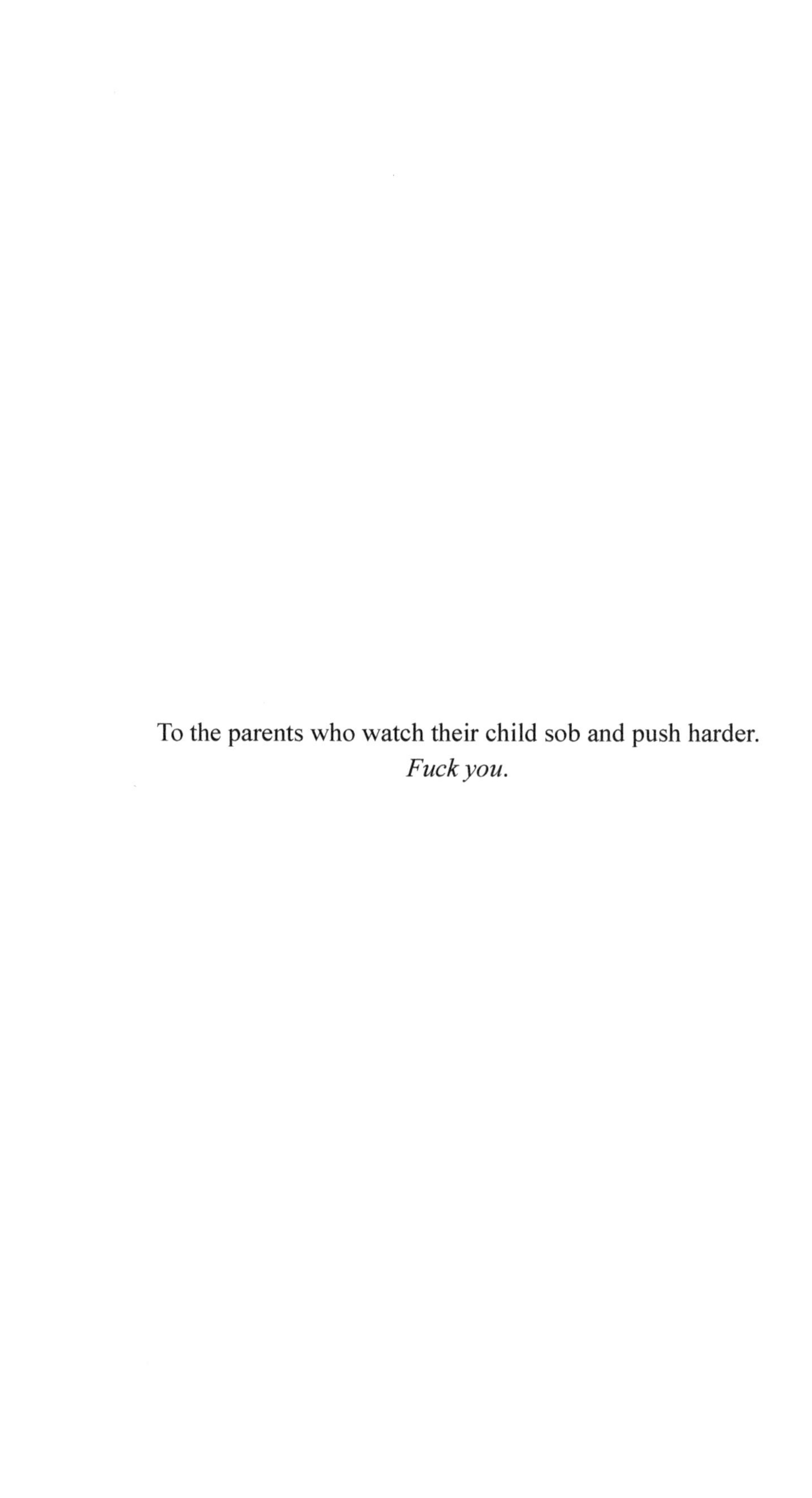

To the parents who watch their child sob and push harder.

Fuck you.

THE KID

"Better to be a winner than a loser. Better to look good rather than not."
—Yesalis, Charles. Phone interview. February 26, 2025.

"Val?" Zahara knocked. "Are you in there?"

She brushed her hood back, staring intently at the wood. The thought crossed her mind that the dealer was indeed absent. But then the door creaked open. Zahara stepped back, gazing at Val— her hollow face beaming with a practiced, stupid grin.

Val placed her hands on her hips. "Look who decided to pay a visit. Ran out already?"

Zahara didn't wait for the response. She flung herself into Val's chest, pressing her face into the dealer's blouse. Val's sweet floral perfume surrounded her in its deep embrace. And soon, she wrapped her own hands around Zahara.

"If you're trying to get a discount—" Val mused. "This isn't the way to do it."

"Shut up, Val." Zahara gleamed. "My mother doesn't care what I spend. As long as I perform well, she couldn't give a shit."

"Such a wonderful woman—" Val spat, choking on her own sarcasm. "Overglorified raisin, that one."

Zahara laughed— really laughed. From her stomach this time. A motion that hurt too much to do a week ago. It still hurt, but now she had an inkling of joy— of *hope*. That small part made the pain negligible.

Val frowned. She cupped Zahara's face, pinching her cheek. "You—" she tilted her head; as if assessing a specimen. "You're different: something happened."

Zahara shrugged, but a hint of blush touched her face.

"Come!" Val led her to her desk. "Sit! Tell me *everything*!"

"Well…" Zahara folded her hands in her lap. "I— I met someone."

Val wrinkled her nose. "Oh, darling. Boys are way below you—"

"No, Val," Zahara chuckled. "It's not a romantic partner. I met a kid."

Val's disgusted face remained. "The snotty things? Zahara please, you're much too talented for baby sitting."

"I'm not baby-sitting her." Zahara said. "And— well… maybe she's not a kid. She's thirteen. And—" she took a breath. "And she wants to be like me."

Val's eyebrows hit the ceiling. "What?"

Zahara smiled. "Yeah."

"Why would anyone want to be like you?" Val snapped. Zahara made a face. "Not like that, love. But with all due respect— you're not exactly… happy."

Zahara sighed, touching the opium rashes on her neck. "I know." She swallowed. "But, her— Leah. I can help her: make sure she doesn't fall into the same hole as me. Or maybe—" she heaved a breath. "Maybe when she falls into the hole— I can lessen the drop."

Val brushed her graying hair behind her back. She leaned forward, placing her hand on Zahara's. The dealer always had such extravagant nails— this time around, they were purple— poppies dancing along the paint.

"I'm sorry I'm poisoning you, Zahara." Val murmured. With the same breath, she pulled the drug from her drawer, the black mush creeping along the glass.

Zahara ran her finger along the opium, the darkness seeming to swallow her whole. "You didn't poison me." She whispered. "The world did. You simply gave me something to help."

She reached into her pocket, grabbing a wad of money. Val took it, not bothering to count the cash. Zahara stuffed the opium into her bag, standing.

"Zahara—" Val called. "This kid…"

Zahara tilted her head. "What about her?"

"I'll take care of her." Val said. "When you're gone. I'll make sure she has what she needs."

Zahara didn't say anything— she didn't need to. Val would take care of Leah just as she took care of her. And when her protégé eventually stumbled into the dealer's den, Val would give her the necessary crutch.

IT'S JUST A GAME

THREE DAYS EARLIER

"Ball!" Leah shouted, clapping. She knew she wasn't getting it. No one on this damned team liked to pass to her. But if she wouldn't get the basketball, at least she could make a ruckus trying. "*Ball*!"

The point guard's eyes flitted to her. Leah's defender was positioned under the basket, eyes filled with panic as she tried to find Leah.

The point guard, perhaps tired of Leah's babbering, flung the ball in the opposite direction. Leah's teammate caught it, squared her shoulders and geared up for a shot.

Leah scoffed.

So she gets to shoot.

The ball rolled off the girl's fingers, the gentle flick of her wrist sending the thing into the air. But the arc was flawed— too flat, shifted too far to the right. The ball bounced off the rim, ascending into the air.

Leah took her chance, racing to the key. Her defender— who had actually managed to locate her— stumbled behind.

Her fingers curled around the basketball's bumped texture. As she looked around, she realized she was fucked. For a five-foot-two seventh grader with the muscle mass of a pigeon— under the hoop was no sanctuary.

As if to confirm her terror, a rush of strong, taller girls came at her. Leah ducked, attempting to dribble to safety. By no means could she handle the ball — the thing bounced erratically, occasionally climbing to her shoulders. But by some miracle, Leah managed to weave between the defense and make it to the three point line.

She stopped, panting. When she looked down, she was shocked to find the ball was still in her possession. She locked eyes with the rim. This was her chance to shoot.

Three things happened at once. First, the coach's tempered screech echoed across the court. Leah couldn't quite catch what he said. She never could.

The next scream came from the point guard. She was clapping, shrieking for the ball like an early morning bird. Her eyes narrowed in rage; there might have been a play that they were supposed to run. Leah couldn't remember. She barely paid attention to that stuff.

And third, her defender, who had finally found her again, was tripping over her own feet in Leah's general direction.

In response to the events, Leah made three decisions. One— she made no effort to decipher her coach's call. Two— she refused to give up the possession to the fiery point guard. And three— she flung the ball into the air, letting the thing soar towards the rim.

It was a bad shot. Her follow through twisted to the right and her elbow stuck out like a chicken wing. The ball was crooked and flat— following a flawed arc that bounded off the rim and right into the defense's hand.

Leah drew a sigh, slouching into a pout. As the opposing point guard raced down the court, she started into her jog. Well, at least she took her shot. She wasn't going to get passed to anyway, so she might as well take her chance.

As she crossed half court, Leah's eye caught a girl waiting by the scoring table. A replacement. Undoubtedly for her. She was lucky the coach even put her in the game. Now, she had fucked up and her playing privileges had been revoked.

An ear splitting screech broke the air. Leah's head whipped around to find the ball had rolled out of bounds. The ref called for the substitutes to enter and Leah's name was called.

She scowled, locking eyes with Fiona, her teammate. Their hands brushed each other's in a half hearted high five.

"Who?" Fiona asked.

"Twenty three," Leah responded, pointing to her defender.

She sulked off the court, clapping hands with her teammates as she moved to the far end of the bench. Just as she reached for her water, a call rang behind her.

She turned to find Coach Ezra. He locked eyes with her, raised an eyebrow, and patted the seat next to him.

There was only one way to describe Ezra Soren— a college frat boy. From his erratic blonde hair to his black hoodie: the way his eyes always held that familiar focus. Much younger than any coach Leah had seen. Much younger than most men.

"Leah," he pulled out his clipboard and a marker. "Draw Scissors."

Ah, yes. 'Scissors;' the play Ezra had been obsessing over since he first learned about it. About every practice Ezra had them rehearsing it. And about every practice, the play went in one ear and out the other.

So, knowing full well she was only going to embarrass herself if she attempted to draw the arrangement, Leah planted the marker on the whiteboard and sketched the cutting material.

Ezra raised an eyebrow. "You don't know it."

Leah snorted. "No, I don't."

The screech of the whistle interrupted their conversation. Ezra's gaze flung up— eyeing the ref.

"Dammit," Ezra growled. "She fowled *again*?" he tugged his hood over his head. "Mikey— go for Franny. Move Fiona to point." Ezra stood, muttering under his breath. "I'm going to pop a blood vessel."

He moved, leaving Leah with the clipboard. She gently set it on Ezra's chair and moved down the bench, planting herself beside her best friend.

"What a load of bullshit," Leah muttered. "Do you think they ever pass?"

"Maybe," Serena smirked. "But not to you."

"Kind."

Serena shrugged. "It's the simple truth. If you want the ball, you're going to have to get it through a rebound or steal."

"Yes," Leah nodded. "And if I happen to do that, I better hang onto it." She crossed her arms. "It's not like I'll get it back."

"Oh?" Serena tilted her head. "Is that why you took that god awful shot?"

Leah scowled. "Just because it didn't go in, doesn't mean it was awful."

"Oh Leah, trust me," Serena grinned. "It was *awful*. You looked like a fish. Honestly, it's a miracle the thing went within ten feet of the hoop."

Leah scoffed. "It was a rushed shot," she admitted. "If they passed to me more, maybe I would get a better opportunity to show off my shooting."

A loud buzzer filled the gym. Leah shot up: she hadn't realized the game was so close to the end. Like clockwork, the teams filtered off the court, replaced with older, taller girls.

"Hey!" a rasp— so sharp it could've cut paper. "Come on! We're doing shooting lines!"

Leah paused, taking a moment to find the source of the voice. Her eyes landed on a woman— long hair tied into a bubble braid; dark skin littered with rashes and intense heterochromic eyes.

She strode through the court like she owned it— the ball in her hands following every command. Her posture was so perfect; every little twist of her features practiced. She was—

"Leah?" Serena tapped her shoulder. "We're giving the other team high fives. You coming?"

Leah wrinkled her nose. Indeed they were. An after game tradition Leah didn't much care for. She found congratulations forced and unnecessary— besides, who would notice if she missed one line up?

A smile cracked her lips. "I think I'll skip this one."

Before Serena could respond, Leah took off. She ran around the court, settling on the bleachers. By then, the woman was arguing with another girl. Her lips moved so fast— such a dangerous urgency. Her efficiency was intriguing.

The buzzer rang a second time. The argument halted— the subject was quickly dropped as both women ran to the bench. The entire team crouched down, leaning next to a young, blonde man.

Wait— Blonde? Young? Leah knew that guy.

The team must've been Ezra's varsity squad: that which he constantly compared Leah's team to. Supposedly they were really good— good enough to run his plays without much direction.

Leah stood, slinging her bag around her shoulder. Her shoes squeaked as she sprinted along the sidelines. By the time she'd reached the bench, the team was already standing on the court. Ezra sat on the bench, hands folded over his lip— the designated thinking position.

Leah's hand landed on his shoulder. "Hey—"

Ezra spun around— startled. "*Holy shit*!"

The man nearly exclaimed it. Luckily nobody seemed to pay mind to his unexpected shriek. Although the woman turned, raising an eyebrow.

The terror in Ezra's eyes died— replaced with a grim dissatisfaction. "It's you."

Leah matched his gaze— a hard feat considering she was a good bit shorter than him. "I don't believe I warranted such a considerable response."

Ezra slinked back into his chair. "You left before high fives. I didn't know where you were. I'm responsible for you, you know."

Leah tiled her head. "Why does that matter?"

“Well,” Ezra rolled his eyes. “If you die I’m assuming I’ll get sued.”

“Oh,” Leah nearly laughed. She moved to sit beside Ezra: ignoring the suspicious look from the coach. “Don’t worry. No one would care if I disappeared. Who’s the girl with heterochromia?”

Ezra raised an eyebrow. “I wasn’t aware you were allowed to sit here.”

“Well I’m glad I could clear that up for you. No one owns the bench.” Leah pointed to the woman. “Who’s she?”

Ezra sighed— Leah could’ve imagined it, but he might’ve held a tint of a laugh in his tone. “Zahara Williamson.”

Zahara. *Zahara*— she recognized the name. She’d heard it before, but she couldn’t place it. Zahara, Zahara, Zahara…

“She’s a pretty frequent picture in the papers. Gives the reporters something to talk about.” Ezra said. Leah gave him a look. “If you’re wondering where you’ve seen her.”

Leah was barely listening anymore. Instead, she watched Zahara. She had the ball at the moment; dribbling with such power. A defender raced up to her, but she cleared the opposition with a simple crossover.

The ball was swung to a girl in the corner. For a split second, a shot was open. She pump faked, sending her own defender into the air and then—

And then she passed it: Leah thought it was a mistake. But then someone caught it. Down at the hoop Zahara laid the ball into the basket. How did she get down there?

Ezra stood, clapping. “Good assist Jen, nice shot Zahara. Maybe stick to the play next time but a point’s a point.”

Zahara met his gaze, saluting him. Ezra rolled his eyes, returning to his place on the bench. But Leah kept her gaze on Zahara— staring. Her fine lines and perfectly crooked features— so amazing in her imperfections.

Zahara met Leah’s stare. So intense— an unbreakable gaze of green and brown. And Leah could’ve been mistaken, but she thought Zahara winked at her.

~~~

Zahara Williamson was the furthest thing from pretty.

Her hair was messy, spiking around her poorly maintained ponytail. Her shoulders were too broad, defined muscles running from her arms to her long, sharp fingers. A blueish, tired tint embroidered her dark skin. The color hung on her sharp cheekbones that shifted just slightly to the right when she spoke.
~~~

Her heterochromic eyes were too small— their sharpness piercing into people with a green and brown stare. The skin hanging on her defined angles was littered with red blotches. They weren't scratches— rather a rash. Leah wanted to ask about them, but something told her not to mention it.

No boys chased Zahara.

There was no doll that even remotely resembled her.

And yet— Leah couldn't look away.

Zahara, in her very essence, was a magnet to eyes. If she strode across a room, the attention of the crowd would be on her within seconds. People copied the brisk of her stride, the cut of her rasp and the end of her shot. They wanted her skill, her knowledge. They wanted her favor with power.

"How did you do that?" Leah snapped, poking out behind a locker.

Zahara jumped back, covering her body with her jersey. "Who the fuck are you?"

Leah had unfortunately only managed to break into the locker room when Zahara was in the middle of changing. She'd caught the athlete in her bra and underwear— and the jersey did nothing to hide her defined abs.

"How did you go from the three point line to the key in like— no time at all?" Leah asked. "How do you swish threes from the volleyball line? How do you—"

"What—" Zahara's jaw was on the floor. "How—" she closed it, taking a breath. "Kid, who are you?"

"That doesn't matter." Leah said. "Answer my questions."

"Answer mine."

"Fine," Leah wrinkled her nose. "Leah. How did you get so good?"

"Leah who?"

"Taven. Answer my fucking question."

An echo of amusement came from Zahara's teammates. The hum was followed by a series of patronizing statements.

"Zahara's got a fan!"

"The kid can swear!"

"*Can it*!" Zahara's rasp ripped through the air. She leaned down, patting Leah on the head— a motion that was ever so condescending.

"Gotta try a bit harder than that kid," She said, pulling on jeans and a t-shirt. "Better luck next time."

Zahara strode past her— a sickly sweet scent following her wake. Leah made a face. Fine. If breaking into a locker room wasn't enough, Leah would try something more *extravagant.*

Leah scurried to the heap of team bags, shoveling through shoes and water bottles to find Zahara's backpack. She'd seen it strapped around Zahara's shoulder when she left the game. The athlete was deep in conversation with her teammate— the same one as before. They were arguing again: as if stopping would kill them both. Leah grinned. Zahara was so invested in her retorts she wouldn't notice that her car keys were missing.

"What are you doing?"

The voice made her jump. She whipped around to find Serena staring at her.

Leah grinned, continuing to rummage through Zahara's things. Her bag contained objects with a very… *interesting* feel. At one point, Leah figured she stumbled upon a bag of small seeds. An interesting choice for a mid-game snack.

"Can you tell your parents I won't be needing a ride home?" Leah asked, now elbow deep in Zahara's backpack.

Serena made no acknowledgement of the request. "Leah, what are you up to?"

Leah's hand locked around a piece of jagged metal. She pulled it out, revealing several silver keys. Among them was an oval of plastic with a gray 'H' implanted on it. Leah grinned. *Bingo*. "I'm about to commit grand theft auto."

"Leah," Serena clutched the bridge of her nose. "You're thirteen, you can't drive."

"I don't need to." Leah stuffed the keys in her sweater pocket. "Zahara's going to drive me."

"She can't very well do that if you steal her car."

"I'm not—" Leah sighed. "Just trust me, okay? I'll see you at school tomorrow."

"Hopefully," Serena extended a hand. "If you're not in county jail."

"Now," Leah met her palm with hers. They intertwined their fingers, commencing their practiced handshake. "You know no prison can hold me."

They met each other's gaze. Leah grinned. Serena frowned. And Leah took off, darting for the door.

She had no idea what Zahara's car looked like, but she knew it was a Honda. She also knew that if she pressed the lock button on the plastic stick in her hand, the vehicle would beep.

So, after a few minutes of wandering around the parking lot, locking and unlocking a random car, Leah located Zahara's Honda. She was surprised it took her so long; the thing stuck out like a sore thumb. Dents and ridges plagued the car's blue exterior and the guts of the front stuck out like intestines. It was arguably the most beat up thing Leah had ever seen.

For a moment, she questioned if she really wanted to drive home in the thing.

Then she was reminded of the way her teammates flocked to Zahara's call, clinging onto her every word like a goddamn lifeline, and she opened the door.

The inside of the vehicle smelled strangely of smoke. But it wasn't marijuana— Leah knew that smell all too well— it was sweeter. But sick sweet, not like candy, but medicine. Leah hacked a cough.

Ignoring the fume, she snuck into the back of the car, rolling under the backseats. She tucked her backpack at her feet and pulled her phone from her pocket. She had a little time— might as well see how Serena's doing.

As expected, Serena's name glowed on the screen. Leah grinned, tapping on the notification.

So, you on the road yet?

I'm not driving the fucker. I'm waiting for Zahara.

Well, wait no longer, she's heading out the door right now.

Leah let out a gasp. Her head bolted up, banging on the seat. She rubbed the bruise, moving to make another attempt at sitting up. She peered out the window— and sure enough— Zahara was headed for her car. Leah ducked, reaching for the keys.

Before she knew it, Zahara was at the door. A rustling told her that she was rummaging for her keys. A zipper opened— she was checking her backpack.

Leah reached for the windowsill. She opened the window just enough to catch Zahara's attention. Sure enough, her head flew up, a flicker of surprise crossing her features.

"Looking for these?" Leah asked, holding up the keys.

Zahara scoffed. “You little shit.” Despite her words, a shimmer of amaze wandered over her face. “You broke into my car?”

Leah shrugged. “You said to try harder.”

“I didn’t mean *that.*”

“Well, in my defense, you were rather vague.”

Zahara huffed a chuckle. “Fine, I’ll drive you home. But first, answer a question.”

Leah crossed her arms. “What?”

“Why do you want my company?”

Leah had the reply before Zahara finished her sentence. “Because I want to get better.”

“No you don’t,” Zahara waved her hand. “Try again.”

“That’s the truth!”

“No it isn’t,” Zahara shrugged. “No one *wants* to get better. Getting better is just part of a piece. Of a goal. So, Leah Taven, what is your goal?”

This time, Leah didn’t have a response. Yes, she did want *something*. Something that Zahara had. But what exactly did she possess that Leah wanted so bad?

“No one really pays attention to me.” Leah crossed her arms, tucking her knees to her chest. “But they pay attention to you. They listen when you speak. They *admire* you. Your achievements are worshiped, but I– I don’t really have any achievements. I guess–” Leah looked at the floor. “I want someone to be proud of me.”

This time, Zahara didn’t reply. When Leah met her heterochromic eyes, nothing but silent acknowledgement lingered in her gaze. There was no pity on her features: no hint of sympathy. Leah was glad to have the absence of it. Instead, Zahara looked like she understood, like somewhere along the line, she had felt the same thing.

“Well Leah,” Zahara said. “I can’t promise people will be proud of you. If anything, they’ll aim to take you down— to end you. But I can swear that they’ll know your name. No matter how they see you, they *will* see you. A hero or a villain, a martyr or a demon, Leah Taven, you will be known.”

~~~

The drive home took about thirty minutes. With that knowledge, Leah figured she had thirty minutes to interrogate Zahara.

As soon as the car departed from the parking lot, Leah realized she had about a third of her estimated time.
~~~

The woman drove like a maniac, speeding onto the slow streets of the suburbs. Leah was thrust against the window as Zahara turned out of the parking lot, the car whiring to a steady sixty miles per hour.

"So," Zahara slapped her hand against the steering wheel. "You obviously have some questions. So what is it? Spit it out."

Leah would have spoke, but the mix of terror and ungodly speed had suctioned her to her seat. It was like she was on a roller coaster— except this thrilling experience had no safety checks.

But nonetheless, Zahara was her ride home. It wasn't Leah's place to criticize her driving, no matter how scared she was.

"Well—" Leah flung forward as Zahara hit the brakes, a wide-eyed pedestrian inches away from her bumper. "How do I get people to follow me like they follow you? How do I get—"

"Noticed?" Zahara finished. The car accelerated from sixty to ninety miles per hour as it sped onto the highway, narrowly avoiding a truck as it merged. "You achieve the unachievable. You make it impossible not to look at you. Break their imagined boundaries— shatter their perception of what players can and can't do. That's how you get people to notice you."

"Right," Leah grasped the door handle as Zahara weaved around the traffic. "And how do you do that?"

Zahara gave a low chuckle. "You give everything."

Leah expected to her continue, but instead, Zahara remained silent, the hum of the car remaining between them.

"What?" Leah finally said. "What do you mean?"

"I mean you give *everything*." Zahara's gaze was trained on the road, not daring to meet Leah's eyes. "Your body, mind, sanity— fuck, every gift you think is granted. It takes your *life*, Leah. A name in the future takes a life in the past."

Leah considered this. Her life? Body, mind, sanity? She ran the words through her head, searching to find aspects that matched. Her mind was nothing special— average grades, no outstanding accomplishments. She wouldn't mind losing it. Body? One of a scrawny child. Building muscle was hardly losing it. And sanity?

What even was sanity? Better yet, what was insanity? There was no definition, no line between the crazed and the normal. What if "crazy" was just a way to describe those who were different?

“I don’t care.” Leah’s voice was low, barely audible compared to the hum of the car. “I don’t care what it takes. As long as I’m worth something, I couldn’t care less what I have to do.”

For a moment, Zahara kept the car’s silence. Her driving seemed to slow— or at least she wasn’t actively trying to cut someone off. She laid a hand on Leah’s leg. “That’s what makes us so dangerous, kid.” She said, her rasp cracking around the edges. “Most people have bounds— limits that they aren’t willing to cross. Us? We don’t have that. We will do anything— and I mean *anything*— to achieve our goals.”

FATHER DEAREST

"Neglect is the most common form of child maltreatment outside of sport and yet is understudied in the context of sport."
— Kerr, Gretchen, "Neglect in Children's Sport."

As expected, Zahara's arrival to Leah's house was not done with grace.

She sped through the neighborhood at a pace triple the speed limit. Leah had been clutching the handle so tight her fingers lost circulation. As Zahara sped past her house, Leah murmured a quiet "here" and the brakes were slammed. The car screeched, skidding on the pavement before sliding to an unsteady stop. Leah was thrown against the dashboard, half expecting an airbag to collide with her face.

"Well?" Zahara said, tapping her long fingers on the steering wheel. Of course she was unaffected by the sudden halt. "This is your stop, isn't it kid? Why not get out of my hair?"

Leah was more than happy to oblige. She scrambled from the seat, grabbing her bag. As soon as she stepped foot on the pavement, it felt as though the world had finally found peace. Leah's stomach, however, was not as lucky and still seemed to be stuck in Zahara's car.

"Where are you going?" Leah asked. It didn't seem right to end the car ride without another question. "In a hurry?"

Zahara scoffed. "I'm always in a hurry."

Leah tilted her head. "Why?"

"You love that word, don't you?" Zahara sighed. "I already told you. This game takes everything from you. I'm willing to give everything."

With that, she slammed the door and drove off, car screeching against the pavement. Leah turned to her house, shrugging. Maybe insane did have a definition. Maybe that definition was Zahara. After all, how much could the game really take from you? When push came to shove, it really was just a game.

Leah flung her bag over her shoulder and treaded through her yard. It was messy and overgrown. Weeds brushed at her knees, hiding the dry, crunchy earth. Massive plants towered over her, bushes so tall they could be mistaken as trees. Her dad loved the tall plants, apparently they kept the neighbors from being nosy. Leah despised them.

No one had really managed the garden in years. It was her mom's thing—she was always out in the wild, reminiscing over her plants. Without her supervision, the things spiraled out of control. Leah, to her great credit, attempted to tame the mess of a garden. Within about an hour of that idea she gave up. The weather was hot and the weeds were ungodly stubborn, refusing to come out no matter how hard she pulled them. Plus, the garden brought too many memories. As soon as she got inside the house, Leah had washed her hands, dirt falling down the drain along with her grief.

Since then, the garden remained a jungle. No one mentioned it. No one made a point to look at it. It was the unspoken contract between her and her dad. One of the few things they agreed on. Don't mention Mom.

Leah stepped into her house, padding against the creaky floor. As soon as she closed the door, the smell of fresh smoke drifted into her nose. Not the welcoming kind, like a barbecue or crackling fire, but a tainted scent.

"Leah?" her dad rasped. "That you?"

"Yes," Leah murmured, her voice low. She slipped off her sandals, making a break for the stairs.

"Be a dear and get me another pack, will you?"

Leah's lip curled. She dug her fingernails into her palm, keeping her voice tranquil and deliberate. "I'm not going to the store, Dad. Do it yourself."

"There's a pack in the cabinets." He hummed. "Fetch it for me, Leah."

Leah flung back her head. Dropping her bag, she headed for the kitchen. She retrieved the cigarettes, opened the tray, and spit on every one of them. Not a large glob, but just enough to sink into the marijuana and make the drug hard to light. Besides, the fact that her dad was smoking her saliva did bring some satisfaction.

She closed the pack, padding to her father's room. As she approached the smell of smoke grew thicker. She pulled her uniform over her nose, continuing her stride.

Gael Taven wasn't old, but *god*, did he look it. His was a thin man, yellow skin matching his yellow hair, yellow teeth, yellow nails—

Scratch that.

Gael Taven was a man of yellow. Not the bright, sunny kind, but the disgusting kind. The kind that comes up with a wad of phlegm. The kind of yellow you see on the sidewalk. Vomit. Spit. Grease. That was Gael Taven. A shell of a man. A servant of the color *yellow*.

"Thank you," he snatched the pack, pulling out a stick of weed. "You can go now."

Leah turned. She didn't like seeing her dad like this. She didn't like seeing him at all. Rotting in his bed, too grief stricken to go a moment without a cigarette. He was pathetic. Drugs had destroyed him. Addiction had taken him hostage. She had witnessed the full power of narcotics— the sweet poison, delicious manipulation of the substance. And each and every time her father smoked, Leah promised not to fall into the same trap.

She was about to flee, to head to her room. But in the doorway, she stopped. She didn't know why— maybe the remnants of the relationship her and her dad once shared. Maybe, after all these years, she still wanted to be noticed by him.

"You know who I met today?" she asked, not daring to look back.

Gael hummed, his tone bored. He didn't bother to answer, but Leah knew damn well he heard her.

"Zahara Williamson." Leah said. She didn't elaborate. The woman had been in the news so many times he was bound to have known her name.

"Zahara?" the words dripped from his mouth like sweet syrup. "The prodigy? The division one?" Gael hummed a chuckle. "Off to Stanford in the fall. That's what the papers say, anyway."

"Yes." Leah nodded. "That's her. She believes that I can be like her. She thinks I have what it takes."

Well that wasn't exactly what she said. Zahara told her the price— what she had to give, and Leah agreed. She agreed to give everything, even though Zahara seemed a bit hyperbolic.

Gael, through his weed stricken high, found this remarkably hilarious.

"Oh Leah," his chuckle dripped from his mouth, curling around the smoke like a snake. "You? Really? Zahara Williamson, the basketball prodigy, the girl who ruled the high school league at fourteen, thinks *you* can be the next D1?"

Leah raised her hand to the doorframe, digging her nails into the wood. "Yes," she swallowed. "She does."

"Leah," Gael's tone was thick, a sludge of sweet, venomous poison. "Let's be realistic here. Zahara is a prodigy, a *legend.* And you? Well, you're simply a girl. A child with nothing but a yearn. A spark of ambition that will be put out next week. You're no Zahara Williamson. You're a little kid, Leah."

She didn't bother responding. There was no point. Gael would only laugh— always laugh.

Leah managed to turn before the tears crossed her waterline. Fresh smoke followed from the room, strangling her with its gray touch. A few drops managed to drop to the floor, splattering on the wood. Leah wiped them on her sleeve, swallowing her pain.

~~~

That evening was an evening of promises.

Leah didn't take off her jersey or undo her braids. Instead she pulled on her basketball shoes and ankle brace, and looked in the mirror.

"I am going to be great." She whispered. "I will be Zahara."

Maybe it wouldn't be this jersey. Maybe it wouldn't be these shoes or these braces. But by god, it would be *her*. The tips of her braids— the ones that only ran down to her shoulders, would see her glory. Her body, her mind, her hair would be worshiped. Every part of her would see the day when she became Zahara.

When she proved her dad *wrong*.

She slept without a blanket that night. She had seen people in movies sleep without them and they were always able to get up early. The blanket made the bed comfortable, therefore making it hard to get out of it. Leah figured that if she did without it she'd be able to get up without a struggle.

The night was cold. Her bare skin felt unprotected without the cover. She didn't sleep well, but she slept. That's all she needed. A bit of rest. That would keep her going.

And when her alarm rang at five in the morning, Leah was more than happy to jump out of bed. She pulled on shorts and a t-shirt, not bothering with a sweater. If she wore one, she would be warm. If she didn't, she would be cold. The cold meant she had to move. Leah took every precaution, sacrificed every ounce of comfort. She made sure the call of the bed wasn't a threat.

The crisp night air bit her nose as she padded into the dark. Bumps formed on her arms— the cold making her shiver. It was dark and frigid. She yearned for the warmth of the inside.

But her father's voice lingered in her head. Just a kid. She was *just a kid*. That wasn't acceptable. She would not live her life as a nobody. She would not blend in.
~~~

Leah broke into a run; her bag draped over her shoulder and basketball pressed against her hip. It was an awkward jog— the backpack bouncing on her back and ball slipping from her grasp. Annoying as hell, sure. But she supposed the extra weight made her stronger. Better. *Closer.*

She sprinted through the park, rounding a corner and spotting the community court. It wasn't much. Cracked pavement, crooked rim and a net hanging by a single strand.

But she wasn't the only one there. Outlined by the moonlight was a slim silhouette. She was close to the basket, shooting a ball with only her right hand. Her hair was slicked back in a high ponytail, the strands falling down her back.

"Zahara?" Leah asked, stepping onto the court.

Zahara took out her earbud, smiling a slick, ambitious grin. "Well," she placed a hand on her hip. "Look who made it. Care to join me?"

Leah nodded, setting her bag on the bench. She approached the basket, shooting the ball with one hand as Zahara had done. In all honesty, she didn't know how to improve. Of course, there were the little drills she did in practice, but those were few and far between. Ezra mostly focused on team plays and set ups.

"Why are you doing that?" Zahara asked, materializing behind her.

Leah tilted her head. "Because you were doing it."

"Why was I doing it?"

Because you know your shit. Because you're fucking Zahara Williamson and you're basically a god. Because I have no clue what I'm doing but *you* do.

Not the answers Zahara was looking for.

So instead, Leah spoke the desired words.

"I don't know."

Zahara nodded, satisfied. "What you're doing is called form shooting. The point is to get your shot consistent— that way you have a solid base to work with. After that, you can move on to repetition."

Leah nodded. The explanation was pretty sound.

"So why only use one hand?" Leah asked.

"The guide hand isn't as important. It's practically just for balance. Besides, using only one makes you stronger."

Leah nodded, continuing her practice. She let the ball rest on her palm, bent her elbow, and extended her arm. As the ball licked the tip of her finger, she flicked her wrist.

The ball tattered around the right side of the rim, eventually falling into the net.

Leah looked at Zahara.

Zahara gave her a blank stare.

She placed the ball back on her palm, replicating the motion. The thing bounced on the same side of the rim, instead falling to the side. A miss.

Leah tilted her head, retrieving the ball. She replicated the shot, and unfortunately, replicated the outcome. The ball didn't even make it to the rim, instead bouncing off the backboard and falling to the ground.

"It needs to go to the left." Zahara commented.

Leah huffed a sigh. "I know. How do I do that?"

"You make it go to the left."

Leah turned to her, glaring daggers. "Are you making a point to be useless? No shit, I need to make it go to the left. But *how* do I do that?"

Zahara hummed a chuckle, immune to her previous insult. "If you take that tone with anyone else, bad things will happen. Lucky for you, I'm forgiving." She tapped Leah's shoulder, her long fingers tracing her skin. "Say it."

"Say what?"

"Go left."

Leah threw up her hands. "The ball doesn't follow orders."

"No, it doesn't." A sick smile curled on Zahara's lips. "But weapons do. You're a weapon, Leah Taven. Now make it go left."

Leah turned to the basket, positioning the ball in her hand. She readied her shot, bending her legs and eyeing the hoop.

Zahara's ice cold hand landed on her shoulder, sweet breath hot on her neck. "Leah," she drawled. "Say *it*."

"Go left." Leah murmured. It wasn't spiteful, and it wasn't toward the ball. It was to her arms, her legs, her shot. When she released the thing, her form changed. Just slightly. The follow through was more crisp, the ball stayed on her fingertips for longer, and it sailed past the rim and through the net.

Leah let the thing fall to the ground, bouncing once at her feet before rolling into the grass.

"How—" she watched the ball like it was magical. "How did that work?"

"Science." Zahara responded. "The subconscious mind doesn't respond to step by step instructions: it doesn't need them. Your brain knows how to execute a goal: all it needs is for you to give the order. Don't take suggestions, Leah. Order your own greatness."

Zahara ran Leah through multiple drills after that. Dribbling, finishing, fuck, even balance— they practiced it all. Leah was instructed to do a thing called Mikan Drill, something she despised with all her might. Zahara told her to stand under the basket and make layups on either side. Simple right?

Nope.

Because every time Leah took a step, Zahara promptly informed her she was doing it wrong. So Zahara demonstrated and Leah watched and replicated. Once she had the footsteps correct, it was onto making the shot. At first, when the ball rolled off her fingertips, it slammed against the rim and came shooting back at her. So she took longer strides, ordered the ball to hit the backboard, and eventually, it lingered around the rim before falling into the basket.

"What do you mean it doesn't count?" Leah hissed, rubbing her aching neck. Another awful detail about Mikan Drill was that it required her to constantly look up. "It went in!"

Zahara shrugged. "Barely. It waltzed around the rim before your luck decided to tip it in."

Luck? Was that what she called an hour of orders and neck pain? *Luck*?

"It doesn't matter how it went in," Leah retorted. "Just that it went through the net. A points a point, Zahara."

"No," she shook her head. "The adrenaline of the game makes the shot ten times harder, not to mention that someone will be guarding you. If it's not a perfect swish in practice, it's not a point in the game."

Leah gave an exasperated sigh, but continued. She did the drill until the dark sky brightened. She did the drill until her neck sounded like a concrete grinder. But most importantly, she did the drill until she made ten perfect shots in a row.

The second the last ball swished through the net, Leah nearly kicked the thing with joy. She looked at Zahara, beaming ear to ear with the largest smile she'd ever shone.

Zahara gave the smallest quirk of her lips, an expression that almost looked pitiful.

"Nice job," she smirked. "Now do this."

Leah watched in horror as she replicated the drill, except this time, backwards. Her neck craned at a near ninety degree angle. Leah wanted to cry.

But she did it. She did all the Mikan— all five versions. Then, she did Zahara's dribbling drills, which were almost worse, but her neck was grateful for the break. Then it was balance and stamina, which Zahara had combined into a special kind of hell.

And when she was done, she was beaming ear to ear. Because even though Zahara had crafted a torture worse than the devil's making, even though the drills made Leah more exhausted than she had ever been, she enjoyed them. Not because they were fun, but because they offered her a promise. A promise of challenges. Challenges only she could endure.

"The fuck happened to you?" Zahara had asked one early morning. Gael had been extra cruel the night before— Leah had attempted to hide her tearstains, but Zahara knew. Zahara always knew.

"What?" Leah swallowed. One last attempt at resilience couldn't hurt. "I don't know what you're talking about."

Zahara gave her a look. One of *her* looks. So fierce and cutting— almost as sharp as a blade.

"Fine," Leah blew a stray strand from her face. "My dad was…" she paused: Zahara didn't want to hear. She'd think she was pathetic— ungrateful. "Well — it doesn't matter. Let's just play."

Zahara tilted her head. Leah expected her to push, but she didn't. Instead, her lips quirked into a grin. "You know what?" she snatched Leah's ball from her hands. "Fuck practice."

"Hey give me that—"

But Zahara had already kicked the basketball across the park. The thing soared through the air, landing in a tree and tumbling through the branches. It brought a few leaves and sticks with it.

"What was that for?" Leah scoffed.

"We're not practicing this morning." Zahara said. "We're getting coffee."

"Okay, well—" Leah frowned. "You didn't have to kick my ball."

"Dramatic effect, kid." Zahara patted her head. "Now go get it."

Leah scowled, dashing to retrieve the thing. Zahara drove them to a cafe right by her school. The D1 paid— despite Leah's many protests. And when she finally caved and told Zahara she wanted a latte, she smiled sweetly and ordered Leah a small hot chocolate.

"Why are we here?" Leah asked, blowing on her drink. The whipped cream spun slowly in her cup, melting into the deep brown. "We could be using this time to practice."

"We could," Zahara agreed. "But I want to tell you a story."

"Is it interesting?"

"No—" Zahara smirked. "But it's useful. Listen."

Leah sighed, resting her cheek in her palm.

"I was born with a ball in my hands," Zahara started. "My parents decided my future for me at an early age. By the time I was seven, I could dribble better than any adult. When I was ten, I was playing with high school girls. And when I was sixteen, that's when my mom told me she loved me."

Leah's eyes widened.

"It was after a big game— I had just been awarded MVP for the first time." Zahara swallowed— Leah could've imagined it, but she thought there were tears bordering her mentor's gaze. "She hugged me so tight: I still remember her cherry scent from that night. It was the first moment I ever felt that she loved me— that everything I'd done was worth it."

Leah wrapped her hands around the mug.

"But by the time I'd gotten that love, I was already brilliant." Zahara breathed. "I had already discovered how to work until I collapsed: until I just wanted to curl into a ball and cry. And when I finally got a taste of my mother's care— all I wanted was more. So I worked harder: got *better*."

A smile touched Zahara's face. Her gaze wandered to the ceiling. "But I still remember the bad nights— the dark days after I played awfully. The horror that followed…"

"What did your mom do?" Leah asked.

Zahara swallowed. "It doesn't matter. I don't want to talk about it. The important part is, that fear lived in my *bones*. It accompanied me throughout the day— never quite leaving. And that fear kept me vigilant: it kept me ambitious— it kept me *brilliant*."

Leah looked into her cup. The tears filling up her eyes broke— trailing down her face. She remembered Gael's voice— his comments about her looks, her skill, her ambition. His words grasped her with their smoked breath. Like a blade plunging into her heart.

Zahara cupped her face, brushing away the drops with a gentle hand. "I don't know what you're going through Leah, but I can imagine your fear."

Her thumb traced Leah's jaw. "And the best piece of advice I can give you is to use it. Take that terror into your game— every time you feel tired: every time you want to give up, remember what happens if you fail."

THE TRAGIC LEGACY OF ZAHARA WILLIAMSON

"Opioid use among professional athletes at any given time, as reported in 2 different studies, ranged from 4.4% to 4.7%, while opioid use over a National Football League career was 52%. High school athletes had lifetime opioid use rates of 28% to 46%."
—Ekhtiari, Seper, et al. National Library of Medicine

Leah continued to improve.

Slowly, through early mornings and late nights, she mastered Zahara's drills. Her neck adjusted to Mikan, and soon, it was a drill of relaxation rather than exasperation. She did it to warm up, making ten perfect swishes effortlessly.

Every time she outgrew a drill, Zahara would provide another. There were the staples, such as form shooting, that she would still do. But soon, mid-range became three pointers. Crossovers became hesitation moves. She added her dribble to the shot fakes. Her layup became a euro step. And eventually, Ezra Soren took notice.

"You know," he said after a particularly impressive game. "I can usually tell when someone will be good. But you surprised me. I never figured you'd amount to anything, but now—" he smirked, a genuine smile. "Five threes as a seventh grader. God damn, Leah. I've got the next division one athlete right here."

After that, Leah ran right to Zahara, quoting Ezra by the word. Zahara had patted her on the back, grinning just as much as Leah was.

"Ezra's a good man," she had said. "Keep him close. He's important."

"He's brilliant," Leah agreed. "He can teach me—"

"Not because of his skills." Zahara said. "Because he's a good man. An ally, Leah. You don't find many people who will be your friend in this game, but Ezra—" a smile touched her lips. "He will."

Leah didn't just practice, she observed. Zahara brought her to each and every game. Watching her mentor destroy teams with minimal effort was like looking into the future. When Zahara made a shot, Leah imagined herself with the same powerful grin. Because she would rule that court one day, striding around, barking orders and drinking the power like syrup.

No one would ignore her then.

When Zahara couldn't make it, she practiced on her own. She made sure to play for at least two hours a day, not including practices with Ezra. If she only practiced an hour one day, she did three the next. It took ten thousand hours to go D1, at least that's what Zahara had said. So that was her goal. Ten thousand hours before her graduation date.

Zahara and Leah's relationship was not one of friends. Not of sisters, and not of mentorship. Sometimes, they were all those things and sometimes they were none. They loved each other, sure. Zahara's eyes would light up whenever Leah came running towards her, and Leah spent every second thinking about her upcoming meeting with Zahara. Their care didn't have a name. It didn't need one. They simply enjoyed each other.

As spring rolled around, so did the end of high school season. The day of Zahara's last game was a gray one. It was as if the sky was in mourning—saying a final goodbye to their basketball prodigy before she was off to Stanford.

Leah didn't let herself feel sad. Zahara's departure wasn't so much a loss, but a gain. At least that's what she told herself. The sooner she left, the sooner people would start looking at Leah.

The crowd that gathered before Zahara's final was massive. High school students, parents, children. Maybe they weren't all here to see the D1, but all of them had to know her name. Leah scurried through the crowd, dipping under adults and running past the pay table.

She settled on the very first step of the bleacher, clasping her hands over her lap. The teams were warming up, Riverside versus Hampton. Zahara had single handedly carried her team to the League championships. It was no surprise, the girls on her team played like startled squirrels, darting all over the court with zero coordination. She knew because both the D1 and Ezra had complained about it on multiple occasions.

As if on cue, Ezra materialized beside her.

"Incompetent fucks," Ezra muttered. "They can't even catch her passes and then complain that she doesn't share the ball."

Leah smirked. "Nice to see you too, Coach."

Ezra turned to her, ruffling her hair. "How are you doing, kid?"

"I'm okay," Leah responded. "How about yourself?"

"I'm about to watch the girl I trained for years dominate her last high school game." Ezra's gaze shifted to Zahara. "It's bittersweet."

His eyes were proud. Like watching his daughter graduate. Maybe that was what it was like for him; watching his kid walk across the stage with a diploma and a wave.

Except Zahara wasn't waving to the audience. Zahara was cussing out her teammates.

"— you fucking *imbeciles*—"

"— are you actually *shitting* me—"

"— you can't pass to someone who's *not there*—"

"— in order to make a shot, you actually have to aim at the *hoop*—"

Leah caught snippets. Ezra only needed snippets to beam with pride.

"You know," he wiped a fake tear from his eye. "I taught her more than half of those phrases."

Leah snorted. She had grown fond of Ezra— not just because of his skills or the fact that Zahara advised it. She actually *liked* the guy. He wasn't afraid to swear or say certain things like most adults were. He gossiped and laughed with her— like an acquaintance rather than a child.

"So?" she tilted her head. "What's the deal with the other team?"

Ezra smirked. He always had information on the opponents. Leah didn't know how he did it but, somehow, Ezra knew the secrets of every girl who stepped foot in this game. Their strengths, weaknesses, traumas and victories. He knew every piece of knowledge there was to know.

And he was more than happy to share it with Leah.

"The team, like any high school one, is an absolute mess," he declared it like he was giving a compliment. "But their mess is thicker, hotter. More tangled. You see that girl—" he pointed to number thirteen. "She despises number twenty— over there— because she was given the shooting guard position. That's because number fifteen spread rumors that she was doping and the coach caught whiff. Now, of course he has no problem with the act, but an unfair advantage would cause the parents to riot. So like any sane person, he benched her so she doesn't have to play and the parents won't have his head."

"Is she?" Leah asked. "Doping, I mean."

Ezra wrinkled his nose. "No. Only the serious players dope. The ones that want to go into college levels. That kid only wants to impress boys."

"Why would a coach be okay with doping?" Leah asked. "Shouldn't they be opposed to that sort of thing?"

"Yes, they should." Ezra's tone held the smallest hint of venom. "But drugs can help a player's performance, most coaches don't much care for the player's wellbeing, only that they play well."

Leah bit her lip, her gaze shooting to Zahara's coach. Coach Viren would be her high school instructor in two years. Did he condone it? How much of her well being would he sacrifice for the win? How much would *she* sacrifice?

"Do you condone it?" Leah asked. "Doping?"

Ezra shook his head. "I— thank god— have my priorities straight. Basketball is not the biggest thing in the world, and it will— at most— take fifteen years from your life. The rest is yours, and drugs can seriously fuck that up."

Leah took a moment to consider this and nodded. The other team was boring; she decided to change the topic. "What do you think of Viren?"

Ezra's gaze darkened. His features had gone hard before, but not in this way. Ezra had looked angry in the game, but it wasn't this. This wasn't just anger. This was a mix of unidentifiable emotions, carving his face like a blade.

"He's an asshole." Ezra drawled, icy gaze resting on Viren. "Don't trust him. I don't wanna talk about this. Let's switch the topic."

Leah was tempted to push. Ezra had dirt on everyone, and by his reaction to Viren's name, it was probably something *really* bad. But by the way Ezra's eyes twitched, Leah could tell the topic was sensitive.

"What about her?" she pointed to number thirty on the opposing team. "She seems to be the best player. What's the dirt on her?"

Ezra's grin returned. "That's Zahara's rival."

Oh shit.

Leah furrowed her brow. "I thought she had multiple."

"Did she tell you that?"

"I assumed."

Ezra chuckled. "Smart kid. She does. This one, however, is most substantial. Daniella Vallran. They've played on the same competitive team since they were in seventh grade. Always together, always rivaling. I've coached both of them since they were tots. They're like my daughters."

Leah tilted her head. Daniella looked so much like Zahara— fine edges, tired eyes, a fire that burned throughout her body. "If you love both of them, why pin them against each other."

Ezra looked offended. "That wasn't me. I hate their dynamic. It's even worse during AAU season when they're on the same team. Their jealousy is the kind that eats people alive. They always want to be the star— the one who gets my— the whole county's— attention."

"So," Leah tilted her head. "If not you, who makes them enemies?"

Ezra gave a low chuckle. "That's a loaded question, kid. It has many answers. I think some of it is their fault, but then again, nothing is really a kid's fault. They just want to be loved, that's it. And they have this view that only one of them can have that love, so they fight for it."

Leah looked at Zahara. She didn't see a kid. She saw a god, a deity of power. But then again, she was only seventeen. Ezra was right; she was a kid. A kid that didn't act like one.

The buzzer rang and the teams flocked to their bench. They had thirty seconds before another loud screech echoed around the court, and the starters took their place.

Leah had memorized this ritual. The calling of the numbers, the announcing of the names and grades. Most people probably found it annoying, but to Leah, it was the best part of the game.

She imagined her name, her number, her legacy echoing around the gym. Everyone would memorize the nature of her syllables as she strode to the score table and shook the hand of her opponent.

Several names were called before Zahara's. She always went last. Perhaps it was the nature of the announcement, but more likely, Zahara had made it that way. Leah didn't know how, but it seemed right for Zahara to be the final and greatest name before the game commenced.

"Number seven, a senior and the current MVP of the League—" the announcer proclaimed, words echoing around the court. The last part wasn't required, but Leah had a feeling Zahara had forced the phrase. "Zahara Williamson!"

Zahara stood from her seat, striding to the score table. She raised her chin, locking eyes with her rival.

"And finally, Number ten, a senior— Daniella Vallran!"

Daniella's stride was longer. She and Zahara held each other's gaze. Their handshake lasted longer than normal— as if they were trying to tear off each other's arms. Daniella was a good bit taller than Zahara, her hair falling in a jagged haircut that rested at her chin. Zahara's biceps were more defined, her gaze was tighter and her hair was pulled into a neat bubble braid.

They finally broke away, going to huddle with their teams. Zahara's stern voice was so loud the audience could hear snippets and Daniella's hand movements were more than enough to grasp the concept of the conversation.

The buzzer blared a third time.

The teams gathered into the formation of the jump ball. Zahara and Daniella were on opposite sides of the court, eyes locked on each other.

The referee put the ball in the center, gesturing for the two tallest players to touch it. For a moment, the tension of the beginning ceremony remained. Then, the ref threw the ball, and the chaos began.

Zahara's teammate got to the ball before her opponent. Unfortunately, she hit it the wrong way and Daniella was able to grab hold of the ball. As soon as the thing was in her possession, she sprinted towards her basket.

Fast, but not fast enough. Zahara raced after her, heterochromic gaze blazing in a determined glare. She caught Daniella just as she began her lay up. Zahara poked the ball from her rival's control, sending the thing rolling.

The two women dove for it. Zahara got there first, pounding it to a dribble. Daniella, once she realized offense was a lost cause, raced after Zahara. She could have taken the ball to the hoop, but Daniella's teammates had already formed a thick layer of defense.

Instead, Zahara slowed the offense. She pulled back, allowing the ball to flow between her legs. Daniella glided in front of her, settling into her defensive stance. She slapped her hands on the floor, the bang echoing around the gym as the audience cooed. Daniella's short, jagged hair hung in front of her wild eyes like a madman. Zahara's loose strands did the same. In some ways they were identical. In others, they had nothing in common.

The game was heated for the entire hour. Shot after shot. Play after play. The score was pretty much always the same. Sometimes Zahara would take the lead, and then Daniella would snatch it right back. At one point, Daniella managed to pull ahead by eight points.

That was when Zahara decided to stop sharing the ball.

She managed to catch up— getting ahead by a three. Then Daniella nailed a shot from the volleyball line, and the crowd exploded.

Adrenaline seeped from Zahara's forehead, dripping down her neck and into her uniform. She wiped a stray strand from her fiery eyes, anger glowing off of her. She looked powerful. Even though the game was tied, at that moment, she held more potential than Daniella. Leah couldn't explain why, but somehow the threat of failure made her a more likely victor.

"Timeout!" Zahara shouted. "Timeout! *Now*!"

Leah looked at Ezra. "You can do that?"

"*She* can do that." Ezra patted her head. "And if you keep on this track, kid, you will too. Not with me, though. If you ever take one of my timeouts you'll never see the court again."

Zahara gathered her team in a huddle, snatching Viren's clipboard and sketching up some sort of plan. It seemed the coach was not permitted in the meeting, because he sat on the far side of the bench watching the court like it was the most interesting thing in the world.

A screech of a whistle later, the timeout was over. Zahara's team organized themselves on the court, preparing for whatever scheme their leader had planned. The inbounder passed the ball to Zahara, and the chaos resumed.

Zahara sprinted down the court, swinging the ball under her legs. Daniella kept her pace, sliding with Zahara's stride.

Zahara shouted an order. Her team made an attempt at something that looked vaguely like a pin-down and flair screen. They failed spectacularly, somehow ending up in the worst possible spot; the key.

"No!" Zahara screeched. "That's not—" Daniella made a jab at the ball. "Nevermind. Clear the floor! *Now*!"

The team scattered. Now it was only Zahara and Daniella. The clock ticked down to twenty seconds, and the championship rested in the hands of two women.

Zahara flung the ball behind her back, making a break for the basket. Daniella stepped in front of her, countering the attack. In response, Zahara twisted the ball through her legs, attempting the opposite direction.

But it was a sloppy crossover. Before she could finish the move, Daniella slapped the ball, freeing it from Zahara's grasp. It rolled into the open court, both athletes racing after it. This time, it was Daniella who managed to gain the possession. She hammered her dribble to life and pushed down the court. Zahara followed, but it was too late. Daniella made the easy layup, giving her a two point lead.

The audience exploded, cheers echoing around the gym. Daniella skipped along the sideline, rolling in her fame. She thought she had won. She thought the game was over— that her rivalry with Zahara was *over*, and she had taken the crown.

Little did she know the D1 was already sprinting down the court, ball in hand, gaze focused on her target. Daniella's teammates made an attempt at stopping her, only for Zahara to weave around them, going for the layup.

Leah thought she was going to make it. She thought her mentor would force the game into overtime. But just when she thought no one could stop her, Daniella came at Zahara from behind, swatting the shot from the air.

Five seconds left.

Zahara didn't react. She raced after the ball, Daniella on her heel. She pulled the thing into her possession, pounding the dribble at her side.

Four seconds.

She pulled out onto the three point line, weighing her options. Daniella didn't poke at the ball— no, that was too risky. Instead, she stayed in front of Zahara, waiting for her to make a move.

Three seconds.

Zahara charged at the basket, Daniella at her side. Just as she crossed the three point line, she halted her momentum, sending her defender flying towards the baseline.

Two seconds.

Zahara flung the ball behind her back, straightening in her shooting form. Daniella recovered quickly, charging at Zahara in a closeout. But it was too late; the ball already tipped off Zahara's fingers.

One second.

Zahara released her shot, sending it with the slightest flick of her wrist. Daniella collided with her just as the thing left her grasp. The girls fell to the ground, watching as the ball sailed through the air.

It was as if the entire gym was silent. They watched the shot fly in a perfect arc. Time slowed, gravity thickened and sound seemed a distant memory. For a moment, the ball held its place, spinning due to Zahara's perfect, practiced follow through.

Time resumed.

The buzzer screeched.

The ball landed in the net, creating a perfect swish.

And the crowd went wild.

Cheers and shrieks erupted in the gym. The audience jumped to their feet, shouting Zahara's name. Her and Daniella stayed on the floor, still watching the net. Neither of them could accept that the ball actually sailed through the hoop. That now, there was a clear victor. One of them had won— one of them had done enough. The other's efforts were in vain.

Except Daniella wasn't crying. She didn't look that least bit defeated. The fire that gleamed in her eyes was more alive than ever. She looked like there was still a fight. Like there was still *something* she could do to change her fate.

No one heard it the first time Daniella spoke.

But Ezra's body tightened, as if he had witnessed the phrase before.

The second time, Daniella screamed it.

"*Sine Luni.*"

The crowd fell silent. You could hear a pin drop. The air was thick as Zahara's fiery gaze returned, centered on Daniella. The two looked at each other, a renewed hatred gleaming off of them.

Leah nudged Ezra. "What's happening?"

Ezra didn't take his eyes off his girls. "A Sine Luni. It's like a one-v-one, but worse. Full court, no rules, no boundaries. Hitting, punching, pulling— it's all on the table. There are three ways it ends. A contestant scores three points, they tap out, or they die."

"Surely they would rather admit failure than lose their lives."

"Really?" Ezra looked at Zahara. "Would she?"

Leah's gaze shifted to Zahara. Her gaze was so hard, so *determined*. She remembered what Ezra had said. *They have this view that only one of them can have love, so they fight for it.* In their head, only one of them could win that love. But from who? Did it matter? Maybe it was everyone's love they were trying to win. Had they ever been loved? Had *Leah* ever been loved?

And would she be willing to die for a chance?

It seemed only she was unaware of the term, because the audience was put in a hush. No one spoke. It seemed disrespectful to do so. But no one left. A Sine Luni might be a solemn occasion, but damn, it was an entertaining one.

Daniella and Zahara stood in the center of the court. Their respective teams had retreated to their benches, each watching with anxious anticipation. The referee waltzed to the middle of the court, holding the ball. He held it out to Daniella and Zahara, who both touched it. No words were needed, no conversation was necessary. The referee simply threw the ball in the air and the duel began.

Zahara got the ball first. She caught it mid-air, bounding off her left foot and towards her basket. This time, Daniella didn't move side by side with her. In the previous game, Daniella didn't foul once. It was almost a surprise when she grabbed Zahara's hair and flung her foot into her back.

Zahara shrieked, toppling to the ground as the ball rolled from her hands. The audience let out a gasp and Leah stood. Her own fire building in her veins. *No one* hurt Zahara. How fucking *dare* she.

A hand laid on her shoulder. Leah turned to see Ezra, a protective grasp steadying her rage.

"Look," Ezra said. "She's getting up. She's okay, Leah. She can do this on her own."

He was right. Zahara got up. Leah was damn sure Daniella broke her spine, but Zahara got *up*. It was like she didn't even feel the pain. She was running, chasing down Daniella like a hungry panther.

"How—" Leah stuttered. "I don't—"

"Me neither, kid." Ezra murmured. "I've never been able to figure it out."

Daniella made the layup; Zahara let that one go. But as soon as the ball went through the net, Zahara grabbed it. Daniella was on her heel, sending punches and pulls her way. But the D1 was ready, dodging each blow like it was a normal part of the game. She sprinted down the court, pulling ahead of Daniella. Just as she was about to make her layup, she stopped. Daniella leaped past her, attempting to block. Instead of her intended goal, she jumped past the baseline and Zahara made a dazzling reverse. Just for show.

Daniella retrieved the possession, but now, Zahara was on her. She was done playing nice, done playing by the rules of the game. So as soon as Daniella started dribbling, Zahara tackled her.

Her fist came like a bullet. Daniella was thrown off balance but managed to keep the ball in her hands. Zahara threw herself at her hair, yanking her scalp back. Daniella gave a sharp yelp and loosened her grip on the ball.

That was all Zahara needed. She slapped the thing from Daniella's hand, pounding it into her own possession. Leah stood, anticipation climbing her bones, it looked like she'd get another point.

Then Daniella sent her fist into Zahara's nose.

It was a clean hit, a sickening crack rewarding her punch. Then the blood came. So much of it, dripping onto the floor in a steady stream. Zahara wiped the red with her sleeve. She looked stunned, watching the crimson drip onto the floor, creating a shiny puddle at her feet.

She recovered fast. Too fast to be natural. Zahara was running before the blood finished falling. She caught Daniella at the volleyball line, but instead of swiping the ball from her hand, she flung her foot into her back.

Daniella cried, stumbling. She didn't quite fall, but she stumbled. That was all Zahara needed. She picked up the ball, but not before slamming her foot into Daniella's ribcage.

Necessary? Of course not.

But the audience loved it.

They roared with cheers as Zahara raced down the court, blood streaming down her cheek. They cheered as Daniella struggled to get off the ground, yelping as the pain consumed her.

But by god, she got up. The girl was impressive, because she got to her feet and started racing towards her enemy. Zahara managed to make the layup before Daniella pushed her to the ground.

This wasn't a Sine Luni. Whatever this was, it wasn't basketball. When Daniella slammed her fist into Zahara's face, over and over and over again, it was clear the ball was no longer the goal. She wanted to *hurt* her rival.

There was blood; cries of pain and restraint. Zahara tried to break free, only for Daniella to force her head back into place and continue her blows.

Ezra looked terrified. Zahara's blood dripped down her face, pooling around her head. He could have turned away, he could have stopped watching. But instead, he kept his gaze. He at least owed them that.

Leah owed Zahara much more.

She dug into her backpack, drawing her lunch fork. Without thinking, she raced along the sideline, fork by her side. She slid the utensil toward Zahara, whose puddle of red was slowly getting bigger.

The audience didn't see the trinket.

But Zahara did.

With bloodied fingers, she reached for the silverware. As soon as it met her grasp, she propelled it into Daniella's arm.

Daniella let out a scream and loosened her grip just enough for Zahara to slip away. As soon as she was free, she made a beeline for the ball. Zahara wasn't interested in revenge— she was interested in winning. That was vengeance enough.

So Zahara wavered around the three point line, waiting— *waiting* for Daniella to get up.

"Come on, *Dany*!" Zahara spat. "Is that all you got? Come and get me. Let's end this with both of us on our feet!"

With these words, Daniella staggered up. Maybe Zahara's voice was enough— enough to get her off the ground, back into her defensive stance.

Daniella didn't dive for the ball. She didn't reach or poke or tackle. She simply stayed on defense, waiting patiently for Zahara to make her move.

Zahara held the same stance, waiting for her opponent. It was as if time stopped again, the steady rhythm of Zahara's dribbling echoing around the gym.

Then, Zahara attacked. Her drive was fast— precise. She ran to the free throw line, retreating as Daniella caught up to her. Her movements were quick, her dribble precise. The threat of a Sine Luni momentarily vanished, and it was just a one-v-one. Leah almost forgot there was blood covering the court.

Zahara flung the ball behind her back, letting it spin in one hand before clasping it with the other. Daniella sprang into a closeout, but it was too late. The shot was already spinning in the air, stopping time and reality to look at its arc.

The ball splashed into the net.

The crowd erupted.

Daniella fell to the ground.

Zahara breathed an exhale, running a bloody hand through her hair. She looked so powerful, standing in the bright gym light. Her uniform was drenched in her own blood, a stain that would never fade. But she wore it like a crown— she bore her injuries, her hurt and her rage like a sword. Because that was what she was willing to sacrifice— *everything*. And perhaps that was what everyone truly admired about Zahara. That there was *nothing* she wouldn't give.

Zahara headed to Leah and Ezra, brushing past local news reporters like they were simply ghosts. Ezra stood, locking eyes with Zahara, and then Daniella. Briefly, they looked the same. Their eyes were a vulnerable gloss as the two gazed at Ezra; each wanting— *begging* him to come to their side. To be there for them in their moment of triumph or failure.

He had to choose.

Two girls who he had called his daughters, and he had to *choose*.

It was then that Leah realized how mad she would be if he didn't choose Zahara.

Not just because she loved her, not just because she was her mentor. But because Zahara *deserved it*. She had fought; given blood, sweat— *everything* into his love. Maybe Daniella had too. But in the end, she didn't give enough. Zahara had. Zahara *won*.

Maybe twisted, awful, misguided jealousy swirled between them, but that jealousy was their life. Maybe untrue, maybe falsified— but those two really believed only one of them could have Ezra's love. It didn't matter the truth of the belief— it was their *life*. Ezra at least had to give them that.

So when he hugged Zahara, it was no surprise. The D1 looked close to tears during the embrace. But she didn't let the droplets break her waterline. She needed to seem calm, composed; *okay*.

Daniella couldn't hold her composure. At first, the tears were silent, starting as Ezra hugged Zahara. Then they got louder; her body started shaking. She pulled her hair, banged her head against the floor, and screamed. Agony, terror, hopelessness— the picture of failure. The consequence of loss.

"Hey," Zahara grabbed Leah's hand. Maybe she didn't want her to see Daniella, sobbing on the ground. It was as if Zahara *didn't* see her rival. Or maybe Zahara was just grateful it wasn't her that broke. "Come on, I have something to show you."

Pulling Leah behind her, she made a beeline to the door. They brushed past reporters with questions and dumbstruck children. Zahara didn't notice the chaos, she was simply sprinting to her beat up car with the knowledge that all her work had finally paid off.

They piled into the vehicle. Zahara backed up without a care of who was in her way. She didn't drive with her usual ferocity, but as a slow, controlled, safe driver.

Leah hated to admit she missed the danger.

"Zahara?" she asked. "Where are we going?"

Zahara grinned. It wasn't forced, it wasn't ambitious. It was one of a teenager. One of *excitement*.

Leah didn't like it. It didn't suit her.

Zahara pulled into a parking lot. Surrounding the dark were the vague shadows of trees. Leah recognized it. This was Village Park. She used to go here with her mom when she was little.

“Come on,” Zahara opened the door, Leah following behind her. The D1 slung her bag over her shoulder. Leah didn’t ask what was in it. She figured she’d find out soon enough.

“Zahara wait—” Leah stammered. “Just tell me where you’re taking me.”

Zahara knelt down, brushing a stray hair from Leah’s eyes. Her face was covered in blood, bruises littering her head to toe. But somehow, even though she was injured, she was glowing. “It’s not so much where I’m taking you, kid.” Zahara said. “But what I’m going to show you.”

“Okay,” Leah touched the back of her neck. “What are you going to show me?”

Zahara didn’t respond— instead she grasped her hand, pulling her through the wet grass of the park. The dew collected on her socks, bleeding into her shoes and sending shivers up her spine. Zahara continued to drag her, nearly skipping to the top of the hill.

The view was remarkable. The shine of the full moon gleamed off the canal, providing a silver, ethereal glow. Just across the water was a building— a hospital. Leah’s mom went there all the time— hooked up to so many machines it was hard to tell where she ended and the drugs began.

Zahara laid down a towel, gesturing for Leah to sit. She crossed her legs, folding her arms to protect herself from the cold. Zahara hummed a laugh, draping her jacket over Leah.

The D1 plopped down next to her, gaze resting on the luminescent water. Zahara brushed brushed her hair away, a smile curving her features. It was rare that Zahara was content— unheard of, even. Peace didn’t get along with her.

“Do you remember what I told you the first day we met?” Zahara asked. “On that car ride?”

Leah nodded. “That you have to give everything for this game. Mind, body, sanity. Everything you think is granted. That’s the price of greatness. That’s the price of being like you.”

“Right,” Zahara breathed a sigh. “I didn’t tell you the whole truth that day, Leah. Yes, you have to sacrifice everything. But when it comes down to it, this game takes more than you can give. It expects you to do things that the human body simply can’t. Humans can’t practice six hours a day— trust me, Leah, I’ve tried. Humans can’t get up after an injury. Humans, by themselves, are simply not enough.”

"So what's your point?" Leah asked. "Are you here to tell me you were made in a lab?"

Zahara gave a low laugh. Leah could have imagined it, but she thought she sensed a tinge of sadness in her tone.

"No," she chuckled. "I'm here to show you how to become better than human."

Before Leah could respond, Zahara dug her hand into her bag. She pulled out a long pipe with a metal pot melded on top. Leah's eyes widened in recognition. She had seen the mechanism before— diagrams at least. In history— the drug trade between China and Britain. Apparently, the device hadn't been used in years— in fact it was illegal to simply be in possession of it.

Leah didn't think she would ever see a real one.

But there, in Zahara's bloody hands, was an opium pipe.

"Why do you have that?" Leah snapped, lunging for the stick. "That's illegal and dangerous and—"

"I know."

"If you're caught with that they might—"

"I know."

"Zahara, it could *kill* you!"

"I know."

"Then *why* do you have it?" Leah didn't think she'd ever been so mad. She was seething, yes— but she didn't feel rage. She felt scared. Scared that something might happen. Scared that she might lose the one person who actually believed in her.

"I have it because this is what it takes." Zahara flicked a match, fire lighting up her hollow features. Suddenly, it all made sense. The rashes on her skin— they were from the drug. Her skin was hollow because she smoked. She was so good— a martyr, a deity— because she *doped opium.*

"It can't take this much—"

"It does, Leah." Zahara's voice was so small. "It takes everything and a bit. People will hit, yell— do *awful* things to you if you don't succeed. But when you do, it feels so damn good. You need their love— *I* need their love. And the only way you can get it is becoming great. Becoming *inhuman*." Zahara lips, letting the smoke pour from her mouth like a dragon. "You can't do it without a crutch, Leah. This is what the game requires of us. The question is, how much are you willing to give?"

THE DEBUT OF A D1

TWO YEARS LATER

"A freshman, number seven— Leah Taven!"

Leah stood from her place on the bench, jogging to the score table and shaking the opposing coach's hand. He gave her a reassuring squeeze, his eyes nearly pitiful.

"Don't be scared," he said, his voice a dripping sludge. "I'll tell my players to go easy. They won't hurt you."

Leah's face contorted into a scowl. It occurred to her that this man, along with many others, genuinely thought he was being nice— that she too believed her age was a hindrance. Leah wanted to gouge his eyes out with a spoon.

But that wouldn't do— no, too messy, too extravagant. Not to mention she failed to possess such a utensil. Instead, she matched his syrupy tone, copied his pitiful features, and hid her boiling rage as best she could.

"A shame," Leah grinned. "I instructed my players to go for your point guard's achilles." She tightened her grip on his hand, jolting him forward with a firm pull. "Listen. I fought my way to this starting spot; and I deserve to be here more than anyone on this court. So you better put your best little dog on me, or I will actually bite your player's ears off."

She didn't wait for his response. Instead she let go of his hand and strode to the open court, meeting her teammates. Reluctantly, they opened up their huddle, letting in the know-it-all freshman.

Leah was about a foot shorter than every one of her teammates. Well, maybe that was an exaggeration, but it sure felt like it. They were all long, had the balance of a limbless rodent and the smarts of a brain dead frog. But at least they listened. To *someone*.

"Hey," Milly started, arms around her teammates. "Try and clear the court for me, I want to get a clear lane to the hoop. The other team typically plays man, so it won't be hard. And if I can't get a shot, I'll pass to one of you on the wings."

Leah scoffed. No she wouldn't. That sentence was just a ploy to get the mindless frogs to follow her.

"That's about the worst idea you've ever come up with." Leah snorted. "And that is saying *a lot*."

Like a pack of angry vultures, the team turned on her. Milly stood at the center of the pack, small lips contorting into her best attempt at a scowl. Milly couldn't really portray any emotion accurately— her eyes were too square to be anything but quizzical, and her mouth was permanently ironed in a fine line.

Still, she had to applaud her effort. The senior put a lot into her hatred for Leah.

Milly didn't say anything. She didn't have too. After all, seniority held more power than skill ever could.

The buzzer screeched and the referee called for her team to line up. Leah took her assigned spot to the side. Milly was given the front, the position to score. The glory angle. She hadn't even fought for it. Viren had simply *given* it to her.

The jumpers tapped the ball. The referee threw the thing, and the chaos commenced.

Leah's teammate hit it forward. The ball basically presented itself to Milly on a silver platter. It baffled her how the senior still fumbled with the thing, letting it slip out of her hands like a fish.

Leah wasted no time. She sprinted towards the ball, pounding it to life and dribbling towards the basket. A defender raced towards her, she swung the thing behind her back. Another girl had planted herself in front of the basket. Leah planted her foot between her feet as she swung the ball over her head. She finished in a scoop, a perfect ending to her perfect euro.

But the ball teetered around the rim, refusing to give her the satisfaction of a swish. Eventually, the thing decided to spite her and tilt off the hoop. Leah lunged for it, but was pushed aside by a larger girl.

She growled, climbing to her feet and racing after her opponent. Her team was already gathered in defense, their arms barely raised above their hips. Leah had tried to improve her teammate's defense, but Milly had shut that down fast. The girl liked her frogs lazy.

Leah matched her opponent's speed, moving in front of them. She dropped into her defensive stance, arms outstretched to catch a stray ball. She watched her girl's hip— something Ezra had taught her. The head could deceive but the waist was honest.

“Taven!” Milly screeched. “That girl’s mine! Fuck off!”

Leah didn’t change her gaze. “Find someone else! I’m on her!”

Milly didn’t respond. Instead, she marched up to Leah and pushed her away, taking over her girl.

She could have fought back. But there was only so much room for infighting in a game. Only so much time, and only so many points Leah would let slide. Fighting wouldn’t do her any good. In this situation, she had to bite her tongue and wipe Milly’s shit off the court.

Leah found her girl, a small guard who looked rather scared. She wasn’t a threat, so Leah sagged off and continued to sweep up Milly’s mistakes.

Just as she predicted, the point guard drove, leaving Milly on the three point line. Leah stood in front of her, hands raised above her head. The girl slammed into her, throwing up the ball. She fell to the ground, letting out an overdramatic grunt.

There was the screech of a whistle. The game halted, eyes turning to the ref who held up an arm. “Fouls on white, seven.”

Leah made a face. That was *not* a foul.

Before she knew it, all eyes turned to her, Milly’s frogs glaring in a practiced stare. Milly shoved past her goons, standing before Leah.

“This is why we don’t let freshmen on varsity.” She snarled, voice barely above a whisper.

Leah ignored her, retort already on her tongue. “You know, Milly, I think the point of defense is to stay with your defender.”

Milly’s tight features twisted into something that vaguely resembled a scowl. Leah straightened her posture— an attempt to seem much taller than she actually was.

But she didn’t want to start a fight. It was too feeble of a disagreement to throw hands over. Leah wanted to save her fists for someone more competent.

She lined up at the free throw line, watching the girl shoot her two shots. She missed both, despite her extravagant free throw routine. This confirmed what she already assumed. High school basketball was an absolute joke.

The inbounder retrieved the ball, stepping out of bounds. The rest of the team filtered backward, except for Leah and Milly, who lingered at the point guard position.

“Leah!” Milly screeched. “Get back! I’m point guard.”

“See I would, but I’d actually like to keep this possession for more than ten seconds.”

Milly’s glare tightened. Leah shifted her gaze to the inbounder, who looked like a confused chicken in a fork-road. It was either upset the favored senior or the hated freshman.

She made the wrong choice.

Leah was sent running to the wing like a fool while Milly hobbled up the court, barely able to keep the ball in her hands. Leah stood at the three point line, waiting for a pass that had a very slim chance of making it to her.

Luckily, Milly was an idiot. She attacked the basket as soon as she crossed half court. Five defenders swarmed her, but none of them got the chance to poke the ball away. Milly did their job for them, promptly dribbling off her foot and sending the ball rolling out of bounds.

Leah made a beeline for the thing, grabbing it a second before it rolled into the other team’s bench. She dribbled at her side, scanning the court for an opening. Milly, unfortunately, had recovered and was screeching from the top of the key.

“Leah, Pass! Leah, I’m open! Leah—” some inaudible screaming. “Leah! Give it to me!”

Fat fucking chance.

Leah saw her opening, and it had nothing to do with Milly. A gap in the defense— one of them had slacked off. She took the opportunity, parting two defenders and leaping towards the hoop. She took a second attempt at her euro, this time dipping the ball under her defender’s grasp. She ended in a smooth scoop and watched the ball fall through the net.

The crowd whistled and cheered in admiration. Euro steps were smooth, beautiful. A dance among a dirty game. The audience always loved them.

The announcer’s voice crackled through the intercom. “Freshman Leah Taven with the euro to kick off the game.”

A pretty solid debut of a D1.

The ball was inbounded before the crowd stopped clapping. Leah raced back, matching up with her girl. Milly, however, was late. The point guard raced forward, stalling at the three point line. Leah relaxed. Maybe she was simply running a play.

“Dammit Savana!” A parents voice hollered from the crowd. “*Drive*.”

Leah saw a flicker of fear sparkle across the girl’s face. She recovered quickly, fire tracing her features. Fire. Zahara’s fire. *Leah’s* fire.

The girl raced into the defense. Leah didn't think she would make it— the drive was too fast, almost out of control. But it wasn't. Savana kept the ball in her hand, placing it strategically between defenders. In one leap, she faked, sending the final layer of defense flying. Then, with a smooth hand, she finished her layup before falling onto the ground.

"Freshman Savana Afren for a extravagant finish!"

A *freshman*?

Leah and Savana met each other's eyes. The girl looked up, bright purple hair falling over her eyes. She smiled, winking at Leah. Leah winked back.

"Timeout!" Viren's rasp came over the game. "Timeout, now!"

The ref blew the whistle and the teams flocked to their respective benches. Leah took her spot, ready to tune out whatever useless bullshit Viren planned to scream in her face.

"Dammit, Leah!" he screeched. "You need to let *Milly* score. She's the only one who can."

A touch of a smirk touched Leah's lips. "*Milly* can barely dribble without sending the ball running to the sideline."

Viren growled. With a smooth motion, he grabbed one of Leah's braids, yanking her to her feet. "You're out, Taven—"

"Is there a problem?" Ezra materialized behind them, laying a gentle hand on Leah's shoulder.

"Ezra," Viren's tone was thick, an unknown past flickering behind his manipulative features. "Do you mind taking your girl? She needs to learn some *manners*."

He emphasized that last bit. There was something behind his eyes, behind his sugary rasp. A past. A secret Leah had no idea about. But she knew there was one. The dude was too shady not to be hiding something.

Ezra led her to the film room— a small closet that smelled thickly of sweat. As soon as he closed the door, Leah collapsed onto the bench, putting her head in her hands.

"Dammit!" Leah drawled. "I'm better than this! I know I am!"

Ezra nodded. "You are."

"I could swish threes from the volleyball line, I could break any press single handedly—" Leah dug her fingers into her temple. "I could win this entire game if I had that chance—"

"You could." Ezra agreed.

"Then *why* am I playing like shit?"

"You're not."

Her head shot up. She met Ezra's blank gaze; as unreadable as ever.

"I'm sorry," Leah slumped against the wall. "Were you watching the same game as me? I'm giving the ball to Milly *every single time*."

"Which—" Ezra began, sitting next to her. "Is not at all your fault. Viren runs the plays for her because he doesn't like you. He wants you to fail, and as of now, he has the necessary leverage to dictate your game."

Leah breathed a sigh. "I hate being helpless."

Ezra's hand landed on her shoulder. "Then it's a good thing you're not."

"Again—" Leah raised an eyebrow. "Are you sure you're watching *my* game?"

"Positive." Ezra raised his chin. "You may not have leverage on Viren, but I do."

Leah rolled her eyes. "And how is that?"

Ezra looked offended. "Leah," he scoffed. "Of course I have leverage on him. I'm Ezra fucking Soren."

Leah made a face. Of course he had a plan: he always had a plan. He was a black hole of schemes and plays. Honestly, Leah didn't see why he opted for a job in sports— the man would've been much better off with a career in politics.

"Fine," Leah raised her hand to her forehead, saluting him. Ezra copied the gesture. "Commence whatever you have up your sleeve."

"Oh," that silky ambition had entered Ezra's tone. He opened the door, the chaos of the game corrupting the previous peace. "I plan to. Go for Milly. I'll deal with Viren."

Leah nodded, heading for the scoretable.

"Oh, and Leah?" Ezra called. Leah turned. "Put on a show for them. Make it impossible to forget."

Leah grinned, flicking stray hairs out of her face. Put on a show. She could do that.

The ref blew the whistle, gesturing for the subsitutions to come in. As Viren saw her, he stood up, anger flickering on his features. Ezra pushed him into his seat, whispering something into his ear.

Leah ran into the court, hollering Milly's name. The bitch pretended not to hear her until Leah grabbed her shoulder.

Milly's stiff features hardened. "What are you doing?"

Leah ignored her, digging her nails into Milly's shoulder.

A trace of fear flashed across Milly's face before she raced off the court. Leah straightened her posture, brushing her long braids behind her shoulder.

My turn.

The ref blew the whistle. The inbounder passed to Leah, sending her running up the court, ball in hand. She was supposed to run one scheme or another. None of Viren's plays ever worked, not that her teammates could run them correctly anyways. Leah was doing her own thing.

Savana planted herself in front of her, locking eyes around her waist. Leah took note of her, and charged down the court. She made a swift crossover, only for Savana to match her pace. Leah tried again with the hesitation move, but Savana only stumbled. Without thinking, Leah flung the ball behind her back, arranging her feet in a step back. She released the ball a second before Savana recovered. The thing sailed through the air, falling through the net.

The crowd went wild.

"Leah Taven for three!"

Savana inbounded the ball, racing down the court. Leah met her at the halfway point, dropping into defense. Savana placed her foot between Leah's stance, spinning around her. Leah caught her pace, regaining her defensive advantage.

"Savana!" a teammate called. "I'm open!"

Savana's eyes flickered. She looked at the girl, then at the stands— at a man. At her *dad*. He gave the smallest shake of his head, and Savana charged.

First a crossover. It was good enough to catch Leah off guard. Savana sped around the second layer of defense, pulling into a jump shot.

Her form was good, Leah was sure the shot would go in. But just as the ball neared the tip of her fingers, she was pushed.

Savana fell to the ground, followed by the screech of the ref's whistle. Leah's teammate hovered over her, eyes wide with guilt.

"What are you doing?" Leah snapped, pushing her shoulder. "You could have hurt her!"

The girl stumbled a response, but Leah wasn't listening. Instead, she bent down to Savana, extending her hand.

Savana took it, hauling herself to her feet. "Thanks."

"Don't mention it." Leah laid a hand on her back. "That's quite a move."

Savana shrugged. "My release should have been quicker. Then it would've been an and-one."

Savana lined up at the free throw line, buying her time. She wasn't catching her breath, but basking in her glory— fully aware that all eyes were on her.

She took her first shot: swish. Her second: swish. And the battle resumed.

Leah took the ball, pounding it to a fast dribble. Savana matched her pace, her defense flawless. They wove around girls like simple obstacles. Take after take, shot after shot. The game was theirs. Just an overglorified one-v-one.

When Leah laid the ball into the basket, Savana followed with a euro. When Savana took a step back, Leah copied her shot. They ran side by side, fully aware the entire attention of the room was on them.

Once, Leah halted in the middle of the court, staring at the audience. For a moment, she let the adrenaline consume her. It coursed through her veins, making her fully aware of the sweat dripping down her skin, the unruliness of her hair and the breath rising from her throat. It was her armor, and she wore it proud.

She only took a second. After it was done, the game resumed. By the end of it, Leah didn't notice who won. When Viren gave his end of game speech about whatever, Leah found herself giving absolutely no shits. The eyes of the crowd were on her and Savana— two prodigies with futures brighter than the stars.

She knew what Ezra was going to ask before he opened his mouth.

"That kid," he said when she came to him in the stands. "Savana…" he rolled the name around in his mouth, searching for the end of it.

"I know who you're talking about." Leah said. "The other freshman. What about her?"

Ezra shot her a glare. "I know you know who she is. She was the only other girl on that court who could dribble. I need to find her last name. Abblefine? Artificial? Aferation?"

"Afren." Leah finished. "Her name is Savana Afren. Why is her last name important?"

"Because I am sending you on a mission." Ezra said. "Kid's got skill. You know who could make her even more unbelievable?"

Leah rolled her eyes. "You?"

"Don't sass me," Ezra snapped. "You know damn well I'm right. I train the best players in the county."

"Oh yes," Leah grinned. "Didn't both Zahara and Daniella go mad by senior year?"

Ezra shrugged. "Keep up your good work, and you'll be just as crazy as a sophomore."

Leah huffed a sigh. Her eyes darted to Savana, who was in conversation with her dad. Well, *conversation* wasn't the right word. The dad was making jarring, aggressive movements with his hands, mouthing words that must've scared the bystanders. Savana sat on the bleachers, eyes trained on the court, occasionally nodding along to what her father was saying.

"Asshole," Ezra muttered. "Go. Use her full name. That makes you seem more official."

Leah blew a stray strand from her eyes. "Why can't you go recruit her? You're the coach."

"Yeah and I'm also a grown ass man." Ezra commented. "These incredible puppy eyes don't work on everyone, Leah. I know it's hard to believe but some people see me as… *intimidating*."

"I can't believe it."

"Anyway—" Ezra continued. "She likes you, or at least I think she does. You helped her up that one time so that earned you points—"

"Ezra," Leah sighed. "I'm going. I'll get her. Just sit down and try not to piss anyone off."

Ezra gave her a lopsided grin. "Like I would ever."

Leah snorted. She headed for Savana, brushing her braids behind her back in an effort to look presentable.

"Hi!" Leah said. Savana's eyes locked on hers. "Savana Afren, right?"

Savana nodded. "And you're Leah."

She smiled. "Nice to formally meet you. Do you mind if I sit down?"

"Not at all," Savana scooted to the side, patting the spot next to her.

"So, if you haven't already figured it out, I was sent to recruit you." Leah said. "Have you heard of Fifth Torch Basketball?"

Savana was about to open her mouth when another voice came over hers.

"She'd rather not play for an AAU team." Her father scoffed. "They're a waste of time."

Leah raised an eyebrow. "And you are?"

"Steven Afren."

Oh of course. The chief of police. He was in the news all the time. Smiling too big, looking too proud. The county loved him— schools invited him to their events to talk about his supposed "heroship." Leah always despised the man. Something was always *off* about him. He was on too high a throne to be morally genuine.

"Oh?" Leah tilted her head, putting on her fake, toxic smile. Ezra used the same expression when he needed to charm someone he despised. Leah, through the years, had learned to copy it. "And what is so *wasteful* about competitive basketball?"

Steven shrugged. "The coaches play favorites and they're never open to… *constructive* criticism. Most of the girls who play don't even get to touch the ball. You're Ezra's bitch, right? That man has about three plays in his handbook and enough of an ego to fill a gym."

Even Leah's syrupy smile was having a hard time remaining on her lips.

"Interesting opinion." Leah had to fight to keep her tone neutral. "Unfortunately, I wasn't asking you. Savana? What do you think of AAU?"

Savana shot a glance towards her father. Leah snapped in her face.

"You're not his dog." She drawled. "You're by far one of the most skilled players in the county. I saw you swish threes from the volleyball line, so a decision shouldn't be a far feat for you."

Savana took a breath, covering her eyes with her purple hair. "I think I'm good." She murmured. Her voice was so small— a songbird in the presence of eagles. "It won't help."

Leah shrugged, getting up to leave. She could tell when a battle was lost, and Savana wasn't going to sway anytime soon. "Well, if you change your mind, here's Ezra's number." She pulled out one of his business cards. Ezra was hardly professional enough to own them unironically. When she asked about them, Ezra just laughed. Leah supposed the cards were a form of mockery. She had no idea towards whom. "You're welcome any time."

She began to turn around, then realized she had one more thing to say. Maybe she couldn't convince Savana with simple facts, but results didn't lie. Ezra had results.

"Oh, and Savana?" she turned her head, braids dripping over her shoulder. "Daniella Zalcman, Zahara Williamson— every single NCAA basketball player you can name has been coached by Ezra. I plan to follow in the D1's footsteps, and I know that when my time comes, I'll be shipped off to Stanford with a scholarship." Leah blew a strand of hair from her eyes. "I have my goal, I have my plan, and I have my mentor. Who's yours?"

DIRT, TOOTH AND NAIL

When people think of sports, they think of the ones held in high school. The over-glorified games filled with cheerleaders and school bands. The so-called "popular" kids who go to parties after winning the big game. In movies, high school basketball is where legends are born.

In real life, high school basketball is a shit show.

The players who barely know how to shoot a ball get praised because their parents are rich, and girls who average a point a game get glazed in the papers. In reality, high school sports are filled with amateurs who barely know the rules of their game.

AAU is where the rough work is done.

Three competitive girls basketball teams resided within the county. Martyn Valley Club, Westside Dynasty, and Fifth Torch Basketball.

Martyn Valley could be described in one word— pathetic. It was founded by an angry father who decided to one day become a coach. As most sports parents were, he was incredibly cocky and had no idea what he was doing. At first, customers flocked to him, as he promised championships and team merch. When his team found out his coaching skills couldn't beat a flock of pigeons and he didn't have two pennies to rub together, they left. The parent was left with only his daughter and her friends— barely holding together a junior varsity team. But when they eventually go off to college, the organization would fade to the back of history, never mentioned again.

Westside did a bit better. They're an organization of high school coaches— Viren being among them. They currently managed three teams. One for middle schoolers, junior varsity, and varsity.

But like every team, they would fail. The coaches were simply guessing; they had no real idea how to teach the game. Sooner or later, their players would leave and the organization would trickle out, just as the rest of them did.

That was always how it was. For years, competitive teams in the city lived and died— a raging river to a simple stream. No one lasted forever. No one could scrape by for more than five years.

Until one man.

No one knew where he came from, but he was different. He actually *knew* the game; studied it. At first, the other coaches hated him. No, not hated. *Disrespected* him. In so many ways, that was worse. But within a matter of weeks, he took girls who had never played before and turned them into all league players. Soon, his team of rag-tag girls was the best in the county.

And so people flocked to him. The competing teams were drowned out in the man's success. They hated him, of course. Nearly everyone in the city despised him. But they knew his power; his ability to snuff out an organization with a simple snap— and they respected it.

Ezra Soren fought his way to the throne with dirt, tooth and nail. No one really knew how or why. No one asked. He was simply the king of the game, and if anyone questioned his reign, their reputation would shatter.

"So," Leah put her hand on her hip. "Which ones your next in line? Who are you gonna move up to the middle school division?"

Ezra squinted, looking at his girls. He had them scrimmage. To them, it was a simple game. But to him, it was a decision. Which one of them showed enough potential to play with the older girls?

"Alina's the obvious choice." He commented, pointing to the point guard. "It's rare to actually know how to dribble at ten years old. She can do it well. And her dads been hounding me to move her up."

"Alina doesn't pass." Leah retorted. "She may be the most skilled, but she doesn't know the game. Some people forget that this sport is a team one. Besides, do you really want her dad oinking poison in her ear that'll affect the entire culture?"

"Good point." Ezra nodded. "Who else?"

Leah scanned the court. The perk about being Ezra's next prodigy is that she was also his right hand. He did her the courtesy of sharing his secrets; in turn, she was his loyal student. The very swish of her threes reminded the other coaches who really owned this town.

"If you are to move anyone, move up Penn." Leah said, eyeing a girl with a wide defensive stance.

"She won't add much to the middle schoolers."

"She won't take anything away, either." Leah countered. "She's quiet, plays good defense and doesn't complain. If anything, she would make the culture better."

“Oh please, Leah,” Ezra waved a hand. “They’re middle schoolers. The culture was fucked when the team was formed. They’re going to eat Penn *alive*.”

“Her skill can hold her own.”

“It’s not her skill I’m worried about.” Ezra said. “She’s sensitive, shy. Those kids are gonna tease her so much she’ll slit her wrists. Trust me, she’s better with the children.”

Leah couldn’t argue with that. She could never argue with Ezra. He had a counter for every point. Sometimes she wondered why he even bothered to keep her around. Perhaps he was lonely— or perhaps he just needed someone to bounce ideas off of. Either way, Leah appreciated his company. It wasn’t like she had better things to do.

“Why move anyone up anyway?” Leah crossed her arms. “Doesn’t seem to do the team much good.”

“Good question.” Ezra grinned. “It's an investment. If a player plays at a higher level than they’re used to, they adapt to said level. Then, when they go back down to their own age group, they’re nearly unstoppable. Besides, playing above gives the player bragging rights. It’s an honor. Works in favor of both parties.”

“Is that what I am?” Leah asked. “An investment?”

“Yes and no,” Ezra said. “You’ve got potential, kid. No doubt. But I also enjoy your company. If a kid’s annoying, I won’t move them up. But I like having you around.”

Leah smiled— the praise sending her soaring. Ezra’s words were the best validation: the only time Leah ever felt like she was enough. .

“Okay!” Ezra clapped his hands. “Wrack the balls. Practice is over.” The children looked at each other, as if Ezra was speaking in a foreign language.

He palmed his face, letting his fingers slide down his chin. “That wasn’t a request. Leah? Can you deal with it? I have some people I need to meet.”

Leah nodded, pushing herself from the bleachers and striding to the kids.

“Chop chop!” she snapped, placing her hands on her hips. “Clean it up, children. If you wanted to be babied you’d have listened to Ezra. Wrack the balls or I’ll hurl them at you.”

This time, she got a reaction. The kids rushed to put away the balls, placing them firmly on the wrack and wheeling it into the storage closet. Within thirty seconds, all twelve of them returned to Leah. They gathered in a circle, placing their fists in a center.

Leah blinked, frowning at the dozen sets of eyes landing on her. "Well?" she snorted. "I'm not going to break it for you. Someone here needs to develop a sense of accountability."

After a few fleeting glances, Penn stepped up. Her voice was quiet but audible. While a lingering fear remained, the majority of her tone was swallowed by a newfound confidence.

"Fifth Torch on me, Fifth Torch on three." She shouted. "One, two, three—"

"Fifth Torch." The team echoed, the sound bounding off the gym walls. The kids dispersed, rushing to their backpacks to chug ungodly amounts of water.

Penn hung behind. She picked up a ball, dribbling to the basket and practicing her left hand layup. It wasn't perfect by any means— the shot was off balance and rhythm. But the kid was practicing. The kid *wanted* to get better.

Perhaps she wouldn't slit her wrists after all.

Leah would make a second endorsement to Ezra.

Speaking of Ezra, the coach was deep in conversation with someone. A girl. Around Leah's age. Blonde hair, shining green eyes, and a nose the size of a baby carrot.

Leah approached her, brushing her braids behind her shoulder. She put on her best smile and stuck out her hand. "Hey, I'm Leah."

Carrot Nose's eyes lit up. She grasped Leah's hand, shaking it with an intensity that scared her. "Swan! It's nice to meet you!"

Swan. *Swan*? Like the bird? Who the fuck named their kid after a *bird*?

"Swan's a starter from West Moon High." Ezra explained. "Been playing since she was five years old."

"I'm the starting point guard." Swan corrected, puffing out her chest.

Leah flashed a grin. "Starting point guard for River. We have that in common."

Swan raised an eyebrow. "I thought Milly Fersak was the starting point guard."

Leah's lip curled. "Yeah well, she's missing a very valuable qualification for the role. The ability to dribble."

"Oh," Swan rubbed the back of her neck. "I suppose."

"Well come on," Leah beckoned to the open court. "I'll rebound for you."

"Just a second," Ezra said. "There's one more person I'm waiting on."

“Oh?” Leah tilted her head. “Who? Anyone interesting?”

“You tell me,” Ezra shrugged. “You recruited her.”

Before she could respond, a girl strode in. Her hair, which was once a dark shade of purple, had morphed to a pastel blue. She clutched her bag in her arms, biting so much of her lower lip Leah figured she might swallow it.

Savana Afren.

Her dad followed close behind— like a guard to a prisoner. His long amber eyes rested firmly on his daughter, as if at any moment, she may bolt away.

Ezra swept in first, greeting his newfound customer with a gleaming smile. “Hey Savana. I’m Ezra. Great to finally meet in person.”

Savana took a nervous breath.

Ezra’s eyes flitted to her father. Their gaze met, a brief flame of recognition radiating between them. Then, Ezra’s posture took on a less friendly stance.

“Closed practice.” He announced. “Parents aren’t allowed to watch.”

Steven Afren’s face contorted. “It’s my daughter–”

“And it’s my court.” Ezra finished. “My rules.”

“They say you train the best girls in the county.” Afren scowled. “I want to see if the rumors are true.”

Ezra scoffed. “They aren’t rumors. Zahara Williamson, Daniella Zalcman— hell, even Reese June, who went to Berkely nine years ago. They *all* went through me. That’s proof enough.”

Afren shook his head. “No it isn’t. Programs can go down real fast. How do I know you still have what it takes?”

Ezra rolled his eyes. “Fine. Leah, if you may?”

Leah grinned, picking up a basketball off the floor. She strode to the volleyball line, sent the ball through her legs, and straightened into her shooting form. The ball tipped off her fingertips in a perfect follow through, spiraling towards the basket.

The thing sailed through the net with a crisp swish. Leah let the ball bounce once before releasing her form. She dropped her hands to her sides, brushing her long braids behind her back.

“There,” Ezra gestured to Leah, who was grinning ear to ear. “The kid just splashed a shot from the NBA line. Is that proof?”

Afren shot Leah a questioning glare. She returned the gesture, sticking out her tongue for dramatic effect.

"Fine." Afren spat. He turned from Leah and strode out of the gym. Once he was gone, she sprinted to Savana.

"Glad you could make it," she said, putting an arm around the girl.

Savana glanced at the doorway, as if expecting her dad to be looming there. "It wasn't easy."

Leah offered her a smile. "I'm sure. But you're here, that's all that matters."

Savana's eyes wavered to the farthest hoop. Swan had found a ball and was swishing threes from the corner. Her focus didn't break. As soon as the ball left her hand, she ran to collect it from the net. She was like a robot— each movement replicated to perfection.

"Who's that?" Savana asked.

"Swan," Leah said. "She's the starting point guard for West Moon."

"*Swan*?" Savana rolled the name on her tongue. From the look on her face, it must have tasted fowl. "Like the bird?"

Leah heaved a sigh. "Exactly like the bird."

"That's a stupid name."

"Yeah," Leah agreed. "Let's just hope she's smarter than the glorified duck."

THE BRILLIANT AND THE BRAINLESS

Children perceive a pattern of emotional abuse in sport from both coaches and other players. Coaches tend to downplay this abuse and it is more prevalent in a performance oriented sports culture.
—Eliasson, Inger. "Breaking the Silence of Abuse in Children's Sports: Experiences and Effects of Emotional Abuse towards Young Athletes in Sweden."

"*Leah*!" Milly screeched. "Pass the fucking ball!"

Leah scowled. She kept the thing in her hand, letting it spin before pounding it against the floor. Viren and Milly had single handedly lost the game for them before it even started. The combination of both's pea sized knowledge had put Leah in an impossible situation.

Viren's plays didn't work. He wanted everyone to set screens for Milly, then get out of her way. The issue was that Milly, as hard as she tried, couldn't dribble for shit. Leah had seen her attempt the act.

But all Milly's frogs were hellbent on the plan. Therefore, whatever Leah attempted, they would only get in her way. The only chance she had at scoring was going one-v-five against the other team. No, scratch that— one-v-nine. Milly wasn't above defense against her teammates.

Well, she was out of options. Might as well give Milly another chance at glory.

With the hardest glare she could manage, Leah passed the ball to the senior. The girl barely caught it, allowing the ball to teeter around her fingers before landing in her hand.

Milly's fist shot up, signaling for a screen. Three of her frogs rushed to her, setting blockades on all sides. Milly crossed over, ball bouncing at her head. Before she had the chance to drive, her defender came at her. She swiped the ball from Milly's hand, taking off down the court.

Milly and her frogs glanced at Leah. Leah shook her head, sending them a grin. They lost the ball. It was their job to retrieve it.

And they didn't accomplish the task.

As soon as the other team made their free lay-up, the whistle screeched. All gazes turned to the referee, who was pointing at Viren's bench.

"Timeout!" they ordered. "White."

Great. Time for another one of Viren's bullshit schemes.

Leah jogged to her bench. She sat down, placing her elbows on her knees and awaiting the flurry of insults.

"*Taven*!" Viren's voice cracked in the middle of the word. The sound came out as "Tav-er-en" or "Tav-ag-en." Leah entertained the witty response on her tongue. Unfortunately, she didn't have the chance to voice it. Viren acted first.

"*Agh*!" Leah yelped as Viren snatched her braid. His grip was strong, just inches away from her scalp. He pulled her close, her face almost touching his lips. His breath smelled like fish on her cheek, sending shivers down her back. She tried to speak, but her mouth wouldn't open.

"Not so spiteful now, are you?" Viren spat, spit flying on Leah's face. "Soren's not here to protect you. Your bitchy behavior won't fly now, will it?"

Leah swallowed. Viren was twice as large as her, defined muscles bulging from his wrinkled skin. His grip was tight, unrelenting. She couldn't fight this man but she couldn't run either. She couldn't get out of this alone.

She looked at her teammates. None of them looked back. Milly's sneer was gone. She looked at the crowd— they *all* looked back. But no one got up from their seats. No one stepped to save her from the predicament. Maybe they thought it was her fault. Maybe they thought she deserved it. Maybe she did.

Viren placed a hand on her chest, shoving her back into her seat. The chair tilted, threatening to fall back, but Viren caught her uniform collar, pulling her upright.

Leah's breath caught, an icy bead of sweat trailing down her cheek. Viren held her still, his breath making the hairs on her neck stand.

"You're going to follow the plays." Viren growled. Leah flinched back. "No more extravagant disobedience. No more of being a nuisance. When Milly asks for it, you better be the first to set that screen." He yanked Leah forward. "Am I understood?"

Leah swallowed, glancing at the hand holding her shirt. "Yes."

"Good." Viren pulled her from her chair, causing her to stumble onto the court. The ref blew the whistle, and the timeout was over. Leah ran a shaky finger over the part of her braid that Viren touched. It felt poisoned.

The ball was passed to Milly. Leah took her place on the court. Her legs felt as if they may break beneath her. She couldn't play. Not like this. No matter how hard she tried, she couldn't break out of the sheer terror that Viren had inflicted. No, not terror. *Helplessness*. No one would ever raise a hand to stop him.

Milly dribbled to the court, surveying the defense. When her fist shot into the air, Leah was the first to sprint towards her. She planted in a screen, letting Milly use her as a shield.

And when her defender swatted the ball from Milly's hand, Leah was already sprinting back to stop the fast break. She blocked the shot, collected the ball and passed it back to Milly.

And when her hand shot up, guess who delivered the screen.

Leah.

And when the ball rolled off Milly's feet, guess who retrieved it.

Leah.

And when she was so tired she could barely breathe, guess who continued to hold down the team's defense.

And when River High lost and Viren went ballistic, guess who took the bulk of it.

And when it was all done and everyone was gone, guess who stayed in the locker room sobbing.

Leah.

Fucking suck up. Zahara hollered in her ear. *Would you lick Viren's boot if he asked you? If he did so much as tug at your hair*?

Leah tucked her knees to her chest. Tears trickled down her face, Zahara's voice clattering in her mind.

Do you think I let him do this? *Do you think this is how I became the best in the county? No. I was better. You need to be better, Leah.*

"I know, I know." Leah murmured. "I know, God dammit. But I can't."

Why? Zahara hissed. *Because you think someone's going to swoop in and save you, just as they always have? You lazy piece of shit. Never doing anything for yourself. I'm appalled. Ezra would be appalled. You should be appalled.*

Leah swallowed. "But he could hurt me. He *would* hurt me."

So? Zahara's voice dripped. *He can't kill you, Leah. Are you willing to risk a few bruises? What are you willing to risk? How much are you willing to give?*

Leah drew a shaky sigh, letting her final tears drift down her face. "Everything."

Good. Zahara drawled. *Because it costs everything.*

Suddenly, someone grasped her shoulder. Leah whirled around, fist ready to hit whatever waited for her.

Serena's hands flung up in surrender, eyes glittering with pity. Leah scowled. She didn't need company.

"What are you doing here?" Leah snapped. "Shouldn't you be home? The JV game ended two hours ago."

"I wanted to see you play." Said Serena. "I saw— I saw what Viren did. That wasn't okay."

"It's reality."

"Right." Serena rubbed the back of her head. "But what he did is the textbook definition of abuse."

Leah snorted. "It's sports, Serena. There's no such thing as abuse here."

"Hm." Serena put a hand on Leah's shoulder. Leah shrugged it off. "Maybe there should be."

"Well there isn't." Leah snarled. "And no magical deity is going to make this go away for me. I have to deal with Viren *myself*."

Serena sighed. "Leah, sit down."

"I don't need—"

"Please," Serena put a hand on her shoulder. "Leah."

"Fine," Leah folded her arms to her chest, slumping onto the floor. Serena joined her, placing an arm on her thigh which Leah quickly slapped off.

"Leah, I've missed you." Serena said. "Ever since you started taking basketball seriously— like, really seriously— you haven't really had time for anything else. Not rest, not free-time, not *friends*—"

"I don't need those things." Leah snapped. "I have my goals. That's all I need."

"You need *support*." Serena countered. "You need someone who can stand by your side! You need—"

"I need you." Leah finished. "Is this what this is about?"

"No—" Serena said. "I mean— I miss you Leah, a lot. We used to be best friends, and then you just didn't have time. But I don't care if that friend is me or someone else. I just need you to be okay."

Leah scoffed, standing. "I am okay, Serena—"

"Your coach just grabbed you by the hair!" Serena reached for her hand. "You were just talking to some imaginary person in your head. You are *not* okay."

Leah yanked her hand back. "Fine. I'm not okay." She snapped. "You wanna know why? Because I'm weak. I let Viren and Milly and all the other incompetent fucks push me around like they're better than me." A low rasp rose from her throat. "But they're *not*. I'm gonna show them I'm better. I'm going to show them *all*."

"Leah—" Serena started, reaching to touch her.

"But you know what doesn't help?" Leah interrupted. "People like *you* treating me like I'm a child. Like a porcelain doll that may shatter. I'm not *fragile*, Serena. I won't sob if someone pulls my hair. So stop treating me like a tiny little *kid*."

For a moment, Serena just looked at her. Her gaze softened, a tear trickling down her cheek. She wiped it quickly, recovering her posture. When she stood, Leah realized just how much taller she was. But Serena didn't grab her braids. This time, she didn't try to touch her. She simply walked away, padding out of the locker room and leaving Leah with her thoughts.

Leah padded to the bench, placing her elbows on her knees and resting her head in her palms. She needed to think. She needed to come up with a way to fix this— to put Viren in his place.

Zahara had done it. She had dealt with Viren so well he didn't even have a say in the plan. The coach was probably glad to have his power back and was even more likely to hold onto it with every ounce of his grip.

But was there something he'd hold tighter?

What had Zahara done? What dirt had she found? Did she use blackmail or pure force? How the fuck does a fourteen year old make a grown man grovel?

"Your coach is an ass." Leah's head shot up as the voice echoed around the locker room. With the tone, the distinct smell of marijuana crept through the air. She wrinkled her nose, locking eyes with her dad.

"What are you doing here?" she asked. "I thought you hated sporting events."

Gael blew a long breath, smoke curling from his tongue. "Maybe I just miss my daughter."

"Yeah right." Leah rolled her eyes. "What password did you forget?"

Gael scowled. "Talk about it later. But for now, it seems you have bigger problems."

"I'll deal with it, Dad." Leah said. "It's not your issue."

"*You're* going to deal with it?" Gael sat beside her. "I don't think so. I think Ezra is going to run to your side once again and defend you. Make all your little problems go away." He mimicked a butterfly with his fingers— a delicate bug that exploded into finger twitches. "Until he finally realizes what a waste of time you are and discards you. I think, if you really want to keep this basketball charade of yours going, you need to find a way to do things *yourself*."

"Ezra wouldn't do that." Leah murmured. "He loves me. I'm like his *daughter*."

"Love is conditional, Leah." Gael took a puff of his vape. "It's only worth it when it's convenient. And Ezra coming to your aid every time Viren points his wrinkly finger at you?" he breathed a smoked breath, the smell graying the room. "Not very *convenient*."

Leah drew a shaky sigh. "So what do I do? Huh? He's ten times stronger than me. I don't hold a finger to him."

Gael shook his head. "You don't need to be stronger. Just *smarter*. I saw how easily that man grabbed you. He's done shit like that before— probably worse. Find that— you've got your leverage."

"And how do you suppose I do that?" Leah snapped. "Break into his office? Go rummaging around until I find something useful?"

Gael tilted his head, standing from his perch on the bench. "That depends." He pressed his vape to his lips, letting the smoke slip from his mouth. "How far are you willing to go? How much are you willing to risk for this game?"

He strode out, leaving her on the bench. But she wasn't alone. Zahara's voice replaced his, whispering the same words, but a different tone. A different accent. A different motive.

How far are you willing to go?

THE WAY WE DO THINGS

"The results show that 0.5% of adolescents experienced sexual abuse involving a coach. When considering all adolescents who experienced sexual abuse in their lifetime (10.2%), it appears that 5.3% of them were victims of sexual abuse by a coach."

—Representative Sample of Quebec Adolescents, *Journal of Interpersonal Violence.*

Leah trained extra hard the following morning.

Her alarm felt like poison in her ears. It crept into her dreams, startling her awake. She grabbed her phone, silencing the ring. The light of the screen glowed with the white 5:00. A half hour earlier than usual— but this morning held an extra task.

She crept out of bed, her muscles screaming from the earlier day. She was always sore. Something always hurt. Leah figured she simply needed better stamina.

She flicked her room light on, the sudden flash blinding her. She wiped the crust from her eyes and blinked away her remaining rest. The cold air nipped her bare skin as she stomped off her pajamas. Shorts and t-shirts littered the floor from days before. She didn't need to step into her closet.

Before she could pull the clothes on, her eyes caught in the mirror. She stood up straight, running a hand along her stomach.

Leah may have been strong, but she didn't look it. While hours of intense work outs may have suggested the appearance of biceps and abs, Leah didn't get that blessing. Her arms held muscle, but they weren't defined. Her legs were too short for her torso, and her stomach was too rectangular. She wasn't pretty— not the kind they showed in movies. No— her boobs sagged and her hip dips were quite pronounced. Not pretty— functional. After all, weapons weren't built for display.

Leah used to watch Family Guy with her mom. It was one of their many hobbies, before the incident of course. Her mother enjoyed the adult jokes which flew over her head and Leah enjoyed her mom's laughter.

But there was one joke she didn't miss. One about the WNBA. The show asked if the athlete's minor skill was worth being hopelessly unattractive. That stuck with Leah. Women didn't carry muscle well. Most people with body image issues could work out or eat healthier, but Leah already did that. Every second of every day. Yet she was still hopelessly ugly. It was a trade off— one of the many sacrifices the game required. If you want to be good, you give up your beauty.

Leah didn't like to think about it. She tore herself away from the mirror, pulling on her shorts and t-shirt. She grabbed her over-packed school bag and left her room, finding her basketball and shoes.

Leah shivered as she stepped into the cold. The beat of rap music pounded against her skull as she shoved her earbuds in. The genre was so unbearably plain, but it sharpened her focus. A worthy sacrifice.

It was still dark when she got to the court. By that time, her fingers had already gone numb around her basketball. It didn't matter, she could still play if none of her limbs had feeling.

She started with form shooting. The five swishes in a row had doubled. On good days, Leah completed her warm up in five minutes. On bad ones, it could take her up to an hour.

Good thing this was a good day, because she finished her form shooting while the sun was still well behind the horizon. Then, she moved to threes.

She made this practice into a game.

Leah required herself to make ten threes from each of the five spots on the court. She had three misses without a penalty. The penalty in question, you ask?

It differed.

When Leah needed to increase her endurance, she would run laps around the court until she could barely stand.

When she needed to get stronger, she did push ups until her arms shattered beneath her.

And when she needed better balance?

There was no punishment for that one.

But the rest of the shots she took that day had to be on one foot.

Leah started from the corner, dribbling the ball between her legs and straightening into a shot. Her release was too loose and the ball twirled off the wrong finger. But nonetheless, it clattered into the basket.

Not a swish, Zahara taunted. *I wouldn't have counted it.*

"Shut up, Zahara." Leah retorted. "I'm too tired for this."

Zahara only laughed. The laugh said everything.

She ran to retrieve the ball, repeating the motion. This time, the three was better. It fell into the basket, plummeting through the net with a crisp splash.

Zahara hummed, pleased.

The third shot missed. Strike one.

The fourth hit the backboard, much to Zahara's displeasure. But, despite the D1's criticism, it fell into the hoop. Leah counted it.

The fifth was a swish.

The sixth was an airball.

Leah swallowed, running to retrieve the ball. She usually didn't miss this much, especially after form shooting. Was she falling behind? Was something wrong? She shouldn't be this bad. Swan wouldn't miss like this. Swan was better. Leah had to be *better*.

She made the next three. But on the tenth, the final shot before she moved to her next spot? She tensed. Her core was off balance, her grasp too tight and her wrist too slow. The ball fell from her hand before Leah permitted it to. Miraculously, the thing made it to the rim. It teetered around the basket before deciding to fall to the side.

Third strike.

Zahara cackled in delight.

Leah didn't bother to collect the ball. She broke into a sprint as soon as her shot failed. Her feet pounded against the ground, ankles brushing the wet grass of the park. She did laps around the court— her record was fifty before kneeling over and vomiting. Her goal was to beat it.

The first ten laps were a breeze. The next few were harder. But when she got to thirty laps, she was exhausted. It felt like there was a squirrel in her lungs, trying his very best to claw his way out of her chest. Her stomach had cramped so badly she was nauseous. By the time she hit lap thirty six, she was limping around the court, gasping for air that never seemed to be enough.

Come now, Zahara drawled. *Keep going*.

Leah dropped to her knees, clutching her stomach.

"I–" she gasped. "I can't–"

So are you done? You failed?

Leah coughed. Her split tasted toxically metallic.

Ah, so you're done with your laps. Zahara laughed. *You did better yesterday. Are you getting worse*?

"No!" Leah blurted. "I– I'm just tired. That's all."

Hm, Zahara hummed. *Such an interesting obstacle— exhaustion. We'll get rid of that in due time*.

Leah spit a wad of pink phlegm onto the grass.

Well? Zahara prodded. *You still have shooting to do. Come now, Leah. Get to it. Don't want to become lazy, now do you. Don't want to become a failure.*

~~~

Leah left her workout an hour early that day.

Not because she was done— no, she was never done. There was always something wrong with her game, always something to work on. But this particular morning, she had a more prying issue on her hands. Something that demanded her immediate attention.

Leah entered River High normally. She strode through the front steps with the other students. They were going to meet with their friends or study. Normal high school things. Leah was not a normal high schooler.

So instead of going up the stairs to her first period, she strode around the first floor, searching for an open classroom. It wasn't long until she found one. The teachers were careless, unsuspecting of students with a motive.

Her eyes flitted to the teacher's desk. There, resting on top of a stack of papers, was a key card.

Bingo.

Leah pulled up her hood and slipped her scarf over her nose. No security camera could identify her.

She snatched the card right off the teacher's desk, not bothering to concealing it. No one would suspect a fourteen-year-old, straight A, innocent freshman of thievery.

Leah wove around the hall, nearly running to the gym. But she wasn't going there to work out. In fact, she didn't intend to touch the basketball court at all. She was looking for a room.

And sure enough, just before the court entrance, there was a black door. It was small, paint peeling around its edges. But in black, serif font was the exact name she was looking for.

Coach Viren Varnette.

Leah knocked. No answer. Of course, Viren didn't show up until five minutes after practice started. The old fuck couldn't get up before noon.

Leah slid the keycard over the handle. The door made a sound and clicked open. She padded inside, shutting it behind her.

The office was a wreck. Not the mess of teachers under stress— papers scattered along the desk. No— this room was slob messy; *pathetic* messy. Beer cans, cigars, molding food, a stench Leah couldn't recognize. Absolutely pathetic.
~~~

Clearly, Viren felt comfortable doing all his shameful activities within these walls. If he had anything worthy of blackmail, it would be here.

Leah wasted no time. She yanked the drawers from the desk, rummaging through their contents. She didn't need to be discreet. After all, she wanted Viren to know she had been here. Wanted him to *know* she defeated him.

But she needed to find something. Something fucking *damning*.

Leah dug through papers, chargers and pens. Spare change littered the floor as she tossed the pennies aside. She was beginning to think there was nothing, and as she yanked out the third drawer, her hope dwindled to a sliver.

But when she pulled a book out of the desk, it rattled. *Rattled.* The way a present might. Leah flipped through the pages and found it wasn't a book at all. No— it was a box. A treasure chest. And what Leah might have just found gold.

A USB.

It was dirty, an unplaceable crust covering the edges. Grease and fingerprints covered the plastic. Whatever this held must've been used frequently.

Leah picked up the hard drive, spitting on it and rubbing the thing against her pants. There— at least she wouldn't gag every time she touched it.

She pulled out her chromebook, Gael's old one. It was beaten up, but it worked. At least for this purpose. She placed it on Viren's desk and shoved the key in the hole.

The screen flickered. Then a white library of data revealed itself. Each file was labeled with the date. They seemed to be in no particular order, perhaps organized with frequency of use. Leah clicked on the first one.

The computer took a second to load. Once it was done, it flashed black, a white triangle in the center.

Leah unpaused the video.

She wished she hadn't.

Viren's face showed first as he set the camera up on his desk. He was younger, brown hairs mixing with his grays. Behind him was a child about Leah's age. He had blonde hair and looked absolutely *mortified.*

Viren spoke first.

"Take off your clothes."

The boy hesitated. "I don't—"

"Take them *off*."

The boy remained still.

Viren's fist plunged into his face.

The boy stumbled back, clutching his bleeding nose. Viren advanced on him, ripping his shirt off. This revealed several bruises on the boy's frame, each matching the size of Viren's knuckles.

Next, the coach slammed him against the wall. With onto his hands, he ripped the boys shorts open. The kid screamed.

Viren shoved a cloth into his mouth.

Then, he unbuttoned his own pants.

Leah's hands flew to her mouth, tears watering in her eyes. Viren's thrusted his penis into the boy, who was now crying silent tears. He kept hitting him, forcing him against the walls, the desk, the floor. *Forcing* him to—

Leah closed the laptop, pulled the trash can to her mouth, and threw up.

A rapist. Viren was a *rapist*. Boys, girls— who knew how many. Leah certainly didn't intend to find out. She didn't want to access those videos *ever* again. She wanted to stomp on that hard drive and destroy every single minute of that footage.

But she couldn't. Because this was leverage. This could get Viren fired. This could get him put in *jail*. She found his weak spot, and now, she controlled her coach like a puppet.

Suddenly, she heard footsteps. Loud ones. Coming towards the door. Leah stuffed the USB in her backpack, taking cover under Viren's desk. The steps got louder— she could hear someone rustling in their bag.

"Viren." A voice outside. Leah recognized it as the athletic director. "You don't usually come in this early."

A laugh. *Viren's* laugh. "Well, I forgot my book here. It's quite good. I'm looking forward to *reading* it."

Oh god.

But wait. She had her leverage— what better time than now to share her strength? It's not like she ever planned on keeping it a secret from Viren. Her blackmail didn't work that way.

Well, Zahara chuckled. *Why not make your point unforgettable*?

"Here," the athletic director said. "Let me unlock that for you. I have my keys right here."

The door clicked, a green light flashing.

The handle turned.

“Thanks, I appreciate it.” Viren stepped into his office, head turned towards his colleague.

“No problem.” The director waved, already walking away. Viren drew a sigh, turning to his desk.

That was when Leah turned around. Slowly, in Viren’s chair. Legs swung over the armrest, braids falling to the floor. And in her hand, positioned between two fingers, was the key.

“Hey Viren,” Leah licked her teeth. “Good book?”

Viren’s face contorted into a scowl. “Taven,” he scowled. “I’ll have you—”

“Have me *what*?” Leah smirked. “Suspended? Expelled? Arrested? Well, I’ll tell you one thing, *Coach*.” Leah slammed the USB on the table, circling it with her finger. “I’m not taking my clothes off for you.”

The color in Viren’s face drained. He was left a pale white, eyes flickering from the hard drive to her.

“You don’t—” Viren breathed, his voice small. “You don’t understand.”

“I understand that you have been *raping* kids.” Leah said. “And I understand that this information could get you fired, ruin your career, and get you imprisoned. I also understand that this—” Leah picked up the key, tossing it in the air. “Holds all that power. Therefore *I hold all that power.*”

For a moment, there was silence. Viren’s panicked breath, Leah tapping her fingers against the desk. They were waiting for the other to speak. Viren was searching for his retort, his *escape*. Leah waited for it.

But it never came.

Gotcha.

“Well?” Leah tiled her head. “I’m waiting.”

Viren met her gaze, pure fire burning in his eyes. “For *what*?”

“For you to beg.”

Viren remained still. Leah shot him a look. And slowly— wonderfully *slowly*— he got on his knees. Leah got up from her perch, striding to where he knelt on the floor. She circled him for a bit, admiring his fallen figure.

Then, she slammed her foot into his back.

The coach kneeled over, gasping. Leah kept her shoe on his spine, forcing him to the floor. She grinned when she noticed tears dripping onto the carpet.

“You know what the difference is between you and me?” Leah drawled. “You get your power from strength. From your muscles. But that’s inefficient. *Weak*. Because you know what trumps brute strength *every single time*?

“*Hunger*.” Leah whispered. “The undying will to succeed. Maybe I don’t have your strength, Viren. But I have something much better. I don’t care what I risk. I don't care what I *lose*. All I care about is my goals, my *victory*. And right now—" Leah shoved her foot into his spine. The coach yelped. "You're getting in my way."

Viren gasped, tears pouring down his face. His lip wobbled and his throat bobbed. Ugly sobs breached his lips, joining the panicked breaths. "What–" he gasped. "What do you want?"

Leah grinned. She released him, leaning against the desk. Before she spoke, she picked his chin up with her sneaker, looking directly at his face.

"You're my bitch now, Viren." Leah breathed. "If I need to score, you lick the bottom of my sneaker. No more bullshit Milly plays. No more using me as cleanup. *I'll* draw the plays. *I'll* hold the strings. And *I'll* be the one who carries this team. Not Milly. *Me*."

Leah tossed the hard drive, catching it between her thumb and her pinky. "All you have to do is be a good little dog and play your cards right. You can take all the credit. I don't mind. Be the brilliant coach. Tell everyone you and I are lovers for all I care. Just be my puppet. Roll over, wag your tail, and go fetch. Because you're my bitch Viren. Do all that, and I'll keep our little secret under wraps."

"You—" Viren picked up his head, glaring daggers at her. "You— Leah Taven— are an *awful* person."

Leah tilted her head. "That's rich, considering your actions."

"I didn't say I was better." Viren drawled. "But believe it or not, I have my boundaries. You don't. That's what's so dangerous about you, Leah. There are no lengths you won't go to. No line you won't cross. To you, there is no price too great for success."

Leah hummed a laugh. "Maybe. Maybe there's no line I won't cross. But every single thing I do, every deed I can't take back— I do it for a reason. You destroy children's sanity and security for fun— for *lust*. That makes you a monster. But me?" Leah leaned down, face just inches from Virens's. "I do it for fame. To be known. To be *loved*. Am I cruel? Maybe. But I'm respectable."

Viren scoffed. "Respectability doesn't mean your moral."

Leah laughed— hard and off tune. She didn't give the coach the courtesy of her response. "Oh, one more thing." She started towards the door, placing the USB in her pocket. "Any more of your disgusting behavior: anything to make me believe that you may repeat your heinous actions—" Leah turned to face him, braids dripping over her shoulder. "And I will *destroy you*."

REMEMBER WHO WINS

"As indicated below, 35% of current athletes and 33% of retired athletes sought help for their mental health challenges. Only 19% of current athletes and 9% of retired athletes felt supported by their sport organization while receiving help for a mental health issue."
—Kerr, Gretchen, et al. "Prevalence of Maltreatment among Current and Former National Team Athletes"

"Listen," Leah placed her hands on her knees, leaning into the conversation. "This game is one of deception. We know Swan's every move— every play she might run. We're ready for her. All we need to do is remember what we talked about."

Her teammates nodded, eyes locked on Leah. They had actually been quite coachable once Leah had taken Viren down. Even hostile Milly bended to Leah's every wish. They still didn't like each other, but she didn't care about that. Milly respected her. That was all Leah wanted.

And in turn, Leah let her take a fair amount of shots. She averaged around twelve points a game, double what she scored under Viren. Though Milly would never admit it, she worked better with Leah's leadership.

"Swan's going to run a series of screens— one after another. She wants us to scramble, to lose our footing. That's when she'll strike. She's taught her team how to deal with every screen counter, so we need to mix them up. Her team hasn't mastered it yet— so the variety should confuse them."

"Are there specific screen counters you want us to use?" Milly asked.

Leah nodded. "Hedge and drop. Oh, and if you are *absolutely sure* that it'll work, we can use blitz. But not against Swan. *Never* against Swan."

There was a buzzer. Leah's eyes darted to the door. The JV game must've ended. It was her turn.

"River High hasn't lost the championship since Zahara Williamson's sophomore year. I want to maintain her record." She placed her hand in the middle of the huddle. Her teammates followed. "River on me, River on three. One, two, three—"

"River!" Leah's teammates echoed. Their fists pumped into the air— a united front. With much work, Leah had actually created a *team*. A rare occurrence in high school basketball.

Leah strode out of the room, teammates following her. As soon as she opened the door, the energy of the gym hit her. Pop music blared from the speakers, the beat rumbling through the floor. As she strode along the baseline, the JV team walked past her. Serena stared forward, not daring to glance at Leah.

They bumped shoulders. Neither seemed to acknowledge it.

"Leah—" Milly scrambled to her side. "Viren's not here yet."

Leah kept her stride. "We don't need him, it's fine."

"*We* don't need him." Milly retorted. "But the game does. What are we going to tell the refs; a freshman is running our team?"

Leah blew a strand of hair from her face. As much as she hated to admit it, Milly had a point. They needed Viren. For show and nothing else. So where the fuck was he? Passed out in the bottom of a pit?

"Let's wait." Leah said. "If he doesn't show by game time, you'll tell the refs that you'll run the show."

"But they won't listen—"

"Yes they will." Leah set her bag down by the bench, grabbing a few balls off the rack. "Seniority, remember? You've been on varsity for three years. They'll listen to you."

Milly dipped her head. Respect.

That was all Leah needed. Milly had her uses— everyone did, at least if they were used right. Once under a capable guide, Milly turned out to be a good ally.

Leah joined the warm ups, mentally preparing for the game. This was it. This was the moment that decided who was the next Zahara. It was her or Swan. One of them would get MVP. The other would go by unnoticed.

And Leah *had* to be great.

The buzzer rang. Leah beckoned her team to their bench. Surprisingly, Viren decided to show up. He looked hungover, bags lingering under his gray eyes. No one acknowledged him.

"Sit down," Leah ordered. "We're gonna run our standard flow offense. Swan's the only outstanding threat, so I'll guard her. She's also going to run a man to man defense, so don't call a play that's meant for zone. Oh, and remember—" Leah pointed to the middle of the court. "The traps are going to come just as you cross halfway. Always— and I mean *always*— dribble up the middle."

The crack of the speakers sparked to life. The starters sat on the bench, waiting for their names to be called. Leah was called first, being the youngest. Swan was called at the same time.

They locked eyes. She looked so *light*. So carefree. Did she not know what was resting on the fate of this game? Did she not understand what was at stake? Did she care?

Or maybe she was just so certain that she would win.

Bitch!

They shook hands, Swan's eyes sparkling as they met each other. She smiled, her gaze glittering. "Good luck, Leah."

Leah returned her grin. "You too, Swan."

The words felt thick in her throat.

Throughout the ceremony, she kept her eyes on Swan. Leah memorized her appearance— her slim legs, hourglass figure and shiny hair put into a perfect ponytail. Her shoes looked too bottom heavy— not enough ankle support. Leah considered going after her weak spots. If Swan were to sprain—

No, no. That was unfair. Besides, Swan didn't deserve to be hurt. They may have been competing now, but she was still a person. An ankle sprain— if it was bad— could take her out for months. Leah did have a moral compass, and as warped as it may be, she had the bounds she wouldn't cross.

Besides, Ezra would actually kill her.

Once everyone was announced, her team gathered in a huddle. "Remember," Leah said. "Once this is done— once we *win*— we won't have to worry about Swan for months.

"River on me, River on three," Leah put her fist in the center, her teammates following. "One, two three—"

"*River*!" they echoed, the sound radiating around the gym. They dispersed, lining up for the jump ball. Leah met Swan's gaze. She was positioned at the other end of the court, eyes never quite resting.

Leah caught her gaze. Swan waved.

Leah returned the gesture.

No point in being rude. It didn't serve her.

The referee held the ball in the center, gesturing for the two girls to touch it. They did. The ref blew his whistle, and the ball ascended into the air.

Leah's teammate hit it towards her. She grasped the ball, slamming it onto the floor and running towards the basket. But the thing was bouncier than she expected— and as she pounded it against the floor it bounded up to her shoulder.

Swan took advantage of this. She dove for the ball, swiping it straight from Leah's possession. Leah sprinted after her, but Swan was already gone. She made the layup easily, her manicured hands laying the ball into the basket.

The crowd went wild.

"Swan Trevor with the fast break!" the announcer said.

Leah slapped her leg. The pain helped her focus. That would *not* happen again.

Milly inbounded the ball, passing it to Leah. This time, she took her time dribbling up the court, becoming accustomed to the way the ball rolled on her fingers. Swan didn't bother to press.

Just as Leah crossed half court, Swan swarmed her. She came at the ball, but her attack had a consequence. Leah spun around her, pushing the thing ahead.

She raced into the first layer of defense. They came at her, leaving the hoop unprotected. It was Milly who made the move, cutting to the basket. Leah flung the pass between her opponent's legs, giving Milly an open layup.

The senior delivered.

"A senior, Milly Fersak, for two!"

Leah backpedaled to the other side of the court, high-fiving Milly as she sprinted back. Swan came quick, bringing up the ball with her post by her side. Leah recognized the play before it happened— a pick and roll.

"Watch the screen!" she shouted. Her teammates bristled, awaiting the upcoming action. Just as predicted, the post set a screen for Swan.

"Switch!" Leah shouted. She sank back with her new defender, blocking the pass. But Swan didn't attempt to hit her teammate. Instead, she stepped back — out of reach from her defender— and pulled into a shot.

There's no fucking way that's going in.

But it did. A perfect swish.

The crowd absolutely loved it.

They cooed and hooted, making enough of a racket to do serious damage to ears. But Leah didn't mind. She dribbled up the court fast, rage fueling her steps. She was not losing this game. She was not losing to *Swan*.

She pushed past Swan using her shoulder. The first layer of defense couldn't stop her, she simply barreled towards the basket, knocking down anyone in her path.

Leah swung the ball over the last defender, finishing with a scoop.

"Leah Taven with the Euro!"

Leah barely heard the scream of the crowd. She had already locked eyes with Swan, watching as she dribbled up the court. She was ready— ready for any move her opponent tried. Eyes locked on her torso, legs spread just wider than shoulder-length.

But Swan did the one thing Leah didn't expect. Something more glamorous than practical.

She punched the ball through Leah's legs, meeting it on the other side. The audience yelped with delight as Leah scrambled to meet her opponent, preparing for the drive. But Swan tricked her. When she noticed Leah's imbalance in weight, she stepped back into a three. Leah lost her balance, slipping to the ground.

The crowd erupted with laughter.

And when Swan swished the shot, the cackles turned to applause.

Leah staggered to her feet, flicking her braids behind her back.

"Leah—" Milly appeared by her side. "She's too good—"

"*She* is a fucking show off." Leah snapped. "You wanna play a game of threes Swan? Fine. I'll make you choke on your own moves."

This time, when Leah dribbled up the court, she did so slowly. She waited for Swan to come at her, and when she did, Leah barged past her. She faked the drive, venturing into the first layer of defense. Swan followed, sticking her long fingers in Leah's dribble. But she was off balance— expecting to guard a layup.

Leah flung the ball behind her back, straightening into her shot.

Swan stumbled.

Choke, Swan. Fucking choke.

Leah swished the three.

And the crowd went wild.

"Leah Taven for three!"

Now, they were cheering for her. Not for Swan, for *her*. So she kept at it. She didn't go for layups, only the far shots. Every time, she used Swan's own moves against her, and every time, the girl fell for them.

But her smile never wavered. It was like this was just a game for her. Just a *game*.

So Leah kept swishing.

And Swan kept smiling.

Maybe that was because her tactic had switched. She wasn't going for threes anymore, she was driving. Plummeting into the defense and stacking up points upon points.

No one could stop her.

So Leah played her game.

She made three after three— the crowd whispering as she made yet another shot. But she couldn't make all of them. No matter how much she practiced— no matter how good her shot was, the probability of a three was much less than one of a layup. She had chosen the harder shot. Swan was playing the easier game.

So with twenty seconds left, Leah found herself down by four points. Four points. Twenty seconds. That was a point per five seconds— a shot every ten. If she could pull this off all of it— *all of it*— would be worth it.

Leah had the ball. She pounded it up the court, weaving between defenders and running through Swan's press. Swan met her on the other side of the court, grinning ear to ear.

She thought she had won.

Choke.

Leah slammed herself into Swan. It was with her shoulder— something completely legal. But the girl tripped backward, falling onto the court. It was over exaggerated. Leah hadn't hit her that hard.

But the referee blew his whistle, moving his hands in a pushing movement.

"Charge on number Seven. White ball."

Charge? A fucking *charge*?

Leah wanted to scream.

But she didn't. She ran a hand through her hair, fingers drifting over her long braids. She could do this. No problem. Four points. Fifteen seconds. She was going to win. She was going to be the *fucking MVP*.

"Press!" Leah shouted. Swan was *not* getting past half court. "Now!"

Her teammates flocked to their places. They guarded the passes. If the inbounder wanted to get the ball in, they'd have a hell of a time trying.

Leah stood next to Swan. They were both exhausted, that was clear. Their chests rose and fell rapidly, lungs stretching the most they possibly could. But they didn't gasp. Leah could run five extra miles if she willed herself to and Swan looked ready to fight an army.

They may have been exhausted, but that was just a feeling. The game was different. That shit was *real.*

The ref blew the whistle and Swan leapt from Leah's side. Leah moved with her, blocking a clear path to the ball. The inbounder locked eyes with Swan, letting the ball roll off her fingers.

Leah grinned.

But the ball didn't come at her. Instead, it sailed towards half court. The opposing center caught it, holding the ball above her head.

Ten seconds. Four points. And counting. The clock was rushing downwards as the post held the ball in the center of the court. Leah was rushing towards the girl before the ball was placed on the floor. When the center attempted to dribble, it was flawed. Too high, very out of control.

Leah swiped it with ease.

With a long stride, she dribbled to the three point line. Before Swan could get to her, the shot rolled off her fingers. Leah released a breath, watching the ball sail through the air.

It hit the rim— Leah tensed. The ball bounced around the basket, teetering around the circle. Eventually, it fell through the net, rewarding Leah with a crisp swish.

Five seconds. One shot. That's all she needed. Then she won. Then she would be MVP. Then people would actually *notice* her.

"Press!" Leah repeated. Her team flocked to her side, matching up with their opponents. Leah stood beside Swan, watching the inbounder like a hawk.

The ball came quick. Too quick. Leah misjudged the pass. She leapt too late. By the time she intercepted the line of trajectory, the thing was already in Swan's grasp.

And she was dribbling up the court. Fast. With a motive. But no particular goal.

Five seconds.

No no no. She was running out the clock. Leah charged at her, feet pounding against the court. But Swan was too far ahead.

By the time Leah reached her, the clock had clicked down to three seconds. She swiped at the ball, but Swan placed it out of reach.

Two seconds.

Swan stopped dribbling, holding the ball in triple threat. Leah grabbed it, tugging at the thing like it was her child.

One second.

Their eyes met. As always, Swan gave Leah that pitying smile. But Leah wasn't angry. When she found Swan's gaze, she didn't find herself wishing fire would rip through her body. Instead, her eyes widened and her rage shrunk. She was left with regret, pleading to win. Pleading for the victory. Because victory meant she would be noticed. Victory meant recognition. Recognition meant *love*.

Swan's gaze softened, understanding drifting over her features.

For a moment, she looked as though she may give Leah the ball.

Then the buzzer went off.

And the game was over.

Swan broke eye contact first. Her smile brightened and she gave Leah's back a soft pat. "You did well."

Leah didn't respond. She was left staring into the crowd— at the people cheering for Swan; *ignoring* her.

A hand landed on her shoulder. Leah turned to see Milly. "Come on, Leah." She said, "We lost. We need to go—"

Leah brushed her hand off, eyes returning to the crowd. She didn't say anything, but Milly got the message. She left her alone.

Leah padded to the bench, watching as Swan and her team cheered. Leah's own teammates had retreated to the locker room, defeated and shrunken. But Leah stayed, elbows resting on her knees, braids draped over her shoulders. She watched the basket, eyeing the slightly ripped net. She could've glared at Swan or at the crowd who worshiped her. But no— her anger was centered on the hoop.

"Fuck you," Leah murmured. "I gave *everything* and you still made me lose. *Fuck you.*"

~~~

No one was surprised that Swan got MVP.

Really, who else would it go to?

But when it was announced, the crowd still went wild. Friends, family and coaches flocked to her side, swarming her with love and admiration. A good sport would've been happy for her opponent. After all, in high school Swan was her enemy but in AAU they were teammates. A good sport would've been among those congratulating her.

Leah was not a good sport.

She sat on her bench, watching as they all adored Swan and ignored her. Savana, who Leah had eliminated from the tournament a day prior, was showering her with praise. Ezra rushed to hug her, whispering something Leah wished she heard.
~~~

When the ceremony was done, Leah stayed behind. No one came to talk to her. No one acknowledged her performance. Why should they? She didn't win. She was worth *nothing*.

She just sat in the gym, unmoving, unfeeling. She simply glared at the net, promising over and over to succeed so many times that this tiny loss would be drowned in her mass of victories.

When the crowd left, Leah stayed. The janitor didn't notice her when he shut the lights off. She was left in the dark gym, making promises to herself and the shadows.

Then, a spark of light lit up the dark.

Leah turned to see a flame dancing along a cigarette. The glow illuminated the shallow, yellow features of the man smoking it. Gael touched the drug to his lips, letting the smoke ooze from his mouth.

"What are you doing here?" Leah snapped. "You never come to my games."

Gael withdrew the cigar from his mouth, releasing a long curl of gray. "You did everything right."

Oh fuck he's so high.

"Yeah, I did." Leah crossed her arms. "Didn't matter much, did it?"

Gael either didn't hear her or chose to ignore the phrase. "Do you know how many threes you scored?"

"It doesn't matter, Dad."

"You made thirteen." Gael answered. "Do you know what the record is for the county?"

Leah was surprised to say she didn't.

"Twelve threes in a game. Set by Daniella Vallran. You broke it."

Leah breathed a sigh. "Well it's not like anyone cares."

"I care." Gael's tone was sweet as syrup. "I underestimated you, daughter dear. You have some potential. The potential for fame. At least in this small town. Do you know that D1 athletes get paid now? You could go to a very good college and a full scholarship. With that kind of money—" Gael chuckled. "Well, let's just say the cash your mom gave us could last a lot longer."

"So what are you proposing?" Leah asked.

"Every D1 athlete has one thing in common. A parent who doubles as a coach. Someone who's not afraid to push their child to the limit." Gael pressed the cigarette to his lips. "I suppose it's time I start paying more attention to my *daughter*."

WHEN THE AMBITION SHIFTS

"One of the main reasons that athletes won't report abuse is because they're trying to protect other people."
—Willson, Erin. Zoom interview. April 8, 2025

"So what are we doing?" Leah placed her hands on her hips. "Shooting, dribbling, conditioning? What have you got in mind?"

Gael pressed a scrawny finger to his lip. Him and Leah stood at the community court, ball resting between them. Gael had decided to join her morning expedition. The man seemed quite eager to teach her a thing or two. Leah knew damn well her dad had no basketball experience, but she was willing to humor him.

Gael shrugged. "I have no idea."

Leah squinted. "What do you mean, *no idea*?"

"I mean you know more than me, Leah." It almost looked like the words hurt him. "You already know what drills to do. I'm just here to provide *support*."

Cheerleader father. All he was missing was a skimpy uniform and pom-poms.

"Fine," Leah snapped. "Do whatever that means. I'm going to start with Mikan drill."

Gael nodded. Before Leah could grab the ball, his hand met her wrist. Leah raised an eyebrow.

"Just one more thing," Gael breathed. "I need to know; how much are you willing to give for this game?"

Leah frowned. "Whatever it takes."

Gael smiled. That's all he did. Smile.

Leah took her position under the basket, starting her warm up. She made the first shot— missed the second. Made the third and the fourth: and the fifth—

"*Agh*!" Leah yelped, falling to the ground. "What—"

"You can't be that weak." Gael growled. "You need to stand your ground."

"You just pushed me—" Gael grabbed her collar, hoisting her to her feet. Hot smoke lingered on her cheek: Leah flinched backward, and for a moment, she was so incredibly sure Gael was going to hit her.

But instead he simply set her on the ground, placed the ball in her hands, and gestured for her to continue.

Leah swallowed, attempting to continue her routine. But now, it was harder. Harder than it had ever been with Zahara. Gael lingered behind her, not moving, not speaking— only breathing. That breath slithered down her back, the smoke choking her in its tight hold.

Shots are a lot tougher to make with a threat behind you.

Not a defender— Leah could deal with that. But Gael wasn't playing defense. This was *not* defense. His shoves were random, mostly only light, but sometimes he knocked Leah to her knees. And sometimes he didn't push. Sometimes he kicked her. Sometimes he scratched— drew blood with only his fingernails.

Leah never really realized how strong he was until she experienced it first hand.

She missed every single shot.

And on the tenth one, Gael's plans had shifted.

"Run." He growled.

"What?" Leah choked. "Why—"

Gael tilted his head. "You missed too many. You need to improve your stamina— that's why you lost to Swan. Come on Leah. *Run.*"

With that, she took off; ball rolling her hands, full sprint. She ran faster than she ever had, up and down the court. That was okay. She could run. She ran by herself. But she didn't realize Gael was chasing her until he screamed.

"Faster!" his voice was like a blade, cutting into her eardrums. "Dribble harder! Go, *bitch.*"

The air left her lungs. Not from the running, but from the shock. From the *fear*. What if she didn't run? Would he hurt her? What happened when she got tired? What then?

So she kept running. She powered through the burn roaring in her legs, powered through her aching lungs. Powered through when it felt as though her chest may collapse. She didn't want to know what happened when she failed.

On lap twenty, her foot caught on a dent in the court. She toppled to the ground, ball rolling from her hand. She tried to get up, but her legs wouldn't move. Her lungs felt like they had exploded and nausea surfaced in her throat.

"Come on," Gael's voice was so soft, barely audible over the panic roaring in Leah's ear. "Get up."

"I—" Leah gasped. "I can't."

Gael didn't respond. Instead, he grabbed her arm, nails digging into her skin. He yanked her to her feet, shoving the ball into her arms. "Run, girl, run." He pressed his yellow teeth together. "Tell me you aren't as incompetent as you look. *Fucking run* Leah."

"Dad, *please*!" Leah heaved. "I can't— I can't *breathe*—"

"Come on Leah—"

"Dad no!" she shrieked. "I don't want it to be like this. It can't be like this. If this—" she choked. "There has to be another way!"

It was then when she realized how many people were watching. Parents, teenagers, grandparents. *Children*. Their heads turned from what they were doing— tennis, playing on the playground, biking, digging in the sand. But those activities stopped as they heard Leah's terrified wail. Everyone watched as Leah was chased and tormented. Everyone saw. Everyone *knew*.

And everyone did *nothing*. They sat there, neither smiling nor frowning, but accepting. No one pulled out their phone to film. No one made any move to stop her father. They all just stood and *watched*.

"Oh come on, Leah." Gael huffed a laugh. "You're being hysterical."

Leah looked around, frantic to find *something*. Someone who would step between her and her father. Someone who would protect her. But there was no such person. No one dared. Because in the context of sports, abuse didn't exist. Gael was just trying to make her better. He was a *good dad*.

No one was coming to save her. The only thing left to do was endure.

She ran. Fast. Even though her lungs screamed at her to stop, even though the phlegm in her mouth was beginning to taste like blood, she ran. She spat her vomit through sloppy strides. She let the tears leak from her eyes as Gael screamed his influx of insults.

Bitch. Useless. Pathetic.

Leah didn't realize when he stopped chasing her. Maybe because the insults didn't cease. In her mind, someone~was still on her tail. The shrieking remained, her own mind hollering louder and louder. She dribbled until the calluses on her hands exploded into bloody welts. She ran until she could barely feel her legs.

But it wasn't energy that was feeding her stride. It wasn't ambition either. Usually, those were the two that kept her walking. But this time, it was pure, shattering *fear*.

Fear, she realized, was much more effective.

Because before she knew it, she had broken her record by ten laps.

~~~

Leah was still shaking when the car door shut behind her. She was thirsty, of course, but nausea kept her water bottle full. She would've been crying, but thankfully, she wasn't hydrated enough to shed the tears. Good thing too, as Gael was positioned in the driver's seat.

"You were lucky with Viren." He began. "Not everyone you come across will have a weakness like that. Sometimes, you'll have to do it without control. You can't care what people think of you. You can't care what people do to you."

Leah kept her eyes on the dashboard, not daring to look her father in the eye. She ran the cloth of her shorts through her fingers— a desperate attempt to keep herself from clawing at her skin.

"Those parents probably thought I was an awful father." Gael continued. "But I don't give two fucks about that. Because they didn't do anything to stop it. They know that what I'm doing will only make you better."

Leah swallowed.

"You best everyone who opposes you, Leah. Deep down, your opponents know that too. Don't ask for permission, and don't ask for forgiveness. Take control like your enemies never even existed."

Leah took a shaky breath. "But people *are* better than me. Swan is. I can't simply act like she doesn't exist."

Gael lit a cigarette. The distinct smell of drugs drifted into the car as he pressed it to his lips, heaving a sigh of smoke.

"You're right." He breathed. "Swan is better than you. That's because everything you've been doing up to this point has been child's play. Believe me, Leah, you may not be the best now, but you will be." Gael pressed the drug to his mouth, blowing a string of smoke. "Not if I have anything to do with it."

~~~

Leah was still shaking when she got to practice.

She figured if she started dribbling she would snap out of her terrified trance. But when the ball tipped off her hands, all she could think about was what would happen if she missed.

Was Gael watching? Was he the only one who would hurt her? What if—

No. Ezra would never. Swan would never. *Savana* would never. Because Leah's brilliance only mattered that much to her father. She needed to be great for him. He reaped the benefits. The only thing Ezra got was a good player.

The shot seemed to hang in the air. Then, it dropped. The ball didn't even hit the rim. Three feet short.

Leah's breath stopped. She was ready to run as soon as the thing hit the ground. Ready to sprint. Ready to flee from whatever was chasing her. Her breath stopped, and as much as she needed to bolt, she couldn't. She was frozen in place, watching as the ball rhythmically bounced against the ground.

"Hey," Leah jumped as a hand landed on her shoulder. "You okay?"

She spun around to see Savana. She looked into her with prying eyes, studying her like a specimen. Savana snatched her forearm, running a finger over the blood and bruises.

She met Leah's gaze, understanding drifting over her face. Leah snatched her hand back, rubbing her sore skin.

"It's nothing," Leah murmured. "Just scratches. Everyone gets them in basketball."

Savana simply looked at her. Not with pity or sympathy, but in understanding.

"You have five minutes until practice starts." She said. "Therefore five minutes to pull yourself together. Splash water on your face, scream— cry if you need to. Just get whatever happened out of your system."

Leah nodded. She strode towards the door, nearly breaking into a run. Before she could reach the frame, someone grabbed her shoulder.

"Hey kid," Ezra looked at her with soft blue eyes. "You okay?"

Leah jerked her shoulder away. "Fine."

Before Ezra could object, Leah bolted out the door. Tears drifted down her face as she ran through the grounds. Ezra rented his gym from an elementary school. Too small for high schoolers— but it was cheap and got the job done. Unfortunately, the nearest bathrooms were far from the court. A long way to run, a long way until her sobbing was no longer a public display.

She slammed the bathroom door behind her, fumbling with the lock. She was alone. She could fall apart *alone*.

Leah's hands slid to her hair, tears cascading down her features. She sunk to the floor, braids spilling over her shoulders. The voice wasn't gone. The insults hadn't ceased. In fact, they were louder.

Incompetent. Bitch. Useless.

Leah's breath quickened. She opened her eyes, letting the tears sting under her iris. She yanked her hair, letting out a screech. Her own yell echoed around the bathroom before falling silent.

When the scream was gone, she started sobbing. Hard, rough belts erupted from her throat, sending rivulets falling down her cheeks. She slammed her head against her knees, letting the droplets slide down her legs.

It wasn't pain she was feeling. Nor was it rage. She cried because her hands trembled. She cried because she was scared. Because she was *helpless*. And she hated it.

She hated the way her father had pushed her. The way he made her run. The things he yelled. She hated how she just *took it*. She hated everything about the experience. But it was necessary. Abused kids took the throne. This ordeal, though awful, was a necessity.

Failure. Pathetic. Weak. The voices resumed. Leah placed her hands over her ears, trying to stop the flashes of her father from invading her mind.

But there was another voice. Not her father's. Refreshing, but dangerous. An ice gold knife plunging through her thoughts.

Five minutes, Leah. Zahara cooed. *Get it out of your system.*

Leah took a breath, steadying herself. Still shaking, she made her way towards the toilet. She rested her forearms on the rim, looking into the clear water.

She took a final breath and stuck her fingers down her throat. She'd learned the trick from her mother, who did it often when the drugs became too much.

"It'll calm you down." She had told Leah. "Narcotic or none, this will help you reset your nerves. Get the past out of your system."

One. Two. Three. Leah pulled her fingers out on the third second. Nothing happened. Maybe she had done it wrong. Then, the nausea intensified. Leah leaned over the toilet, gagging into the water.

The vomit came with her second heave. Yellow, clumpy stuff that matched the texture of her breakfast. It came in waves. One moment, a rush of bile overwhelmed her. The next, she was heaving for air, expecting the next round of throw up.

When it was finally done, Leah wiped her mouth. Using the toilet as a crutch, she got to her feet. She gurgled water, blew her nose, and wiped the tears from her eyes. Miraculously, no vomit had gotten on her shirt.

You're going to have to get better at handling this. Zahara scolded. *This kind of breakdown is most inconvenient.*

"I know," Leah growled. "I'll handle it better next time."

You're lucky I put up with you. Zahara's voice was tainted, it held a darker edge. Leah realized it may not be her mentor's tone at all. A new figure had entered her mind to taunt her.

Ungrateful bitch. Some girls would be more than happy to have a dad who puts even the smallest grain of effort into their greatness. Gael cooed. *Stop with this existential crisis and get on the court.*

"Dammit," Leah banged her fist against her head. "I know, I'm sorry. I'll—" she took a breath. "I'll do better."

Good girl, Zahara was back, her voice as sharp as ever. *Now get out there and show how much you're willing to sacrifice.*

RENO MEMORIAL DAY TOURNAMENT

Parental involvement may be interpreted as pressure by athletes. Athletes respond best to praise and encouragement.
—Bonavolontà, Valerio, et al. "The Role of Parental Involvement in Youth Sport Experience: Perceived and Desired Behavior by Male Soccer Players."

"Holy shit." Savana marveled as she, Leah and Swan strode into the vast gym. It was the largest thing Leah had ever seen. Courts stretched farther than the eye could see; a game occurring on each one. Parents and players filled the gym, lining the courts and waiting for the next big shot. "It's fucking huge."

Leah elbowed her. "Worth the long drive?"

"Are you kidding?" Savana was jumping up and down now. "How long do you think it took to set this up? How many courts are there? At least fifty I bet."

Swan chuckled. "The real question is, how long will it take to find our court?"

Leah looked at her phone, pulling up the schedule. "Ezra said we're playing on court forty eight."

"Brilliant, Leah." Savana smirked. "And which one of these sixty something courts is that?"

"Was that sarcasm?" Leah scoffed. "Didn't think you had it in you."

"Guys," Swan grabbed Leah's hand, leading her down the walkway. "Forty eight is this way."

"And you know this, how?"

"The courts are numbered. They're in rows, just like every other tournament. The only thing different about it is the scale." Swan tilted her head. "See? One, two, three. And over there— eight, nine, ten. So I would guess that forty eight is somewhere—" Swan scanned the area. "Other there."

Leah looked at Savana. Savana looked back. Their eye roll was synced.

Savana nudged Swan. "Well aren't you just brilliant."

Swan gave her a smile. She led them through the maze of games, eventually finding one with a large '48' taped to its backboard. Ezra was waiting at the other end of the court, arms crossed as he watched the current competition.

When he saw them, a smile replaced his focused frown. “Well look who it is,” he said. “Timely as always.”

Leah smirked. “That’s why you have us arrive thirty minutes early.”

“Thank god for that,” Ezra hummed. “I fear if I don't, you may never show up.”

“I’d miss you too much.”

“I’m flattered, Leah.” He turned back to the court, his firm stare resting on a girl with a blue headband. “See her? She’s the best player on that team. MVP of her league. Supposed to be really good. From what I’ve seen, she’s no better than our own MVP.”

Leah scowled. Swan’s flattery was subtle, but Leah picked up on it. She always did.

“So what do you want from me?” Leah asked.

“How do you know I need something from you?” Ezra raised an eyebrow. “What prevents the fact that I’m simply sparking conversation?”

“Your personality.” Leah replied.

Ezra shot her a glare. “Touche, kid. I want you to figure out what that girl’s non-dominant hand is. Oh— and find her preferred method of shot.”

Leah furrowed her brow. “Simple enough. Couldn’t you have done that yourself?”

“I could’ve.” Ezra agreed. “But I thought I’d save the task for you.”

“How considerate.”

Ezra grinned, clapping her on the back. “Have fun.”

The girl, as it turns out, was remarkably hard to scout. She dribbled with both hands fluently, switching like it was nothing. She was well practiced— Leah could respect that, but it was unfortunate for her.

Her shot selection wasn’t any easier. The girl took a wide range of takes, from post-ups to threes. Her accuracy was average— she made around twenty five percent. But they couldn’t guard all of her attacks, especially with her variety.

That’s when she saw it. As the girl dribbled up the court, Leah noticed her dribbling. At first glance, nothing was out of the ordinary. But everything about her handle was slightly *off*. She dribbled too high, too far in front of her and not hard enough.

Leah grinned. A tight press would destroy her.

She turned, heading to where Ezra had gathered her team. When she approached, he smiled.

“Well Leah?” Ezra gestured to the circle. Leah took a seat. “What side should we play too?”

Leah smirked. “Beats me. The girl might as well be ambidextrous.”

“Well isn’t that splendid.” Ezra groaned. “And her shot selection?”

“As random as a roulette wheel.”

Ezra drew a sigh. “Well you aren’t smiling like that just for fucks, are you? What did you notice?”

Leah grinned, scooting closer into the circle. “The girl’s handle isn’t great. They aren’t pressing her now, but I bet with the slightest bit of pressure, she’ll panic. All we need to do is press and the game is ours.”

“Right,” Sarah crossed her arms. “What about when she passes? Do you have any insight on them?”

She had her there. Leah hadn’t noticed the girl’s passes. She’d have to work on that in future.

“It doesn’t matter.” Ezra answered. “If she can’t dribble, that means she doesn’t have the correct tranquility to make those passes. And even if she manages to shoot a fast one, we’ll have people there to intercept it. Well done.”

Leah raised her chin.

As always, Ezra’s game plan was incredibly hard to follow. Apparently, because this ‘wasn’t an important game’ he felt the need to introduce a new, incredibly complicated action that was apparently ‘too mystical’ to run in practice. Whatever the fuck that meant.

“So—” Ezra pointed to his clipboard. “Then this player sets a screen for the post, and the post sets a screen for the point, and that goes into the action Riens—” he tilted his head, looking at the team. “Are you even listening?”

Swan rubbed the back of her neck. “To be honest, you lost me on that last part.”

Leah jutted out her jaw. “I’ve been lost since your flurry of flare screens.”

Savana folded her arms. “I was never there.”

“Fine,” Ezra twirled his pen. “Let’s start again.”

Remarkably, by the time the game started Leah had figured half the play out. Swan seemed fluent enough to teach, and Savana—

Well Leah had no idea. She just hoped the girl’s grasp was strong enough not to get her benched.

The jump ball was a disappointing affair. The referee’s throw was awful and neither team could get a solid hold on the ball for a good ten seconds. Finally, Swan came through and dribbled the thing up the court.

"Break!" She yelled. It took Leah a moment to realize what she meant. In her head, she'd called the play 'Ezra's latest obsession.'

Leah ran to her spot, preparing for her turn to screen. She was supposed to set the flare after Savana did… something. Leah only had enough brainpower to memorize her part. She'd learn the other later.

Savana, it seemed, didn't learn. Because she stood in the middle of the key, eyes wide like a dear in headlights. Leah didn't know where she was supposed to be, but it definitely wasn't *there*.

"*Savana*!" Swan screeched. Leah didn't know she could yell. "Set the screen!"

Savana just stood there, frozen.

Leah brushed her braid over her shoulder, running to Swan. "Go! Around the three point line! We'll run our regular thing!"

Swan shot her a look. "But the play—"

"Fuck the play." Leah held up her hands, gesturing for Swan to pass. She did. "It's not going to work this time. Next possession."

The ball spun in Leah's grasp as she scanned the court. Savana was in the corner, watching the stands. She was looking for her father. He wasn't there— Swan's family had driven both of them to Reno— but she still looked for him. Still terrified.

Leah drove, drawing the defense inward. Just as she got to the basket, she passed the ball to Savana.

At first, when the pass hit her, Savana looked startled. She made eye contact with Leah, unsure of what to do. Leah gave her a curt nod. Savana seemed to gather herself enough to shoot. The shot rattled around the rim before falling through the net. Hopefully the small victory would soften the blow for her.

The whistle blew. Leah turned to the referee.

"Timeout," he said. "White."

Leah glanced at Savana. She moved like a ghost, making her way to the bench with cautious, heavy steps. By her side, her hands were shaking. Leah didn't know what she was expecting— but it must've been *awful*.

Savana started speaking before Ezra could. "I'm sorry—" she blurted. "I didn't know what to do and I didn't listen—"

"Kid you're good," Ezra laid a hand on her shoulder. "Go sit down. Get some water. Kelly's in for you."

Savana looked at Ezra like he just grew a tail. Then her expression morphed to one of gratitude. She ran a hand over her forearm, breathing a sigh of relief.

“Look,” Ezra said. “I shouldn’t have expected you to run an action that you just learned. That’s on me. We can work on it later in practice. Right now, try and run the stuff you feel less confident on. Also, have fun.” He flashed a smile. “That’s what we’re here for, right?”

“But you told us to run Break.” Swan blurted. “If we need to—”

“No, we’ll learn it in practice.” Ezra said. “No point in struggling here. Too stressful. Just make sure everyone scores, okay Swan? Our main goal is to just have a good time.”

Swan nodded. The ref blew his whistle, signaling for the game to resume. Leah was about to step onto the court when Ezra tapped her shoulder.

“What’s up?” Leah asked.

Ezra glanced at Savana. “I saw what you did for her. Getting her that three was a nice thing. Make sure she’s alright, okay?”

Leah nodded. “Of course.”

“Oh,” Ezra’s expression changed. “And put pressure on the point guard. Let’s see if her handle is as weak as you claim.”

The handle, as it turns out, was God-awful. Leah was one hundred percent accurate in her scouting. The girls game was as random as the weather, but her dribbling was her achilles heel.

When she crossed over, Leah’s hand met the ball, swatting it from her possession. When her dribble climbed too high, Leah poked it into her hand. And when she attempted the pass, Swan was there to intercept it.

Together, the two made the score climb higher and higher. Once their lead breached twenty, they decided not to score anymore. Instead, they created shots for their team, making sure everyone got at least one basket.

“Kelly!” Leah screeched, pulling to the top of the key. The ball spun her hand as she waited for an open player. “Cut! Go to the nail!”

Kelly stared at her like she was speaking Latin. It was Swan who came to Leah’s rescue— setting a screen practically shoving Kelly to the basket. Leah took advantage of the opening, flinging the ball to her teammate.

The ball slid through the hoop, sparking the eruption from Leah’s bench. Her teammates clapped and cheered, shouting Kelly’s name. Ezra was the only one who was silent. He smiled at Leah. She smiled back.

The rest of the game was a breeze. Her and Swan took over the court, galavanting from hoop to hoop like it was simply a playground. They swung the ball behind their back, flung it between their legs, and created shots for every teammate that entered the game.

The cheers filled the gym, loud and infectious. Leah felt the cold sensation of power climb up her limbs as she gulped the essence around her. The ball spinning in her hand, the shout of her teammates and the cheers from the crowd. She drank the attention. She saw the glory. And for just a moment, she felt like Zahara.

Savana wasn't herself. When she was subbed in, she stayed on the outskirts of the court. She held her own and didn't make any large mistakes, but she wasn't noticeable. She looked timid, eyes flitting from Ezra to the stands. She was expecting something. Expecting *someone*. Leah knew all too well who.

No one really wanted the game to end. So when the buzzer rang for a final time, Leah felt like she could play another few hours. Everyone was ecstatic, gossiping about their own points.

Savana lingered in the rear, eyes trained on her shoes. Leah fell back, matching her stride. She didn't say anything. She didn't need to. She simply walked with her, letting Savana know she wasn't alone.

"Well," Ezra said once the team had gathered in a circle. "Not much to say about that one, guys. Well done, we blew them out of the water."

The team purred in agreement, pulling their shoes off and sliding on their slippers.

"I think everyone scored." Ezra grinned. "I love those types of games. Everyone walks away happy and better. I think that's all I have to say. Anyone care to add anything?"

This, like many other things, was a test. Those who spoke up got the respect of the coaches and players. They were viewed, in some perspectives, as a leader. Coaches liked that. And most importantly, *colleges* like it.

"We work really well together." Leah started, not incredibly sure where she was going with the speech. She glanced at Swan.

"I agree," she added. "Everyone knows where to go and me, Leah and Savana know where to pass. It's a playless chemistry— the kind where a scheme isn't needed."

"That's the best kind." Leah agreed. "It's unstoppable. We know each other like the back of our hand. No instruction necessary, we'll beat the opposing teams just on instinct."

Leah glanced at Savana. She met Leah's eye. Leah gestured to the circle, inviting her to talk.

Savana cleared her throat. "I think the most dangerous thing about a team is how easy it is to mess up. We aren't just competing against the other organizations, you know. We're competing against each other. There are only five starting spots. Only five players are deemed good enough to participate in the jump ball. And only one player can be the best. The one colleges notice. The one they pick." Savana took a breath. "It's kind of a miracle competition hasn't broken our peace yet."

Silence followed Savana's speech. No one knew what to say. There weren't any words to reciprocate her claim. Her words kept spinning in Leah's head. *Only one. Only one.* There's only one MVP. There's only one player who outshines the rest. There is only *one* Zahara Williamson.

Savana didn't wait for the response. She picked herself up from the floor and strode from the huddle. No one tried to stop her.

Leah watched her go. She watched her weave around the courts, disappearing into the mass of people.

Ezra met her gaze. Leah tilted her head up. Ezra nodded, and Leah raced after her teammate.

Savana was hard to find. She hid herself well, blending in with the mass of people and players. But Leah had her location down to a science— or rather, down to relation.

When Leah played poorly, she found salvation in the bathroom. There, she could pull her hair, punch her face, and sob as much as needed in the privacy of her own company. So when she found the empty restroom, she was almost positive Savana was hiding in there.

"Savana?" Leah called. "Savana?"

A muffled sob confirmed her suspicion. She was in one of the stalls— Leah had no clue which one. And she wasn't about to slide under the doors in hope she found her teammate and not some shitting grandma.

"I know you're in there." Leah said. "If you wanna talk, I'm here."

Only silence answered her.

Leah shrugged. "Fine. I'll leave you then. I'm gonna go talk with Ezra. I'll be on court forty eight when you're ready to come out."

She turned on her heel, striding out the door. Just as she was about to cross the frame, a bathroom stall creaked open.

Savana looked awful. Her messy, blue ponytail had been pulled down and strands of hair stuck to her tear stained cheeks. A red, puffy gaze followed Leah— an empty glow illuminating her eyes.

Savana pressed her arms against her ribcage. "I'm never going to be good enough, Leah."

"What?" Leah started towards her. "Savana you started on varsity as a freshman—"

"That's not what I mean." Savana said. "It doesn't matter what I achieve. It doesn't matter what I do. As long as someone else is better, my contributions fade into the background." Savana sank to the floor. "You see it too, don't you?"

"See what?" Leah asked.

Savana tilted her head. "That you're never going to be better than Swan?"

Never going to be better than Swan? *Never going to be better than Swan?* Oh that bitch! Savana thought Leah was a hopeless case. That she would never be number one. That she would never be *noticed.*

"Get up." The sympathy vanished from Leah's tone. "Get the hell up."

Savana just sat there with an unreadable expression.

"Oh for fucks sake—" Leah grabbed Savana's uniform, yanking her too her feet. She let out a tiny scream, flinching back. "Oh come on, Savana. You think you're going to survive if you're always in this pity party?"

"Leah what—" Savana stammered. Leah slapped her. Hard.

"Do you know what will happen to us if we don't succeed?" she snarled. "If we don't become number one? Because I know damn well what will happen to me." Leah's hands began to shake. She clenched her knuckles. The weakness couldn't show. Not now, not ever. "My dad's going to push and shove and scream at me until I'm just a machine. He's going to chase me down that court screaming insults and profanity— and he won't stop until I'm better than the day before. Day after day. Night after night. Until I am number one." Leah drew a shaky sigh. "And if I don't become the best— he'll cast me aside. I'll be left in the dirt. Unloved, unnoticed, *nothing*."

Tears started pouring down Savana's cheeks. Leah backhanded her.

"*God dammit* Savana!" Leah screeched. "I am trying to *help* you. If my guess is right, you have the same stakes with this game. Your dad is the same as mine. He leaves you with bruises and tells you how lucky you are. Do you want more of that? Do you want something *worse*?"

Savana shook her head. The motion wasn't fast, but slow and controlled. A fire had returned to her eyes, drying them with the heat of her rage.

"It's never going to stop, is it?" Savana asked. "All of it? It's never going to go away."

Leah shook her head. "Not until you meet your goal. Not until you become the best."

"Not until I go D1." Savana finished. "What if I can't?"

"You can." Leah said. "You can't think about what happens if you can't. There is no failure. You can't afford to think about what happens if you don't win."

THE BEAUTY OF OUR PAIN

"Knowing we can be replaced and our careers are on the line, you are regularly forced to ignore issues or maltreatment out of fear. I have witnessed blackmail, intimidation, favouritism, experienced verbal and mental abuse personally. We are silenced or put down if you ask questions. I am fearful that after I speak out, I will be punished."
—Kerr, Gretchen, et al. *Prevalence of Maltreatment among Current and Former National Team Athletes.*

Ironically, tournaments were the most restful part of Leah's life.

The only thing she was required to do was play a few games— a small feat compared to the four hours of basketball a day she held herself too. The games, however, were risky. If she played well, she would be ecstatic for the next week. If she played poorly, the following moments would be spent in the bathroom pulling out her already thinning hair.

Fortunately, right now, she was blessed with the pure euphoria that came after a good performance. Usually she would put that happiness to use— going on a run or practicing for an extra few hours. But unfortunately, she was lacking both a ball and a court, and she wasn't about to go gallivanting around Reno like a lost deer.

So, with no better thing to do, she decided to go back to her hotel room. She had paid for it with the amount of money her mom had left for her. That was basically what she and Gael lived off of. Her father was too lazy to work even before the incident and with her mother's high paying profession, he never had to.

As soon as Leah hit the bed, she slipped into unconsciousness. She didn't even have time to take off her uniform. Her body must've sensed the opportunity of rest and snatched it before Leah could object.

She didn't know how long she slept for, but when she awoke, the sky had darkened. She wiped the crust from her eyes and picked up her phone. Ezra's name glowed on her screen.

Where are you? Bowling starts in ten minutes.

Bowling? *Bowling*? Oh right, Ezra's fun idea of team bonding. Leah couldn't criticize it, a strong team relationship was important. But the thought of holding a ball that weighed anything more than two pounds disgusted her.

Nevertheless, she scrambled out of bed, took a frigid shower, pulled on the closest pair of pajamas and scrambled out the door. A perk of being an athlete was the ability to sprint across any surface. Whether it was a court or a hall, Leah sprinted at quick pace.

She leapt down stairs, weaved around crowds, and made a valuable use of elbows to push past drunk gamblers. Luckily, the bowling location was at the bottom of the hotel. Unfortunately, the hotel was fucking massive. Leah found herself sprinting around random corners in hope she saw a teammate.

"Leah?"

She turned around to see Savana. The girl looked like she came from practice. Sweat beaded on her forehead and her blue hair sprouted in frizzy tangles. Surprisingly, she was looking at Leah like she was out of place.

"You look like you just fell out of bed." Savana said.

Leah wrinkled her nose. "You look like you just ran a mile."

Savana shrugged. "I was practicing my dribbling."

"With what ball?"

"I asked Ezra for one." Savana responded. "Then I went to the games. Plenty of room if you look for it. If you wanted to practice, you would."

Oh shit. She was right. Should she have been practicing? She just wasted a few hours on a stupid nap. If she kept up her laziness, she would never be like Zahara.

"Well good job you," Leah's smile felt toxic on her teeth. "Any clue where the bowling alley is?"

Savana pointed to a sign. Displayed in white letters was the word 'bowling alley' with a small arrow pointing to the right.

Leah shrugged. "I'm not great with signs."

Savana only smiled. "Then you're lucky you found me."

Bowling was, as expected, exceptionally boring. Leah hated it; mostly because every ball she threw wound up in the gutter. Everyone else had trouble remembering their turn— too focused on the fries that kept appearing at their table.

Leah couldn't eat any. Gael said unhealthy food made her look sluggish and she didn't need to get any bigger. Her muscle mass was ugly enough. If she had the chance, she'd buy herself a salad.

Savana didn't eat any either. She kept glancing at the food like it might sprout claws and kill her. Leah supposed she had similar reasons— the more time she spent with Savana, the more she realized how parallel they were. Two girls with enough ambition to kill and success as their only path.

Leah supposed Ezra wasn't satisfied with the hangout, because as their bowling experience came to a close, he suggested that they get ice cream. The team, of course, flocked to the nearby store, leaving Leah and Savana sitting with the half eaten fries.

"Aren't you going to go with them?" Leah asked.

Savana offered a small smile. "I was going to ask you the same thing."

Leah shrugged. "My dad said I shouldn't eat unhealthy stuff. Makes me a worse player."

"Yeah," Savana breathed. "It's a similar story for me."

"Well," Leah tucked her knees to her chest. "I guess it's just you and me."

"Leah?" Savana asked. "Do you do anything outside of basketball?"

Leah snorted. "No. What kind of question is that?"

"I don't mean hobbies." Savana said. "Hobbies are stupid. They amount to nothing. I mean for fun."

"Basketball is my fun."

Savana let out a rough cackle. "You're hilarious."

Leah raised an eyebrow. "I'm being serious."

"Of course you are." Savana grinned. "But do you wanna have some *real* fun?"

Leah tilted her head. "What do you mean?"

"Come on," She grabbed her hand, pulling her to her feet. Savana led Leah through crowds of people— all too drunk to walk in a straight line. She slunk behind a trashcan, watching the bar in front of her.

"Savana what—" she placed a finger over Leah's mouth, shushing her. They watched as a young couple ordered a bottle of wine. Moments later, two small glasses and the crimson liquid appeared.

"When they turn," Savana gestured to the couple. "Take that bottle and run."

"I never agreed—"

"Trust me, Leah." Savana put a hand on her shoulder. "It's worth it."

With that, Savana rose from her perch behind the bin. She strode over to a group of hammered gentlemen and bumped their bottle with her hip. To anyone else, it would've looked like an accident.

"Oh my—" Savana placed a hand over her mouth. "My apologies, I didn't mean—"

"That's alright." One of the men stood, moving much too close to Savana. "It's just liquid."

Savana batted her lashes, noting that the man's eyes were on her ass. She played it up, however, bending over in an attempt to clean the mess.

The couple at the bar, noticing the spill, moved next to Savana. "Do you need help, miss?" the man asked.

"Here," said the woman. "Let us get paper towels."

Leah didn't hear the rest of the conversation. As soon as the couple fled from their stools, she raced to the bar. She grabbed the bottle and ran. Heart beating out of her boobs, hands slipping with sweat, she made her way into the crowd.

She slowed her pace, blending in with the passersby. Leah may have been fifteen, but she had the stress lines to pass for twenty five. No one would bat an eye at the bottle in her hand. Of course, her heart didn't slow. She had to physically control her breath to keep herself from hyperventilating.

A hand landed on her shoulder. Leah jumped, whirling around to find Savana grinning.

"Was that so hard?" she flicked the bottle. "Now we get to drink it."

Leah wrinkled her nose. "I don't want to drink."

Savana tilted her head, like this was a foreign concept. "Why?"

Leah shrugged. "My dad's addicted to cigarettes and he's about the most pathetic man I know. I don't wanna end up like him."

"You won't get addicted." Savana said. "It's just alcohol. Everyone drinks it. And Leah, it makes you forget everything."

"What?"

Savana blew out a breath. "It's like, just for a moment, all of your thoughts are just blocked out. Nothing holds meaning. It's a feeling of detachment. Like— you're only in the present." She smiled. "Sort of a meditation, if you think about it."

Leah looked at the bottle, then at Savana. She supposed there was no harm in a single drink.

"Fine." Leah said. "Let's go back to my room though. I don't want anyone seeing us."

~~~

Drinking alcohol was like touching a hot stove.

No matter how many times Leah willed herself to take a sip of the liquid, she couldn't. When the wine got too close to her mouth, she would start shaking and then shove the bottle down.

"Come on, Leah." Savana had already taken a large swig. "It won't hurt you."

Leah took a breath. "I know. But—" she tapped the bottle, making the wine ripple. "I'm kind of scared, you know?"
~~~

“Leah,” to her surprise, Savana chuckled. “If you’re anything like I think you are, you’ve been through much scarier things than an alcoholic beverage. Here—” Savana moved beside her. “Close your eyes. I promise, once you drink it, in a matter of minutes, it’ll make all the stupid thoughts go away.”

Leah swallowed. She closed her eyes tight, imagining she was simply drinking a glass of water. Savana placed the bottle in her grasp and Leah pressed it to her lips.

She expected the wine to taste sweet. Like grape juice. After all, that was what it’s made of. But no— it was bitter. Not the bitterness of an unripe berry, but coffee bitter. About as light as light roast can be with a slightly fruity flavor.

It was absolutely horrid.

It took all her might to swallow it. And when she did, she was met with a burning sensation in her throat. No drink did that— something must’ve been wrong.

“Oh fuck—” Leah mumbled. “I did it wrong—” she made a beeline for the toilet, finger already in her mouth.

“Leah, Leah.” Savana put a hand on her shoulder. “*Leah*. What’s wrong?”

“It burns.” Leah gasped. “Savana it really fucking burns. Something’s wrong. I have too— I have to vomit—”

She turned to the toilet, leaning over in her practiced position. But before she could hurl Savana grabbed her shoulders, yanking her back.

“Leah. Is it a burning sensation in your throat? Just after you swallowed it? Like heartburn almost?”

“Yes,” Leah was beginning to panic. “Will vomiting not work? Do we need to call poison control? Fuck, Savana. Ezra’s gonna kill me—”

“*Leah.*” Savana wasn’t panicking. Savana looked like she was holding in cackles. “Listen to me. That burning? It’s just the alcohol. It’s completely normal, okay?”

Leah wasn’t convinced. She kept glancing around, looking from Savana to the wine to the toilet. The thought that Savana might be trying to poison her flashed across her mind. She ignored it.

“Okay,” Leah took a breath, trying to stop her heart from fluttering past her boobs. “So um, how long until it kicks in?”

Savana chuckled. “Should only be a few minutes. It’s sort of hard to tell since you’ve only had a sip. But since it’s your first time, I suppose your tolerance is pretty weak.”

“Cool,” Leah tucked her knees to her chest. “So, uh, what do you wanna talk about?”

Savana scoffed. “That’s an awful way to start a conversation.”

“Oh yeah?” Leah smirked. “Why don’t you try then.”

“Easy.” Savana said. “Why are you doing it?”

“Doing what?”

“Doing *this*.” Savana waved her arms. “Sports. Why are you working so hard?”

Leah shrugged. “Because I enjoy it.”

Savana gave her a weird look. Not a smile— not quite. More of a frown, a glare, maybe. A studying look; somewhere between pleased and angry. When she finally spoke, the word came out like a melody.

“Bull*shit*.” Savana sang, landing hard on the last ‘t.’ “You don’t enjoy it Leah. Try again.”

Leah threw up her hands. “That’s the truth!”

“No it isn’t.” Savana leaned forward. “You know, I have you figured out. You’re like me. The drive, the fire. It isn’t a want. It’s a *need*. You recognized what would happen to me if I failed. Now Leah, I want to know what happens to *you*.”

Leah simply stared at her. She had two options for this— play it off like Savana was crazy or tell her the truth. But the truth made her look weak— like she couldn’t handle what was a necessity. But gaslighting— well, Leah was never very good at that.

“Fine.” Leah snatched the bottle, taking a large swig of wine. The liquid washed away all emotions attached to the words when it slithered down her throat. “The truth is, I don’t know. I know what has happened to me. But that was minor. One faulty game and—” her voice cracked. She willed the alcohol into effect, leaning into the burn. “And all of a sudden, he was interested. All of sudden, I realized the real price of greatness.”

Savana nodded, leaning back against the wall. She took a sip of wine, closing her eyes as she swallowed. “My dad was always like that. It wasn’t even my choice what sport I played. I suppose it is a luxury to choose your cage.” She took a breath, as if blowing out smoke. “It’s for the best though. They’re only trying to make us better. They’re doing it for love.”

“Love.” Leah rolled the word through her mouth. What was it? Why did she need it? Why was it used as a pawn? ‘I love you’ was more of a blade than a hug. How much was Gael allowed to do to her because he simply loved her? Did the word ‘love’ know any bounds to its cruelty? “Why does it matter?”

Savana blew out a breath. It took her a while to answer— a stark contrast to the freeflow of her tongue. "It doesn't." She murmured. "Love is just a word. An excuse. A reason to do terrible things. Our dads can scream and hit and curse at us all they want and society won't care. As long as they claim to love us."

THE GREAT COMEUPPANCE OF VIREN VARNETTE

"I left [sport] because I was the favorite target of an abusive Coach. I was so afraid of him and "what he would do to me" if my Mom found out what he had done - I usually felt sick. Could not really concentrate. I left this sport because of fear."
—Kerr, Gretchen, et al. *Prevalence of Maltreatment among Current and Former National Team Athletes.*

Fucking hangerovers.

Leah hadn't actually had one before but she'd heard of them. She had just assumed they'd be something that would be easy to shake off, like any regular headache.

This, however, was not something she could simply ignore. The pain pounded in her head like a thousand drums beating in sync. She tried drinking water to no avail— and food didn't help either. It seemed the only pleasant thing to do was stare at the bright lights of the gym and let her mind configure them into shapes.

She was smiling at an imaginary light bunny when Ezra laid next to her. She barely noticed him at first, as the blinding ceiling was much more interesting in her post-drunken state. Leah only gave her coach a worthy amount of attention when he spoke.

"How's the hangover?"

Leah jolted up, her headache slamming against her skull. She winced at the pain, rubbing her temples. "How did you—"

"You really think I didn't notice you and Savana slinking off with that bottle?" Ezra smirked. "She seems to be doing fine though. First time?"

"Ezra you can't tell—"

"Oh relax kid." He ruffled her hair. "I won't. Besides, you deserve a break. I'm just glad you didn't do one of the more harmful drugs."

Leah rubbed the back of her neck. "Yeah. I don't want to."

Ezra flashed a smile. "And hey, be careful. Addiction's a motherfucker and I don't want you caught up in that."

"Thanks," Leah tucked her knees to her chest. "Don't wanna lose your next D1, huh?"

Ezra's face fell. "What? No! Leah I—"

"Ezra!" Savana's voice interjected. "Leah! Look who we're playing."

Leah got to her feet, jogging next to Savana. There, across the court, was Viren. He was dressed in all gray, basketball positioned between his arm and his hip. Next to him was the varsity team of Westside Dynasty.

"They have such a stupid name." Savana groaned. "Westside Dynasty my ass. Who comes in and calls themselves a fucking dynasty?"

"It's as if the janitor of Buckingham Palace started calling himself King." Leah said. "All talk, no merit."

Savana shot her a grin. "Good thing we're about to kick their butts."

Leah returned the expression. "This is gonna be fun."

"Hold up." Ezra appeared beside them. "Don't underestimate them. They're still an opponent."

"Barely," Leah scoffed. "Ezra, their team is made up of mediocre high school players. The only reason they can put the ball in the basket during school season is because me, Savana and Swan give them the shot on a silver platter. They have the illusion that they can play because of *our* plans."

"Doesn't Viren come up with your plays?" Swan asked. "He is the coach."

"Only in technicality."

Ezra took a breath. Leah could've imagined it, but she sensed the smallest tremble on his tongue. "We *won't* underestimate them. If we underestimate, we lose. And I will not lose to *Viren*."

"Fine," Savana shrugged. "What's the plan?"

"We're running a box and one." Ezra said. "Savana you'll be on Milly like glue. Make sure she doesn't even touch the ball."

"Ezra—" Leah began. "With all due respect, box and ones are typically meant for one dominant player and Milly is hardly… well, dominant. Besides, I've played with her before. If we're going to run a box and one, I'm the best one to guard her."

Ezra's eyes met hers— they were neither perpetrating nor kind. The only emotion his expression gave was a deep, unrelenting ambition.

"I'm not taking chances." Ezra drawled. "Savana's the best defender here. She'll guard Milly. The rest of you can match up with whoever you please. Make sure no one can drive. I'm okay with them taking threes, but none of Viren's girls get layups. Clear?"

"Yes coach." The team responded. For most of them, the words were instinct — something they didn't even have to think about. But that wasn't Ezra's doing. They had learned if from other coaches, Ezra was different. He treated them like friends, not weapons.

Most of the time, at least. But with Viren he changed. Leah couldn't pinpoint it, but something about him shifted. As if all of a sudden, he found his own fire. And all of a sudden, not even Satan himself could keep him from victory.

~~~

Ezra's insanity continued right up to the jump ball. While waiting, Leah caught him yanking on his blonde locks, eyeing Viren with an expression between fear and undying rage.

Leah let her eyes roll into her head. The game would be no problem—whatever blossoming butterfly of doubt Ezra had in his head, Leah would make sure it died as soon as the game sped into motion.

But for now, everything was tense. She stood in the middle of the court, waiting for the refs to locate a suitable ball. Swan stood on the opposite side, screaming something Leah was happily ignoring. Savana stood a few strides away from her. When she saw Leah, she waved.

Leah supposed the hangover had done next to nothing in hindering her jolly attitude.

"Leah," she nearly jumped as Milly strode beside her. "Long time no see."

Leah snorted. "Enjoying playing for that porn addicted pedophile?"

Milly smirked. "You're one to talk, your coach looks on the verge of a panic attack."

"Yeah," Leah rubbed the back of her neck. "Something's up with him. He'll calm down once we're twenty points ahead of you in the first few minutes."

If Milly registered the insult, she didn't show it. Instead her face darkened, a hint of concern touching her cheeks. "Leah listen, you have to be careful this game."

"Ezra tells me that each tournament and I go at it with the same reckless shit every time." Leah said. "What makes you think your suggestion will have any sway?"

"I'm not suggesting, Leah." Milly's tone was low. "I'm begging you. Be careful, or you're going to get seriously hurt."

"Are you threatening me?"

"No," Milly shook her head. "But there are people here who are going to do much worse."

Before she could respond, the whistle screeched. The ref threw the ball into the air, and the game began.

Leah didn't think. She lunged for the ball, pounding it to life. Swan was running to the wing, wide open for the pass.
~~~

As soon as the ball hit her hand, three defenders swarmed her. Swan barely blinked when she carved right through them. On cue, Savana sprinted to the basket. She didn't need to call for it— Swan saw her. And given the defenders hadn't gathered their wits, she flung the ball at Savana, who tipped it into the hoop.

Leah smiled, backpedaling to defense. Her hands brushed Swan's and Savana's, then she sprinted to find her defender. Savana stayed near half court, waiting for Milly to dribble up.

The girl made short work of her. As soon as Milly crossed half court, Savana swarmed her, poking the ball from her possession and sprinting down the court.

‘ Leah didn't bother to follow. Neither did Swan. They both knew Savana was going to make the layup.

Milly's next few attempts at dribbling didn't go too well. On the off chance that Savana didn't swipe the ball, it was Leah or Swan that intercepted the pass. Most of their offense consisted of fast breaks, all of which were pretty straight forward. Dribble down, shoot and— if you weren't an imbecile— make the bloody shot.

When their lead climbed to a steady twenty points, Leah, Swan and Savana decided to have a little fun.

"On your left!" Leah hollered. Swan flung the ball between her legs, halting her momentum. Her perpetrating defender slid forward— unready for the sudden change in motion. Before she could recover, Swan flung the ball to Leah.

It took her a split second to weigh her options. Split second too long— a good team would capitalize on that mistake. Luckily, West Side Dynasty was not a good team.

No shot, no available drive. That meant the only good option was to pass. Savana was three steps ahead of her, already sprinting to the corner. Leah flung the ball at her.

She caught it, sent her defenders in the air with a pump fake and drove to the basket. Swan sprinted to the key; Savana's pass landing in her palm. Now, it was Leah's turn.

Swan flung the ball behind her back as Leah sprinted towards the block opposite her. She caught it and laid the ball into the basket.

There weren't really crowds in Reno. More like small flocks of spectators. But at that moment, a full *crowd* of people had gathered at their court. And when the ball fell through the net, that *crowd* went fucking wild.

Swan, Savana and Leah basked in the glory. Felt the power— the *admiration*— seep through their veins and crawl into their minds. This wasn't like normal. They weren't cheering for one dominant star. They were cheering for the game they played together. The legends they became *together*. No one above the other, everyone equally a spectacle. And for a moment— just for a moment— it was brilliant.

"*Timeout*!" Viren's voice pierced the air. Leah turned to see him striding along the baseline, anger radiating from his beaded sweat. "Timeout!"

The ref blew the whistle. The teams flocked to their respective benches. There they found Ezra doing just a tad better. He had stopped pulling his hair, which was a positive sign. Now his anger had been replaced with a blank stare.

A blank stare directed at Viren.

"Hey coach," Leah tapped his shoulder. "Are you feeling okay?"

Ezra cleared his throat. "Fine, fine. Thanks."

Leah took a breath. "Are you sure—"

"I'm fine, Leah." Ezra stood. He moved like a ghost, as if his formal self had been ripped from him. His eyes were glossed, his skin was white. Leah was half sure her vision had malfunctioned because for a moment Ezra Soren looked… *scared*.

"Get some water guys," he breathed. "What's the score?"

"Fourteen to thirty seven." Swan said. When Ezra's face grew paler she added. "We're winning."

"Okay, okay." Ezra sighed. "I guess we're winning by quite a bit." He laughed. No one knew what at. "That's good. That's good."

Savana raised an eyebrow. "Hey can I get you some water? You look like you're about to pass out."

"No, no I'm alright." Ezra put on a smile. It was the fakest shit Leah had ever laid eyes upon.

The whistle blew. They walked back onto the court, gathering at the halfway point. Leah glanced at Viren, who was still lecturing his players. The whistle blew again, this time followed by a stern voice.

"Coach, your timeout is over."

"Just a second." Viren retorted.

"Must be some play." Leah murmured.

Swan raised an eyebrow. "I thought Viren isn't good at plays?"

"Who knows?" Leah shrugged. "Maybe he's broadening his horizons."

“That—” Savana squinted at the coach. “That doesn’t look like a play.”

“Yes Savana, because obviously they’re baking a cake over there.”

“No.” Swan shook her head. “She’s right, Leah. That looks like a human anatomy lesson.”

They were right. Viren was pointing to his leg like it was a diagram, shifting the limb in every position imaginable. The players were watching him like he might kill them, a slight wince of fear in their eyes. And maybe, just maybe—guilt?

“Woah.” Leah said. “He really is broadening his horizons.”

“*Coach.*” The referee’s voice escalated to a holler. “Your timeout is over. If this continues, I’m going to give you a technical.”

“Fine.” Viren gave his players one last look. “Remember. Don’t half ass this one. Execute it.”

“White ball,” the ref said. Leah inbounded it to Swan; her and Savana jogged with her as she dribbled up the court. Whatever Viren’s new play was, it must’ve been defensive. The position of his girls was completely different. He had put the smallest girl at the bottom of the basket and the tall girls near the three point line. It was like he was just *begging* her to drive.

Swan must’ve seen it too, because she passed Leah the ball. “All yours,” she said, “I think you have the lowest point count between the three of us.”

Leah snarled. “Thanks for reminding me.”

Nevertheless, she did as requested. The drive was simple enough, given Viren’s play-making skills had actually managed to get *worse*. The girls who guarded Leah couldn’t match her speed or her moves. She got past two defenders at once with a simple hesitation move.

The next layer of defense was a bit more tricky. An average sized player, but damn was she strong. Leah found out the hard way when she tried to muscle her way through. It was like her shoulder hit a wall, and when the girl didn’t budge, she realized a different method was necessary.

Leah planted her foot between her opponent's stance. Letting the ball spin at her waist, she spun around the defender. This method was much more effective.

The last layer of defense was the easiest. A small girl— obviously out of place. She was a point guard, not a post. If adrenaline hadn’t taken hostage of all emotion, Leah would’ve felt bad for her.

The move was simple. Actually, there was no move. She simply went up for the layup like the girl wasn't there. She didn't seem to mind— she made no effort to stop her.

Leah didn't have time to look if her shot went in. Her feet didn't have time to hit the ground. Because before all of that could take place, a pair of hands landed on her back.

Leah gasped as she was pushed forward. Her body lunged, landing on her leg. Her knee turned inward.

A snap.

She toppled over, gazing at the court in a haze. She saw Savana, eyes just darting to Leah's fallen figure. Swan, already running towards her. Ezra, looking absolutely mortified. And Viren, who wore the smallest hint of a smile.

Then, all of that vanished; replaced with so much fucking *pain*.

THE ONLY SOURCE OF PITY

Athletes are prone to several mental health conditions and disorders because of "early attrition from sport, a higher risk of injuries, negative effects on sports performance, burnout, and lower levels of academic and occupational functioning."
—Reardon, Claudia L. "The Mental Health Crisis in Sports: The Perfect Storm of Contemporary Factors."

Leah couldn't recognize the faces hovering over her.

At first, the blurry people must've been her teammates. Then, they were brushed away, new faces replacing them. She supposed the blonde one was Ezra.

The pain was strong. Really fucking strong. She clutched her knee, afraid to let go. Somehow her tight grasp kept the pain from slithering past her thigh.

"... think it was…"

"... it went inward…"

"... *no*…" Ezra's voice. "Not *that*…"

Hands. On hers. Drawing them away from the injury. No! Through the pain, Leah managed a word. "*Stop*! Please."

"We have to view…"

"No." Ezra again. "Take her to the medic. She's in too much pain."

Quiet.

"... identify…"

Ezra's voice was rock hard. "She's in pain. She needs help. Real *help*. That's all that matters."

Hands. Again. But this time, they weren't invading. They lifted her, careful not to touch her injury. Through her tear coated eyes, she saw people. All staring at her. Swan and Savana walked alongside her, terror molding their features.

The infirmary smelled like mint. Not the good kind, but the kind that made your heart speed up. The kind that reeked of chemical inflicted death.

She was set on a table. The faces hovering over her vanished, replaced with new, unfamiliar ones. Then, the hands returned. When they landed on her knee, Leah screamed.

Not a yelp. Not anything small. No, this was a belch. Her back arched, tears trickled down her face and a mortifying screech erupted from her lips. The pain rushed through her blood, ripping her muscles and tearing her ligaments.

"...hysterical…"

"...her knee…"

"...ACL sprain…"

The hands left her, replaced with her own. She clutched her leg, halting the blood flow to her knee.

The doctors left. She couldn't hear them anymore, but she could barely hear anything. She was only focused on the tears in her eyes and the pain pumping from her leg.

The voices returned.

"...sedate…"

"...pain meds…"

"*...morphine…*"

They were going to drug her. Leah would've thrashed, would've begged them not to give it to her. She had sworn off of drugs long ago— when the stuff with her mom happened. Normally, she would hate the idea of morphine. But now…

She just wanted the pain to go away.

So when she saw the blurry form of a needle, she didn't fight it. When the tip touched her skin, she didn't squirm. And when it entered her flesh, all she felt was relief.

The morphine was cold— an icy river coursing through her body. The drug sloshed against her limbs, digging into her flesh. It was like she was doused in an ice bath, and when the water trickled off her body, as did the pain.

She was left with euphoria. A strange happiness that seemed to sprout from the air. It encased her thoughts, and for a moment, everything painful and sad vanished.

Then, she drifted into a drug induced slumber.

~~~

Savana was there when she woke up.

She stood over Leah's bed, a stupid grin plastered on her face. "Hey," she said. "You look like shit."

Leah sat up, rubbing her head. Her gaze wandered to her knee. It was wrapped in bandages that were so tight she thought it might cut her circulation. Over them was a large, ugly brace. It looked almost dystopian— with gears and metal to keep her leg in place.

She wiped the sleep from her eyes. "How long was I out?"

Savana shrugged. "Few hours. Maybe more. The medics wouldn't let us in so I have no clue when you fell asleep."
~~~

"Where's Ezra?"

Savana snorted. "Well hello to you too. He's waiting outside the facility."

Leah wrinkled her nose. "Why?"

"Well," Savana's smirk grew. "You missed a few things, Leah. After he carried you here, he got into a *small* disagreement with Viren."

"How small?"

Savana's smile grew. "If the ref hadn't pulled them apart, Ezra might've killed him. He thinks your injury was Virens's doing— on purpose."

Leah raised an eyebrow. "Is it?"

"Oh most definitely. But these kinda things are hard to prove, especially with Viren's 'merit.'" Savana scoffed. "I don't think I've ever seen Ezra so angry though. They kicked him out. Swan's with him; I suppose she's safeguarding his surroundings. Between you and me—" Savana leaned closer. "I think he's arson level mad."

Leah gave a laugh. For a moment, she forgot anything was wrong.

"So," Savana leaned foreward. "Hows the pain?"

Leah's gaze drifted down to her leg. The morphine hadn't quite worn off. Leah was grateful for the fact— she wasn't ready to face that pain again, and besides, the euphoria was actually quite enjoyable.

"Don't feel anything." Leah said. "They gave me a powerful painkiller. Actually, I feel almost manic."

"Shit," Savana raised her eyebrows. "Someone's getting the good drugs."

"Snap your ACL and you'll get them too."

Savana's expression darkened. "Wait— is that what it is?"

"I think so," Leah shrugged. "The doctors mentioned it."

"Oh Leah," Savana cupped a hand over her mouth. "I'm so sorry."

Leah furrowed her brow. "Why? Is something wrong?"

"Leah," she released a breath. "An ACL sprain is one of the most devastating injuries an athlete can endure. If you're lucky, you'll be out for only six months. If you're not—" her gaze wavered. "You could never play again."

~~~

At first, Leah allowed herself to rest.

Ezra drove her home, shaking behind the wheel. Leah couldn't tell if anger or regret caused the trembling. The entire ride was filled with orders and advice for her sprain.

Leah barely listened. She couldn't. All she could think about was the long days ahead. Watching her teammates improve while she sat on the bench. Useless— pathetic.
~~~

When she got home, she managed to limp to her bed. Gael stood in her door, a quizzical expression touching his lips. They stared at each other for a good long while.

"I suppose you're not going to practice for a while, huh?" he said.

Leah couldn't meet his eye. "I suppose not."

She laid in bed for the next few days. Not reading, not watching television — barely sleeping. She just laid there, staring at the ceiling.

It must've been days. Leah didn't count. No one came to check on her— to make sure she was still alive. She didn't read her texts— she couldn't find the energy.

She just kept thinking about the game. *Her* game. Savana's words rang over and over in her ear. She could never play again? What was she if not a basketball player?

Other kids had their friends, hobbies, relationships— that's what gave them a purpose; an *identity*. But Leah didn't have that. She had basketball. She had her fire. She had her need to succeed. That's all she was. That was the only thing she was allowed to be.

She eventually got up. To go see a game. One of Ezra's games. He requested she be there. For moral support, she supposed.

They didn't seem to need her. Swan and Savana did their thing— playing together like two pieces of a puzzle. It was a close game, their team losing by three points. But Leah didn't much care about the score. She cared about the team. *Her* team. All getting better while she remained the same. The *same for months*. Shooting for the stars while Leah fell behind.

When she got home, Gael offered her a solution. They would bring a chair out to the local court. Then she would shoot. For hours. All while he was there — watching.

But he wouldn't just watch. No, Leah knew better than that. He was going to scream at her— criticize her to no end. Make every day miserable and degrading. People would walk by that court, stopping to watch the spectacle. But no one would intervene.

And even though she knew it would be awful, Leah agreed to the proposal.

"Dammit Leah!" Gael screeched. "Your form is lazy."

"Fix your stance."

"Stop stalling."

"Your shot is pathetic."

"You are pathetic."

Leah let the tears roll down her face. It was pointless to try and stop them. Gael didn't normally talk to her like this. Only when she played. It was to make her better— stronger. But right now, Leah felt so unbelievably weak.

But she kept going. Even when Gael hollered right in her ear, she kept going. Over and over and over again. Because if there was even a chance that she could keep her game, she would do *anything* to keep that flicker of hope alive. *Anything.*

She was given morphine— just a small bottle of pills. But she kept it away — never reaching for the bottle. She wouldn't become addicted to the drug. It didn't matter how much pain she was in— she would not become her father.

Three months into recovery, she hit rock bottom. First, it was panic. Her mind took her to dark, dark places. Images of failure flashed through her mind — never being able to play again, or worse, being too dog shit at the game to be considered of worth. Ezra, Savana and Swan would cast her to the side, never talking to her again. And then there was Gael.

Nothing physical would happen. At least she didn't think so. But she would see the looks. The subtle remarks that she was getting fat. The disrespect. The connotation of failure. The *hate.*

That was so much worse than whatever he could do on the court.

She considered killing herself in the deepest depths of the night; when it seemed her ACL would never heal. It was still swollen; still an ugly shade of blue and purple. And it still hurt. A lot.

She had tried to sleep, she really had. But the voices were strong. Ezra, Zahara, Gael. They all screamed in her ear. Telling her she was nothing without basketball, telling her she would never heal or amount to *anything.*

They told her to kill herself.

She limped down to the kitchen, clutching the wall for support. She hated her goddamn crutches— it was easier to hobble around on one foot, even if others called it reckless.

Her fingers grazed the counter, gripping its smooth stone. Pots and pans littered her surroundings, old food crusted in the ceramic. Gael never bothered to clean up and now Leah was unable to perform that duty for him.

She attempted a hop. This time, the ground didn't meet her foot; instead her toes touched a glass bowl. The thing slipped from under her feet, shattering as her weight tipped onto it.

Instinctively, her sprained leg rushed to the ground in an attempt to stabilize her. As soon as her injury touched the concrete, pain shot to her knee, cascading through her body.

"*Agh*!" Leah collapsed to the ground, clutching her throbbing injury. She dragged her fingernails up her flesh, trying to distract from the pain gnawing within her skin. "No no no no *no*!"

Tears began to drip down her face. At first, she tried to wipe them, but they kept coming, blurring her vision. "Stop it! Stop hurting. Go away!" she didn't know who she was talking to. Zahara? Gael? Herself? It didn't matter. Whoever they were, they wouldn't listen.

Look at you. The voices molded together, so intertwined they could've come from one vocal chord. *On the floor, unable to walk. Unable to move. You can't even get up without someone to lift you. Dependent. Helpless. Pathetic.*

"Stop it." At first, the words were just a murmur. A whisper meant only for the voices in her head. But they didn't listen. So the words got louder. "Stop it!" a screech. "*Stop it*!"

Leah reached to the counter. She grabbed a glass, hurling it across the room. It hit a cabinet, shattering on impact. "Get out of my head!"

The voices stalled.

Leah broke into a sob. She let it happen— let it shake her shoulders with a mix of anger and pain. She let herself scream. She let herself yank her hair— unwoven from her usual braids and spread around her in a blanket.

"*Aaaahhh*!" she screeched. "Ah-hah— *haha— aahh*!" her knuckles slid to her temples as she began to punch herself. "I'm never going to go D1. I'm not even going to *play*! Because— because—" the cackles hurt when they came from her throat. "Because I'm fucking *broken*!

"Swan and Savana are getting better. Surpassing me. Leaving me *behind*." The words dripped from her mouth like poison. "And I am just *useless*. How long until Ezra leaves me too? How long until he realizes that I am *never* going to scratch my potential and I'm better off *slitting my fucking throat*."

Her words echoed off the walls of the house. Not even Zahara dared speak. So no one tried to stop her when she reached for the shard of glass.

She raised the piece to her throat, breathing a shaky exhale as the edge dug into her skin. Tears stung her eyes, drifting down her cheek as she tightened her grip on the shard.

Leah. This time, it was only one voice. Ezra. Soft, clear— almost gentle. He wasn't there, but his memory was. All the moments they shared together. And for once in her life, Leah saw the relationship clearly.

We'll find a way. His voice was so real. *This isn't the end, Leah Taven. You'll play again. I don't care what it takes, I don't care what we have to do. Your legacy does not end here.*

Leah put the glass down, replacing it with her trembling hands. For a moment, she glazed over the possibility that maybe, just maybe, she had underestimated her worth.

She was expendable. That was for sure. But maybe her potential was something hard to come across. Replaceable. But possibly hard to replace. At least for Ezra. He would be willing to work for her future— to take a risk. One minor setback was not going to deter the faith he had in her.

She was a powerful weapon. And powerful weapons weren't simply cast aside for a scratched trigger. No, they were shined and oiled. Kept in comfortable facilities that protected them. They were given all the spoils of the world, as long as they did their job.

And as long as Leah did her job, that meant she had a reason to live.

THE GAME, THE GOAL AND THE CONSEQUENCE

"Although injuries are a common and rather expected part of being an athlete, the most glaring findings of this study included: 35% of current and 53% of retired athletes perceived that their injuries impacted their quality of life; 28% of current athletes and 40% of retired athletes perceived they lost support (e.g. attention, resources, funding) due to their injury; 33% of retired athletes perceived their injury to lead to retirement; and 63% of retired athletes perceived inadequate support for their injuries post-retirement."
Kerr, Gretchen, et al. *Prevalence of Maltreatment among Current and Former National Team Athletes.*

Seven months into her recovery, Ezra let her play a high school game.

She had been waiting for his word; his permission to start playing again. To get it, she had been working with him non-stop, attempting to brighten the chances that maybe— just maybe— she could get on that court again.

It was a random Tuesday when he gave her the okay. Leah had come to the workout barely awake. So when Ezra said the words, it took her a few seconds to acknowledge the gravity of the situation.

"Wait—" Leah's eyes widened. "*What*?"

"If at any point it hurts, you need to get out of there. I don't care if you just walk out in the middle of a play. And you have to wear your brace— double check that everything's okay before the game starts. And do the pregame exercises I taught you. Twice—

"Hold up," a smile was beginning to creep along Leah's lips. "You're saying I get to *play*?"

"With certain precautions, yes," Ezra said. "Preferably, I would have you wait a few more weeks but I think if you sit still much longer you might combust."

"Oh my god…" Leah was on the verge of tears. "Oh my god! Thank you, thank you, thank you!" she flung herself at Ezra, catching him in a hug. He was startled at first. Then, cautiously, he wrapped his arms around her.

"Just be careful, okay?" Ezra gave a small smile. "I don't want you getting hurt."

"I won't!" Leah was jumping up and down now, her brace squeaking with excitement. "I won't. I promise."

Her next high school game was in two days. That was two days to prepare. She practiced before and after school— from dusk until after dawn. Sometimes, she would be out past ten, legs aching and eyes so droopy she could barely see the hoop.

But she kept going. She needed to. She needed to prove to *everyone* that she wasn't useless. That this wasn't the end. She would still be the next Zahara Williamson.

When she showed up to the game in her uniform, Viren did a double take. Everyone seemed to look at her like she was a ghost— risen from the dead to drag them down with her. Leah just smiled.

"You're back." Viren said.

"I am," Leah agreed.

Viren led them to the locker room. Surprisingly, the plays seemed pretty decent. Complicated enough to work but simple enough to understand. This was out of character for Viren. Ezra must've pulled some strings.

Leah tightened her brace while he talked. It was a large, bulky thing. So many different parts and gears. Ezra said she'd have to play with this for the rest of her career. Frankly, Leah would rather cut her leg off and play like that.

But that was impractical. The brace, though annoying, worked to some degree. Well, hopefully it would.

The pregame rituals seemed to fly by. Leah went through them buzzing with excitement, preparing for the adrenaline to climb through her veins and rush through her body.

But when it was time for the jump ball another feeling tumbled inside her. Instead of the tinge of excitement, her fingers started to tremble. Her legs felt shaky beneath her and all of sudden she was very, very aware of her knee.

Every step felt like a risk. Her breath would catch in her throat as her foot touched the ground. She was waiting for the snap— for the rush of pain. For the horror of the past few months to repeat itself over and over again.

Holy *fuck*. She could not do this *again*.

The referee blew the whistle. The ball was thrown into the air and hit. Right towards *her*. She managed to catch it, hands trembling.

Usually, she would sprint the court, instinct taking over her senses. But this time, instinct was absent. All of her skills, all of her practice, had simply vanished.

Leah just stood there— *terrified* to move.

A girl lunged at her, swiping the ball from her hand. She watched as she sprinted down the court, going for the open layup. Leah remained paralyzed, her heart climbing into her throat, blocking her breath.

"Leah."

Her teammates were looking at her. Everyone was looking at *her*. Expecting *her* to tell them what to do. To lead. But she couldn't. Right now, she couldn't even speak.

"Leah?"

The ref blew the whistle. He picked up the ball, counting down from five. She had five seconds. Five seconds to get it together. But she couldn't. She couldn't. There was no way… she couldn't— she couldn't—

"*Leah*!" the noise made her jump. A hand landed on her shoulder. She expected someone to hit her. "Are you alright?"

Serena looked so kind, so compassionate. Nothing but good intentions glowed on her face. Nothing but *love*.

Fucking liar!

"Go!" Leah screeched. "Go! Get the ball!"

Serena looked taken aback. Then, she backed away from Leah, hurt etching over her fake compassion. It was also fake. *Everything* was fake. No one cared for her when she was like this.

Serena inbounded the ball just in time. Leah managed to get her bearings and move. Every step shot pain through her knee. She wasn't even sure the ache was there— just a phantom event. But every time the buzz trickled from her knee, her heart rate climbed.

Serena passed her the ball. When Leah turned she saw the full might of the other team was gathered in a back court press. Her opponents charged at her — two at a time.

Leah panicked. She crossed over, but it was sloppy. The ball hit her foot, breaking into a roll. She tried to chase it, but she tripped over herself, falling on her knee. More of the phantom pain erupted from her injury, cascading through her body.

Her defender picked up the ball, finishing in an easy, wide open layup.

As the ball fell through the net, Leah realized she was holding back tears.

Failure. Failure. Failure. Failure. Failure. Failure. Failure. Failure.

And then Gael's voice. Murmuring something in her ear. She couldn't hear the words, but she knew that tone. The tone that meant *danger*.

She stood, her legs trembling under her. She needed to get up. She needed to finish this game. She needed to ignore all the feelings swirling inside her and fucking *play*.

"I'm not weak." Leah murmured. "Come on, Taven. You're not weak. Go get that ball. Go get the *fucking ball.*"

But it was too late. The referee blew the whistle and her substitution came in. The girl grasped her hand, looking at her with thick *pity*.

"Who are you guarding?" she asked.

Leah didn't respond. In all honesty, she didn't know.

She jogged to the bench, her ACL brace tugging on her knee. Viren was waiting for her, the smallest hint of a grin touching his lips. As soon as she got within range, he grabbed her braid.

"Dammit Leah!" Viren screeched. "What the *fuck* was that?"

Leah gasped, staring at him with wide, wild eyes.

"'Oh, I'm just gonna stand here while my teammates do the work.'" Viren pulled her closer, face inches from hers. "'Because I'm too good for this game,' aren't you Leah? Too good for us?"

"No–" Leah blurted. "I'm sorry. I'm so—" she choked; tears burning in her eyes. She couldn't stop them. They rolled down her cheeks without permission. When Viren saw them, his grin widened.

He pushed her into the bench, turning away. "If you want to cry you can do it off the court. You're benched."

Benched? No no no. *Fuck*!

Her foot started to shake against the wood. Her breath grew thick; the air caught in her throat. Tears streamed down her face, leaving a salty residue on her lips. With blurry eyes, she scanned the crowd.

Gael was sitting in the front row of the bleachers. He was leaning forward, chin resting on his wrist. He was looking directly at *her*. His ice cold eyes bore into hers with a promise. A horrible, ugly *promise*.

Viren kept yelling. The game kept going and they kept losing. And Gael kept staring. Unrelenting. He was watching her. He was *always* watching her.

Leah put her head in her hands, foot bouncing against the floor. The air stuck to her throat, unable to come out. Her eyes stung with pain and her heart pounded like a drum. Everything was loud. Everything was too much. But at the same time, the world seemed so unbearably quiet.

~~~

Leah closed the car door behind her as she climbed into the front seat. Gael sat beside her, staring at the wheel. At first no one moved. Then, her father lit a match.
~~~

The light flickered around the car, dancing in the dark. Gael touched the cigarette to his mouth, the fire dimming to an orange glow. Smoke oozed from his lips, curling down his torso and landing on his lap.

"Well," Gael puffed a wad of gray. "That was pretty pathetic."

The tears returned to her eyes. Gael was right. She was pathetic. That's probably what hurt the most. The fact that he was right.

"Oh come on," Gael rolled his eyes when he saw the tears. "I'm not insulting you, I'm telling the truth. Stop with the crocodile tears."

Leah's breath began to feel short. "Dad I'm not—" she stuttered. "I promise they're not fake. I know I'm weak. I know I'm pathetic. I know I'm *worthless*."

Gael pressed his cigarette to his mouth. "Oh stop with the pity party. You are. But that doesn't mean we can't do something to fix it."

Fix it. Fix it. Fix it. Fix *her*.

"I think the first thing we need to address is your fear." Gael pulled the car into drive, speeding from the parking spot. "It's hindering you. You're like a squirrel running from a car. Where do you think that fear is coming from?"

Leah brushed her hair over her red eyes. "I don't know."

Gael pulled onto the road, smoke seeping from the cigarette between his lips. "Yes you do. Come on Leah. You know you do."

She did. She just didn't want to say it. "My… my injury."

"Exactly." Gael said. "You think it's going to snap again. You're expecting that pain— that sudden moment when your entire life is flipped on its head. So you know what we're going to do?"

Leah swallowed. "What?"

"I'm going to foul you on every layup. Push you to the ground whenever I can. You won't expect it, and trust me, it will hurt. Not your knee, but the rest of you." Gael released a murky breath. "And you're going to let it happen, do you know why?"

Tears drifted down Leah's face as she spoke the words. "Because this is the only way I'm going to be good enough."

"Correct." Gael smiled. "I'm doing this because I love you, Leah. I'm doing this because I want you to be the best you can possibly be. And I know that we can fix you."

He let out another breath. This time, the smoke ascended to the ceiling, coating it in a sea of foggy gray. "We can fix you *together*."

~~~

As soon as Leah shut her bedroom door, she collapsed. Not into tears, not into exhaustion; but into a pool of panic. Her memories twisted and turned, flashing through her consciousness.

First it was the events of the day. Her frozen body in the middle of the court, fear stricken. *Weak.* Her brain played it over and over, all different angles. Sometimes, she could hear Viren scream.

Then it was her dribbling. The sound the crowd made— pitying, almost. But it wasn't pity. Pity required some sort of sympathy. That didn't exist.

They cooed and yelped— booing as she let the other team go for the layup. She let it happen. She just *let it happen.*

Weak. Pathetic. Incompetent. Unloveable.

Weak. Pathetic. Incompetent. Unloveable.

Weak. Pathetic. Incompetent. Unloveable.

And then it was Viren. Yelling at her. Pulling her hair. Shoving her onto the bench. She thought of what he did to that little boy— the way he forced himself on him in such a brutal, cruel way. Could he do that to her? Would he?

And then there was Gael. Flashing through her mind like a gunshot. Chasing her. Pushing her. Screaming at her. Over and over and over again. It would never stop. Not until she reached his enormous expectations.

No mistakes. No mistakes. Ever. Mistakes meant pain. Mistakes meant no one would ever love her. Mistakes mean *pathetic.*

Leah intertwined her fingers through her braids, yanking them downward. An ache of pain shot through her scalp. Her nails drifted to her head— pressing harder and harder until the warm ooze of blood drifted down her face.

Leah fell into the fetus position, covering her ears while another round of flashbacks enveloped her. Too real— too accurate. A telling of the past, maybe. But it felt like they were predicting the future.

Leah thrashed as images of her father cascaded through her mind. She tried to scream but all that came out was a mute gasp. Her foot swung forward, attempting to collide with the wall. But it hit something else. A paper bag tilted over, spilling its contents at Leah's feet.

She sat up, the panic thrumming at the back of her mind. There, just before her toes, was a pill bottle. Little white tablets dwelled inside. Rolling on top of one another.
~~~

Leah picked it up, examining the pills. She twisted the capsule open, dropping a tablet into her hand. She rolled it between her fingers, letting it slide between her grasp.

"You." Leah tilted her head. "You can make it all better, can't you?"

She pressed the pill to her lips, savoring its cold touch. But she didn't let it enter her mouth. She just felt it, like she was assessing a clothing item for purchase.

Leah withdrew the pill from her lips, dropping it back into the bottle. She moved with a purpose, with a new hope. This would fix everything. This would make the fear go away. This would stop her pain.

With a smile, Leah stuffed the morphine into her bag.

CAN'T DO IT WITHOUT A CRUTCH

Regularly administered doses of morphine increase pain tolerance in athletes even when they were given a placebo. The morphine makes the athletes perform better through pain tolerance.
—Benedetti, F., et al. "Opioid-Mediated Placebo Responses Boost Pain Endurance and Physical Performance: Is It Doping in Sport Competitions?"

"So, how'd the first game go?" Ezra asked as the two walked towards the gym.

Leah bit her lip, contemplating how to respond. She was going to lie, of course, but her lie had to be believable. So much so that Ezra wouldn't question it.

After that devastating game, Leah and Gael had spent the following days training. It was gruesome— her heels were so bruised from overuse that Leah had to fight to keep herself from limping. But she was better. That's all that mattered. She didn't freeze when she stepped onto the court. And besides, she had something else to help her.

Leah put on a smile. "My knee didn't hurt once."

Ezra matched her expression. "Good. That's what we want. This game, let me know if there's any pain at all."

"Will do," Leah nodded.

Just then, Savana ran up next to them. Her blue hair had turned a deep, blood red. She locked eyes with Leah, eyes widening.

"Shit, are you playing today?" Savana grabbed her shoulders. "I thought it wasn't fully healed— ya' know, with all…" she gestured to her knee brace. "*That*."

"Unfortunately," Leah rubbed the back of her neck. "The brace may be a permanent thing."

"Oh," Savana leaned down, tapping the gear. "Well, it certainly adds a lot to your look."

"My *look*?" Leah raised an eyebrow. "What's that supposed to mean?"

Savana shrugged. "Well, you're pretty recognizable." She picked up one of Leah's braids. "You're fucking Rupunzel. Hair runs down past your ass. And that mechanic thing—" she gestured to the brace. "Makes you look almost cyborg. I dunno, seems like a pretty great character design to me."

Leah snorted. "You're one to talk. It looks like you dipped your hair in a pool of blood."

Savana smirked. "Awh, you really think so?"

Leah huffed a laugh. The three of them padded into the gym, weaving around screaming parents and stressed out officials. The rest of their team was sitting on the bleachers, deep in conversation with one another.

Ezra started talking as soon as he sat down. "So, is everyone familiar with the play Hands?"

Some of the team nodded. Others, mostly the newer ones, didn't. Ezra pulled out his clipboard, quickly going over the action.

Leah didn't listen. She didn't need to. More important things required her attention. Her gaze trailed to game. Two teams— scrambling for the win. Players fell to the ground, skinning their knees and scratching their skin.

All of a sudden, that snap was ringing in her ears. Over and over— then her blood curdling scream as hands were on her knee. The way the doctors laid her on that stretcher that smelled like mint. Sickening *mint*.

Then her father. Pushing her. Her ankle twisting— shots of pain errupting over her body. Pain. So much *pain*. The months of healing, the hours of being hollered at while she could do *nothing*— and those long nights with glass held against her throat—

All pain. Always pain. Forever in *pain*.

But there was something that could make the pain go away.

Zahara's voice sang in her ear. *How far are you willing to go?*

This time, Leah answered.

As far as it takes.

"I need to go to the bathroom." Leah blurted, standing.

Without waiting for confirmation, Leah ran to the restroom. She scrambled into a stall, locking it and standing on the rim of the toilet. She dug her hand into her bag, fingers stretching to find the container hidden at the bottom.

Her hand curled around the bottle, lifting it into her gaze. The little tablets of Morphine rolled to a halt, settling at the bottom of the plastic. Leah unscrewed it, taking a pill between two fingers.

The thing was so small. Just a few milligrams. Could this tiny circle fix everything? Fix *her*?

Zahara's voice reappeared, but her tone was different. Still hateful— still ever so condescending. But the tiniest bit of grief touched her tone. Like the way she talked when she smoked that opium. The only time Zahara ever looked human was when she taught Leah how not to be.

This is your crutch. She hummed. *My opium, your morphine. They numb you— make your pain vanish. It's how you become legendary, how you achieve the impossible. How you become inhuman.*

Leah took a breath, rolling the pill between her middle and ring finger. "What are the effects?"

Does it matter?

Zahara didn't phrase it like a question. She said it like a fact. Because it didn't matter. If she was really good enough for this game, if she was good enough for Gael, for *Ezra*, those consequences wouldn't matter.

Gael's voice was in her mind again. He was yelling at her. There were swears— there always were. But that wasn't the worst part. The worst part was the critiques. Her dribbling was wrong, her shooting was wrong, she was *wrong*. And as long as she was broken, those long days with Gael would continue. The sleepless nights, the endless hours she spent with the edge to her throat. The days she ran until she threw up. The scars and bruises that healed too quickly to be a problem. All because she was *broken*.

The morphine would fix her.

Well, Zahara cooed. Suddenly, she could almost smell the sweet opium smoke. *What are you waiting for*?

Leah took one last look at the pill. The little thing clasped between her fingers. It would either save her or kill her. Maybe neither. Maybe both. But in the end, Leah didn't care about the consequences. She just wanted it to work.

So she shoved the morphine into her mouth.

~~~

Dread was slowly becoming more intertwined into Leah's subconscious. It slithered up her limbs before the game, never quite leaving. It flared when she made any mistake, and when she put her head into her hands on the bench, it throbbed like a gash.

Leah had made the dumb assumption that the morphine may make the dark feeling vanish. If anything, the pill enhanced the anticipation.

As she stood at the jump ball, she could barely keep herself from trembling. Her heart beat so fast it hurt and waves of panic nearly pushed her to the floor. But she stood, not daring to look at anything other than the ball until the morphine came to her rescue.

The ref blew his whistle and the game flew into motion. Swan grabbed the possesion, taking off down the court. Savana flew past Leah, sprinting to the corner.
~~~

The entirety of both teams raced by her at a speed she couldn't seem to comprehend. Her braids flew with them, as if pulling her towards the competition— to victory.

But she couldn't. She couldn't move. Couldn't *play*. She kept hearing that god awful noise. That snap. *Snap snap snap snap*— and then snap, she was gone. Back into that hole. Back with the shard of glass. Back with Gael—

Her legs collapsed, her brace screeching in anger. She put her hands over her ears, trying to stop it. To stop time, to stop the game— to just make everything *stop*.

"Get up," tears brimmed her eyes as she said it. "Get up Leah. Get the fuck *up*."

Slowly, she stood. Her knees threatened to buckle and her panic rose to her throat. But still, she got up.

As soon as she staggered to her feet the ball came spiraling at her. She managed to catch it, barely. She simply stared at it— like she was holding the moon in her hands— mesmerized by its presence.

"Leah!" Swan's voice. "What the hell are you doing? *Wake up*!"

She nearly jumped. On instinct, she put the ball on the ground. She expected the thing to come back to her hand. But instead it hit her foot, rolling right into the other team's hands.

She gave them a fast break. A free point. But that wasn't the worst part. The worst part was Swan's angered face, Savana's disappointed one; Gael, sitting in the crowd with a sadistic smile. And Ezra—

Sending Sarah to take Leah out of the game.

Leah was so unbelievably sure that Ezra was going to hit her.

She deserved it, didn't she? All her mistakes— she fucked everything up. *Everything*. She deserved to hurt. She deserved to get hit.

Savana inbounded the ball, passing it to Swan. A full court press had gathered at the front. Leah gathered her bearings, running to the half court line. Before she knew it, the ball was sailing at her. She caught it, turned, and saw an army of defenders standing in front of her.

The panic got caught in her throat. Her ACL flared with heat and a phantom sting. Her head was pounding— it was all too much, she couldn't do this. She couldn't—

Then the bullet of mania hit her.

Her anxiety evaporated. The trembling that shook her fingers halted. Time slowed as the morphine crawled through her veins, running down her arms and sending pure, frigid power to her fingertips.

Leah exploded off her back foot, bursting through her opponents. She flung the ball between her legs, letting it hover in her hand. With a burst of power, she bolted past the three point line and to the basket.

When she jumped, she seemed to stay in the air— below her, the game had halted. But she was moving. The ball twirled from her grasp, spinning in the air. It fell into the hoop with a crisp swish— cutting the air like a blade.

Time resumed when she landed. Leah fell in the thick of defenders. Someone pushed her off the court. She stumbled backward, ramming her head into the hard wall.

She expected a wave of pain. She expected her head to burn and her ACL to scream. But the misery never came. There was no gripping panic, no stinging ache.

It didn't hurt when Leah reached back and touched blood.

Holy shit.

She couldn't feel pain. Leah was feeling everything and nothing at once but by *God*; she couldn't feel *pain*.

Swan was by her side, offering her a hand. Leah refused it, standing on her own accord.

"Oh my god, Leah," Swan clapped her on the back. "What are you on?"

Leah blinked. It took her a second to realize her special ingredient was probably best kept a secret. It took her an additional second to realize that Swan did not know about her doping and was simply stating a phrase.

Doping. Leah was *doping*. No loophole, no metaphor. Straight up *doping*.

She decided not to respond— she didn't have the words anyway.

The rest of the game was hers. All *hers*. Famous coaches and sports scientists often talked about something known as the zone. A state in which there were no thoughts or feelings— only instinct. Often, Leah had attempted to replicate the feeling. Sometimes, she'd even been successful— playing her best games in pure focus.

This wasn't the zone.

The morphine made her powerful. The morphine eliminated her fear and the *morphine* made her excellent. It dug into her flesh, intertwining the euphoria with Leah's very being. It felt cold, refreshing and gave the slightest sting.

Leah pounded the ball up the court, weaving around defenders like they were objects. She wasn't afraid of going fast, she wasn't afraid of hitting anyone. For the first time in nearly a year, the brace hugging her knee seemed to disappear.

Leah flung the ball to Swan, who was running along the three point line. She grounded herself, extending into her shot. The ball swished through the hoop, cutting along the net.

The game was over shortly. They had won, of course. Losing seemed vaguely possible with the amount of excellence Leah now held at her fingertips.

"Holy *shit*!" Reese clapped Leah on the back. She was a new freshman, someone who Leah believed had a lot of potential. "Leah, that was *insane*!"

Leah let her smile show. The compliment cascaded over her body, resonating into her heart. "Thanks," she breathed. "That means a lot."

"Hey kid!" Ezra grasped her shoulders, beaming ear to ear. "Well fucking done!"

Leah matched his expression. "Thank you Ezra,"

"You did so well," Ezra's voice was soft, no one but her could hear. "You're doing so well. Honestly, Leah, you're the most resilient person I know. I am so, so proud of you."

The tears came without warning. Leah grinned, attempting to hide them from view. She managed to blink them back into her eyes. She could only smile in response. Hopefully, that smile could convey half of what those words felt like.

Suddenly, arms wrapped around her. Leah flung around, ready to land a punch in her attacker's face. But instead of a stranger, she saw the eyes of her father.

Gael picked her up, swinging her in the air. When she landed on the ground, he engulfed her in a hug. "Oh my god, Leah." He murmured. "I knew all your work would pay off. I knew *it*!"

The same tears pricked her eyes again. She couldn't tell if it was the smell of marijuana or the words, but either way, she couldn't keep the tears in. She allowed three droplets to slide down her cheeks, seeping into her dads shirt. Then, she blinked them away, finally finding the courage to look at him.

"Hey," Gael pulled apart from her. "What do you say we get ice cream after this? Your moms favorite spot."

Leah swallowed. She hadn't done something as simple as getting ice cream in years. Even before she started playing, Gael hadn't shown this much interest in her since the incident with her mom.

"Sure," she managed. "That sounds… wonderful."

As they strode from the gym, the crowd's eyes stayed on Leah. But they weren't prying, they weren't judging her. They watched her with admiration. They watched her like they watched *Zahara.*

Just as she was about to exit the building, something rammed into her shoulder. Leah spun around, staring straight at Savana. Tears ran down her cheeks— trailing from her bloodshot eyes. She looked like a starved lion who just lost a gazelle.

"Hey, Gael," she put on a smile— a sickly sweet one. "Can I steal her for a bit."

She didn't wait for his reply. Savana dragged Leah to the bathroom, tugging on her wrist.

"Savana what—" Leah stammered. "Are you alright?"

She didn't answer. Her eyes were in front of her, not daring to move. Tears dripped from her gaze, splattering onto the floor. She yanked Leah inside the bathroom, slamming the door behind them.

"What was that?" she snapped. "What did you *do*?"

"I don't—" Leah stammered. "What are you talking about?"

"*Dammit Leah*!" Savana lunged forward, backing Leah against the wall. "I worked for this! Every day I worked!" she staggered back. "But then you come along— after the *biggest* injury one can get— and just— and just—"

Savana let herself break. Droplets streamed down her face, trembling enveloped her body and for a moment, Leah thought she might collapse.

"Savana…" Leah murmured. "It's okay—"

"*No*!" she screeched. "No. No. No. No. *No*!" she raised her palm to her face, wiping her tears. "You don't get to act concerned. You don't get to act like you care about me. I'm the competition. An *opponent*. And right now—"

Savana let out a scream. Loud, unfiltered rage. Leah was familiar with it. It had come out of her own throat.

"And right now you're *winning*!" Savana screeched. "How are you winning? How are you *beating me*?"

"Savana—" Leah started.

"No no no." Savana placed her hands over her ears. "He's going to hit me. He's going to hit me!" her breath quickened. She grabbed a fistful of her bright red hair, pulling hard. "I didn't win. I'm not going to win. And he's going to hit me. Again and again. *He's going to hit me*.

"And now—" Savana drawled, turning to Leah. "Your dad is going to take you to fucking ice cream. *Ice cream*, Leah! Dammit because you won! How the fuck did you *win*?"

Leah thought that was yet another question Savana asked herself. She didn't even feel like a part of the conversation. It was just Savana and whatever version of Zahara that whispered in her ear.

Savana took a step towards her. When she spoke, her voice was surprisingly steady. "Well?" she tilted her head, fire blazing in her black gaze. "How did you do it?"

"Savana I promise," Leah raised her hands above her head. "I don't know what you're talking about."

"Oh, you don't?" she phrased it like a question. When the words breached her lips, Savana was calm. But there was a danger lingering beneath them. "No one can get over an ACL like you did. *No one*. I don't care what special techniques Ezra taught you and I don't care if that brace is made from the flesh of Stephan fucking Curry. The way you just played—" Savana took a breath. "It just isn't humanly possible."

This time, Leah found her composure. She straightened her posture, flicking her braids behind her back. Savana didn't shrink away when she strode to her. Instead, her opponent stood tall, matching Leah's stance.

"That's the point." Leah drew, barely a whisper. "Maybe I'm better than human."

Leah brushed past Savana, letting her braids run along her shoulder before falling with her stride. She walked out of the bathroom, fire burning in her gaze. She was so focused on the heat blazing behind her eyes that she didn't realize her father stood just behind the door.

THE NEW GENERATION

Athletes don't report because of fear that they'll be punished by an authority figure or person in power. They believe that what is happening to them is normal because of conditioning and harsh expectations in sport.

—"Why Athletes Do (and Don't) Report Abuse in Sports." *Psychology Today.*

"That girl is a problem." Gael said, closing the car door. "A big *problem*."

Leah crossed her arms. "No, it's okay Dad. She's my friend."

"*Friend*?" Gael nearly laughed. "Friends don't talk like that. And friends don't threaten each other's victory. That girl sees you as nothing more than an obstacle. An *opponent*. I think it's time that you respond to her in kind."

"Dad no," Leah shook her head. "She was upset, that's all. We all get like that. It's just something that happens. She's suffering. She didn't mean it."

Gael raised an eyebrow. "Fine, Leah." He thrusted the car into reverse, backing out of the parking lot. "Just don't blame me when she takes your place."

Savana didn't text her for the next few days. Leah attempted to get in contact with her, but her messages were left on read. For a few quick seconds, she let herself worry. She entertained the possibility that Savana may also find herself with a shard of glass to her throat.

But Leah didn't drown in the worry. She drowned in ambition. For the next few days, she threw herself into her sport. Early mornings into nights that flew into the morning. She even let Gael practice with her. Just as rough as ever, her father put his full effort into the workout. Leah left every one with bruises and weak knees.

The panic had lessened. Because now, she was in control. Every time the workout ended, Gael expressed his admiration for Leah. His *pride*. And every time, the words made her close to tears.

She saved the morphine for the games. No drugs unless necessary— unless she needed to perform. She had seen first hand what they could do to someone. She didn't want to end up like either of her birth givers.

She got her driver's license a few days after she first found her crutch. It was a massive relief— not having to rely on her father for transportation anymore. She drove her mothers old stick shift car, but she didn't mind it. As long as she could get to and from, she was happy.

Leah pulled up to practice on a rainy day. The water pounded on her windshield, the sound slowly putting Leah to sleep.

She stepped out of the car, putting her coat over her head. It did little for her. By the time she made it inside the gym, she was soaked. Her braids dripped on the floor, falling droplets following her stride.

"Oh shit," Ezra raised a brow. "Rain caught you?"

Leah twisted her hair, water splattering onto the floor. "Yeah. No good parking."

She made her way to the balls, spinning one on her finger. Savana was deep in conversation with Swan. They were laughing, a genuine smile on both of their faces.

Leah met Savana's eye, grinning. Savana looked away quickly, sending Leah something that could've been a scowl.

No, no. Probably nothing. Savana didn't hate her. Savana wasn't leaving her. She wasn't going to *lose* her.

"Hey!" Ezra stood in the middle of the court, drawing them over. With him was a girl Leah didn't recognize. A new kid. "This is Tina. She's trying out."

Leah nodded, making her way over to Tina. She looked nervous, fingers tugging at her shorts. Before she could offer her greetings, Savana stepped in front of her.

"Hi!" she exclaimed. "I'm Savana, and this is Swan." She put an arm around her teammate. "Swan's literally the only one who can make a shot."

What? *What*? Leah nearly slapped her. The familiar hot grasp of rage climbed through her limbs. Swan was not the best and Leah was not *incompetent.*

Leah laughed. It sounded so fake it stung her throat. "That's so funny, Savana." She hoped no one saw the malice behind her tone. "But trust me, Tina, this team is not a one man show."

"Oh come on, Leah." Savana copied the fake cackle. "Have you ever seen either of us do anything without Swan? She's amazing! *Inhuman*."

Then Leah understood. This wasn't about Swan. It was about her. About hurting her. Swan was Leah's weakness— the one who could match Leah's skill without having to try.

Leah shifted her gaze to Tina. The girl looked back, clearly uncomfortable. "Tina, go warm up with the others." Leah cocked her head to where the rest of the team practiced. "Go on, don't be scared, they don't bite."

Tina scurried past Leah, joining the girls in shooting lines. Leah watched her go before turning back to Savana. They met each other's eyes, leveling their glare.

"Outside," Leah growled. "*Now.*"

Savana raised her chin, red hair swishing as she tilted her head. "As you wish."

The two stood under a shelter, the rain pattering against the narrow overhang. They lingered as far apart as possible, as if one of them was infected with the Spanish flu.

"What do you think you're doing?" Leah drawled. "First you don't answer my texts and then you start acting like *Swan* is the only one who can hold a fucking ball?" she took a step closer. "What game are you playing?"

Savana's lip curled. "I'm playing the same game I've always played. I told you Leah— from the very get-go— only one of us can be the best, and right now, neither of us holds that role."

"Oh?" Leah tilted her head. "And Swan does? Is she the threat you've created?"

Savana hummed a chuckle. "No. Swan may be good now, but she isn't interested in long term play. For her, it's just a game. Just for *fun.*" She advanced towards Leah, face inches from hers. "You wanna know who the real opponent is, Leah?"

Leah flashed a toxic grin. "Oh, please Savana." She said, "Tell me."

Savana tilted her head. "It's you."

"What?"

"See I didn't clock you as an enemy at first." Savana strode around her, like a vulture circling prey. "I thought you were just a cocky, unstable child who played Ezra's perfect prodigy. But now—" she chuckled. "You know, after that game I realized something. We're more alike than we realize. Sure, we both have this pressure ticking down like a clock that might end one day, but there's something much more special about the two of us."

Savana lunged forward, coming face to face with Leah. "We have no limits. No deed too awful for our goals. You know, Leah, we might be the only two people like that."

"Fascinating," Leah's drawled. "And because we're alike, you immediately regard me as an enemy?"

Savana let the slick grin slip. "There can only be one prodigy, Leah. And right now, there's one too many." She flicked her hair, heading back into the gym. "Good luck, you'll need it."

Leah watched her go. For a moment she let herself feel grief. Sadness for the friendship she had lost. She let a tear leak from her eye, caressing her cheek like a hand.

Savana's betrayal was an unfortunate sacrifice. A friend she wished didn't have to go. But no matter how much it hurt, Savana still left. That made her an opponent, someone who had to be crushed.

I smashed everyone who got in my way, Zahara cooed. *If she's not on your side, she's in your way. Those who prevent your goals need to be decimated.*

Leah closed her eyes, droplets curving down her face. She dropped to her knees, betrayal burning like a flame. Savana left her. It didn't matter how much Leah cared, she left.

How long until everyone else abandoned her too?

Leah raised her gaze to the sky and let out a long, cracked scream.

~~~

Leah was quite shocked when Ezra invited her to one of the middle school practices. To help him with *logistics* he said. When Leah texted back asking for specifics Ezra responded with the skull emoji and turned his notifications off.

Of course, Leah had offered to help coach middle school before. Whenever she proposed the idea the most response she ever got was a laugh coming straight from Ezra's stomach.

Savana had told her that apparently she was a 'bad influence' on children. Leah personally didn't see it but she couldn't very well ask Savana for clarification now.

When Leah walked into the gym, Ezra was leaning against the bleachers. Three little girls crouched next to him, watching the scrimmage unfolding before them.

Leah strode to him, letting her braids fall at her waist as she stopped. Ezra met her gaze, grinning. Leah matched his smile.

"So," Leah tilted her head. "You finally gonna give me context on why the hell I'm here?"

Ezra shrugged. "Figured it might be beneficial for you and another party."

"Right," Leah said. "And is that beneficiary you?"

"Oh please, Leah." Ezra leaned against the bleacher. "Every action I take will benefit me in the long run. But that doesn't mean I don't take other people's goals into account."
~~~

In front of them, a girl dribbled down the court. Defenders surrounded her, attempting to poke the ball from her grasp. The girl flung the ball behind her back, swerving away from her opponents. She let the ball rotate in her hand before gathering into her shot. The ball flew from her fingers in a perfect arc, swishing into the basket.

"Holy shit," Leah chuckled. "Who's that?"

"The second party." Ezra said. "Trisha Lively."

Leah turned to him, raising an eyebrow. "Where'd you find a girl like her?"

"I didn't." Ezra smiled. "She came in with her dad about a year ago. Unprovoked; I think they were practicing outside. Anyway, her dad asked if she could scrimmage with us. I'm not one to refuse free competition. I offered her a place on the team as soon as she swished her third three."

Leah recentered her gaze on the court. Trisha had reclaimed the ball and was now dribbling it down the court at top speed. This time, her defense was trying a different approach. Instead of coming at her, they waited behind the three point line. Leah would've taken the three, but Trisha decided against it.

With a smile, the girl drove into the opposition. She planted the ball just out of reach, weaving through her defenders like a string through a needle. When she reached the basket, she euro stepped around the last opponent and finished with a scoop.

Trisha watched the shot glide through the net, grinning with anticipation. When the ball fell, she sprinted back down the court, brushing stray strands of hair from her face.

When she saw Leah, she froze.

They made eye contact. Leah waved.

Trisha just stared.

Leah pointed down the court. Trisha's defender was dribbling past the half way mark. Well, *dribbling* wasn't the right word. It was more like the ball was dribbling her. It seemed to have a mind of its own, bouncing off the girl's foot and running towards the sideline only for the handler to retrieve it right in time.

Trisha swiped the ball without trouble. Her teammate was already sprinting to the corner, wide open for the three. Trisha flung the ball towards her. The girl caught it, setting up her form and letting the ball flow from her grasp. The shot was close, but instead of swishing it tattered around the rim and fell to the side.

Trisha bolted into the three point line, coming at the ball with the speed of a cheetah. She leapt into the air, ascending to an impressive height. She caught the ball and tipped it back into the hoop— all before landing on the ground.

"Lively!" Ezra screeched, blowing the whistle that hung around his neck— a birthday present from Leah. "You're out. You—" he put his hand on one of the scrub's backs, "Go in for her."

Trisha high fived the girl and skipped back to where Ezra was perched. When she realized Leah was still there, she froze.

"Trisha," Ezra began. "I'm sure you're aware of Leah Taven."

Trisha looked at Ezra, then at Leah, and nodded profusely.

"She never shuts up about you." Ezra whispered. "You're her idol. Thought it might be beneficial for you to show her some things. She'd love it."

Leah smirked. "Hey kid," she said, "Can you show me your euro step again?"

A smile stretched along Trisha's face, lighting up her eyes. She nodded, shaking her head so vigorously Leah thought her neck might snap. She led Trisha to a side hoop, looking her up and down.

She was pretty small. Not child small, just short. Her skin bulged with the beginnings of muscle. Every feature pointed to the fact she may be confident, but the girl walked with her arms pressed against her chest. Her eyes stayed on the floor, occasionally darting up to meet Leah's. And on the top of her head—

"Hm," Leah chuckled, flicking her braids. "Nice hair."

Trisha gave a small smile. She reached to touch Leah's braids, which had fallen at her waist. Her first instinct was to pull away, maybe slap the child. No one really came at her hair without ill intention. But Trisha just held the weave, as if the very presence of it mesmerized her.

"Pretty cool, huh?" Leah asked. "Can I tell you a secret?"

Trisha raised her eyebrows and nodded.

Leah took her braid, holding it between two fingers. "You know, I tell people that my hair is this long so I can whack people on the court. The acceptable answer, right? But the real reason I have these—" she let the braid fall from her grasp. "It's so I don't look like every other basic bitch on this court."

Trisha raised a hand to the stray strands running down her face. "I have that too."

"Oh?" Leah leaned down, brushing the hair behind her ear. "Is that what the hooker strands are?"

"Hooker strands?"

"That's what they're called."

Trisha shrugged, brushing the other lock from her face.

"Hey," Leah undid the action, letting the two strands loose. "Keep them. They look really pretty."

Trisha smiled, a slight redness glowing on her cheeks.

"So," Leah flicked the ball onto her finger, spinning it. "Show me that euro step again— I wanna see it up close."

Light flashed across Trisha's face. Leah flung her the ball. Trisha barely let it touch her grasp before she pushed it between her legs, pounding the dribble to life.

She moved to the top of the key, dribbled the ball behind her back, and swiftly crossed over. The thing rolled in her hand for a moment before she pushed forward, darting to the basket. Two steps in she bounded off her inside foot, landing on the opposite side of the hoop and laying the ball into the basket.

Leah cupped a hand to her mouth. "Holy shit."

The words were neutral, not an opinion amongst them. The phrase was an accident— not meant to come out, She meant the words in amazement and awe, but Trisha seemed to take them in offense.

The kid crossed her arms, leaving the ball's bounce dying at her feet. She didn't meet Leah's eye. "Sorry, was it bad?"

Leah raised an eyebrow— giving herself a second to be confused. "What?" she rushed to Trisha's side, grabbing her shoulders much like Ezra held hers. "No no no. Trisha that was *perfect*."

This time, it was Trisha's turn to be confused. "What?"

"*Perfect*." Leah repeated. "Jesus Christ, Trisha, I couldn't critique that if my life depended on it. God, kid. How old are you again?"

Trisha blushed, letting a small smile tint her lips. "Really? Perfect?"

"Not a flaw," Leah agreed. "Now how old are you?"

Trisha pressed her arms to her chest. "My dad said that you would tear every aspect of my game to shreds if I ever met you."

"Your dad's an idiot. Trisha— how many years have you been on planet earth?"

This time, the kid gave a response. "I'm thirteen."

"Shit," Leah brushed her braids behind her back. "When I was thirteen, I could barely get the ball to reach the hoop."

Trisha's eyes widened. "Really?"

Leah thought for a moment. "No. That's a hyperbole. I could reach the basket— my form was just… well, fucked."

The kid tilted her head. "You swear a lot."

"Astute observation."

"Thank you," Trisha said. "What do we do now?"

Leah grinned. "Show me your three pointers."

Trisha's eyes fled to the ground. "They're not very good."

"Bullshit." Leah said. "You said that about your euro and it was one of the best I've seen."

"But you haven't seen—".

"Right, but I've met you." Leah responded. "And in these few short minutes, I've gathered that your standards massively outweigh those of everyone else. What you think is horrible must be at least above average." Leah tilted her head. "So, Hooker Strands, I wanna see you shoot."

A smile touched Trisha's cheeks. She picked up the ball at her feet, jogging to the three point line. Her shot was near perfect; legs bent just enough to get a powerful spring. The only fault was her arm placement, which strung out to the side.

The ball rattled off the rim, falling to the side. Trisha's face fell.

Leah picked it up, passing it back to Trisha.

She shot it again— everything perfect but that one mistake.

Leah caught the ball. "One more time."

Trisha straightened into her shot for the third time. Exactly the same— the shot rattled around the hoop before falling to the side.

Leah let the ball fall to the ground, walking up to Trisha. The kid's eyes were on the ground, and Leah could've imagined it, but she thought she saw her tremble.

"Hey, kid." Leah placed her finger on Trisha's chin, raising her gaze to meet hers. "You okay?"

Trisha's voice was barely a murmur. "I missed."

She phrased it with confusion— like something was meant to happen, but didn't. It wasn't a statement; it wasn't an order. It was a 'why?'

"Chelsey Plum misses." Leah said. "It's not something you can avoid."

Trisha shook her head. "Not the easy shots."

"Trust me, Trish, she does." Leah retorted. "And also, Chelsey Plum isn't fucking thirteen. Look, everyone misses— everyone fails. To not fail means you don't succeed— and isn't that a failure in of itself? The important thing is that you learn from your mistakes, just like you can right now."

Leah took the ball, straightening into her shooting position. "Look. Your shooting form is perfect— except for one thing; your elbow. It goes like this." She stuck her arm out— like a chicken wing. "See? Makes your shot go all wonky and to the side, but if you straighten it—" Leah fixed her from, releasing her shot. The ball tattered around the rim before falling to the side. Leah made a face.

"Can't make all of them." She shrugged. "But you get what I mean."

Trisha folded her arms over her chest. "My dad said that having my elbow like that gives me more power."

"Yeah I'm starting to really not like that guy." Leah said. "He trained you, right?"

Trisha nodded. "I started when I was three."

Leah chuckled. "Well that explains your skill. Although from what I've heard, it seems that the man is nothing short of an imbecile. I'd wager you did most of the work yourself."

"He's the one that makes me practice."

"Right," Leah crossed her arms. "But it's you who does that practice. Your work kid. You made yourself, not him."

For a moment, light touched Trisha's face. It vanished quickly, but Leah caught it. She let a smile of her own spread across her lips.

"Tell me," Leah knelt down, flicking one of Trisha's braids. "Does your dad know who I am?"

"Oh yes," Trisha nodded. "He talks about you all the time. Reads about you in the paper. The people who report on high school games really like to talk about you."

"Yeah, well I give them something to talk about." Leah snorted. "Keeps me in the headlines. Does your dad like me?"

"Of course," Trisha said. "You're my goal— at least according to him. I want to be like you. Exactly like *you*."

"Oh," Leah said. "Well that makes this easy. Hooker Strands, tell your dearest father that you are now shooting with your elbow tucked in. Oh and if he decides he wants to argue—" she tilted her head. "Tell him Leah Taven says to shove the fuck off."

THE TRUTH WE IGNORE

Children describe a feeling of being "sick" after a bad game or after being scolded by a coach. Several children described patterns of emotional abuse by their coaches and teammates.
—Elliason, Inger. "Breaking the Silence of Abuse in Children's Sport:Experiences and Effects of Emotional Abuse Towards Young Athletes in Sweden."

"Why are seniors always on varsity?" Trisha asked. "Even the ones that suck?"

"Because they're sensitive incompetent beings and are making a last ditch effort to make their high school career anything better than pathetic." Leah said, tapping her fingers against the steering wheel. "The coaches take pity."

Leah had been Trisha's chauffeur for the last few games— a task that was enjoyable for both of them. Leah now found herself in Zahara's position, answering the never ending questions that came from her protégé. Thankfully for Trisha, Leah didn't drive like she was being chased by a fucking dinosaur.

"Why do all the other coaches give Ezra such weird looks?" Trisha asked. "Like he's a demon or something."

Leah smirked. "He might as well be to them. It's because he's skilled—beats the others with minimal effort. His very presence is bad for business. Oh, and he's not an asshole to his players; that also adds to the alienation."

Trisha nodded, digesting this. Usually, one question did not lead to another corroboration. That either meant Leah was very good at providing answers or incredibly bad at it.

"Why do you drive a manual?"

Leah furrowed her brow. "That's not a basketball question."

"Astute observation. Why do you drive a manual?"

Leah chuckled, shifting the car into fifth gear. The machine's pitch sped to a high frequency as she passed a rather slow car that seemed permanently planted in the left lane.

"You really wanna know?" Leah asked. "It was my moms. I taught myself. Father dearest wasn't incredibly keen on teaching me and I wasn't ecstatic to spend unnecessary time with him either. So I just drove around my little neighborhood."

Trisha tilted her head. "Why doesn't your mom use it?"

"She's gone."

"Where?"

"I don't know, Trish. Wherever people go when they leave. Ask another question."

Trisha studied her for a long moment— taking in every inch of her face. It was as if the kid was trying to memorize her features, searching for any hints about Leah's emotions. She didn't find any.

Eventually, she gave up. "So, am I allowed to sit with the big kids?"

Leah raised an eyebrow. "You mean the varsity team?"

"Yeah, the big kids."

"Frankly Trish," Leah turned on her turn signal, speeding into the exit. "You can sit wherever you please. If that means with my team, go for it. Not my personal choice, but who am I to dictate what you do?"

Trisha's eyes widened. "Do you not like your teammates?"

"Some of them piss me off."

"Why?"

"They're assholes."

"Why?"

"Because they're assholes, Trish. I don't wanna talk about this."

Trisha tucked her knees to her chest. "You don't wanna talk about a lot of things."

"Astute observation."

Leah pulled into the parking lot, sliding her car into one of the narrow slots. She put the thing in park and turned to Trisha, who had another question tipping off her tongue.

"So what's your beef with Savana Afren—"

"Okay," Leah held up a hand. "Q and A's over. Give me your hair."

"Why?"

"I'm redoing your braids, that's why." Leah pulled a brush from her bag. Trisha, to her surprise, didn't argue. In fact, she seemed quite ecstatic about the makeover, barely containing her smile.

Before, Trisha's hair had been… something. Two braids right on the top of her scalp; nearly pointing straight into the air. Leah had a deep suspicion they were supposed to resemble her own style. When she asked the kid about it, she only blushed.

She removed the ties from Trisha's hair, careful not to pull the stubborn strands that knotted around the rubber band. Slowly, she untangled her hair—brushing it with careful precision.

The new braids were carefully done. Two weaves starting from the bottom of Trisha's scalp, cascading down her back in two neat patterns.

When Leah finished the last braid, Trisha was nearly bouncing up and down. Leah chuckled, pulling down her car mirror. The kid sat up, admiring her new style.

"Like it?" Leah smiled. Trisha nodded, grinning ear to ear.

"You know, I was a lot like you when I was your age." Leah pressed her knees to her chest. "Although, you're much better than I was. But I used to go on car rides like this— ask so many questions my mouth would run dry." Leah chuckled.

"I had a mentor— like what I am to you." Leah looked at her feet. "Her name was Zahara. The greatest woman I've ever known. I thought she was a fucking goddess. Maybe I still do. But she was the person I wanted to become, and now, with you, I'm realizing—" she smiled. "Maybe I've already become her."

Trisha looked at her, prying blue eyes meeting her brown gaze. "Where is Zahara now?"

Leah shrugged. "College. Stanford University."

"Do you miss her?"

"Sometimes," Leah shrugged. "Sometimes I just wonder how she ever achieved what she did. Sometimes I just want to call her and scream— but mostly—" Leah shook her head. "Well, I don't know. I guess I filled her shoes, and now I'm the new Zahara. Now people wonder how I do it, and I don't even know myself."

Trisha tilted her head. "Do what?"

"Do—" Leah halted, plastering on a sweet smile. "You know what? It's not important. Let's go inside."

~~~

Chaos, as usual, resonated inside the gym. Savana, Swan and the rest of her teammates sat clumped together on the bleachers. Savana's red hair was tied in a high ponytail, the strands cascading down her back. Sleeves lined her arms— a strange change. Savana hated undershirts; some sports superstition of hers.

When she saw Leah, a malicious smile curved along her features. She turned to her teammates, brushing her hair from her shoulder. "Why do you always freeze up at the beginning of the game, Leah? It's like you can't move. What the hell is up with that?"

Leah scowled. "Well hello to you too."
~~~

"I mean seriously," Savana cackled. "Do you really expect to get into NCAA basketball when you're virtuously useless at the beginning of the game?"

Leah sighed. She looked down at Trisha, who was gazing back at her with curious— and a bit angry— eyes.

"Trish," Leah said. "Cover your ears."

Trisha gave Leah one last questioning glance before placing her fingers into her ears and shutting her eyes.

"What's the matter Leah?" Savana cocked her head to the side. "Don't want the kid to see how much of a *psycho* you are?"

"Precisely." Leah advanced on her. "What the fuck is your problem? Is insulting me the only thing that fills that never-ending hole of not being good enough? Criticizing my game is not going to make yours any better."

Savana laughed. "I'm just being honest."

"Oh, are you?" Leah copied the laugh, mockery coating her tone. "Well then, Savana, allow me to be *honest*. You don't have enough power in your shot and to get that power you compromise the integrity of your form. Your dribbling is mediocre at best— and don't pretend like we haven't seen the ball running to the sideline whenever you handle it. Oh, and your defense?" a malicious smile curved her lips. "You may pretend like you're the best in the county, but let's be real, you couldn't guard a duck with a basketball taped to its back if it *sat on your feet*." Savana stood, anger curving her features. Leah met her gaze with carefully constructed cruelty. "Ezra only praises your defense because he *pities you*."

Savana didn't say anything. She just stared at Leah, fire flickering between her gaze. She clenched her hands into fists, raising her chin to match Leah's.

"Hey guys," Trisha, who had uncovered her ears halfway into Leah's string of insults, pointed to the door. "Speak of the devil."

Leah turned to see Ezra waltzing into the gym. He chatted with the referees as he walked, a smile spreading on his features.

Leah huffed a sigh. "Excuse me."

She brushed Savana's shoulder, striding along the sideline and into the privacy of The locker room. It was quiet in there: it always was. Leah reached into her bag, pulling out the morphine. The cap snapped off and two pills slipped into her hand.

One didn't cut it anymore. Not at all. Leah had noticed the effect slowly lessening and her terror creeping back like a snake curling up her leg. Squeezing and squeezing until slowly, she suffocated.

Leah popped the pills in her mouth, drinking a swig of water to wash them down. There— the nerves should vanish in a few minutes.

A clattering rang throughout the room. Leah jumped up, scanning the lockers for anyone who saw her. Her heart beat like a hammer, weakening her knees. If anyone had saw—

No. *No*. She was imagining things. No one was there. And even if someone had seen it, they would assume it was antidepressants or allergy medication.

"Hello?" Leah snapped. "Who's there?"

Nothing but silence rang around the locker room. Almost silence. But Leah could've sworn she heard breathing.

Just then, Ezra led the team into the room. Leah stuffed the pill bottle into her bag, disguising the sudden movement as the action of pulling out her shoes.

Ezra raised his eyebrows, gaze flitting from Leah to her bag. "Someone's eager."

Leah flashed a smile, red blooming on her cheeks. She didn't say anything— if she did, it would just add to Ezra's suspicion.

"Alright," Ezra forced his gaze away from Leah, pulling out his clipboard. "The game plan's pretty simple…"

Leah didn't bother to listen. She knew what it was; the last few plays they'd done in practice. This was no game out of the ordinary. She had done this kind of thing a million times.

What she wasn't used to was Savana glaring at her with such ferocity. But it wasn't just anger that rested in her gaze, but curiosity. *Suspicion*. Her gaze kept flickering to Leah's bag, as if trying to see inside it.

Leah caught her gaze, lifting her chin. Savana held eye contact, tilting her head. For a moment, they simply let the fire flicker between them, heat rising in their bones.

Then, Leah mouthed two simple words. Subtle enough only Savana could see.

Fuck off.

~~~

The ref flung the ball into the air. Sarah hit it forward to Leah. As soon as the ball grazed her hand, she took off down the court. The layup was easy— not a defender in sight. And best of all, not once did she think of the terrible snap of her ACL.
~~~

The ball glided into the basket, falling at her feet. A loud cheer erupted throughout the gym. The praise added to Leah's euphoria, pushing the morphine deeper into her veins.

She inbounded the ball to Swan, who turned to see the back court press surrounding them. Swan crossed over, trying to make it by herself. She beat her own defender, but a second girl met her two steps later. She retreated, letting her own opponent catch up.

"It's a man to man," Swan spat. "We need everyone to—"

"*Clear*!" Leah shouted. "Get out!"

The team obeyed, scattering down the court. Leah followed, leaving Swan with her opponent. When she crossed over, her defender followed. Swan countered by flinging the ball behind her back; this caused the opponent to stutter and just like that, the press was broken.

Leah raced down the opposite side of the court, eyeing Swan. Her own defender hadn't located her yet— she was wide open for the three.

She didn't have to call for the ball— Swan had already seen her. She was open for only a moment before her defender found her bearings. The pump fake sent her opponent flying, allowing Leah a clear path to the basket. Her eyes met the corner, seeing Savana wide open for the three.

Well fuck.

The ball flew from her grasp, landing in Savana's. She hadn't stooped to the level of icing her own teammate. But when Savana made the shot, a tiny spurt of anger flared inside her heart.

The crowd shrieked— screeches and wails cutting through Leah's anger. Still, she ran beside Savana, face twisted with malice.

"You're welcome," she murmured.

"Keep your dick on, Taven." Savana retorted. "No one cares about assists."

Leah swallowed her anger, sprinting down the court. She found her defender perched in the corner, anticipating a pass. Leah quickly stopped that possibility, but was met with yet another issue.

"*Move*!" Savana screeched. "That's my girl!"

"No, it's not," the player backdoor cut, sending Savana and Leah with her. "I got here first and I called her at the jump ball."

Savana scowled, not backing down. "Ezra assigned me to her before the game!"

"I heard no such order!"

"Well that doesn't mean it didn't happen, does it?"

"Leah!" Swan ordered. "Go get someone else! In case you have forgotten, we have a fucking game going on."

Leah closed her mouth, biting back the retort. Bickering would do no good for either of them. Being the bigger person would be seen as admirable. Even if it meant letting Savana have this one.

She sprinted to the open girl, dropping into her defensive stance and strangling the rage boiling inside her.

The rest of the game was as hostile as ever. Her, Swan and Savana ran the show as always, creating shots and making passes faster than the human eye could capture.

The bickering didn't stop. Leah and Savana spent every spare moment making remarks about each other's skills and Swan spent every spare moment telling them to knock it off. They didn't of course.

But despite the rivalry, Leah thought she played pretty well. The morphine did its job— keeping her head above the murk of terror.

Leah raced after the ball, diving for it. She managed to grab the possession, quickly passing it to Swan. After staggering to her feet, she raced down the court.

Swan saw her immediately, the ball plummeting into her hands. Leah straightened into her shot, letting the ball fly from her grip. It rattled off the hoop, falling into the grasp of the opponent.

Leah cursed, running back on defense. She ran her gaze across the crowd— just a quick, almost accidental glance. But then she saw him.

Brown eyes, long greasy hair, cigarette positioned between two fingers. The yellow teeth, the yellow fingernails and that yellow, stone cold gaze that promised *horror*.

Leah froze, staring right at her father.

The morphine evaporated from her veins, leaving behind the icy grasp of fear— it encased her like a prison; and there was no way out of this cell. No. *No*! He wasn't supposed to be here. Leah hadn't told him where the tournament was— he wasn't even supposed to know there was one. How—

And suddenly Leah was rethinking the entire game. The shots she took, the shots she *missed*. Every single pass. *Every single time* she didn't dominate. He noticed, he always noticed. He always saw *everything*.

"Leah!" Swan shouted. "Come on!"

Come on Leah. Zahara ordered. *Get your shit together. Come on, move. Fucking move!*

But she couldn't. She was stuck in one place. Her heart rate kept climbing, her hands started to tremble and her eyes—

Her eyes were stuck on her father. Meeting his yellow gaze— that knowing *gaze*. It made her want to vomit.

Then the flashbacks started. Climbing up her throat and infecting her mind. Chasing, chasing, chasing. She needed to run. She needed to get away. But no matter how hard she tried, no matter how many times she swallowed that morphine pill, she could never run fast enough.

The crowd erupted in triumph. Someone must've scored. But Gael remained seated, hand pressed together and chin resting on his knuckles. Knuckles. Knuckles. Knuckles.

He's going to hit me.

Someone pushed her. She spun around, face to face with Savana. Her eyes were filled with fire, but Leah couldn't muster the anger. Not now, anytime but *now*.

Savana's eyes suddenly softened. Understanding crept into her gaze; the rage fizzled out. But then the fire sparked and gasoline lit up her entire being.

"What are you doing?" she shrieked. "You can't just fucking sit and stare, Leah. If you want to be lazy, you can do that on the fucking bench!"

The whistle blew. Leah didn't respond. She just ran. Ran past the bench and into the locker room. She didn't think about the game, she didn't think about anything. She just *ran*.

She collapsed onto the locker room floor, choking on her own breath. It came out ragged, scarred with sobs and cries. Her hands crept to her face, nails digging into her skin. He was coming. She knew it. He *had* to be coming.

And he could *not* see her like this.

Leah tried to stand up, but the weight of her own terror held her down. Tears streamed from her eyes, entangling the hair that escaped her braid. She coughed on the salt, sending her into another struggle for air.

Suddenly, a pair of arms wrapped around her. She jumped up, but the grasp didn't leave. She was ready to run, ready to pick herself up off the floor and sprint until she threw up.

But she didn't have to. Because there, tightly wrapped around her waist, was Trisha. She didn't say anything, she didn't have too. She just held Leah, pressing her face into her chest.

Leah just stared at the kid. She didn't believe she was real. That someone was just holding her because she needed it. Someone wasn't trying to hurt her.

Carefully, Leah wrapped her arms around Trisha, letting her heart steady itself. The kid's breath was soft, steady and rhythmic. Leah copied it, allowing herself to match Trisha's tranquillity.

Leah pulled apart first, wiping her eyes. Trisha followed, crossing her feet under her. At first, they just looked at each other— as if trying to memorize the other's features.

"Are you alright?" Trisha asked.

Leah breathed a shaky sigh. "Yeah, just got a bit scared, that's all."

Trisha didn't push. Instead, she gazed at Leah with her bright blue eyes. She let a smile creep along her lips, kindness radiating from her features. "Do you want me to drive?"

It took Leah a second to comprehend what she said. "What?"

A laugh cracked Trisha's composure. "Do you want—" she snickered, "Do you want me to drive?"

Leah let herself smile. Not because the joke was funny—it was so far from funny— but because of its irony. She was supposed to be playing. Later, she would hate herself for not playing. But for now, she was cracking jokes with a middle schooler who held herself together better than she did.

"Tell you what, kid." Leah ruffled her hair. "One day, I'm gonna take you to a parking lot and I'm gonna teach you how to drive."

Trisha tilted her head. "I'm going to crash."

"I would expect nothing less."

Suddenly, footsteps filled the hallway. Soft, but heavy. Loud, but quiet. A combination of everything. A combination of everything Leah feared. The sound that told her the monster was coming.

"Trish," Leah grabbed the kid's shoulders. "You need to go."

"What?" Trisha's eyes flashed with confusion. "No—"

"Trisha *please*." Leah's eyes watered with tears. "You can't be here when he comes—"

"I'm not leaving you—"

"He's going to find me no matter what." Leah's voice wavered with trembling. "But you need to leave. I'll be alright."

"*No*—"

"*Trisha*!" a tear rolled down Leah's cheek. "There's a back exit. *Please*, take it."

For a moment, they simply stared at each other. Leah's pleading eyes, and Trisha's worried ones. They met and Leah's fire vanished. Instead, she was met with pure love. Not the manipulative kind, not the dangerous feeling. But a feeling of *care*. She couldn't explain it, but somehow, she *loved* this kid.

The door handle turned. Trisha took one last glance at Leah and bolted to the door. Leah watched her go, only letting her heart slow when Trisha escaped.

That's when the door opened. Sure enough, there was Gael. When he saw Leah, collapsed and pathetic on the floor, he laughed. A cold, hard cackle that echoed around the room. Leah flinched.

"Get up." The chortles left with the words— clean and cold cut. "Get the fuck up, Leah."

She tried. To her credit, she really tried. But she couldn't. *She could not move*.

Gael advanced toward her, grabbing her collar. She let it happen, let herself be shoved against the locker and let her father breathe smoked air into her face.

"What the *fuck* was that?" he snapped. "Is there something wrong with your legs, Leah? Or is it that you're too fucking lazy to move?"

"Dad—" Leah stammered. "I couldn't—"

"'*I couldn't—*'" Gael mocked. Then, a stout laugh erupted from his throat. "Yes you can. Your legs work, Leah. So don't bullshit this like you always do. *Why didn't you fucking move*?"

Leah didn't answer. Her mouth had sealed itself shut, and even if she could speak, it would do no good. She had fucked up, and now, she had to bear the punishment.

"You'll never go D1 if you keep acting like this. Oh, and those passes?" Gael scoffed. "They have to stop. You are giving your own future away to your opponents. If you want to be like Zahara you have to start acting like it."

"Dad—" Leah gasped. "They're my friends."

"No," Gael shifted his grip, slamming her onto the bench. A hand slapped her across the face, leaving a red mark. "No, they're your competitors. You don't win by *giving your opponents the fucking ball*."

Leah let out a cry— it wasn't voluntary and the tears came down without her permission. "No—" she choked. "I'm sorry, I'm sorry…"

"Sorry?" Gael cackled, smoke dripping from his lips. "No, don't be sorry. Be better."

He turned around. But not before backhanding Leah in the face. His knuckles connected with her cheekbone, leaving behind a cascading pain.

"Fix your shit, Leah." Gael drawled. "Or I'll fix it for you. Both of our futures rest on your success." He strode to the door, letting the noise of the gym seep into the locker room. "Don't forget it."

Leah didn't relax when her father pulled the door closed. She barely even noticed his absence. Because in her mind, he was still there. *Always there*.

The shaking consumed her. She slipped onto the floor, tucking her knees to her chest. No one was here this time, no one was going to save her from herself.

"*Stupid*!" Leah slammed her fist into her forehead. "God dammit! Fucking *imbecile*!"

He's right Leah, Zahara's crisp words echoed around her skull. *Right about everything. You're a useless, pathetic creature who can't do jack shit on her own.*

"Shut up…" Leah covered her ears. "Shut up, shut up…"

Do more. Be more. You're not enough. Gael's tone seeped into her mind, infecting her with his thick poison. The voice seemed so real— so vivid. For a moment, she could've sworn she smelled smoke. *You will never be enough.*

Tears poured down her cheeks as the voices howled on. They mixed— her father and her mentor going at her like wolves.

Pathetic. Weak. Useless. God dammit, Leah.

You're awful.

"Dammit!" Leah screeched. "Fuck *I know*!"

She slammed her head against the locker, the bang resonating throughout the room. The voices flickered. Leah reached up to her forehead, touching the blood trickling from her hair.

Then they returned. Cruel and evil. But true. Always true. Forever *true*.

Leah laid her head in her hands, crying loud, ugly sobs. They interrupted her breath, catching the air in her throat. Soon, the cries became chokes. Giant heaves that didn't seem to get any air into her lungs.

The tears kept coming, the panic swelled in her chest. She coughed, but no air came out. Her skin was too tight— tugging at her fingertips. She needed to get out; she needed—

"Hey," a hand landed on her back. "It's okay, breathe, breathe—"

Leah jolted away, scrambling away from the figure. She wiped her tears, attempting to get her panic beneath the surface.

"Ezra?" she gasped. The word came out like a laugh. A joke. "What?"

Ezra simply tilted his head, keeping his radiant blue eyes locked on her.

"I—" Leah wiped her cheeks, blinking the tears from her eyes. "My dad—how much of it did you see?"

Ezra's expression was unreadable. He looked caring, but he couldn't be. Leah knew he wasn't. No one genuinely *cared*. "I only saw what you want me to see."

"You can't—" Leah gasped. He hit her. *Gael hit her*. Violence— child protective services. No! "You can't call them. Don't tell anyone. *Please* Ezra, I'm *begging* you—"

"Hey," Ezra grasped her shoulders. "It's okay, I won't. I promise I won't."

Leah's eyes widened. "But CPS—"

"CPS won't do shit." He said it in such a gentle tone. "Abuse that happens within sports doesn't count to them. It's a loophole in the system. A CPS call will do nothing but hurt you." Ezra swallowed. "I'm not going to hurt you, Leah."

She wanted to believe him. Oh, she wanted with all her heart to believe him. But she couldn't shake off the fact that those blue eyes were filled with nothing but deception. That it was just pain wrapped in care. Suffering in a warm coat of love.

I'm not going to hurt you, Leah. It seemed so genuine. Like he meant it. He couldn't— could he?

But she meant it to Trisha. She truly did care about the kid. She wouldn't use her, wouldn't do anything to hurt her. Not if a knife was at her throat.

Maybe that's what she was to Ezra.

She let her face crumple. She let the tears pour from her eyes. And she let Ezra hug her. She let him wrap his arms around her, let herself cry into his shirt.

She grabbed fistfuls of the cloth, pressing her face deeper into his chest. Ezra didn't ask questions, he didn't ask her to explain anything. He just held her and *let her cry*.

"I'm sorry," Leah choked. "I'm getting snot on your shirt."

Ezra chuckled. "That's why washing machines exist."

Leah pulled away, rising to her feet. She was still shaking, but less so. Wiping the tears from her eyes, she met Ezra's gaze.

"You did great today, kid." He said.

Leah laughed. "I ran away mid way through. That hardly qualifies as a 'great game.'"

Ezra's face sank. "Don't beat yourself up for that." He said. "We all have moments. And with your… situation, it's understandable."

"My dad," Leah breathed. "He does it because he loves me, you know that right? He's hard on me because he knows that's what it takes. I have to be able to take it."

Ezra simply stared. He studied her face— searching for any sign of grief, anything that would give a window into her past. Leah didn't wear it. Her eyes were rock— hardened with what she believed was the truth. Because somewhere deep inside her, she truly believed her father loved her.

"That—" Ezra sighed, "That's not right."

"Yeah, well, it's the dad I've got. I'm just lucky he loves me."

Ezra was silent. He opened his mouth, but closed it, trying to phrase his words perfectly. Leah waited for the sentence, arms tucked close to her chest.

"Maybe he does love you," Ezra said. "But not as a good parent should. He doesn't love you as a daughter. He doesn't care about you because he's your father. He loves you as a tool; for what you can bring him." He took a step forward, putting a hand on her shoulder. "I'm so, so sorry, Leah. But he loves you as a *weapon*."

Leah took a shaky breath. Her gaze wandered down to her hands, calloused and rough. Scars littered her arms, just light enough to be noticeable. They were from Gael— battle scars. From when he pushed and shoved her. They were just scratches— nothing that prohibited her from anything. It wasn't the blood that hurt her— but the carelessness in which the cuts were dealt.

No consideration for how it may feel. No permission to use her until she collapsed. She was a tool— tools were used until they broke. Then discarded and quickly replaced.

She looked at her skin. It might as well have been made of metal.

That's how people treated her. Like she was made of *metal.*

And at that moment, she let herself be what she was truly made of. Skin and bone.

The tears came again, rushing down her face in rivulets. She didn't bother to wipe them away. Instead, she flung herself into Ezra's arms, engulfing him in a tight embrace.

Ezra reciprocated the hug, resting his chin on her hair. They didn't talk— no words were needed. For once in years, Leah let herself cry. Let herself sob without feeling the urge to yank out her hair. Let all of the stress and pain and grief and anger come out in the tears rolling down her cheeks.

Leah glanced over Ezra's shoulder. Her eyes landed on the locker room door. Just above the handle was a tiny window. And Leah could've sworn she saw a flash of red hair.

THE STASH RUNS DRY

Up to 40% of patients seeking treatment for substance dependence report a history of suicide attempts .— Christine Yuodelis-Flores MD, Richard K. Ries MD. "Addiction and suicide: A review."

Leah dug through her bag, attempting to find the pill bottle. The thing wasn't usually this hard to find. She entertained the possibility she'd forgotten it. But she couldn't— no, that was impossible. The thing never left her bag. Unless someone—

Nope. Her heartbeat slowed to a steady pace as she pulled out the bottle. Her eyes focused and her arms tingled with anticipation; ecstatic for the thrill of pure power that was about to rush through her system.

But when she peered inside, her panic re-rose. She felt the familiar shards dig into her lungs as she peered into the plastic, realizing that nothing remained

"No…" At first, the word was just a breath. "Oh fuck. No no no no."

She shook the bottle, searching for any last tablet. There was none— no rattling that signified her success. It was gone.

She shoved the bottle to the side, digging into her bag. Her nails scraped the bottom, catching dirt and dust from her basketball shoes. With shaking hands, she dipped her bag over, spilling the contents onto the locker room floor.

Nothing. Absolutely *nothing*.

She buried her head in her hands, tears stinging her gaze. Her blood bulged against her skin— as if calling for the morphine. But she didn't have it. *She didn't fucking have it.*

Her head flung up, a scream ripping from her throat. The sound echoed around the locker room before slowly dying in an echo. Leah grabbed one of her shoes, hurling it across the room. It rammed into a mirror, shattering the thing on impact.

Leah stood, ignoring the glass shards at her feet. She picked up her shoe, brushing off the blades. Then she started pacing— back on fourth, feet crunching against the shards.

"Oh, no no no," Leah dug her fingernails into her scalp, pulling on her hair. She was playing in thirty minutes— this was supposed to be a quick moment; one she barely even thought about. But now, the morphine was gone. Her skills were gone. Everyone who loved her was *all gone*.

So? Zahara snarled. *Are you so dependent on your drug you can't go a game without it?*

Leah covered her ears. "Shut up, Zahara. I don't need your antics right now."

Antics? A laugh. *His* laugh. Leah froze, swearing the smell of smoke was drifting into her nose. *Is that what you call criticism? She's right, you know. You are your drug— pathetic without it.*

"Stop it, Dad." Leah muttered.

Let's start the show. You lazy, incompetent bitch, let's see how you fare without cheating. Level the playing field, shall we? He seemed to lean closer; the smell of smoke followed. *Maybe then Ezra will see how worthless you actually are.*

"*No*!" Leah screeched. She grabbed the empty pill bottle, throwing it across the room. It landed in the shattered glass, rolling to a halt. "*Shut up*!"

Then shut us up, Taven. Zahara drew. *Play well— show that audience out there that you can do this by yourself. And then maybe you'll finally be good enough.*

Leah stood, running her shaky fingers through her hair. She brushed the stray strands behind her ears, flinging her braids behind her back. When she stood, she was surprised to find her legs were steady.

"I'm gonna fucking show them." Leah breathed. "*All of them.*"

~~~

The ref blew the whistle, flinging the ball into the air. A blur of hands whacked at the ball, sending it flying in Leah's direction. She should've caught it— she willed her hands to reach for the thing flying at her face. But she couldn't. *She couldn't move*.

The ball slammed into her cheek, leaving a red mark. Leah stumbled back, collapsing to the floor. A blur of red jerseys rushed at her, lunging for the possession. Before Leah could react, they were gone— speeding down the court and making the layup.

Her teammates stared at her— unmoving. It was as if her fallen figure was more interesting than the ball they had to retrieve. All the eyes of her team— all the eyes of the gym— landed right on *her*.

Her gaze wandered into the crowd. Gael sat in the crowd, hands pressed together. His knuckles bruised from when he had hit her. A promise— a prophecy.

But for once, it wasn't him that Leah was scared of. Her eyes flew deeper into the crowd— meeting a brilliant blue gaze.
~~~

"*Go*!" Leah screeched. "Get the ball!"

She willed herself to move, her ACL brace squeaking under her. Gathering her steps, she sprinted to her teammate, signaling for them to pass to her.

The ball felt like a blade in her grasp. She pounded it against the floor, turning to see a full back court press. She grit her teeth, assessing her situation. Their pattern wasn't organized and changed whenever Leah's teammates moved.

"Clear!" she shouted. "It's man to man! Get out."

Her teammates obeyed, scurrying out of her way. Leah charged up the court, swinging the ball between her legs to throw off her defender. It worked, she got the edge and sprinted to the three point line.

But when she attempted to dribble, the ball didn't land on the floor. It slammed into her foot, rolling to the side. Leah scrambled to catch it, but the thing passed her grip, running to the out of bounds.

She watched it go, cheeks turning red. She brushed her hair behind her back, fully aware that she had just made an absolute fool of herself in front of a crowd.

But that didn't matter to her. She looked past their gazes— the disappointed droop in their expression. Her vision had filtered them all out, making a black void around one man.

She met Ezra's gaze, trying desperately to read it. She couldn't— he just gazed back, no emotion, no anger— fucking *nothing*.

"Fuck," Leah breathed. He was judging her— assessing if she was still worth it. Why else would she care? A tool. A tool. A tool. Maybe Ezra pretended he loved her, but she was still a weapon. And right now, she didn't fucking *work*.

With a smooth hand, she slapped herself. The sound echoed around the gym with a following silence. Leah took a breath, grounding herself.

Get a grip, Zahara scolded. *He won't love you if not*.

Leah rushed to the inbound. Her opponent had already grasped the ball and was looking for someone to pass it too. Leah squared her shoulders, brushing her braids behind her back.

The guard inbounded the ball, passing it to their teammate. Leah grazed the thing with her fingertips— just enough to intercept its path. She charged at the loose ball, grasping it and starting down the court in the opposite direction.

She didn't let herself mess up again; she carved through her opponents, not caring what reached to intercept her. But this time, without the morphine, she felt every blow that came at her body.

She laid the ball in the hoop just before the shove came. Her breath caught as she fell to the ground. This time, she couldn't gather her feet. Her brace squeaked against the floor as all her weight toppled onto her knee. Pain erupted throughout her body as her head collided with the wall.

Snap. Snap. Snap. *Pain.* So much fucking *pain.* It spread from her knee, infecting her body— infecting *her.* Making her useless. Fucking *useless.* And then there was the glass, raised to her throat.

Her skin got tight— the air stuck to her throat.

Pathetic. Goddammit. Bitch.

"Stop it Dad."

You're so fucking lazy Leah. Get up, get the fuck up!

"*Please.*"

"Leah?" a hand landed on her back. She looked up to see Serena, eyes drenched with concern. "Are you alright?"

Leah was flung back to reality. Her hands reached for her knee, flexing the muscles around her leg. She bent the joint, testing its mobility without a breath.

It was fine. She was *fine.*

Leah's shoulders sunk, her breath resumed. She managed a smile. "Yeah, I'm fine."

"Are you sure?" Serena tilted her head. "You're bleeding."

Leah reached to touch her nose. Sure enough, her finger came away red. She wiped the blood on her jersey— not caring about the stain. Serena offered a hand but she refused it, getting up on her own accord.

She looked around, wondering why everyone wasn't already back on defense. They seemed to all be staring at her, expecting her to do something.

"Leah," Serena tapped her shoulder. "You're shooting free throws."

"Oh," Another stream of blood rushed from her nose. She wiped it before it could trickle to the floor. "Right."

Her shot was off. Too much to the right, not enough spin. It barely grazed the rim, falling short by a few inches. The cold returned to her— a missed shot. Two mistakes. She could *not* miss anymore.

Leah ran back on defense, shaking the errors from her palm. The bruise on her knee radiated pain— the infectious ache spreading throughout her body. She had to struggle to keep herself from limping.

Her opponent came rushing down the court, ball in hand. Leah widened her stance, keeping her eyes on her defender's torso. As the guard came down the court, the ball swung to the right. Leah followed it, hands tracing the rough grip.

But the girl crossed over. Leah's knees collapsed, faltering her balance. She fell to the floor— her stumble followed by the crowds admiring coo. The guard charged into the court, laying the ball in the basket.

Leah stood, cheeks burning with embarrassment. Her eyes found Ezra's. He was still watching her— no trace of emotion on his features. No— there was something. The tiniest tilt of his eyebrows, the curl of his lips. Anger.

Leah's eyes widened. All motion went still. Her breath caught in her chest.

He's going to hit me.

The whistle blew. Leah turned to see her teammate Mia running straight at her. Her body tensed as she saw Viren, fuming on the bench.

"Leah!" Mia called. "You're out."

Leah nodded. There was no anxiety when she strode to the bench. When Viren screamed at her, she barely heard a word. She simply sat down, put her head in her hands and let her foot bounce restlessly against the floor.

He's going to leave me.

He doesn't love me.

Not anymore.

He's going to hit me.

He's going to hit me.

He's going to hit me.

~~~

Leah stumbled into the locker room. She clutched the wall for support, legs shaking under her. She tried to stand. Tried to pretend that she was okay. She took a breath— running her trembling hands along her braids.

She failed.

Leah collapsed to the floor, tears burning the edges of her eyes. She tucked her head between her knees, letting the droplets drip onto the floor. The voices howled in her head— shrieking through her skull.

He's going to leave you, Zahara cooed. *He loves the drug, not you. He loves your skill. He loves you as a weapon.*

"I know," Leah sobbed. "I know, I know…"

Dammit, Leah. You've fucked everything up. Her father rasped. *No one's left to love you now, no one cares. Only me. I'm the only one who will ever love your broken, fallen figure. I'm the only one who can fix you.*
~~~

"Shut up," Leah murmured. The phrase wasn't accusatory or angry, but broken with apology. "I'm sorry, I'm sorry…"

I believed in you. Ezra's voice. *I believed in you and you failed. How could you, Leah? I thought you were something and you turned to nothing. Absolutely worthless.*

"I know," Leah closed her eyes, letting the droplets run down her cheek. "I'm sorry, Ezra. Oh, no, no, no… I'm *so* sorry."

Sorry doesn't fix it.

Worthless.

Awful.

Unloveable.

"Dammit!" Leah placed her hands over her ears. "Dammit *I know*!"

The voices paused. They were still there, but stunned. For once, quiet.

Leah picked herself up from the floor, leaning on the wall for support. Her knee screamed in protest, but she kept going towards the sink. Her hands found the white ceramic as she pressed her head to the faucet.

What she did next she wasn't proud of.

Mostly because there were much more efficient ways to do it.

Leah turned on the water, pushed her head under the rushing liquid, and attempted to drown.

She let the water seep into her nostrils, choking as it rushed into her body. Her lungs begged for air, but she didn't let herself breathe. She didn't open her mouth, didn't give herself the pleasure of cool, thick breath. The water dripped down to her esophagus, burning the edges of her throat like it was boiling.

The edges of her vision blurred. Tears seeped from her eyes, mixing with the liquid. A dizziness overtook her, shattering the balance of her legs. She closed her eyes.

Something grabbed her braids. She was yanked upward, banging her head on the faucet. Her attacker didn't seem to care much for her head's safety, only that she was out of the stream.

Leah collapsed, coughing up water. The liquid dripped from her face, splattering onto the floor. Slowly, her vision cleared to reveal a figure standing in front of her, arms crossed.

"What the *fuck* are you doing?" Leah gazed into the eyes of Serena— about as fiery as she'd ever been. "You were going to drown!"

Leah attempted to stand, ultimately failing and falling back to the concrete. The second option of defense was to attempt to talk herself out of the situation. Leah opened her mouth, only to be met with a spew of hacking coughs. Soon, they turned to dry heaves, and then she was vomiting water onto the floor.

The hurling seemed to go on for minutes, barely giving Leah time to breathe before the next round of throw up made its appearance. She took a shaky breath, slowly getting to her feet.

Serena was still standing in front of her, lips straight with expectancy. Leah wiped the vomit from her lips.

"So?" Serena's eyes were stone cold. "Explain yourself."

Leah shrugged. "I was washing the blood off my nose."

"And you started inhaling the water?"

"I—" Leah took a moment, considering her alibi. "I feel asleep."

"Oh?" Serena scoffed. "Fell asleep? *Fell asleep*? Leah, if you fall asleep under the water, your body immediately wakes you up when your breath is compromised!"

"I was…" Leah bit her lip. "Really tired?"

"Cut the shit, Leah!" Serena screamed. Leah flinched back. "You were trying to kill yourself."

"Serena—"

"No," she shook her head. "For the last few years you have been ignoring me— leaving me for— for whatever the *fuck* this is!" she gestured to the sink. "Dammit Leah! Look at you! This is not healthy!"

"It's sports," Leah said. "Just exercise."

"No!" Serena laughed. A cracked, rough cackle. "This is not just exercise. You are *hurting* yourself. For fucks sake, Leah, look at you!" Serena grabbed her arms. "You're pale as a fucking ghost! Clammy skin— oh, God you're so cold!"

"I—" Leah took a step backward. "Serena—"

"Shut up, Leah!" she screeched. "You have to stop this! Before you do some serious fucking damage!"

She stopped yelling and raised her chin, expecting a response. Leah didn't have a response to give. They simply stared at each other. Leah took a breath, finding the fire buried deep in her heart.

"Fine," Leah drawled. "Fine. It seems you don't completely understand the situation. I'm not like you, okay? I never have been. For me, care isn't granted — *love* isn't granted. But with this—" Leah dug her nails into her palm. "With this game, I can get that. My dad, Ezra— fuck everyone loves me when I do well." Leah advanced on her. "But when I don't— oh, they all hate me. Every single one. I'm their tool, and when I don't work, they discard me."

"Leah—" Serena began. "You're not a tool."

"*Yes I am*," Leah snarled. "And right now, I'm broken. That has to change. So to answer your question, yes, I was trying to kill myself. Because when I fail, everyone is cold. The entire world is cold because I don't deserve its warmth. And what is the point of living if no one loves you?"

"Don't you see?" Serena grasped her shoulders. "Someone can love you. If you leave. Leave this game— leave it all behind. Leah—" she brushed a stray strand of hair behind her eyes. "*Please*, come with me. We can fix this."

She paused. A flash of consideration sprang across her mind. She considered going to Serena's house without telling anyone where she went. Not even Ezra. Hiding; getting better. Really *better*. Maybe the fantasy of skin and bone could come true—

Idiot.

Failure.

Unloveable.

Awful.

You think you can escape, Taven? Not even that girl cares about you. Not at all. You're a weapon, no matter how many times someone says otherwise.

Leah staggered back, hands flying to her temple. The voices got loud, hammering the past into her skull. Leah grasped the ceramic of the sink, digging her nails into the smooth surface.

"Shut up." She murmured. "Shut *up*!"

"Leah—" Serena began. "Are you—"

She was cut short by Leah's cackle. She turned, braids wavering around her body like a shield.

"Liar." Leah hummed, her voice a cracked sugar. "Liar, Serena."

She said the words so softly— like she was only stating a fact. But as if she had grown another head, Serena staggered away.

"What do you want?" Leah asked. "Because I know you didn't mean what you just said. I'm sure of it. So what do I have that you *need*?"

"Leah—" Serena's black hair fell in front of her face, as if she was trying to hide behind it. "I'm not trying to get an edge—"

“Viren sent you, didn’t he?” Leah’s eyes widened, the fire vanishing. She stepped towards her, attempting to touch her friend. “Did he do something to you? Serena—”

“What?” Serena stepped back, refusing her touch. “Leah I don’t know what you’re talking about—”

“I’ll *kill* him!” Leah screeched. “If he lays one hand on you, I’ll destroy him. I have the power. Just say the word, Serena. *Say the word.*”

“Leah *stop*!” Serena’s screech was loud— piercing the air. “Viren didn’t do shit. I barely ever talk to him. It’s yourself that you should be worried about. Because if you don’t stop this—” she waved her hands in the air. “All of this — it’s yourself you’re going to kill.”

For a moment, Leah simply examined the girl. Head to toe, searching her body for any signs of abuse. There was none. No redness along her lips, no bruises creeping up her thighs. Leah heaved a sigh, turning back to the sink and letting the fire slither through her veins.

“Serena,” her voice was steady when she said the name. “Don’t you think I know that?”

THE OTHER NARCOTICS

"Opioid withdrawal syndrome is a life-threatening condition resulting from opioid dependence. Opioids are a group of drugs used to manage severe pain and include morphine, heroin, oxycontin, codeine, methadone, and hydromorphone."
—Mansi Shah, Martin R. Huecker. "Opioid Withdrawal."

Gael was already home when Leah opened the door. He was sitting on the couch, a steady stream of smoke curling from his mouth. Leah tiptoed past him, hoping to evade the lecture about how dog shit she played.

She was halfway to her room when he spoke. "You're lucky that coach of yours has the merit of a god."

Leah turned. "Sorry?"

It was then she got a good look at her father. The usual daunting yellow had splotches of ugly blue and purple. His lip was split and crusted blood paved a trail down his chin. He spat a wad of red into a handkerchief.

"I'd shoot that man if I had the means." Gael scowled.

Leah only stared, mouth a gape. "Ezra did that?"

"The blonde pretty boy?" Gael pressed a bag of frozen peas to his lip. "Yes. That one. Something to do with you. I wasn't really listening. I was too busy being socked in the face."

"Ezra beat you up…" Leah breathed.

"Yeah, I thought that was clear." Gael switched the peas with his cigar— the distinct smell of marijuana graying the room. "You're lucky I'm letting you continue to go to his practices. I care about you more than I care about my grievances. Don't forget it, Leah."

~~~

Leah hadn't realized truly how dependent she was on the morphine until she went a few days without it. Of course, it didn't start bad— simply a flare up in the overwhelming panic.

By day five, it escalated. More of her nights were spent in the corner of her room, shivering as the cold slithered down her spine; her legs glued to the floor and heart beating so fast it hurt. Her teeth rattled against each other as she lifted her trembling hands into her hair, attempting to lodge the locks from her scalp.

Gradually, the anxiety got worse. It spread throughout the entire night, affecting her mornings. When she did sleep, she woke up clutching her throbbing chest, convinced someone was chasing her— whether it was Viren, Gael or Ezra. Oh, the worst nightmares were about Ezra.
~~~

He was the cruelest. Not because of his words or actions— all the voices in her head held the same level of malice. But Ezra was different. He told her he loved her, told her he wasn't using her.

Told her he would *never* hurt her.

He never did anything to lose her trust. Never hit or hollered at her. But Leah knew. She always knew. Everyone *always* left.

And she knew it would be her fault.

When she let him down; inevitably revealed her true self. The unloveable part. The angry, crazy part. The *lazy* part. The *useless* version of herself.

But she couldn't lose him. Couldn't bear it. Because every time she imagined him hugging her— every time he entered her dreams to tell her he was proud, tears budged the corners of her eyes.

She *wouldn't* lose him.

Slowly, the morphine withdrawals wrapped Leah in their burning embrace. The nausea came next— the most awful flu-like symptoms Leah had ever experienced. She spent her next few days trembling on the floor of her bathroom, wrapped in a blanket and hurling whenever she moved. She hadn't eaten in days and her ribs were beginning to peak out from her stomach. She had convinced everyone she had a rather bad case of the flu. No one questioned it— even though she hadn't shown any previous symptoms.

The nausea didn't subside. But after a week of constant throwing up, Leah found herself fed up. She stumbled into the kitchen, head light and dizzy, and swallowed enough Tums to kill a horse.

Practice, by far, was the worst.

The panic attacks increased tenfold when she entered the gym doors. Sweat poured down her skin in salty rivulets which soaked her shirt before she even picked up the ball. Suddenly, her heart had sped to a dramatic pace, thundering in her chest.

And when Ezra met her gaze, it all got worse.

Oh no no no no. Tears stung the edges of her eyes. *No no no. He can't see me. Not like this.*

She didn't wait for Ezra to approach her. She simply bolted, running straight to her car and punching the gas. If he saw her weakness he would leave. Leah would *not* allow him to leave.

She stepped into the house to meet her father's glacial glare. A cigar was pressed between his lips as the smoke seeped from his mouth like glass serpents shattering within the air.

"You look awful." Gael commented.

Leah ignored him.

"No," he stepped towards her, lifting up her arm. Leah recoiled at the touch. "What's wrong with you? You got something up with your liver or something?"

"Nothing's wrong, Dad." Leah snapped. "I'm just— tired. Can't I be tired?"

Gael gave her a look. "Watch your tone, daughter. Exhaustion—" he tapped her right between her boobs. "Is not a viable excuse."

The weeks trickled by painfully slowly, and yet Leah couldn't seem to keep up with the time. She spent most of her days laying on the floor, trying to keep her nausea inside her body. But the sick wasn't the worst part. Neither were the aching pains dissolving her skin. No, the worst part was the cravings. The physical urge— the need— to put the morphine in her blood. Her body physically crawled towards her drug, the narcotic pulling her in like a chain.

She knew the morphine would fix it. It always fixed *everything*. But she didn't have it. She *couldn't* have it. Her very possession of the drug may have been breaking the law before, but to actively seek it out? That was a line of illegal that felt dangerous to cross.

Leah lifted her head from the floor, wincing as pain cascaded through her temples. Over the days, her hair had unraveled from her braids, pooling on the floor and drifting over her face in dark amber strands.

She helped herself to her feet, the nausea bubbling up her throat. Her legs shook— threatening to shatter under her weight. Her ACL brace lay on the far edge of her room— Leah didn't bother to grab the wretched thing.

At that moment, she made a decision. It was in no way a good one, but Leah figured that if she couldn't take morphine, maybe another narcotic would suffice. A substitute.

Leah stumbled out of her room, clutching the wall for support. The windows shone with the light of the full moon— ascended completely into the sky. She tripped to the kitchen, lifting herself onto the counter. Her stomach lurched with the effort, threatening to spill her empty insides over Gael's unusually clean counters.

Leah grasped the cabinet handle, pulling it open. Inside were bottles of red and golden brown liquor. Each and every one of them were opened, and the corks were put on rather poorly. Leah popped one open, sniffing the liquid and quickly recoiling.

Her stomach lurched, attempting to dislodge the imaginary toxins. Leah collapsed over the sink, bottle clattering against the counter. She dry heaved for about a minute before her body finally gave up and realized the poison was much deeper than her esophagus.

"Bitch—" Leah gasped, "There's nothing to fucking throw up. You expelled everything already."

Her gaze shifted to the hallway— empty as always. Gael was probably in his drug induced sleep. Leah could fire a gun next to his ear and he would simply roll in his sleep. The clang of the bottle did nothing to disturb him.

Leah didn't bother to pour the whiskey into a glass. She simply tipped the bottle back, letting the alcohol burn her throat as it made its way into her body. Her stomach grumbled— unhappy with its new found contents. When she felt the similar rise of nausea, she gulped another swig.

"You want a drug?" she told her body. "This is a drug. Maybe it's not the drug you want, but it's what you get. I may not have the morphine, but right now I can focus every ounce of my ambition on getting as drunk as physically possible."

~~~

"Leah?" Serena pushed the door open, peering at Leah's figure in the dark. "What— what are you doing here?"

Leah slumped into Serena, burying her face in her chest. Her hair hung down around her as she let the bottle slip from her grasp, shattering on the floor. Serena gazed down, wrinkling her nose when she smelled the liquor.

"Hey Serena," Leah hiccuped. The drunkenness had her spinning— the world moving in blurry circles around her. "I knew you would be up— I just knew it."

"Leah—" Serena grasped her shoulders, black hair pouring over her shoulder. "Are you drunk?"

Leah hiccuped again. "No."

Serena's eyes darted to Leah, then at the bottle shattered on the floor. "Okay," she breathed. "Let's get you inside."

Serena led her to the couch, beckoning for her to sit. Leah obliged, leaning her head back on the pillows. They were so soft— she let herself melt into the sofa.

Leah didn't realize when Serena left her, but when she came back she was holding a glass of water to her lips. Leah jolted away, eyes wide. The water splashed on her legs, goosebumps surrounding the droplets.
~~~

"Hey, it's okay." Serena held up her free hand. "But Leah, you need to drink."

Leah considered this. Her drunken gaze blurred the surrounding areas. All she could see was Serena— her sparkling green eyes and soft, wavy hair. She outstretched her hand, gesturing for the water.

Serena handed it to her, plopping down on the couch. Leah slowly nursed the cup, savoring the cold of the glass. Serena didn't try to talk to her. She didn't ask if everything was okay, didn't attempt comfort, didn't try to reassure her. She just sat there, hands resting in her lap.

Leah placed the glass on the table, making a light clang. She swallowed, centering her gaze on the drunken blur. Then, very slowly, she began to cry.

She didn't know if Serena noticed or not. Truthfully, she didn't care. The words came with the tears, pouring from her mouth with no bother to stop them.

"I used to enjoy it." At first, Leah spoke quietly. "I really did. Back when I played with Zahara. I used to love the attention. The bad games sucked, but now—" Her voice broke. "All I do is fail. I can never seem to get anything right."

Serena tilted her head. "What's so bad about failing?"

"They hurt me."

Her eyes widened, showing the tiniest hint of panic. "Who?"

"My dad." Leah said, touching the part of his face where he'd hit her. "He hurts me when we play— bruises and blood. But that—" Leah took a breath; she was surprised to find it was shaky. "That's not the worst part. The worst part are his words."

"What does he say?" Serena asked.

"He says—" Leah's voice cracked. "He says I'm lazy. He says I'm a failure. And— and a liar whenever I tell him I can't go any longer. And then—" a sob escaped her lips. "And then he tells me he loves me."

"Oh," Serena began. "Leah, what is failure to you?"

Leah shook her head. "I don't know." She whispered. "I don't know what anything is to me. Sometimes— well sometimes I think I don't have a real personality. Only these demons who run the show. But— I know what my dad's definition of failure is."

"What's that?"

"I have to dominate." Leah's voice cracked. "Always. Every game. I have to destroy my opponents— and my opponents are *everyone*." Her face crumpled. "Even my friends."

Serena tilted her head. "Am I an opponent?"

This time, Leah found the strength to look at her. A tear trailed down her face, curving along her sharpened cheekbone. "*Everyone* is an opponent."

"Those are impossible expectations." Serena said. "You would have to be inhuman to never have an off game."

Leah swallowed. "I solved that problem. I took… something… before every game. But now—" she swallowed. "I don't have it any more. And— and I'm sick. Really sick. Not just in the mind this time."

"Withdrawals." Serena breathed. "Oh, god Leah."

"CPS won't help. Anything sports related is a loophole. And— and then the healthcare system will tell my dad— and then—" she gasped, her fingers began to tremble. A shudder ran through her body and suddenly his fist was coming at her face— and she could hear his voice. Yelling, screeching— so much *screaming*.

"Hey," Serena grabbed her hand. Her grasp was warm, bringing her back to earth. Leah met her eyes; the tears made her vision blurry but through them she saw Serena's glistening green eyes. "Hey, it's okay. *You're okay*."

Leah held her gaze— then she let herself completely break. A choked sob escaped her lips as she collapsed into Serena's chest.

"I know you think I'm a horrible person." Leah choked. "And I am— I know I am. But this is why. This is why I'm so awful and horrendous and sick —"

"Hey," Serena hugged her. "Its okay. You don't need to explain anything to me."

Leah let herself cry that night— let all the droplets rush down her cheeks in tiny rivulets and sink into Serena's shirt. She let herself be held. She let herself sob. She let herself be human.

Leah didn't know when she fell asleep. And she didn't know when Serena had carried her to her car, laying her in the backseat. She had small glimpses of Serena lifting her into her room before falling unconscious. She was vaguely aware of Serena placing her into bed and pulling the covers to her chest.

She felt Serena press a warm cloth to her head while she stroked her cheek. And then— just maybe, after she removed the cloth, Leah felt the soft touch of lips brush against her forehead.

HAD ENOUGH YET?

When Leah woke up, she didn't remember what happened the night before. There were small glimpses of her stepping into the cold night— and somehow, she remembered someone kissing her before she dozed into the empty void of sleep. Other than that, her memory had gone completely blank.

She had about three seconds of bliss— from the time she arose from slumber to when she remembered why she smelled like alcohol.

The stench covered her clothes— intertwined with her hair. It was especially potent on the patch of skin between her lip and her nose.

The nausea came like a rush— Leah scrambled out of bed, bolting to her bathroom. She made it to the toilet right as the bile rushed from her mouth. The vomit was more acidic than usual, burning her throat with a hot sting. It was a golden brown color— tinted slightly more yellow than when she had swallowed the whiskey.

The smell was god awful— alcohol that had been fermenting in her dysfunctional stomach overnight. Leah gagged, shakily getting to her feet and flushing the toilet.

She moved to her bed, picking up her phone. The time showed 10:30— Leah hadn't slept in that late since she was in middle school. Below glowed Ezra's name; Leah tapped on the message.

Hey!
Havent seen u at practice in a while. U sure ur only sick with the flu?

Leah let the phone slip from her hands— barely noticing the sound as it clattered to the ground. Her breath stopped and her hands began to tremble. She sank to the floor, vision blurring with the prick of tears.

"Oh, no no no..." Leah gasped. "He knows. He knows. Fuck! He's going to—"

Leah dug her fingernails into her scalp, pulling at her hair. "No no no. No— oh god *no*!" the tears leapt from her eyes, splattering onto the carpet. "*Fuck*!"

"Shut up Leah!" Gael shouted from downstairs. Leah barely heard him.

She banged her fist against her head. She needed the morphine— God she needed it. If she didn't get better soon, Ezra would get more suspicious. And then— and then—

No. She couldn't think about that. She *wouldn't*. Because she'd find a way out of this. She'd find a way to get the morphine back. *She swore it.*

Leah stumbled to her feet, grabbing the bed for support. She wiped the tears from her eyes— breathing a shaky sigh.

Then she strode from her room, waltzing down the hall and unlocking the room she wasn't supposed to go in.

"Come on, Mom." Leah murmured. "Come on. You have to have left *something*."

Her mother's study was messy— as always. A thick layer of dust covered the papers littering the floor. Contracts— things she had to sign. Her messy signature was sprawled across the documents; sometimes dried tear stains smudged the ink.

Gael wouldn't clean the room. He wouldn't even go in there. Sometimes Leah caught him staring at the door, eyes glossy with grief.

But now, for the first time in nearly eight years, the room was disturbed. The dust lifted from the papers as Leah padded around the room. She didn't bother to weave around her mother's belongings— instead stepping on the crumpled documents without a bother.

The desk was smothered with a mixture of needles and notebooks. Any reminiscing drug had long expired. There wasn't a drop of useful narcotic left in the needle. Leah's face contorted into a scowl; she slammed the object onto the table, glass shattering under her palm.

Leah moved to the desk drawers. She pulled each out with ferocity— not caring which of her mother's belongings she destroyed. "Dammit." She cursed. "God dammit, Mom. Why can't you be *useful*?"

Another drawer was torn from the desk, papers flying at her feet. A journal fell to the ground, landing on Leah's toes. She lifted it, blowing the dust from its cover. The pages were crumpled and weak— years of use crinkling its past.

Leah opened the book, holding back tears when she saw her mother's handwriting. It was so neat— so clean. Talking about some business venture that Leah didn't understand. But the way her letters curved and connected— it was so her.

Leah flipped through the pages— watching as her mother's handwriting morphed to scratch. Tear stains pinched the pages— smearing the black ink. Slowly, the words moved from professionalism to addiction. Drawings of needles and pills and demented humans littered the pages until they looped with the letters.

But the last page was clear— print almost cleaner than when the first line. Leah ran her finger across the words, finally letting the tears fall from her eyes.

My dearest Leah,
When you've fallen into the hole I've left you, call this number.
They'll help you.

Leah ripped out the page, running out the door and padding to her room. Once the door was closed, she moved to her bed, sitting crossed legged on her sheets. She pulled her phone from its charger— punching in the number written beneath her mother's message.

Her fingers didn't shake when she hit dial. She'd done this dance before— the drugs, the deception. This world was nothing she wasn't used to, so what was taking one more step into the morphine's cold grasp?

The phone rang so many times Leah thought no one would answer; that her mother's last attempt at guidance had been a failure. But then a muffled, low breath came through the speaker.

A woman's voice. "Maragret? Is that you?"

"No," Leah drawled. "I'm her daughter. And I need your help."

~~~

Valania told her to drive to the south side of town— the dangerous side. Leah hadn't asked any questions. When the dealer hung up she showered, pulled on dark clothes, and twisted her braids into a bun.

She waited until night to slip out. With a mask pulled over her nose and her hood concealing her hair, she backed out of her driveway. The journey was somewhat peaceful— Leah felt a strange sense of tranquility wash over her as she watched the stars above.

As early as she could remember, people told her not to go to the south side. The streets smelled of piss and drugs and addicts fell deep into the gutters. Thieves lurked along the town's dark alleys— prepared to kill anyone for a penny.
~~~

“If you step out of this car—” Leah’s mother had told her. She had driven to the south side for an “errand.” Only now did Leah realize what her mother’s true intentions were. “Some bad people are gonna snatch you up and then—” her mother had smiled. “You’ll never see me again.”

Leah hid under the car seat for what seemed like hours— occasionally peeking out the window to check that her mother wasn’t dying just inches from the door.

When she finally made it back carrying a paper bag, Leah let a tear slip from her eyes. It was the first real sense of abandonment she’d ever felt— watching her mother disappear into the dark streets knowing that she may never come back.

Her mother didn’t notice her rivulets dropping from her waterline. She spent the car ride humming a gentle, happy tune to herself.

But now her mother wasn’t here. And now, Leah was the one about to disappear into the treacherous streets.

She grabbed her bag, swinging it over her shoulder. The knife in her pocket pried against her leg as she strode into the cold night, leaving the safety of her car alone in the dark.

The first thing she noticed about the town was the smell. A lot of piss, yes. But amongst the urine was a different scent. A sweet smoke— seeping from the deepest cracks of the city. Leah was surprised to find she recognized it from all those years ago— when she first stepped into Zahara’s car.

She padded along the pavement, keeping one hand on the hilt of her blade. Surrounding her were numerous pairs of eyes— watching her with a mixture of anger and envy.

Leah didn’t pay much mind to the people on the street. She knew better than to approach them— they’d kill her; or do something much worse. But she didn’t look down on them. If her father cast her out— she might wind up in nothing but rags and drugs, ready to stab someone for another hit.

Relief crashed over her as she saw crooked, purple lights that displayed “Nia’s Diner.” Leah padded in, tipping back her hood as the safety of warmth embraced her.

The place was almost completely empty— except for one man haunched over a beer. Leah let her mask fall off her face as she approached the bar, attempting to display a facade of confidence.

“Hello?” the bartender scrunched his nose. “Can I do something for you?”

“I’m Maragret’s daughter.” Leah said. “I’m here to see Valania.”

The bartender snorted. “No one can simply *see* Valania. I’m going to need a little more information than that.”

Leah scoffed, a hint of a laugh mixing with her tone. “Fine,” a smile etched upon her features. “I’ll give you more *information*. Ever since my mother fell too deep into those drugs— my dirt bag father figured out that all of mommy’s money might not last too long. The solution?” Leah pointed a gloved finger at her chest. “His dearest daughter. You know how I’m expected to replenish that money and success? Sports— become so good that a college pays for my presence. But that— oh that isn’t easy.” Leah cocked her head to the side. “So I need a little help jumping down the same hole that swallowed both my parents.”

For a moment, the bartender remained silent. He seemed to study Leah’s face for a long while before his features lit up with recognition.

“You’re Leah Taven!” he exclaimed. “I’ve seen you in the local paper— they interviewed you—”

“Where’s Valania?” Leah cut him off.

The man hesitated. He soaked up her features for one last moment, then pointed to a door. “That’s her office.”

Leah nodded, pulling her hood over her head. She didn’t bother to knock— these dealers had wasted enough of her time.

Valania was an older woman— not the type of body that’s displayed in movies. But she held the same remarkable beauty as Zahara. Gray hair that ran loose down her back, an expensive waistcoat hanging from her shoulders. Jewelry littered her long fingers, giving her skin a golden shine.

She stood, green eyes widening. “Leah?” Valania extended a hand, as if to touch her. Leah stepped back. “Oh, you’re the spitting image of your mother.”

Leah didn’t respond, only tightening her glare.

Valania tilted her head, extending her bony fingers to Leah’s hood. She flinched back, hand flying to her blade. But Valania didn’t shy away, instead tilting back to cloth to reveal her face.

“Oh,” her face was a mixture of admiration and pity. “You’re gorgeous.”

Leah withdrew a wad of cash from her pocket. “I want morphine, Valania.”

“Please, call me Val.” Valania padded back to her desk, “Come, sit.”

“I’d rather not, *Valania*.”

“Leah, please, it’s Val.”

"We aren't friends," Leah hissed. "I'm not calling you by a nickname."

Valania raised her chin, eyeing her with a piercing blue gaze. A tingle of fear flashed over her, rattling her bones. She sat at Val's desk, grip still resting on the knife.

Val smiled at her, crystal white teeth flashing in the light. "You don't belong here, do you?"

"I don't belong anywhere."

Val chuckled. "Neither did your mother. Always a misfit, my Maragret."

"I am not my mother." Leah snarled.

"Oh, most certainly not, my dear." Val drummed her manicured nails against the desk. "By the time Maragret met me, she had already given up. But you—" Val licked her teeth. "Oh, you are something else entirely. Whatever you're working towards, you really want it— no, *need* it. And you're willing to do whatever it takes to achieve that goal."

"You don't know me."

"Of course not." Val leaned forward. "But I did my research. Tell me, how's that coach of yours doing? The blonde one?"

Leah drew the knife from her pocket, lunging at Val's throat. She didn't move when Leah pressed the blade to her neck— in fact Leah was the one who trembled.

"If you tell Ezra—" Leah began, her voice quivering. "I'll kill you. *No one* will know about this interaction."

"Woah, a feisty one." Val tried to lean forward again. Leah tightened her grip on the knife, digging the blade deeper into her skin. Val shrugged, leaning back in her chair. "Don't worry, I keep all of my customer's secrets— no one will hear a thing from me."

"Good," Leah withdrew the weapon, slamming a wad of cash on the desk. "I want the morphine."

"How much?"

"As much as that's worth."

Val grinned. She took the money and began counting, her sharp green nails running through the paper at a practiced speed. When she was done, she stuffed the cash in her pocket and unlocked her desk drawer. Out of it she drew a large flask of clear liquid and a bag of syringes.

Leah's eyes widened. As soon as the surprised look crossed her face, she pushed it down. But Val saw.

"Hm," Val pushed the drug forward. "Pill popper, huh?"

"Don't call me that."

"There's no reason to be scared." Val said. "It's the same drug. But the needle method works quicker— given it gets shoved right into your blood stream. You'll thank me later."

Leah didn't respond. She simply took the drugs and flung her hood over her head. Before she stepped out the door, Val's voice rang behind her.

"Oh, and Leah?" she smiled that twinkling grin. "Tell your father that Val requests he masturbate with a cactus. I think he'd benefit from it."

The hint of a smirk lifted Leah's lip. She turned, letting Val see only a moment of her smile. "Will do."

~~~

The night was colder when she stepped under the stars. Her bag hung by her side, the morphine sloshing with her steps. She retraced the steps back to her car, quickening her pace.

But slowly, more and more eyes seem to fly towards her. And then footsteps. At first, Leah ignored them. But then they got louder, and the simple pad of shoes turned into a hammering crowd.

Someone tugged on her hood. Leah whirled around to find several pairs of eyes sinking into her face. She scanned the gathering of filth before her, tightening her grip on her blade.

The man who yanked her hood narrowed his gaze, tilting his scrawny little neck. "You don't belong here."

"Everyone keeps reminding me that."

"Pretty little girl, aren't you?" the man mumbled, gazing down her flank. "Strong too. So what—" he crouched by the morphine, sticking his nose in Leah's bag. "What are you doing with… *that*."

Leah didn't bother answering.

"Well," the man murmured, running a quivering hand through his greasy hair. Leah wrinkled her nose at the familiar smell of sweat and marijuana. "I don't— I don't think you have much use for that… do you?" his scrawny rat hands reached for her bag. "I'm sure you don't mind if I—"

Leah flung her fist into his face. The man tumbled to the floor, a bruise already blossoming in a deep violet purple on his cheek.

Leah didn't wait for the response. She took off as soon as her knuckles collided with the man's bone. Footsteps pounded in her ear, and she could almost see her attackers foaming at the mouth to get her drug. But she was faster, stronger— physically superior in all ways that mattered.
~~~

But she couldn't fight off a crowd. Not by herself.

Fortunately, she didn't have to.

She rushed into an alleyway, pulling her hood above her head and ducking behind a trash bin. She withdrew the flask of morphine from the bag, unscrewing the top and dipping a needle into the liquid.

She withdrew as much as the capsule could hold, letting the drug drip back into its container. With careful hands, she put the morphine away and flung the strap over her shoulder.

Her bun fell from its hold; braids falling down her back. The blinding flash of distant police lights flickered in the distance— not for her, but they illuminated her skin just the same.

You ready? Zahara asked.

Leah grinned, "Always am."

She placed the syringe between her thumb and her pointer, took a breath, and shoved the morphine into her forearm.

YOU FUCKING LOST!

"This [morphine] increases the dopamine release in the nucleus accumbens which determines the feeling of pleasure."
—Listos, Joanna, et al. "The Mechanisms Involved in Morphine Addiction: An Overview."

This morphine was quicker, the cold sensation rushing through her bloodstream like a flood. The glacial drug carved her veins, spreading to her legs in a matter of seconds. Power surged into her limbs, evaporating the fear and plunging an icy focus into her body.

Leah walked through the alleyway slowly, braids drifting behind her. Her attackers were still on the main street, aimlessly wandering.

Leah didn't speak. She didn't need to. But as she held up her hand, syringe squeezed in her fist, heads turned. As eyes landed on the needle; she crushed it, shards of glass dropping from her grip. The men scrambled at her feet, trying to taste the reminiscing morphine on the shards.

The remaining men kept their gaze on her— focused on the bigger prize. Leah didn't wait for her opponents to take the offensive— instead she ran. Not away, not frightened. No, she ran right into the crowd.

They grasped at her— nails digging into her skin. She didn't bother to dodge, instead letting the blood drip from the gash. The knife hilt was flung into her attackers— causing them to stagger back.

When she cleared the crowd, she bolted; faster than ever before, heels pounding against the wet concrete. The men were behind her, but she couldn't hear them anymore. The only sound was the rush of morphine beating in her ear.

A rusty ladder lingered behind the corner. She leapt for it, hands slipping as they grasped the cold metal. The men were behind her, crawling over themselves and foaming at the mouth for any taste of the drug.

Leah let the morphine take over her movements as she climbed. She wasn't in control anymore— the opioid had taken the wheel, and Leah was happy to let it do so.

When she reached the roof, she ran. Her shoes hammered against the shingles, occasionally tearing one loose. She never slipped, never messed up. Her feet hit the roof with practiced perfection— *inhuman* perfection.

Her perpetrators followed behind her, yelping incomprehensible babbles. Leah turned her head, a tint of a smirk touching her lips. They were so far behind. Not even Savana could catch her now.

Leah sped up her sprint, her breath thrumming through her throat. She turned, veering with the direction of the roof, and stumbled to a stop.

Shingles came loose with her skid, falling onto the street and shattering. A gap. There was a *gap*. Leah's breath caught— the morphine faltering. She turned, eyes widening as she saw the mob charging closer and closer— ready to sink their yellow fangs into her skin.

Her eyes flew to a wood plank— moldy and splintering. Not perfect, but it was the only chance she had.

She grabbed the wood, laying it between the fall. Splinters fell from the plank as she set it down; a silent threat of collapse.

Leah began with careful steps, her support groaning below her. The fall was terrible— at least thirty feet. If not death, she would at least receive a crippling injury.

But the board held strong, only wobbling slightly as Leah placed one foot in front of the other, careful not to upset the bridge. The crowd's screech intensified, and the morphine finally woke up.

Leah started running— not paying any mind to the weakened support that kept her alive. With one gratifying leap, her front leg landed on the roof. The second foot, however, was not so lucky. It plunged into the wood, a devastating crack ringing through the air.

Her weight toppled backwards, tipping towards the drop. A gasp escaped her lips as her stomach landed on the singles, slowly slipping towards the massive drop. Her feet dangled over the ledge, pulling the rest of her down. Leah slammed her knife into the shingles— attempting to get a grip. The blade cracked the ceramic tile, sending pieces cascading onto the road.

Her torso slipped over the side. She dug the blade into a glimpse of wood. It stuck— barely, but it stuck. Just enough for Leah to pull herself from the drop.

She stood, shocked at the steadiness of her knees. The men had just begun to cross Leah's makeshift bridge— toppling over themselves to get to her. The plank was weak— but it would hold long enough for a few of them to get across. A few too many.

Leah waited until a few were halfway across the wood, watching their hungry eyes drift towards her satchel. A grin crept along her lips as she held the blade above her head, thrusting it down and into the weakened bridge.

The plank splintered, collapsing in two. Stray pieces of wood flew into the air— holding their position for only a moment before falling through the dark oblivion.

The men did the same. When the crack of wood rang through the night, they only stared at Leah— yellow eyes round with shock. Then the plummet took them to the ground.

The remaining crowd stared at her with disbelief, slowly lurking back into the shadows. Fear reclaimed her slaves, sending them quivering back into her dark obis. She spared Leah, leaving her surrounded by the cold night.

Leah sank to her knees— shingles shifting beneath her weight. The knife fell from her hand, clattering on the ceramic. She wanted to sob. She wanted to break into a million pieces and fall apart. God— so wanted to cry so much.

But a different sound came from her mouth.

She started to laugh; hard cackles resonating with the night air. Then she started screaming— the shriek mixing with her chortles to create an awful, off tune symphony.

"You lost!" Leah cried, louder than she ever yelled before. "Do you hear me? You fucking lost!"

Her words were left to echo into the stars— no one to receive her message. And yet she screamed again and again. So many times that her throat started to burn, so many times that the words seemed to become one with the streets. And when the stars rolled their eyes and the echo no longer bothered with her words, she kept screaming— perfectly satisfied that the only one hearing her screech of triumph was the darkness.

THE WARTIME SIMULATION

"And yet, some studies have shown that between 2% and 6% of male athletes have suffered sexual abuse in the context of their sport."
Parent, Sylvie, and Joëlle Bannon. "Sexual Abuse in Sport: What about Boys?"

Leah pulled into the parking lot, stopping her car and taking a deep breath. Trisha was sitting in her front seat, gathering her stuff. It seemed the kid's bag had vomited all over the floor, and she was quickly scrambling to pick up her belongings.

Leah laughed, letting herself watch for a moment. Trisha's braids bounced up and down— a messy, uneven sprout of the kid's doing. Leah had stopped trying to correct her hair, instead appreciating the style's... uniqueness.

"Hey, Hooker Strands." Leah called, tapping the kid's arm. Trisha sat up, wide eyes focusing on Leah. "Before we go to the game, let's talk."

Trisha raised an eyebrow. "Is everything okay?"

Leah shrugged. "As fine as it usually is." She tried a laugh— ultimately giving up and shifting her gaze to her feet. "Look, I need to show you something, and you have to *promise* to keep it a secret."

Trisha just stared at her, mesmerized.

"*Trisha*," Leah repeated. "You have to promise."

The kid held out her pinky, "I promise."

Leah took it, showing a hint of a smile. "Good." She breathed a shaky sigh. "Trish, do you remember when I told you about Zahara?"

Trisha nodded. "Your mentor— the one that went to Stanford?"

"Yeah, her." Leah said. "When I was about your age, I went to her last high school game. She was playing against her rival, Daniella. They were both— well, *amazing*. Little me was absolutely mesmerized. But in the end, Zahara was able to pull off the win. A buzzer beater— probably the greatest one I've ever witnessed."

Trisha tilted her head. "You aren't telling me this story to convince me how great Zahara was."

Leah chuckled. "No. I'm not. It's what happened after the game that's important. Trisha, do you know what a Sine Luni is?"

The kid's eyes widened. "I thought they were a myth."

"No," Leah shook her head. "They're very real. And after the game, Daniella was so defeated— so *broken*." Leah swallowed. "She knew it was either her or Zahara. Both of them couldn't earn the all-consuming love that came with the game. So she challenged Zahara to a Sine Luni.

"I watched them fight. I watched Daniella shed so much of my mentor's blood I thought she would die. But she *didn't*. Every blow, every punch, every single time Daniella sent Zahara to the floor, she was able to get up and keep playing. Keep running. Keep *fighting*."

Leah swallowed. "At the beginning of the fight, Daniella kicked Zahara's back. The entire audience gasped— we all thought that was the end of her. But Zahara just got up— like it was nothing but a scratch. It was—"

"Inhuman." Trisha finished. "Like you."

Leah paused. She looked at Trisha, eyes shifting through emotions. "Yes," she breathed. "Exactly like me.

"After that game, Zahara drove me to a park— that one where you can see right to the hospital. She led me up the hill and sat me down, showing me the same thing I'm about to show you now."

"What did she do?" Trisha asked.

Leah looked down, suddenly realizing how shaky she was. Her hands moved to her lap as she banished the sting of tears from her eyes. "She pulled out an opium pipe."

Trisha's breath caught. She began to tremble, chest rising with a mixture of panic and fear.

"What I'm about to say *cannot* be repeated," Leah said, keeping her eyes ahead. "Okay?"

Trisha whimpered. "Okay."

"Zahara pulled out the drug and smoked in front of me. She looked so calm— so happy. Zahara *never* looked that happy. But with the opium, it was like a part of her had been restored, a part she could never live without." Leah's voice trembled as the words poured from her mouth. A tear fell from her eye; she quickly brushed it away. "She told me that this game would take everything and a bit from me. Everything I took for granted gone if I really wanted to succeed. And Trisha, trust me—" Leah shifted her gaze, meeting the kid's eye. "I *needed* to succeed."

She took a breath— the air barely reaching her lungs. "And she told me that the game would take things I didn't have. It would require abilities I couldn't physically do. That I—" Leah stopped, looking up at the gray sky. "I would have to be better than human. And the only way to do that—" her eyes flooded with tears— she blinked them away quickly. "Is to have a crutch."

There was silence, Trisha shifted uncomfortably in her seat, hands folded in her lap. Leah kept her eyes on the steering wheel— not daring to let the tears slip past her waterline.

"Was she–" Trisha began. "Was she correct?"

"*Absolutely*."

Another round of quiet. Then, Leah reached into her bag. She lifted a locked box from a pocket— twisting in the code and clicking it open. Inside was a single morphine syringe— little remnants dripping onto the box.

"What—" Trisha scurried away, pressing her back against the door. Her little eyes filled with terror; looking between Leah and the morphine. "You can't— *please*—"

"Hey," Leah closed the box, the lock clicking shut. "Hey—" she reached to touch Trisha's arm, only to realize she was shaking. "Kid, it's okay, it's not for you."

A moment of relief flooded over her— quickly replaced by the previous caution. Trisha brushed off Leah's touch, pressing her arms against her chest. "Then who's it for?"

"Me."

The kid seemed to go through several emotions at once— each one coming and going before Leah could recognize it. Finally, Trisha's features settled in an expression of concern. "If you don't mind me asking, um, what drug is it?"

"Morphine." Leah said.

"Oh," Trisha's words returned to their fearful default. "Will I— will I take the morphine?"

"No," Leah shrugged— then thought about it and corrected her mistake. "I mean, maybe. Honestly depends on the circumstance. I don't take the same drug as Zahara— she took opium. Both opiates, both painkillers, both depressants. But they're different. You just gotta find what works for you."

Leah said it like she was discussing a brand of laundry detergent. Not a narcotic often referred to as "the death drug." The discussion of doping came off her tongue like a simple necessity.

"Do I—" Trisha's breath caught. "Do I have too?"

Leah chuckled. "Of course not. It's always a choice. For me, I was playing so shit after my ACL sprain that my dad was going to—" she stopped, heart beginning to climb at the subject of Gael. She swallowed the matter, forcing her hands to stop trembling. "Well, you've seen the man. The point is Trish, I *had* to play well. And I wasn't— I *couldn't*. Every time I got on that court it felt like my knee was going to—" she stopped, taking a breath and running a hand along her ACL brace. "You know, snap. So when I found the morphine— I was ready to give up everything to play well."

Leah sat up, plastering a fake smile on her face in a poor attempt to lighten the mood. "But by all means, kid. If you can avoid doping, do it. And if you can manage that, I applaud your resilience." Leah opened the car door, grabbing her bag from the back. "Think of this as a warning— an honesty. I'm just letting you know what might come your way."

Leah lifted herself from her seat, pulling her backpack with her. Just as she was about to stand, Trisha grabbed her wrist. Leah turned, staring into the kids wild blue eyes— every part of her filled with absolute terror.

"Leah, wait!" she started, tears pricking the corners of her eyes. "Morphine; I know it's powerful. And the withdrawals—" Trisha let a tear fall down her cheek. "It could kill you."

Leah didn't respond. Instead, she brushed off Trisha's grip and strode into the gym without letting her mind resonate with the phrase.

~~~

Humans, by nature, were violent.

That was why countries sprang at the chance to kill over the smallest quarrel. Sports, Leah figured, resembled war. Just as humans took joy in killing, she took joy in winning. Perhaps it was relief; the freedom from a coach's demanding stare and a father's furious screech. But then again, it wasn't simply her safety that made her grin, but the loss in an opponent's eyes. Leah could tell when someone failed. There was a tint in their gaze, a slump in their shoulders and a nervous glance to wherever their parents had placed their rump in the bleachers.

The symptoms— they gave her power. No, power was the wrong word. *Insurance*. Because she knew that no matter how awful she played, there was always the show of humiliation. If Gael brought up her shortcomings, she would counter with her victim's failure; his sneer would twist into a pleasurable grin and Leah would be spared. Instead of criticism, they would gossip about the girl's broken features. Coaches, parents, players— they all took joy in a child's doom. In a way, watching a little girl cry was like watching a soldier squirm under a blade.

Sick, gruesome, and absolutely *wonderful*.

Leah sat on the bench, surrounded by dazed seventh graders. Most of the kids were staring off into space— so mesmerized by the ceiling it may have been a meteor. Two of the middle schoolers, however, were chatting beside her. Lost in some conversation about their amateur love life. After listening in for a while, Leah realized that the gossip actually wasn't so *amateur*.
~~~

“Hey!” Leah snapped, nudging them. “Pay attention, the game’s starting.”

The girls sneered at her— practicing that perfect middle school glare.

Leah replicated the expression. “Give me that look again and I’ll tell your parents exactly what’s happened with that boy.”

This shut them up. They directed their gaze to the jump ball. Trisha was standing at the front of the operation, staring intently at the competition. The referee flung the ball into the air, and the game commenced.

The possesion was flung towards Trisha. She caught it, starting down the court. The thing spun in her hand as she reached the three-point-line. A defender crossed her path, but Trisha didn’t blink. She plunged towards the basket, sending her defender into the air and laying the ball through the hoop.

The bench, finally waking up, erupted with cheers. Trisha didn’t seem to notice her applause, instead sprinting up the court and falling into her defensive stance.

The other team dribbled up the court, the point guard shouting orders at her teammates. A play was run— Leah couldn’t quite figure out how it worked, but it was effective.

The point guard swung the ball to the corner and a flurry of screens began. The defense collapsed, confusion replacing the careful organization. The ball was passed to a tall girl in the post, who laid the thing into the basket.

The opposing team exploded with celebration. They jumped up and down, shouting their teammate’s names with an orchestra of praise.

But overshadowing that symphony was Trisha’s powerful squeak. She was so quiet around Leah, but on the court she transformed. The little mouse morphed into a lion, roaring orders at her teammates as the ball twirled in her grasp.

Trisha punched her fist into the air, calling a screen. It came quickly, her teammate creating a barricade. Trisha drove into the defense, diving through the chaos. Her teammate followed, wide open for the layup. But Trisha didn’t see her, instead going for her own shot.

There was a loud slap. Trisha’s shot was knocked out of the air. A post stomped around the key, flexing her muscles and screaming like she was Haley Jones. Leah rolled her eyes.

Trisha however, was not celebrating. She wasn’t even moving, just staring into the crowd. Terror had etched over her features as she scanned the bleachers, searching for *someone*.

Leah knew who.

"Ezra," Leah strode to the coach's side. "You need to take Trisha out."

Ezra blinked. "She made one mistake. Other than that she's doing well—"

"I only need a minute—"

"Leah," Ezra breathed. "Are you sure—"

"Ezra please," Leah begged. "Take it from someone who's stood in that kid's shoes. Take it from someone who's been frozen still because of a mistake. Trisha—" she swallowed. "Give her a break. I just need to talk to her."

Ezra nodded. "Okay," he offered a smile. "I trust you."

Leah breathed a sigh of relief, dipping her head. Ezra sent another girl in for Trisha. After a quick exchange, she walked to the bench, a practiced doom tracing her steps.

Trisha sat down, putting her head in her hands and bouncing her leg on the floor. Her chest was heavy with quick gasps; her breath speeding faster and faster as her foot rushed to a higher pace.

"Hey," Leah knelt down, placing her hand on the kid's knee. "Hey, Trish, look at me—" she lifted her chin. "It's okay—"

"No—" Trisha gasped, the tears slipping down her chin. "He benched me—he benched me Leah! I can't—"

"Woah, woah." Leah took her hands, clasping them between hers. "Trisha, *I* took you out. Ezra will put you back in a minute."

Trisha's red eyes filled with fear. But instead of scanning the bleachers, all the horror was directed at Leah. "What? Are you—"

"I'm not going to hurt you." Leah said. "It's okay. He's not here, remember? No one here is going to hurt you."

"You don't know—"

"Trisha, trust me, I do." Leah said. "I know more than most people ever will. But whoever hurt you, they're not here right now. I drove you here. I'm taking you home. I'm not going to hurt you, Trisha."

Zahara's voice came again— the same accusatory tone lingering in her ear. *That won't help.* She hissed. *The kid doesn't need to be babied— she needs scolding. She can't just break down in the middle of the game.* Leah tightened her jaw. *Go on, scold her.*

Leah looked at the kid, features bordering on the line between broken and hopeful. She was supposed to hurt her— supposed to screech. That would make her excellent; it's what Zahara would've done. But Trisha was her mirror, a reflection of Leah's younger self. She opened her mouth— summoning the insult. But she couldn't say it. She couldn't become the monsters who made her.

"I'm not going to hurt you, Trisha." Leah repeated. "It's okay to make mistakes— that's what makes us human. And to expect someone to be better than human, well—" Leah offered a smile, squeezing Trisha's hands. "That's just crazy."

"But people *do* expect that of me—"

"I know," Leah said. "They expect it of me too. But it's not right. And those people— they aren't here right now. The people that are here— me, Ezra, your teammates, we all think you're amazing. We won't hurt you."

Trisha swallowed. "Promise?"

Leah lifted her hand to the kid's cheek, tucking a strand of hair behind her ear. "Promise." Her grasp moved to Trisha's shoulder. "Go get them, Hooker Strands."

Trisha ran from the bench. Ezra leaned down, whispering something in her ear. The kid smiled, running to the scoring table and waiting for the ref to sub her in.

Leah sat in her chair, tilting her head back and resting her eyes on the ceiling. Gyms were always so dreamy— like they weren't even real. Too bright, too loud— too unnatural.

You're doing that kid no favors. Zahara murmured. *You should've—*

"Shut up Zahara," Leah retorted, letting out a puff of breath. "Just shut up."

~~~

Trisha was smiling by the end of the game. Her face glowed with happiness as she skipped off the court, chatting with her teammates. Life had returned to her eyes— lighting up her face with colors of joy.

Ezra moved to Leah's side, placing his hands on his hips. "I'm proud of you, you know."

Leah raised an eyebrow. "For what?"

"For being the guide that girl needs," Ezra grinned, watching the girls gossip while taking off their shoes. "She used to only look up to you— want to be you. But now she thinks of you as an older sister." His ice blue gaze met hers. "As someone safe."

A touch of a smile formed on Leah's lips. Tears pricked her eyes, threatening to fall down her cheeks. Leah wiped them away quickly, blinking the grief from her eyes.
~~~

The varsity game was scheduled just a half hour after Trisha's. When Ezra and Leah made their way to the court, Savana and Swan were already there, deep in conversation. When they saw Leah, the talk halted.

"Taven," Savana scowled.

Leah raised her chin. "Afren."

They stared at each other for a while, as if debating whether or not to fight in front of Ezra. Leah had the insult on the tip of her tongue, but kept it there. And from the look on Savana's face, she was holding back a similar blow.

They looked at Ezra, who was absorbed into the game in front of them. The man was like a magnet to any kind of conflict, especially within his team. Leah breathed a sigh.

"Not here." Leah said, turning to Savana.

"Not here," Savana agreed. The first thing they'd agreed upon in months.

Warm ups were anything but dull. In fact, Leah felt her blood pressure rise as Savana positioned herself behind her in line. Her presence made it immensely hard to focus on the shooting lines.

"You missed." Savana hissed after Leah's previous three rattled off the rim.

"Oh really?" Leah shot back. "Like your layup that didn't even make it to the backboard?"

Savana laughed. "I don't know what you're talking about."

"Yes you do," Leah snapped. "The one that bounced off the bottom of the rim— made that huge bang? The whole team saw."

"At least I don't freeze up in the middle of a game just because something spooked me."

"At least I can *play* a game."

"Leah," Ezra called; both Leah and Savana turned towards him. "It's your turn."

"Sorry," Leah murmured, leaving the malice in her tone behind. She ran to the three point line, receiving the pass and gathering her feet in a step back. The ball flew from her fingers— perfect form. The shot swished into the basket, barely touching the rim.

Leah shot Savana a look. The girl was pretending to look away. Leah rolled her eyes.

"Hey," Ezra beckoned her and Savana forward. "I need to go talk to someone. Can you guys run the warm ups?"

“Sure,” Leah and Savana said simultaneously. They shot each other a glare.

“Awesome thanks,” Ezra, seeming not to notice the obvious conflict, took off. “I’ll be back in ten.”

By that time, Leah and Savana weren’t listening. They had fixed their gazes on the other, trying desperately not to claw each other’s face off.

Savana turned away first. “Hey!” she called to the team— their heads snapped towards her. “We’re doing free throws.”

“No,” Leah retorted. “Why would we do that? We just shot!”

“Well, Leah, obviously your shot could use more practice. So I think it’s better that you don’t air ball every time you touch the ball.”

Leah huffed a cackle. “You’re one to talk,” she snorted. “I suppose you're avoiding your relationship with the ball. Seems you can only get it to roll away.”

Savana stepped forward. Neither of them were talking to the team anymore. Leah raised her chin, looking into Savana’s fiery eyes. When Savana spoke, her voice was low, every syllable laced with venom.

“I don’t know exactly what you’re doing, Leah.” She snarled. “But I do know you won’t be as excellent without your crutch.”

Leah saw red. Before she knew it, her hands were going at Savana’s face. Savana had the same idea, lunging for Leah’s torso. Leah would kill her. *She was going to fucking kill her.*

“Woah!” Swan stepped between the two of them, holding out her hands. “Hey, calm down. We’re all on the same team here.”

Leah’s seething died. She stared into Savana’s flame lit eyes, her gasoline slowly fizzling out. It was just then she realized how ill Savana looked. Eye bags lingered under her dead gaze and her skin was ghostly gray. Her hands were crumpled into fists, but trembled every few seconds. And her arms, which were usually bare, were covered with long, dark sleeves.

For once, Leah didn’t see Savana as an enemy, but as a mirror. So alike, so broken, pinned against each other by the world. For the simple fact that only one of them could get the love and attention each needed to survive.

“What happened to us?” Leah asked, her voice low with sorrow. “We used to love each other.”

Savana’s anger wavered. The flame in her eyes died, leaving behind the empty, tortured daze of a kicked child.

“We were kids back then,” Savana said. “This game kills all its children.”

The buzzer went off. Everyone turned to see Ezra was walking towards the bench. He beckoned them to follow. Leah shot Savana one last look and took off towards Ezra.

“Starters sit,” Ezra said. Leah collapsed on the bench, folding her hands on her knees. “This team runs an offense through their post. It’s an old fashioned kind of game, but they’ve made it work.” He brought out his clipboard, pointing to the block. “Their primary goal is to get the ball to the block—where number forty-three is.” The team glanced at their opponent’s bench. Forty-three towered over their teammates, standing at what Leah would assume was over six feet.

“Um,” Savana raised her hand. “Who’s guarding her? We’re pretty much a team of guards.”

While Leah hated to admit it, Savana did have a point. It was physically impossible for any one of them to guard a post player as tall as Forty-three. Even with the morphine, Leah couldn’t jump higher than a foot; besides, if she could, she wasn’t near strong enough to defend someone in the post.

“Great question.” Ezra said. “Since their offense is run only at the block, that means we don’t have to worry about threes. Savana will be on Forty-three, but she won’t be alone. We’ll exaggerate our defensive spacing, sagging into the post. Then we can swipe at the ball whenever Forty-three gets the possession.”

“And what if the ball gets passed out to the three point line?” Leah asked. “That’s a long closeout that can easily be turned into a drive or a three.”

“The drive will be stopped by the layer of defense we already have at the post.” Ezra said. “And I can live with a three or a mid-range shot. This team doesn’t have shooters. As long as we keep their shots from the post to a minimum, we should have this game in the bag.”

The buzzer rang and the referees called the teams onto the court. Leah strode to her spot in the jump ball, matching up with her defender. Savana had the unfortunate task of doing the jump— as there was no one else better suited for it.

The ball was thrown into the air. Forty-three whacked it forward, right into the opponent’s hands. Leah dropped into her defensive stance as the point guard darted up the court, attempting to confuse Leah’s footing with a crossover.

Leah slapped the ball from her hand, taking off in the other direction. A defender darted in front of her, intercepting her path. Savana was already running, calling for the ball. Leah passed it, sprinting past half court.

"Savana!" she called. "I'm open!"

An opposing girl was gaining on Savana, cutting off her path to the basket. But she kept going, crossing over and backing out to the three point line. She tried to throw the ball through her legs, but the thing bounced off her foot, running to the sideline.

The ref blew the whistle, signaling for a switched possession. Leah marched up to Savana, pushing her shoulder.

"What the hell was that?" Leah screeched. "I was wide open at the basket."

She expected a glare or an angry retort. At least some show of disdain. But the fire had vanished from Savana's gaze. She wasn't even looking at Leah, instead gazing into the bleachers.

Leah followed her gaze, meeting the eyes of Savana's father. He was silent, hands pressed to his mustache. His eyes held danger— the same danger that Gael's had. Instead of rage, Leah felt Savana's fear creep into her own veins.

She laid a hand on her teammate's shoulder— not anything perpetrating, but nothing kind either. "Go get Forty-three."

Her words weren't meant to be a mercy— there was nothing forgiving in her tone. But she wasn't hostile. Not quite a friendship, but not the phrase of enemies either.

Savana, unfortunately, didn't reciprocate the truce.

"Fuck off Leah," she murmured, already starting down the court. "I don't need your *pity*."

Leah sighed, flicking her braids from her shoulder. The game followed pretty much the same pattern after that. Leah thought she played decently; the morphine did what it was supposed to. Swan was well… Swan. But Savana—

She never quite recovered from that moment with her father. Once he wrapped his icy grip around her, it was hard to pry off. Slowly, Leah watched Savana fall apart from the inside and out.

The ball rolled off her foot and she missed easy layups. And every single time she did so, her hands would shoot to her face to either punch herself or yank her red hair.

They lost the game by ten points. By the end of it, all their spirits were pretty low. Leah even caught Swan with a grim expression on her face. Ezra's after game talk was nothing special— just the speech about how 'we could've won that' and 'we'll get them next time' that Leah had heard a thousand times over.

Savana didn't stay for the meeting. Right as the game ended, she ran into the locker room. In a moment of curiosity, Leah followed. She wasn't exactly sure why— it wasn't to comfort Savana and Savana certainly didn't want comforting. But something drew her to whatever was happening within those walls.

She padded into the locker room, careful not to alert anyone of her presence. Before her was the door, a small window engraved into the wood. She pressed her body against the wall, glancing into the glass.

Leah's chest dropped. Her hands slithered into her hair, pulling the locks from her scalp. Tears gripped the edges of her eyes, trailing down her cheeks as she looked at Ezra and Savana.

Hugging each other. Savana's tearstained face— and he was hugging her. He was supposed to love *her*. Supposed to support *her*. But he was embracing her nemesis— he was going to leave her for *Savana.*

Leah tried to tear herself away from the window. But she couldn't— she just kept staring— *knowing*. Knowing damn well that Savana was going to say something— about her. And then— and then—

And then Ezra would hate her. *Leave* her. He was going to leave. He was going to leave. He was going to—

Anger slithered up Leah's limbs, creeping into her heart. It was so powerful —more than any drug she had ever taken. She clenched her jaw, letting the tears flow from her waterline.

Ezra looked up from Savana's shoulder, meeting her gaze. Leah paused, staring through Ezra's blue eyes. Then she ran, her braids swishing behind her as she darted towards the door.

She broke into a sprint, tears falling down her face. She ran through the crowd, pushing through players and parents alike. The breath coursing through her throat grew thicker as her heart pounded in her ear.

Leah bolted out the door— letting out a tearful yelp. A scream ripped from her throat as she collapsed against the wall. Her hands found her face, slamming her knuckles into her cheek bone.

Air caught in her mouth— letting nothing but choked sobs escape her esophagus. The rivulets coursed down her face, leaving a salty residue on her lips.

Leah brought her knees to her chest, ACL brace squeaking with the movement. She placed her head on her legs, a deranged screech breeching her lips.

He's going to leave me. He's going to leave me. He's going to leave me.

She dug her nails into her skin; wanting the blood to pour from the scratch— God, but what was one more trail of blood when it already felt like the red was draining from her heart?

No one was looking at her. She had hidden herself well— but even if someone did come around the corner, she wouldn't care. What did anything matter? Now that he—

He left her.

Leah let another sob breach her lips. She jolted her head into the wall, slamming her scalp against the concrete. The tears cascaded down her cheeks, seeping into the loose strands that fell from her braids.

"I was going to come find you."

Leah snapped her head towards the voice. Ezra was standing before her, hands plummeted at his sides. She scrambled back, palms scraping against the rough concrete.

"Liar." She snarled. "*Liar*."

"Leah," Ezra put his hands in the air. "I'm not lying."

"Yes you are," Leah breathed, scrambling away. "I saw you. Saw you with *her*. What did she tell you, huh?" Leah cackled. "That I'm crazy? That I'm dangerous? That I'm taking—"

"We didn't talk about you." Ezra said. "We talked about *her*."

Leah huffed a laugh, squeezing the drops from her gaze. The rivulets fell from her cheeks, splattering on the hot concrete.

She let a smile spread on her lips. Demented and fake. But she smiled. "I hate you, Ezra."

She said it like someone admitting their love. But she didn't mean it in a caring way. She didn't want to manipulate him. As the words left her mouth, she strode away, letting her braids drift behind her.

"You're not the only one who's fucked up, Leah."

Venom. *Venom* behind his tone. Ezra's voice was always smooth— at the boundary between a rasp and a pitch. But now— now it was darker; deeper. The entire weight of a past weighing his vocal chords into his chest.

Leah turned, centering her gaze. He stood, but his hands shook at his sides. The confident, calm man was gone. Leah hadn't met the one who remained.

"Sit down." Ezra drawled, his voice low. Leah obliged, slumping against the wall. Ezra followed, resting his head against the concrete. He blew out a breath. That was when Leah realized he was trembling. "I'm going to tell you something important. So listen."

Leah nodded, wiping the dried tears from her eyes. Ezra drew a shaky sigh, opening his mouth to speak. No words came out at first.

"I—" he began, then faltered. He swallowed, raising his hands to his head. "I was raped by my high school coach from my freshman to senior year."

Leah's eyes widened. She opened her mouth, but found she couldn't speak. She just looked at Ezra— the man who seemed so strong, so *stable*. And he was— if anything this made him more so. As Leah looked at him, all she could do was gape.

"Every day before and after practice." Ezra's voice was so small. "Half an hour each time. I had to arrive early. And if I refused—" his breath caught. "He would hurt me. Shove me against the wall and—"

He took a breath, steadying himself. His nails dug into the concrete like it kept him steady.

"At first I didn't tell anyone." Ezra drew. "At first I couldn't. He filmed it every time— threatened to release it. Threatened to tell everyone *I liked it*." He spat the last part— as if it tasted sour in his mouth. "After I graduated I decided I'd had enough. That no one was going to suffer the way I had. I went to the school board— told them everything. But they said—"

His voice caught in his throat. He mouthed the words— over and over. But they wouldn't come out. Every time a hint of his tone broke his lips, he flinched. Like they physically hurt to say.

"They didn't believe me." A tear rolled down his cheek. "Said I was just trying to get him fired because I was *spiteful*. They wouldn't even search his office. No hint of suspicion, no cause for concern. *They just ignored it.*

"I went to many places after that. The school board, city council— they all ignored me. Said that I was *lying*. Apparently they couldn't do anything without *evidence*." He pressed his teeth together, blue gaze staring straight ahead. "Then he found me. Told me he knew. And that I needed to back off. And when I refused—" his voice cracked— probably the only time Leah had ever heard it falter. "He beat me. So hard he knocked me out. I spent the night on the curb— people walking by me like I was any other *drunk*." He took a breath, the rage leaving his fingertips and seeping into the ground.

"That day—" his voice was calm. "That day I gave up any hope that this game could be changed. I accepted that those rapists and pedophiles and abusers in power could never be removed. But—" his gaze shifted to Leah. His eyes were still the brilliant shade of blue, but they had darkened. Not the color, but the light. Every form of brightness holding Ezra Soren together vanished. Now, she looked into a lifeless gaze filled with pain, grief and so much resilience.

"But those people can be replaced, Leah. That's why I coach. That's why I'm so different from everyone else in this game. I see the side that no other coaches are able to. The side of the player— the side of the *victim*." He drew a breath. "I'm a coach because I know that if I wasn't some other asshole would take my place— and you and Savana and Swan would have to go through the same thing I did."

Ezra stood, grip surprisingly steady at his side. "I can't make all the bad things in this world go away, and I can't erase what has been done to my girls. But I can be a support. For *all of you.*" He offered a small smile— nothing radiant, but it was real. "To me, this game isn't about winning. It's not about being the best or getting into the most prestigious college. It's about family." He gazed at Leah, the light slowly returning to his gaze. "And family looks out for one another. *Always*."

THE OLIVE BRANCH

There are three types of morphine tolerance: pharmacokinetic tolerance, learned tolerlance, or pharmacodynamic tolerance. Each tolerance primarily affects the pleasureful or positive feelings of the drug but not the withdrawal symptoms; causing negative symptoms to worsen over time.
—Listos, Joanna, et al. "The Mechanisms Involved in Morphine Addiction: An Overview."

"Where's Val?" Leah snapped, leaning on the counter. "I need to speak to her."

The bartender shrugged. "Out."

"What do you mean, *out*?"

"I mean she's not here."

"*Not here*?" Leah grit her teeth. "Its five fucking AM. Where the hell else would she be?"

"Well, not here." The bartender said plainly. "Check a few other places down the block and you can find her using the process of elimination." He ran the rag along his glass. "Better question, why are you up so early."

"Nevermind that." Leah retorted. "Why are you awake? Morning isn't exactly prime time for alcohol."

He chuckled. "You forget, Val runs a casino. Every hour is prime time for alcohol around here."

Leah looked around. Sure enough, slot machines lined the walls. People leaning on the bright, cheerful gadgets dug into their purses, eager to find another penny to throw away. They were like zombies, ripping flesh from their own thigh if it meant the smallest chance of riches.

"What's the chance that they'll win?" Leah asked. If Val wasn't here, she might as well talk to her employee. "If there is any?"

The bartender grabbed another glass, shoving his dirty cloth into it. "No clue. There hasn't been a win in thirty years."

"So how do you know there's still a chance?"

"We don't." He said. "And the gamblers don't either. But they know that the smaller the chance, the more money they'll get if they do happen to win. Millions, probably. And they'll give everything they have just for that small chance."

Leah sneered, averting her gaze from the machines. "That's idiotic."

He stopped scrubbing. "You're hypocritical."

Before Leah could hiss at the remark, a woman strode in. Val, surprisingly, looked relatively normal. A grey hoodie was draped over her shoulders, along with jeans that hugged her legs. Her grey hair was pulled into a messy bun, too loose hooker strands hanging over her face.

Leah suddenly felt the urge to cut them with her knife.

When Val saw her, a look of surprise flashed across her face. It was quickly replaced by a smile that made Leah's guts flip. "Leah!" she strode towards her, going for a hug. Leah stepped back, making it abundantly clear that she did not reciprocate the embrace. "Ugh, fine. You're so stand-offish. Your mother was nothing like this."

"Good thing I'm not my mother."

Val, seeming to ignore her comment, approached the bar. "Hey Grant. Can you bring me a glass of milk in my office?"

Leah snorted. "What are you, five?"

Val flashed her a grin. "She'll take one too."

Leah rolled her eyes, folding her arms across her chest. Val slammed a wad of cash on the counter— way too much for two glasses of milk— and strode into her office, beckoning for Leah to follow.

"Come now, dear." Val said, sitting behind her desk. "You know the deal. I won't do business with you if you don't sit."

Leah scowled but obliged.

"You know," Val leaned back in her chair. "I really didn't expect you to make it back to your car."

Leah's eyes widened. "What?"

"You know, with all those people—" she shrugged. "I saw them find you. I knew they would, but I wanted to see—"

"You *watched*?" Leah hissed, standing up. "You watched them almost *kill* me?"

"Oh don't be so dramatic." Val waved a hand. "They wouldn't have killed you. Just hurt you a little bit— taken your morphine, you know. But what I didn't expect was for you to make it." She tilted her head, letting out a cackle. "Tell me," Val leaned forward. "How did you do it? Find a way into the sewers? I hardly doubt you have much skill with that blade and I didn't see any dead bodies or blood—"

"I'm not a killer!" Leah screeched. "I would *never*—"

"Oh, we're all not killers until suddenly we've plunged a weapon into another's neck." Val flashed a grin. "No one is really too far away from being a murderer."

“Well I’m not,” Leah sank back into her seat. “And I don’t plan to cross that line any time soon.”

Val shrugged. “Suit yourself, but—”

Just then, the door swung open. The bartender padded onto Val’s rug, carrying two wine glasses of milk. He set them on the desk without a word and strode out.

“As I was saying,” Val took the glass, pressing it to her lips. “You—” she choked on her drink.

Once Leah had finished pouring the entirety of the milk onto the table, she dropped the glass. It didn’t quite shatter, but a few pieces broke off from the rim. The shards scattered in the white liquid, slowly bleeding onto Val’s papers.

Val sneered, moving the documents out of the trail. “That was unnecessary.”

“Yes, well I found it enjoyable.”

“Given the obvious hints,” Val pulled a rag from her desk, placing it in the spill. “I gather that you’re quite fed up with small talk, so let's get right to the point. Ran out quite quickly, didn’t you?”

Leah scowled. “That’s none of your business.”

“Oh, but it is,” Val snatched her wrist, pulling down her sleeve. Leah attempted to pull away, but the woman’s grip was iron. “Your skin’s so yellow it might’ve been colored with a highlighter. And these scars—” she ran a hand over the several scratches. Suddenly, right between her forearm and bicep, Val pushed her nail into Leah’s skin.

Pain shot up her limb. This time, Leah was able to jolt away, pulling her sleeve over her arm and backing towards the door. “*Don’t touch me*!”

Val didn’t seem to hear her. “Several scabs on your median cubical vein—fresh enough to bleed. And they’re not just puncture marks; you have scratches. Signs of trembling.” She tilted her head, that awful smile gleaming on her features. “Oh, my dear. You’re more like your predecessor than you realize.”

“I told you,” Leah hissed. “I’m *nothing* like my mother.”

Val huffed a laugh. “Oh, I’m not talking about Maragret.” For a moment, Leah thought she saw sadness in her eyes. “No, I mean the girl that came before. The one who trained you. Your *mentor*.”

Leah staggered back. “Zahara came here?”

“Of course,” Val said. “A lot like you, that one. I knew as soon as you came in that you were hers. She told me about you, you know.”

"What did she say?" Leah demanded, slamming her hands on Val's desk. "*What*?"

"*Calm yourself*, child." Val drew. "Take a seat. Stop running around like a chicken who can't find its feet."

Leah seethed, sitting back in her chair. She didn't say anything else, just crossed her hands in her lap. Val rested her jaw in her palm, smirking.

"Zahara was quite remarkable." She said, "But desperate. I think she might've wandered in here by accident, but when I saw her, I knew she needed my *help*." Val landed on the last word like she was firing a rifle. "She told me everything and I gave her what she needed. She came back many times and each visit she looked sicker and sicker.

"Then one day she came looking slightly less ill. She still had those opium rashes and her eyes still drooped lower than they should. But for once, she had light in her iris." Val looked at her desk, running a manicured finger along the wood. "She told me about a kid. A girl who wanted to be like her. A parallel—a glance into the past. And she told me that she wanted to help her. Help her live a better life, the life she never had."

Leah swallowed, looking down at the wood. Tears stung the edges of her eyes, dripping onto Val's desk. A hand lifted her chin and Val wiped the droplets from her cheek.

Leah slapped her hand away, using her own fingers to recover the rivulets. "Well she failed, okay?" she hissed. "Zahara didn't make it better for me. I follow the same path that she did, because that's the *only* fucking path to follow."

Val only tilted her head. "Oh, I know Zahara failed." She drummed her manicured nails against the desk. "If she didn't, then you wouldn't be sitting here today. But this does beg the question, my dear, will you follow in your mentors' footsteps? And if you do, can I expect another D1 sitting at my desk in a few years time?"

Leah shook her head, trying to keep the tears behind her waterline. She pulled the empty canister out of her bag, the metal clanging on the desk as she set it down. "Just give me the morphine, Val."

"One more thing—"

"*Val*."

"Leah, please." Val's tone was almost vulnerable. "I just want to ask a question." She laid a hand on Leah's. This time, she made no effort to jolt away. "You aren't just taking it for games anymore, are you?"

Leah swallowed, shaking her head.

"Are you taking it before practice?"

"Yes."

"How often do you inject it?"

"When the last dose wears off."

Val took a breath. She reached into her desk, pulling out another canister of morphine. Slowly, she began emptying it into Leah's bottle.

"Val—" Leah's voice shook. "You have to understand, the withdrawals—"

"Leah," Val's tone was solemn. "I'm a dealer. Of course I know about the withdrawals."

Leah let out a sigh, placing a wad of cash on the table. Val passed the morphine to her before taking the cash and shoving it into her drawer. Leah placed the bottle into her bag, starting towards the door.

"Oh," Val's voice rang after her. "Leah, I know it's not my place, but please be careful."

Leah huffed a laugh— a small motion that made her shoulders jolt upwards. "I can't afford to be *careful*."

~~~

Leah let the ball roll off her fingers, the thing briskly falling into the net. She rushed to retrieve it, making her way back to the three point line.

Her second shot wasn't as perfect. Her follow through tilted to the side, causing the ball to ricochet off the rim and run towards the sideline. Leah cursed, starting her sprint.

"Care for a rebounder?" Ezra was standing in the doorway to the gym, a stupid grin plastered on his face.

Leah's face lit up. She forgot about her runaway ball and rerouted the sprint towards her coach. Surprise crossed Ezra's features when Leah embraced him, but he quickly adjusted to the hug, wrapping his own arms around her.

"So?" Leah said. "You offered your rebounding services."

"I did."

"Well," Leah cocked her head to the side. "There's the ball."

Ezra made a face. "Oh, that one was loose before I got here. Therefore, it is your responsibility to get it."

Leah scowled. She gave Ezra one last look and made a beeline for the ball. She passed it to her coach and ran to the three point line.

"So?" Ezra flung the possession into her grasp. "What did you do this morning?"
~~~

Leah bounded into her shot, flicking her wrist as the ball left her hand. "I had a meeting with an acquaintance."

"Oh," the ball rattled into the hoop— Zahara wouldn't have counted it as a make. "Friend of yours?"

"No." Leah caught Ezra's pass, flinging it through her legs and extending into her shot. "An old bitch who asks too many questions."

"Sarcasm?" Ezra caught the ball.

"Not a smidge."

"Interesting," Leah's shot swished into the basket. Ezra flung the ball back to her. "By the way, Leah, we need to start the college admission process soon."

Leah choked, her arm twisting. The ball bounded off the backboard, making a loud clank. "What?"

Ezra crossed his arms. "Well, you're almost done with your junior year. I've already had a few colleges contact—"

"Stanford." Leah blurted. "Has there been anything from *Stanford*?"

"No," Ezra shrugged. "But you have some interest from Berkeley if you want to go to California."

"I need to go to *Stanford*." Leah repeated, landing on the name with rushed panic. "Or else— or else all the work I've been doing will be for *nothing*."

Ezra touched the back of his neck. "I feel like I should know this about you, but are you like hell bent on being a lawyer or something?"

Leah blinked. She hadn't really thought about what she would do after college. She really didn't think there would be an after college. Honestly, it was hard for her to imagine an after high school.

"No," Leah mumbled. "It's just—" she sighed. "That's where Zahara went."

"Hm," Ezra nodded. "Look, I'm not going to dictate where you should go. I'm only here to help. But you're not Zahara. You're similar to her, but definitely not her. You're Leah. Your own person with your own choices and your own hopes and dreams." He approached her. "If you want my advice, focus a little less on being the next Zahara Williamson and focus a little more on being the only Leah Taven."

Leah frowned. Her whole life had been centered around Zahara. The figure that forever lived in her head. The woman who criticized her to no end. The person she always strove to be. She was Zahara— or as close to Zahara as she could be.

Be the only Leah Taven. But what if there was none of her left? She was only a copy and paste personality— a mixture of ambition, goals and drive that morphed into nothing but a weapon whose only purpose was to fight.

"What about Viren?" Leah asked, snapping out of her trance.

Ezra's eyes widened. "What?"

"Don't I need some sort of letter of recommendation from him or something?"

"It's not quite a *need*." Ezra said, his face relaxing. "It would help, sometimes, but college coaches know that high school is only a piece of the puzzle. An amazing AAU record is really all you need."

"But—" Leah sighed. "Would a recommendation from Viren help?"

Ezra shrugged. "Maybe. In my opinion the more the merrier when it comes to college admissions. But I don't really see how you'll get one." He lowered his voice, leaning closer. "From what I've observed, your relationship isn't exactly *prospering*."

Leah chuckled. "I have my ways."

Just then, the door to the gym creaked open. Savana walked in with a bag strung over her shoulder— red hair a darker shade than usual.

"Hey Ezra," Savana waved, a smile plastered on her face. She seemed not to notice Leah.

"Hey Savana!" Leah cried. "Did you re-dye your hair?"

Savana looked like Leah just asked if she drenched the locks in blood.

Leah swallowed, crossing her arms. "It… it looks good."

Savana ignored this, pulling her shoes from her bag. Leah scowled, holding back the insults begging to breach her tongue. She looked at Ezra, who seemed very interested in the ceiling.

"Fine," Leah mumbled. She strode to Savana, watching as her fingers slipped under her shoe lace. She brightened her voice to the highest, fakest octave and spoke the words she'd been rehearsing since that conversation with Ezra.

"Hey, can we talk?"

Savana looked up. Slowly, deliberately, with a look of such disgust you may have thought she literally ate shit. Her upper lip curled into a scowl: she folded her hands in her lap, meeting Leah's gaze.

She stood, her anguish turning into a mocking smile. "Do you remember the last time we had a 'talk?'"

“I do,” Leah responded, biting her tongue to hold back additional thoughts on their last heart to heart.

“Well then,” Savana cooed. “Be my guest. Let’s have a *talk*.”

“Great.”

“Great.”

“*Great*.”

Leah held her smile. As did Savana— though it seemed less fake and more patronizing. Eventually, Leah let down the act of joy and returned to her natural glare.

“Outside.” She drawled. “Now,”

If Savana had an insult, she didn’t use it. Instead, she followed Leah to the soccer field. Whatever screaming match likely to take place would be safe from any echoes.

Leah’s braids wavered around her as the wind ruffled her clothes. Savana’s brown skin reflected the building lights, shining with an eerie glow.

“Well?” Savana tilted her head. “What did you want to talk about?”

“Look,” Leah breathed a sigh. “I—” her words fumbled; and suddenly they weren’t there anymore.

Savana rolled her eyes. “This was a waste of time—”

“I’m sorry, okay?” Leah blurted. Savana froze— and just for a moment, her anger vanished. She looked at Leah like she was fake— like an apology was simply a myth.

“What?” Savana breathed.

“I’m sorry for all that I said.” Leah said. “I’m sorry for relentlessly demeaning your game. I’m sorry for competing with you every second I got. For all the little comments, Savana. I’m *so sorry*.” Leah paused, taking a breath. “I— I miss our friendship. I miss when we got drunk together in Reno, and I miss being there for you.” Leah blinked the tears from her eyes. “I know what you’ve been through, Savana. I know because the same things happened to me. And I know you think only one of us can be the best— that only one of us can get that love that’s been deprived of us, but—” this time , Leah let the drops break her waterline. “But maybe we can be loved. Maybe there’s enough room on the court for the both of us. And maybe—” she extended a hand— a gesture of peace. “Maybe we can be friends again?”

Savana’s gaze shattered. Her eyes glossed over with tears and her hands shook. Leah was about to fling herself around her, press her face in Savana’s chest and forget every moment of the last year.

But then Savana's features hardened. She swallowed, tears vanishing. Then, a smile cracked her lips. Not a kind one, not anything close to remorse. But the smile Leah was recognized. The one used so many times on the court. The smile Leah learned to fear.

Savana's next movement was not a hug, but a fist at Leah's face.

Blood rushed to her nose. A crack collided with the air, quickly absorbed into the cold. Leah collapsed as pain ricocheted through her face, sending rivulets cascading down cheek.

She lowered her hand, realizing it was soaked with red. Leah gazed at Savana, who gazed at her knuckles like they were a blade.

Savana's grip forced Leah's chin up. She tried to jolt away but Savana's hand was strong, nails digging into her skin. They just looked at each other for a second, Savana's fiery, powerful gaze pouring into Leah's.

Then, Savana laughed.

"Did you really think that would work?" she cackled, throwing her head back. "I mean honestly Leah, I'm not an imbecile. Just because I'm winning doesn't mean you can win me over with your '*kindness.*'"

"Savana—" Leah gasped. Crimson tears dripped down her face, pooling on Savana's hand. "I thought—"

"'*You thought*?'" Savana mocked. "You thought you could forgive me? Oh, well in that case, Taven, let me make things very, *very* clear for you. I'm not looking for forgiveness. I'm not looking for your friendship and I'm not looking for any kind of love you can earn. My definition of success is victory. Me standing over your pathetic figure on the ground with a crowd chanting my name. *My* college acceptance letter. *My* fame. *My* glory." She tilted her head, red hair hanging over her glowing eyes. "And the best part of all this? You won't have *any* part in it."

Leah choked a sob. Savana released her, letting her bloodied chin fall onto the wet grass. Savana stood, wiping her hands on her shorts. She took one last look at Leah's figure crumpled and strode away, leaving her in the field.

Leah let out a screech, banging her fist against the ground. "Fuck!" tears tumbled down her cheeks, soaking into the grass. She looked up, eyes slits of anger. "God *dammit*!"

Come on, kid. Zahara's voice. Calm and poised— always a constant. Her mentor may have been mean; cruel even. But she would never leave her. Whenever she was broken on the ground, tears tumbling down her cheeks and mixing with her blood, Zahara was there. Whispering in here ear and telling her to get *the fuck up.*

Come on. Zahara murmured. *Not once have I ever seen you give up. Not once have you not bounded back. You know your power, you know your rage, and you know your potential.*

Leah stood, wiping her blood on her sleeve. Her heart pounded slower, but heavier. Rage encased her body, curving up her limbs and joining the morphine coursing through her veins.

Go ahead, her mentor cooed. *Let it consume you. Become your ambition. That's how you'll survive. Become your goals and stop at nothing to achieve them.*

THE CYCLE

"Power and funding rules over athletes, and there is nowhere for them to go otherwise that doesn't spit them back into the NSO pocket. Like it, deal with it, or your out, that's what we are told."
—Kerr, Gretchen, et al. *Prevalence of Maltreatment among Current and Former National Team Athletes.*

Leah pulled into the parking lot, circling into the nearest spot. She preferred to drive as close to the gym as possible— and as the rain was pattering hard on her roof and Leah's need for shelter had doubled. She didn't want to play the entirety of the game soaked.

Trisha, who was sitting in the front seat, had been unusually quiet. Her eyes were blank, and the lips that usually breached with so many questions barely opened.

Leah yanked the parking brake back and twisted the key from the slot. Her gaze drifted to Trisha. Her two front strands were pulled neatly into a tight bun— Leah didn't like it; the perfection didn't suit her.

"What's this?" Leah asked, cupping her hand over the bun. "Where's the braids? And the hooker strands? They're like your signature look."

Trisha's laugh was forced. Her shoulders shook forward, and when the huff was done, she flinched. Her hands shot instinctively to her stomach as she winced in pain.

Leah gave her a look. She extended a hand to Trisha's shoulder, but the kid shot away.

"Hey," Leah said. "I'm not going to hurt you."

Trisha didn't respond, gaze resting on the dashboard.

"Is everything okay, Trish?" Leah asked, worry creeping into her voice. "You look— really dehydrated. Do you have water?"

This time, Trisha made a move. She reached into her bag, pulling out an empty water bottle. Remnants of liquid remained at the bottom, but only a few drops. Leah made a face. "Well, there was an attempt at hydration."

"I filled it up, Leah."

Trisha's gaze stayed ahead, tears glimmering behind her eyes. Something had happened. Some part of her knew, but didn't want to believe it.

"I was playing with my dad—" Trisha swallowed. "Before you picked me up."

Leah took a breath.

"I kept missing my shots. I don't know what was happening, but the ball wouldn't go in the hoop." Trisha took a trembling breath. "He got mad— really mad. Then made me run— like a lot. I almost puked. And when it was over I tried to get some water—" her voice caught; a tear slipped from her eye. "And he poured it all out. Told me to go back to shooting. I made all my shots after that."

Leah sat still— perfectly still— eyes flickering with hot rage. Some part of her expected this— some part of her knew it was necessary. Trisha didn't become a prodigy from shits and giggles. Abused children became the spectacles of the world— a shining, broken star who burned with its own light. After all, Leah had her fair share of scars from Gael.

But Trisha was a kid.

Trisha was *her* kid.

No one fucking touched *her kid.*

"Trish," Leah dug her water bottle out of her bag. "Drink."

Trisha gave her a weary glance. "Are you sure—"

"*Trisha.*"

The kid tipped the water bottle back, the water dribbling down her chin and soaking her shirt. When she pulled the thing away from her lips, it was empty.

"Sorry," Trisha murmured. "I had all of it."

"Don't apologize," Leah said, her voice steady. She reached into her car door and pulled out an energy drink. "Drink."

Trisha unscrewed the top and downed the red liquid. The juice trickled over her neck, dying her already soaked shirt a bloody red.

"Good." Leah raised a protein bar from her bag. Trisha lunged for the food but Leah held it out of reach. "Show me the bruises."

Trisha gave her a blank stare.

"Oh don't play dumb with me," Leah scowled. "You think my dad didn't do the same? I can tell it hurts to laugh, Trish. *Show me*."

Trisha nodded, picking up her shirt. Dark blotches scattered her rib cage. Leah gasped, covering her mouth with a hand.

"May I?" Leah asked, reaching to touch Trisha's stomach.

The kid gave a small nod, and Leah's fingers gently grazed the bruises. She tried to be gentle, but every time she touched a blue mark Trisha flinched.

"How?" Leah drew, removing her hand.

"I'll tell you," Trisha pulled down her shirt. "But you need to give me that bar."

Leah extended her hand and Trisha snatched the food. With trembling hands, she tore off the rapper and devoured the thing.

"Trisha," Leah drew. "What did your dad *do*?"

Trisha wiped her mouth. "He— he's a good dad. All he wants is the best for me."

Leah released a rough cackle.

"Promise me, Leah." Trisha said. "Promise me you won't tell anyone."

Leah extended her pinky, offering a small smile. "You can trust me, Trish."

Trisha looped her finger through Leah's and nodded. "I'm—" she faltered. "I'm really bad at catching passes. My dad knows this— so when we're training together, he throws balls at me. Like— really hard. I've gotten better at catching them, but sometimes I miss. That's when the bruises happen."

Leah swallowed, anger bulging in her throat. "What else does he do?"

The kid tucked her knees to her chest. "He'll play really rough defense. Sometimes he'll scratch me— draw blood. But the physical stuff isn't that bad. He yells at me in public. Insults. I've gotten good at tuning them out. But when I'm in a game, I don't hear anything."

"What kind of things does he yell?" Leah asked.

"Pretty basic stuff," Trisha shrugged. "Incompetent. Bitch. Demeaning comments. Oh, and he'll hit me sometimes when I mess up. That's scary."

This time, Leah didn't ask anymore questions. She dug her fingers into the leather of the car, trembling with thick rage. Her eyes stayed in one place, not daring to meet Trisha's stare. Slowly, her vision turned red.

"Are you—" Trisha stammered. "Are you mad?"

Leah pressed her lips in a fine line. "Yes," she turned, hot gaze resting on the kid. "But not at you."

Trisha tilted her head. "Who are you mad at?"

Leah's lips quirked into a smile. She raised her fist and banged it against the steering wheel. The car horn screeched. Trisha flinched.

"*Everyone*." Leah drawled. "I'm mad at everyone who dwells within this game. It's fucking obvious, you know? Parents yell at their kids while playing —they're so fucking stupid they abuse in public. But no one gives a shit because—" she raised her octaves into a mockery tone. "*They're so talented; who cares about what mental struggle the kids go through? Those athletes should be grateful! Their parents are amazing*!" Leah banged her fist against the wheel. "Bullshit. That's why players like you and me and Ezra and fuck— even Savana— end up with bruises and nightmares that attack us every time we close our eyes. Because that is just *good parenting*."

Leah fell silent, her chest heaving with enough rage to fuel a dynasty. She dug her nails into the steering wheel, resting her head against its leather.

"Leah," Trisha started. "He's a good dad."

Leah couldn't help it. She laughed. Just a chuckle at first; but as the tears touched her eyes it morphed into a screech. She gasped, letting the rivulets plummet down her cheeks as morbid heat crawled into her lungs.

It was all hitting her at once. Every time Gael had hit or scratched or bruised her while playing. It was supposed to be an "accident." But what kind of accident happens every *fucking* day? With another cry, Leah was sent back to Gael's nails digging into her skin. She was fifteen again. Sobbing. *Begging* him to stop.

That was the last time she ever expected mercy.

"No," Leah rested her head on the steering wheel, strands of hair sticking to her tear stained face. "*No*. That is not good parenting, Trisha. That is *abuse*."

Trisha flinched at the last word.

"Here," Leah dug into her bag, pulling out a blade. It was just the kitchen knife she used when she visited Val. As much as she had contemplated digging the tip into the dealer's neck, it would never happen. "Take it."

Trisha tilted her head. "What for?"

"Next time your dad pulls shit like that," Leah drawled. "You take this, and you shove it up his dick."

The kid took the blade, examining the metal. She flipped it over, the metal reflecting against the light. Trisha tucked it into her jacket pocket, careful to conceal the hilt within the cloth.

"Why do you do it?" Trisha's voice was so quiet. "Why do you play?"

"I don't have a choice." Leah's chuckle was so dry. "You think my father would let me quit? You think yours would let you?"

Trisha swallowed. "But what if you had a choice? What if you were able to just walk away? Never pick up a basketball again." She looked at Leah. "Would you?"

Leah laid her hands on the wheel, staring into the rain. What if she was free? What if she could just walk away? Would she? Could she leave what she spent her entire life trying to accomplish? What was she without her sport? What was she without the fire of her own ambition burning her alive?

"No." Leah murmured, shaking her head. "No. I've spent my entire life working towards the NCAA goal. My entire being is surrounded by basketball. I'm nothing without this game, Trish. So no, I wouldn't leave."

Trisha took a breath. "Do you even want to go to the D1 level anymore?"

Leah's grip tightened. She didn't want to think about that question— it was too sad of one to answer. She swallowed, placing her head against the leather.

"I don't know, kid." Leah breathed. "I just don't know."

THE GREAT COMEUPPANCE OF EZRA SOREN

"20% of current athletes and 21% of retired athletes reportedly experienced at least one form of sexually harmful behaviour while only 12% of current athletes and 19% of retired athletes reportedly experienced at least one form of physically harmful behaviour."
—Kerr, Gretchen, et al. *Prevalence of Maltreatment among Current and Former National Team Athletes.*

Leah strode into the building, Trisha trailing behind her. The team was gathered on the bleachers, watching the game before them. Her eyes darted to Savana, hands curling into fists. But her enemy didn't look hostile— instead Savana was smiling. *Smiling*.

The motion made Leah's stomach flip. She clenched her jaw, fire crawling up her throat and pressing against her lips. Savana turned, catching her eye. Leah kept her gaze level— her eyes morphed into a glare. But Savana wasn't hostile, in fact, she looked calm, *kind*.

Then she waved.

Waved?

Waved.

"Hey," Trisha tugged on her jersey. "Everything okay?"

Leah sighed. "Fine. All fine, Trish.

Ezra was bristling against the wall, watching the game with unwavering intent. His eyes followed the ball religiously— like if he took his focus off the court he might burn.

Then he saw Leah.

She remembered exactly how his face shifted. Every detail of the way he looked at her in that moment. First his eyes widened; then his lips parted and he heaved a breath. The soft gaze Leah had almost managed to trust twisted into ferocity. Ezra's blue eyes tightened on her, like a rope wrapping around her neck.

It was only when she approached him when she realized how pale he was.

Not only that, but bruises peaked from under his sleeves. The light in his eyes had vanished, replaced with a blank, knowing stare.

"Ezra?" Leah extended her hand. "Are you okay—"

The coach slapped it away. Leah recoiled, swallowing. "We need to talk." Ezra drawled. "Outside."

He hit her shoulder as he passed, nearly running to the door. Trisha gave her a look.

"It's okay, kid." Leah smiled. "I'll be fine, alright?"

Trisha nodded, Leah offered one last grin and sprinted after Ezra, braids flying behind her.

Ezra was standing in the rain— the tiny droplets tracing his features as they dripped to the floor. He didn't look at her; instead his gaze was locked on the ground. Leah could've imagined it, but she thought she saw tears accompanying the water.

"Ezra?" Leah called, placing a hand on his shoulder. "Hey is everything—"

As soon as she touched him, Ezra spun around. Leah barely comprehended the blow coming at her face. It was as if it didn't happen. Her mind didn't want to believe that it *had* happened.

But a mark reddened on her cheek and she toppled to the wet concrete. There was no denying that Ezra was looking down with enough rage to burn a forest.

He hit her.

Ezra Soren, her coach, friend and found father *hit her.*

"Ezra–" Leah stammered. There was a tint of a laugh in her voice. She wanted to believe that maybe— just maybe— this was all a sick joke. "What—"

"Don't play dumb with me, Leah," Ezra breathed— his voice was so low. "I know what you did."

What had she done? Maybe there was some mistake that occurred and that was why Ezra stood over her, trembling. Why was he *trembling*? Had she done something to make him this angry?

But when she looked closer she didn't see fury in his features. No, there was barely any rage at all. Instead, Ezra held a composure of vulnerability. His lower lip twitched and tears pricked the edges of his ice eyes. Amongst his fingers was a light twitch. He looked broken, shattered, *scared.*

Ezra wasn't angry. He was hurt.

And Leah had never done *anything* to hurt him.

"I trusted *you*," Ezra said, his low rasp quivering. "How could you, Leah?"

It was only then when the full reality of the situation hit her. She didn't know what she did, but she had done *something*. Something *awful*. Something large enough that Ezra was going to *leave her*.

Ezra hated her.

"Ezra I swear—" Leah cried. "I don't know what you're talking about. Please— I didn't do—"

"Anything?" Ezra finished. "Anything, Leah?" he let out a stout cackle. "Oh, I should've known. The likes of you are reckless, selfish creatures. You're just like the rest of them, aren't you? Just like your father, just like every single person in this game. Ambitious enough to *kill* for it, aren't you, Leah?"

"Ezra—" Leah began. "I swear to you, Ezra. I don't know—"

"*Viren*!" he screeched. Leah flinched away. "I gave everything for you, Leah. I did everything to make sure he didn't— he didn't…"

And then she understood. The dots connected, the stars aligned. It was Viren who had raped Ezra. that was why he hated him. That was why he was so protective of his girls. He was protecting them from *men like Viren*.

"My number, Leah," Ezra murmured, more to himself than to her. "My address. You gave him my goddamn *address*."

Leah had done many things for this game. Bought from the black market, doped morphine, isolated herself, given her body— her soul— for her goals. But Ezra was the only man she had ever trusted— ever *loved*— in her life. She would do anything for this game, but Ezra's safety was the line she wouldn't cross.

"Ezra." Leah began. She was surprised at the tranquility of her tone. "Listen to me. I know what happened was awful— I know you're angry—" Leah got to her feet, arms outstretched in front of her. "But you know me, Ezra. I would do anything for this game, but I wouldn't betray you. I don't know who sent your address to Viren, but please; *It wasn't me*."

Ezra's gaze melted. The anger and betrayal sunk from his face, leaving behind a blank haze. Was he about to apologize? Was he going to hug her and tell her he was sorry? How fast would she forgive him? Would she simply ignore the bruises on her face or would she retaliate? Could she ever truly hate him?

As it turns out, she never got the chance to find out.

"Liar," Ezra's drawl was simple, quiet. The tone was deep, but light enough to mistake as an unimportant mumble. At first, Leah thought she heard wrong.

"*Liar*!" this time, Ezra hollered the word. He advanced on her, the familiar shatters of emotion scraping his features. "Why do you lie, Leah?"

Then she realized: really *realized*. This was a hurricane, a thousand bricks, a million bullets she herself had fired. Ezra wouldn't believe her because she was the only one who was this extreme. No one else could ever go this far for their goals, this *game*. No one else could give— could *take*— this much for their ambition. No one. No one…

No.

One person.

Savana.

Goddammit *Savana Afren*!

"It was Savana!" Leah blurted. "I swear, it was Savana. I don't know how, but trust me Ezra—"

"Stop *lying*!" Ezra's knuckles plummeted into her face. "This isn't something you can just blame on her! Enough with this stupid game, Leah! You did this. *You* pay the price."

It was then that Leah started hyperventilating.

"No no *no*!" Leah gasped. "Ezra, you have to believe me. It wasn't—" her balance broke into a million pieces. She fell to the ground, nails digging into the cold concrete. "It wasn't me! *Please*, Ezra! You know me!

Another blow flung into her cheek. The air choked her, each breath burning her throat.

"Do you know what it's like, Leah?" Ezra drawled. "Do you know what it's like to have to fight someone twice your size? To be helpless as they tear off your clothes and touch— oh god—" Ezra punched her shoulder. Leah screeched, scurrying away from him. "He came to my house last night. I had to fight him to keep him from doing it again. I was ready to kill him. Do you know what it's like to have a blade in your hands; to know that at any moment you may have to shove it into a man's heart?"

Leah couldn't respond. Even if she did have words, her lips wouldn't open, She clutched her chest, scrambling on the wet floor. Ezra loomed over her, tears trailing down his cheeks. He looked broken; betrayed .

But that betrayal was scarred with anger. Ezra's features twisted and contorted with rage, all pointed towards her.

"Ezra *please*!" Leah begged. "I didn't— I swear Ezra, I didn't do it! I would never do it!"

"*Liar*!" Ezra hollered. "Stop *lying*!"

His fists kept coming. Leah tried to dodge them, swinging her head to the side as Ezra's blows drew blood and bruises. She squirmed away, but his grip landed on her shoulders, preventing her from moving.

"No no *no*!" Leah sobbed. "Ezra I promise! I would *never* do that to you. I—" it was then she dared to open her eyes, to see his face looming over her, tears pricking his eyes and lips curling into a scowl. "I *loved* you."

This time, Ezra didn't say anything. He didn't call her a liar, didn't protest her statement. Leah managed to capture a twinge of grief in his eyes— only a moment before Ezra's pain resumed.

Maybe part of him believed her. Maybe he wanted to believe her. But love was confusing; love was *hard.* Love played favorites. Hate didn't discriminate.

And that's why his punches came at her face. That was why he held her throat tight, not relenting when she screeched in pain. He didn't let up. Not when blood flew from her tongue, not when her nose cracked, and not when the cries turned to suffocating sobs.

He wasn't going to stop. No matter how hard she pleaded, he would keep punching her. The man who cared was gone, replaced by a haze of rage and hurt. In the moment, the only safe thing to feel was rage.

Leah's emotions evaporated. She let the blood seep between her teeth and roll down her cheek. She found the euphoric sensation in her bruises. In her demise, she found power. Just like the morphine coursing through her veins, there was power in this pain.

Ezra stopped when she smiled.

"Oh come on, *Ezra*!" Leah spat. "Finish me off. Leave me bleeding in the rain. Kill me. Maybe you couldn't end Viren, but you can sure as hell end me. What are you waiting for?" Leah ran her tongue along her red teeth. "*Kill me*."

Ezra didn't say anything. He didn't try to protest, didn't shoot back with hate. He let the tears slip down his cheeks as he raised his fist.

Leah locked eyes with him, her gaze metallic with the crimson on her tongue. She watched his pain, watched the way his eyes flitted between scared and angry. And as she watched his suffering, she tried her best to suppress the pang of empathy.

His knuckles came at her. Time slowed. Leah closed her eyes, letting a tear slip down her cheek. It wasn't because of the pain— it never was. It was because after everything, Ezra had turned against her. Like every single person in her life, he *left her*.

But as his fist neared her face, a third body entered the space between them. She leaped onto Leah, turning to Ezra. With a smooth, deliberate movement, Trishy Lively pressed a blade to Ezra's throat.

Leah's expression twisted.

"*Stop*!"

She hadn't realized she yelled until Ezra froze. They held their position. Ezra's tear stained face, Leah's bloodied lips and Trisha's blade, held steadily at Ezra's skin.

Trisha was first to move. She released her knife and clung to Leah's blood stained uniform, refusing to let go.

"Get off!" Leah squirmed. "Get out of here, kid!"

Trisha didn't relent.

Ezra drifted off of her, wiping the splatter of red from his cheek. He simply stood for a second, looking down at Leah's broken figure.

"I'll coach you until you leave for college, Leah." He finally said. "But from here on out, don't talk to me. Whatever stain of a relationship we had is gone. Washed away. The only reason I'm allowing you to continue playing is because you're skilled. Good for universities." He huffed a cackle. "Good for advertising."

He turned. Walked towards the gym. Walked away from her. Leah was left on the ground, legs folded beneath her, rain washing the blood that poured from her nose. Trisha sat beside her, head buried in the uniform. The blade rested on the ground, shining as the rain pattered on the metal.

Leah looked at Trisha. Tortured, hurt and misunderstood, Trisha Lively embraced her. The dead and the dying. The blade and the hilt. The future and the past.

Trisha was running Leah's path. Leah ran Zahara's. Zahara ran some other girls. Each found their crutch, each found their ambition, each found their anger. And each and every one was willing to *kill* for the game.

Hell. A torture. The worst part of the game was that there was no way out. Once you doped, once you gave enough of yourself you couldn't escape the competition without leaving most of yourself behind. The sport had already eaten Zahara, Leah was too far in. But Trisha—

She only had one foot in the door.

What were a few toes?

"You need to go," Leah murmured, her voice barely audible over the rain.

Trisha picked up her head, gazing into Leah's eyes.

"You need to run, kid." She stood, her legs shaky beneath her. "You need to get out of here. Quit. Get as far away from this game as you can."

"What?" Trisha stammered. "Leah, my dad—"

"Tell someone what you told me." Leah retorted. "A teacher, a counselor— I don't care. They're mandated reporters. What you've experienced is the textbook definition of abuse. Child protective services, Trish. They'll get you out of there."

"No they won't, Leah!" Trisha's tone was fierce, an edge Leah never heard scraping her syllables. "Sports abuse is praised, remember? Definitions don't matter. This game is a loophole. A loophole no one dares trust."

"I don't care!" Leah blurted. "Run, doesn't matter where. But Trisha—" she swallowed. "You *have* to get out of here."

She leaned down, grasping Trisha's shoulders. "Me, you, Zahara, whatever unfortunate girl came before her— we're stuck. Funneled into this game by our parents and unable to escape. Unless you *run*."

"Leah—" Trisha choked, tears trickling down her face. "Leah, I can't—"

Leah wiped the rivulets with her thumb. "Don't cry," she whispered. "You can't afford it."

Trisha swallowed, dabbing at the droplets. She stared at Leah, looking into her face like it was filled with poison. Then her features twisted with horror. She grabbed Leah's jersey, tugging her.

"What about you?" Trisha shrieked. "Come with me! Leah *please*, I need you!"

"I can't leave." Leah murmured. "My withdrawal symptoms would kill me within a week. That is if I didn't kill myself first."

Trisha grabbed onto Leah, wrapping herself around her. "So what will you do?"

Leah turned, gazing at the gym door. The yellow light illuminated the court, the rhythmic sound of basketballs pounding against the floor.

Ezra was in there.

Savana was in there.

Leah took a breath, wiping a drop of blood trailing down her lip. "Embrace my fate with open arms."

THE SINE LUNI

Leah strode into the gym, water droplets splattering on the floor as her braids flew behind her. Blood trailed from her wounds, retrieved by Leah's sleeve before it splattered to the floor.

Savana was in the midst of warm ups, talking to her teammate. Her dark skin glowed in the light— separating her from the rest of the crowd. Her hair hung in a pony tail, the strands coming loose and falling around her face.

For a moment, she looked innocent.

Leah planted a hand on her shoulder, pushing her forward. Savana's expression took on a glaze of panic. When she saw Leah, it shifted to one of confusion, and then mild amusement.

"What happened to you?" she squinted. "Did you get into a tift with a badger?"

Leah let out a laugh, her voice higher than it had been in a long time. "To think I once *trusted* you." She snorted. "You vile, disgusting, attention whore of a person—" she shoved her again, but it escalated to a brawl, and soon Leah found her nails climbing to Savana's face. "I'll—"

And then hands were on her. They grabbed her shoulders, pulling her backwards. Leah turned to see her teammates, yanking her away from Savana.

"Hm," Savana touched Leah's nose; she snarled. "Really Leah? Over-dramatic much? Well—" she turned away, blood red hair pooling over her shoulder. "I suppose you always were a bit over kill. Hey, maybe you should go to the hospital. That badger might have had rabies." She chuckled. "I would hate to see you become even more barbaric than you already are."

Leah lunged at her, only to be held back by her teammates, and suddenly someone had a hand over her mouth— muzzling her like a wild animal. Tears slipped from her eyes, dripping onto the floor with her blood. Panic crept up her limbs, infecting her heart with the cold touch of defeat and failure.

Stop it. Zahara. Always, forever Zahara. *Pull yourself together. It's not over yet. You haven't failed.*

But I have! Leah lowered her head, letting her tears splatter onto the ground. *There's nothing else, Ezra's gone, Trisha's gone, Savana's gone—*

So avenge them. Zahara drew. *You have me, you have yourself and you have your fire. That's all you need. Beat that bitch— maybe you've lost everything, but make her lose even more.*

Leah closed her eyes, breathing a heavy breath. She sunk into her memories, into her rage. She spiraled back into Zahara— that very last time she saw her mentor play. An extension of herself— the only personality she ever cared to have. A martyr, a legend and someone so incredibly powerful. Zahara could do anything; Zahara wasn't afraid to sacrifice *everything.*

But she had a parallel. A girl just like her— identical in every way except appearance. Just as legendary, just as driven; always that same fire. The only difference was when the time came, she lost.

And suddenly, it wasn't Zahara anymore.

Leah could've sworn that Daniella Vallran was standing in front of her.

She had never once formally met her, but she remembered her presence. The powerful, strong woman— every inch of her placed just slightly off of perfection.

Do it. Daniella's voice was like a million shards of glass all shattering together. *And this time, win.*

Leah raised her head. She blinked the tears from her eyes, evaporating the sting with her rage. She said the words slowly— each syllable hot in her mouth. But every word was deliberate, loud, and undeniably clear.

"Sine Luni."

Her teammates released her, backing away. Leah barely felt their hands retract. She stood straighter, picking up her chin. The gym had gone silent— all eyes on them.

Savana turned, her eyes widening. "What?"

"Goddammit, Savana." Leah wiped a drop of blood sliding from her lip, "*Sine Luni.*"

She nearly screeched the last bit, the words coming from her mouth like serpents— strangling the room in and squeezing every bit of breath from the game's lungs.

Savana swallowed. She reached back, tightening her pony tail. Then her hands fell to her waist, clasping behind her back.

"Is that what you want, Leah?" she asked. "Even if you lose?"

Leah fixed her glare on Savana, brushing her braids behind her back. "I don't *lose.*"

Savana chuckled, a glacial smile spreading across her face. She ran her tongue along her teeth, her words tainted with sugary poison. "Fine," she took a step forward. "You want a fight, Taven? I'll make sure you never forget it."

The entire gym was silent by the time they gathered at half court. Honestly, the audience had faded into oblivion, Leah's rage swallowing their presence. Savana stood in front of her, eyes glazed with heat. She wasn't staring at anything in particular, but her gaze held a fiery power that consumed her being. With the amount of ambition lighting up her features, her red hair might have been made of fire.

Leah's braids wavered behind her as she approached the center line. When she stopped, her hair swayed, halting at her waist. Savana matched her expression, finally meeting Leah's gaze. Fire on fire, staring iris to iris. They held the other's gaze until it burned; until both of their rage threatened to turn to ash.

The referee approached them, holding out the ball. Leah and Savana both touched it, fingers briefly sliding over each other.

The ball was thrown into the air— it halted for a moment, hesitating to commence the battle. But it fell none the less, and the massacre of both their lives began.

Leah leapt in the air, hands brushing across the object's surface. She pushed it forward, managing to get a hold of the possession.

Her head jolted back. She stumbled to the floor, realizing Savana had grabbed hold of her braids. Leah spun around, grabbing her opponents hands and yanking them from her hair.

But Savana was already bolting for the ball. Leah scrambled to her feet, the morphine dripping power from every pore of her body. Just as her enemy grabbed the ball, Leah tackled her. She went for Savana's waist, pushing her to the ground,

"*Agh*!" Savana screeched as Leah's knee dug into her chest. Leah didn't play any mind to the scream. She was already sprinting down the court, ball rolling in her hands.

Leah extended into her layup, tipping the ball off her hand. But just before she could finish her form, something slammed into her back.

She toppled over, weight slamming forward. She managed to turn, gazing into Savana's wild, ferocious eyes.

Leah collided with the wood, the crowd roaring in her ears. Pain exploded through her skull as it hit the court and black folded over her eyes. The ball was rolling out of bounds—

Her hands hit the wood, attempting to haul the rest of her up. But before she could get to her feet, Savana laid her knee on Leah's throat.

She clawed at her neck, attempting to dislodge the limb blocking her airway. Savana cackled, throwing back her head. She pressed her weight deeper, spitting on Leah's face.

The basketball rolled farther and farther towards the sideline. Leah gasped, choking on her own skin. Savana could've easily gotten it— scored the point while Leah caught her breath. But she didn't— she stayed, suffocating her enemy first.

"Savana—" Leah choked. "The ball—"

Savana tilted her head. Her gaze drifted to the object laying on the floor, then back to Leah. "Oh, that?" she snorted. "Why on earth would *that* matter now?"

Leah gasped, the air around her suddenly very cold.

"This isn't about the game." Savana leaned down, lips brushing across her ear. "It was never about the game. You know that. That ball was just a pawn like every other thing within this gym. All pieces in the real goal—" she lifted her head, and before Leah could comprehend the blow, Savana's knuckles pounded into her face. "That only one of us can have—" she withdrew her fist. "The glory—" another punch. "The safety—" Leah's lip slit, blood dribbling down her chin. "The *love*."

Leah choked as the red crept through her lips, the metallic taste landing on her tongue. She turned her head, the sidelines fading into the vision. Ezra stood there, arms crossed over his chest. He didn't wear any emotion over his face— no grief, no anger, no sadness. And he stayed perfectly still, watching her demise without a flinch.

Trisha wasn't here. No one was going to slide a weapon to her like she had done for Zahara so many years ago. Serena wasn't there to pull her out of her thoughts this time, Val wasn't going to help— she never did. And her mom—-

She was the first one to leave.

No one was going to save her.

Not now, not ever.

She had to get out of this one on her own.

Leah closed her eyes, summoning every bit of her drug, her ambition and her fire. Every inkling of pain and suffering and torment she endured throughout her life was brought to the forefront of her mind. The morphine joined the hurt, running through her legs like a tiger begging to strike. And with every ounce of her agony, Leah swung her knee into Savana's stomach.

Her enemy gasped. Savana's grip loosened, just enough for Leah to squeeze from her trap. She sprinted to the ball, pounding it to life and moving to the three point line. Her shot hadn't left her hand when Savana's fist collided with her throat.

Leah doubled over, the blood returned to her mouth. She hacked a cough, the red flying onto her hand.

A cheer erupted from the crowd. Leah turned to see Savana sprinting down the court, a smile gleaming on her features. She had scored— of course she had. One up on Leah— an advantage. And her enemy stood there— soaking up that advantage with gluttonous pride.

Leah stood, the morphine pushing her to her feet. Her vision narrowed, squaring in solely on the court. The ball pattered against the floor, laying right where Savana left it. She picked it up, letting the thing spin in her hand before punching it against the wood.

Savana was on defense now, legs bent in her stance. She grinned, slapping her hands on the floor before they flew to her sides, creating a makeshift barrier.

Leah crossed over, sending a glance to the right before barreling through her opponent. In normal circumstances, the move would've worked. But as she dodged Savana's defense, another tactic hit her.

Her knees buckled as Savana's foot came into the small of her back. She collapsed on the ground, the air leaving her lungs once again. The ball slipped from her grip, rolling to the side.

This time, Savana didn't bother with Leah's fallen figure. She raced for the object, sprinting down the court and laying the ball in the basket.

The crowd screamed. Two in a row. Two in a row. One more and Savana would win it. Tears began to sting Leah's eyes as the rage slowly trickled into defeat.

Shut up! Zahara's voice. *Dammit shut up, Leah*!

Her mentor had been angry at her before— at least in her head. But she had never sounded it. Her voice was always smooth; like she really couldn't care less if Leah lived or died. But now her tone had an edge, a spark.

Zahara had won her Sine Luni.

And she would not let Leah lose hers.

Get up. She snarled. *Get up Leah. Fight back. All of this— all your late nights and early mornings and sacrifices— they were not for nothing. That girl took everything from you. Ezra, your kid, and your friendship*.

Leah picked up her head, tears cascading down her face. The morphine was back; her tears seemed to glow a toxic blue. The drug rushed through her body— summoning the hate back into her heart.

You may not be able to get your life back. Zahara said. *But you can sure as hell take Savana's*.

Leah stood, power radiating from her finger tips. The morphine had absorbed her pain— every loss, blow and bruise had been transformed. Hurt was no longer a part of her. Right now, the only safe thing to feel was *rage*.

She picked up the ball, sprinting down the court. Savana stood before her, red hair hanging over her shoulder. Just as she approached her enemy, Leah stopped.

They paused, years of unspoken history lingering between them. The anger didn't leave, and neither did the competition, but for the first time, they both seemed to acknowledge how irredeemably fucked they were.

"All of us were pawns to you, right?" Leah breathed. "From the very beginning, you used us."

Savana didn't bother to deny it.

"First, you used me to gain skill and social status. You took my relationships with the team and Ezra and everyone— just for your own leverage. Then, when you didn't need me anymore, you abused my envy," It seemed the only sound in the gym was the constant rhythm of the ball pounding against the court. "That's when Swan comes in. She was always your puppet— you played up her excellence to get under my nerves. But you didn't believe a word of praise that came from your filthy mouth. You said it yourself— Swan didn't have what it takes, and eventually, she would fall off. I was the only obstacle from becoming the best." Leah's gaze wandered. Swan was standing on the side of the court, the biggest pawn in the world, only realizing how insignificant she was. Tears drifted down her cheeks— betrayal revealing she heard every word.

Leah actually felt bad for her. Savana— possibly her only friend in this game, always used her. Maybe Swan was oblivious and naive to everything,

everything, but she still had her own battles. And because of Savana— because of both of them, her life had just gotten so much worse.

Leah raised her chin, letting a tear slide from her eyes. "And then there was your final blow. Ezra. You found his weakness, abused it, and put the blame on me." Leah didn't look at her coach. She couldn't bear it. "Destroyed the only guidance I had in the world. And then you just laughed."

Savana simply stood in front of her, neither denying or confirming Leah's words. There was no emotion on her face, no show of care or remorse. Maybe she couldn't even feel anymore.

"You *laughed*." The anger returned to Leah's voice. "Laughed at me, laughed at Ezra, laughed at Swan. All these people who once cared about you, and you betrayed them, and for what?" Leah tilted her head, scoffing. "A title? A college scholarship? The bragging rights of defeating *me*?"

Savana took a step forward. A smile curled along her face— as vile and disgusting as a grin could be. "Well," her voice was small, laced with every bit of cruelty in the universe. "It worked, didn't it?"

Leah met her eyes, the morphine boiling up her veins. Then she crossed over, ball flying to the side. The drug flew from her eyes, leaving its trace in her wake.

"No," Leah smiled, heading for the basket. Savana followed, dropping into her defensive stance. "That's where you're wrong. See, I'm not a pawn. I'm not someone who can be manipulated or tricked—" Savana aimed a blow at her back, but Leah spun around it. "I am still very much your *opponent*."

Leah let the ball spin in her fingers. She could've easily gotten around Savana with a hesitation or spin— but this wasn't just about basketball. It was never about the game or the team.

It was about besting the other.

Leah slammed her knuckles into Savana's face.

She stumbled back, clutching her nose. Blood splattered her lips, dripping down her chin and falling on the court. Savana's gaze flew up, filled with cold, sweet shock.

She was surprised Leah hit her.

Leah sprinted into the key, shoving past Savana. Her layup was smooth, swishing through the net and landing on the floor.

The crowd erupted with chaos, thrilled at the sudden rise of competition. Leah barely heard the applause— she couldn't lose focus.

Kill her! Zahara snarled. *Absolutely destroy her*!

The figures in her mind wanted blood. Leah vowed to deliver it.

Savana dribbled up the court, red dripping onto the wood as she ran. Leah bent into her defensive stance, but instead of following Savana's moves, she lunged for her waist, tackling her to the ground.

They collapsed on the floor, the ball slipping away. Leah scrambled towards it, only for Savana to pull her braid. She shrieked, retaliating with a fist at the girl's face. Savana swerved, making her way towards the ball before Leah tackled her to the ground.

Leah placed her hands over Savana's throat, holding her head in place. "Get off!" she screamed. "Dammit—"

"Tap out, Savana." Leah drawled. "*Tap out*!"

But she didn't. Savana continued to struggle, bringing up her knee into Leah's stomach. She was knocked off, allowing Savana to escape. But Leah was faster; she grabbed the ball, sprinting down the court in the opposite direction.

Her head was yanked back. She reeled, eyeing Savana with her braid. Her enemy sprinted forward, lunging for the ball. Leah went for her legs, sending her to the ground.

Savana yelped, hands flying to her ankle. Leah didn't pay any mind to her, instead seizing the possession and racing down the court. Her shot was simple — off the backboard and from the block. But when it fell, the entire gym erupted.

Two even. A tie. The next shot won. The crowd was calling for blood, Zahara was calling for blood; *everyone wanted blood.*

Leah ran down the court, not giving the audience the grace of her glance.

Savana was still on the floor. Her legs folded under her, pain etching her features. She pressed her palms against the floor, attempting to haul herself to her feet. When that didn't work, she collapsed, a small wail escaping her lips.

"Tap out, Savana!" Leah screeched. "You've lost!"

She turned, face painted with enough hate to light up a town. Her eyes, traced with tears, ignited with rage. The hair dripping over her face was blown aside, and slowly, Savana managed to stand.

Maybe it was a drug, maybe it was a crutch, or maybe it was simply pure will, but Savana Afren dribbled up the court, coming at Leah like nothing ever happened.

Leah wasn't on defense anymore. When Savana's blow came at her face, she wasn't playing basketball. The wartime simulation had molded into a battle and one of them would be the casualty. Leah ducked, swiping for the ball. She managed to touch the leather before Savana crossed it between her legs and charged at the basket.

She went up for the layup, ball gliding off her hands. The entire gym slowed to a stand-still, watching as the shot sailed through the air. It only made it a few feet before Leah swatted it and pummeled the ball to the floor.

The crowd roared— the sound almost nonexistent. She turned to Savana, aiming a blow at her face before sprinting after the ball. Her enemy's blood stained her knuckles, dripping down her fingertips.

But Leah didn't notice it. She didn't notice anything. The morphine had taken hold of her senses, ripping away everything that made her human. She dribbled down the court, Savana at her heel.

A punch slammed into her spine. Leah doubled back, the breath rushing from her throat. But as she fell, her drug caught her, absorbing her pain into its never ending obis.

She regained her dribble, but not before Savana made the gain on her. Leah threw the ball between her legs, hovering along the three point line. Her opponent matched her stride, lunging at her face. Leah twirled around the attack, heading for the basket before Savana yanked her back.

The ball slipped from her grasp. Leah reeled on her opponent, plummeting her fist into her neck. With the spare time, she regained her dribble, backing out of the key.

Savana recovered quickly, closing out. Leah waited— then stepped back into her shot. The ball slipped off her finger tips, sailing in a smooth, clear arch. Savana stumbled into her, sending both of them to the floor.

They just watched for a moment. Not enemies anymore— just kids. Like Daniella and Zahara had been. Kids watching a shot that decided if all that they'd worked for— all that they'd sacrificed, all the terrible things they'd done were worth it.

The ball flew through the net, finishing the game with a crisp swish.

The crowd erupted. Cheers and screeches echoed around the gym, making the floor thrum with excitement. The rush of morphine faded from her ears, finally allowing her glory to sink in.

But her gaze wasn't on the crowd. Not yet. Her focus remained on Savana— the loser. She just stared at the net, her eyes blank. Leah expected her to break down; to start sobbing like Daniella had. But she wore that same look that gave away absolutely nothing.

Leah actually felt bad for her.

She left you, Zahara's cold rasp— so hard it might've been real. *Destroyed Ezra and made Trisha leave. Don't you dare take pity.*

Savana stood. She didn't bother to look at Leah, instead striding to the locker room with practiced proficiency.

Leah watched her go, the fire slowly dying in her gaze. She took a breath, wiping the blood from her face.

When she strode to half court, it wasn't rushed. She did so with purpose— making sure everyone saw her movement. Leah ran her fingers through her hair, clearing the strands running down her face.

Then, she took a bow, her braids pouring over her shoulder. She extended her arms like a bird preparing for flight. Her words were slow, the rasp lower and darker than it had ever been. Because she had won. By god, she had finally fucking *won.*

Leah stood straight, her blood trailing down her lip. "I hope my sacrifice was worth your pleasure."

HOW FAR ARE YOU WILLING TO GO?

Everything was quiet after that night.

Leah didn't bother to practice— what was even the point? No more early mornings, no late nights. No more driving to games or picking Trisha up or running errands for Ezra.

Who even cared anymore? They all left her— everyone. She had shattered her world to win, and now no one was there to pick up the pieces.

She continued to go to school— keeping her grades just above ninety percent. AP tests were in the spring— and she still needed to pass those. D1 athletes needed to be excellent at every part of life, not just their sport. If Leah wanted any chance at Stanford, she needed to claw her way through these last agonizing months.

But after school she would go home, unravel her braids and lay on her bedroom floor. Gael gave her looks as she walked through the door— the smoke attempting to grab at her ambition. But there was none left— she had beaten Savana Afren and now her fire was snuffed out.

"You really should be practicing." Her father would comment. "You'll be rusty when you start playing college ball. They'll kick you off the team."

Leah wouldn't respond. She'd just shrug and walk back to her room where she rotted on the floor.

The morphine lived by her bed, and slowly, she got sicker and sicker. The nausea, the aches, every bit of pain pulsing through her body. She couldn't move— her limbs wouldn't allow it.

The drug was the only thing that ever helped. When the panic seized her at night, capturing every inch of her mind. When images of her father, Ezra, Trisha, Serena, Savana, Zahara and her mom flashed through her mind— everyone who betrayed her, who left her.

The doses of morphine kept getting larger. First it was only a full syringe, then it transformed into one and a half, then two, then three. And soon she was going to Val's every week— getting closer and closer to death each time.

But the morphine fixed it. It always fixed everything. Every inkling of pain and grief went away as the liquid infected her veins. When it wore off, the effects got so much worse, but who cared? Leah would simply inject another syringe and then it was like everyone who abandoned her had never even been in her life.

Ezra texted her one evening. There wasn't any emotion in his words— no feeling at all. It was like he wasn't talking to a person, as if to him she was already dead.

Game tonight. River high school. Be there.

Leah sat up, hands sliding to her face. The tears came without permission, flashes of memory invading her head like they owned the place. The same man who promised never to hurt her, the same one who held her and allowed her to cry. The same man who she believed to be a second father. And now he hated her.

Like every person she ever came to love. They all left. All abandoned her. First it was her mother, then her father, and then a cascading domino of people who promised never to hurt her like the rest had.

And then they did so much worse.

Leah pressed her knees to her chest, tears rolling down her cheeks. A sob escaped her lips, the salty rivulets curving into her mouth. All alone. All alone. All alone. All alone.

She had always been alone. Ever since her mother left, she'd been alone. People came and went but the only true company was loyalty— and no one was loyal to her.

Leah was poisonous. Her entire life she believed she was a rifle— a weapon that could pinpoint an enemy and kill them. But she didn't get a choice who she killed. Anyone who dared to get too close would recoil as she slowly destroyed them.

Her hand curled around the syringe, dipping it into the flask and extracting the drug. She pressed the needle to her forearm, the liquid rushing down her spine and silencing every thought that dared cross her mind.

The euphoria recovered her, encasing her body in a beautiful cage. The chains of the drug lashed out, grasping her wrists and binding them to addiction. Slowly, the poison was pumped into her veins; so sweet as it killed her slowly enough to feel good.

Leah sat up, blowing out a breath. She weaved her hair into its usual braids, letting the locks drift down her shoulder. As she stood, the morphine flask tipped over. The liquid splashed at her feet, drenching her carpet.

To the normal eye, it was nothing but water. Just a simple spill. But for Leah, it was just as important as air. She picked up the bottle from the puddle, sighing. She would make a visit to Val's after the game.

The gym, as always, was buzzing. When she walked in, a hushed silence doused the crowd. Leah didn't give them the pleasure of her glance. They had already played too large a part in her tragedy.

Ezra and her team sat on the far end of the bleachers. Like the rest of the gym, they were silent. But they didn't pay any mind to Leah— she was simply invisible.

Instinctively, she moved next to Ezra. It took her a moment to realize he didn't want her anywhere near him. The only reason she was allowed to come to this game was because of her performance. She really was a delicious poison.

Savana sat beside Ezra, arms crossed over her chest. Bruises littered her arms, ones that Leah hadn't given. Her hair was in disarray; her pony tail plagued with tangles.

It was then that Leah realized she had never seen Savana without sleeves— at least not for a while. Bandages wrapped her wrists, extending all the way to her elbow. Something new she was trying to hide. Or maybe she'd been hiding it all her life and now she simply didn't bother with the cloth.

The buzzer went off. Slowly, the previous game trickled off the court, leaving behind a messy warm up routine. No one really bothered to try. What was the point? This game didn't matter, neither did the next or the next. The real competition was over and the rest was simply protocol.

Leah wasn't as rusty as she expected. Surprisingly, her shots went in with minimal effort. Her doping held up every part of her game and now she was more drug than human.

The whistle blew— only a minute until game time. The team jogged to the bench, Ezra already preparing his next round of plays. But he stopped; looking around like there was a piece missing to his masterfully curated puzzle.

"Where's Swan?" he asked. "She's usually late, but she's cutting it close."

Leah leaned back in her chair, running a hand over her face. She blew out a breath— the morphines' power wavering for only a moment.

Just then, the door creaked open. Swan strode through, wearing a dress that wandered at her knees. In her hand was a folded jersey— wrapped neatly in a ribbon. She jogged across the court, boots clicking against the wood floor.

"Here," she pressed the jersey into Ezra's chest. "I thought you might want this back."

"I—" Ezra was reluctant to take it. "You can't—"

"Can't what?" Swan tilted her head. "Quit? Why?"

"Why?" Ezra dropped the jersey, the thing flopping onto the ground between them. "Why— why would you want to?"

"I don't." Swan said.

"Then *why*?" Savana placed a hand on Swan's shoulder.

"Because I don't want to be like you." Swan picked up Savana's hand, holding it like it was contagious. "I don't want to end up like you and Leah. I want to live, and after seeing what you too have become—" Leah stood, her and Swan's eyes met. "Let's just say I don't want that."

She turned, her heel catching on her old jersey. With care, she lifted her boot, gently releasing the cloth and laying it on the bench.

"Swan wait—" Savana lunged forward, grabbing her shoulder. Swan spun around, pushing her back. A flicker of rage flashed across Swan's features before she regained her tranquility, running a hand through her hair.

"I hope you have a good life, Savana." Swan breathed. "Oh, and for future reference, friends are for much more than a strategic gain."

Then she walked away. Looking nothing like an athlete, Swan walked away from the game she bested everyone at. It looked like it didn't even hurt— like it was simply a necessity.

Savana watched her go, rage flashing through her like electricity.

God, how fucking ironic. Savana was right. After everything, she was *right*. But instead of how she imagined it, her own plan bit *her* in the ass!

A snicker escaped Leah's lips. She covered it with her hand— the restraint doing nothing to hinder her cackle. Soon, the laugh escalated and the eyes of her entire team rested on her.

But who cared? Who *fucking* cared? What were they going to do? *Leave*?

~~~

Leah didn't know whether they won or lost the game. She couldn't be bothered to care. After the last buzzer rang, she left. Didn't even stay to untie her shoes.
~~~

The morphine began to wear off and slowly the pain crept back into her bones. She got to her car and stepped on the gas, quickly switching into fourth gear and speeding onto the highway.

It was a twenty minute drive from River High to the south side. It took Leah about five minutes to get there. Five minutes and about an eighth tank of gas.

She parked in her usual spot, stepping out and striding along the streets. It was night by the time she got there, the sun well set behind the horizon. The sound of police sirens wailed in the distance— Leah pulled up her mask.

Val's door was unlocked. Leah didn't bother asking for permission anymore —she was such a frequent customer that the dealer allowed her to stride in as she pleased.

As usual, Val was sitting at her desk, legs flung over the table. Leah sat in her chair, pulling a wad of cash from her pocket.

"I wasn't expecting you." Val grinned. "Did you really use up all that morphine in three days?"

Leah scowled. "Not that it's any of your business, but I spilled it."

"Did you?" Val raised an eyebrow. "Where, exactly?"

"On the fucking constitution, Val."

The dealer sighed, removing her feet from the table and setting them on the ground. "You get less and less chatty every time I see you."

"I was never very chatty." Leah retorted.

"I never said the bar was very high." Val placed a glass bottle on the table, sliding it to Leah.

Leah pushed it back. "That's not even enough for a full syringe of morphine."

Val smiled, pushing the vile back. "This isn't morphine."

Leah picked the glass up, threatening to throw it at the dealer. "I don't really come here for watered down apple juice— so if you please, the *morphine*."

"Oh, trust me—" Val snatched the vile back. "This is much better than anything you've had before. Fentanyl. About a hundred times stronger than your current drug."

"I'm not interested in an overdose."

"Of course not, dear." Val flashed her white teeth. "Not yet. But this will last you a little longer— less of a strain on your blood stream, if you will."

Leah reached for the glass, weaving it through her fingers. "This thing has killed so many people…"

She had heard stories— news articles depicting the drug as dangerous; killing in mere minutes. People had taken it by accident, only a few milligrams. If this thing could murder so easily…

Leah looked up, centering her glare on Val. "Why would you try to kill me?"

For the first time ever, Val looked taken aback. "I'm… not?"

"I know, bad business move. I'm far too much of your profit by now. But that just begs the question, why are you trying to give me the death drug?"

Val raised an eyebrow. "Morphine's the death drug, darling. Fentanyl just speeds up the process."

Leah had a retort on her tongue— something she would never get to use. A clash rang through the walls— the shattering of glass following the noise. Val jumped up, eyes blazing with alert.

"Police!" a man's voice. "We're looking for Valania Frank."

"Shit!" before she knew it, Val was stuffing as many things as she could fit in her pockets. "We've been busted!"

Leah pulled up her hood, stuffing the fentanyl in her bag. "Do you have a way out?"

"Of course I do," Val snarled. She pulled up her carpet, revealing a metal hatch. "Come on!"

Leah followed the dealer into the hole, sliding down the ladder. The scent smacked her as soon as she hit the ground— the stench curling into her nose and making her gag.

"Where are we?" Leah choked, covering her face with her collar. "What's that smell?"

"Let's go." Val snapped, ignoring her. "We don't have much time. Do you have a phone?"

"Do you not?"

"No." Val shoved her to the side. "Don't fall in the sewage. Give me your phone."

"The *sewage*?"

"It's that or prison, Taven!" Val held out her hand. "Phone!"

"It's in my car!" Leah shoved her hands in her pockets, digging around. "I have a light."

She withdrew one of Gael's matches and created a flame. The underground was illuminated by dancing colors— the gray walls suddenly vibrant with orange and red.

Val snatched the fire, holding it in front of her. They jogged through the tunnels, the thick air catching in Leah's throat. Val, however, seemed relatively fine. Despite her age she ran with little struggle— and when she halted at the ladder, the dealer was barely short of breath.

She climbed out of the sewer, Leah on her heel. The night air was extra crisp in contrast to the muck of the underground. As soon as the oxygen touched her lungs, Leah doubled over— coughing out the thick sewage oxygen.

"What now?" Leah stood, turning to Val. But the space was empty where she stood just moments ago. Only the smell of her flowery perfume remained in her wake.

Leah looked into the sky. Police lights flickered around the city, flashes of blue and red lighting up the sky. Val had led her out of immediate danger then left— the dealer always looked for her own benefit. Leah couldn't blame her— she'd have done the same thing.

But now there was the issue of getting back to her car. She was a few blocks from the flashing lights where the cops had caught Val's operation. If she took the rooftops, she could assess where she was without rising suspicion.

A rusty ladder hung off the side of a building, swaying gently in the night wind. Leah leapt onto the metal, wrapping her fingers around the bars. She climbed it with speed, causing the ladder to squeak under her weight.

The shingles split as she raced along the roof. Her braids pulled behind, catching in the cold night hair. Leah held her hood over her face, sprinting to the cascading lights echoing around the south side.

She halted when she reached Val's building. Police cars surrounded the area, men carrying out crates loaded with vials and flasks. Leah peered down, recognizing the gruff figure held by Savana's father. His hands were planted firmly on his hips, an arrogant shine blooming from him in flashes of red and blue.

A cold wash of fear hit her, and suddenly, Leah was incredibly sure that if that man found her with Val, he would've killed her.

She shook off the terror, catching sight of her car in the distance. It was just a few blocks away— no more than a ten minute trek; five if she sprinted it.

Leah backed up, heels digging into the shingles as she leapt across the alley. Slowly, the blue and red lights faded into the distance as she ran along the rooftops, finding another old ladder and sliding to her car.

It unlocked with a click, the lights flashing. Leah slid into the driver's seat, thrusting down the parking brake and starting the car. Her feet landed on the clutch, the car sputtering to life as she switched to the gas.

She sped onto the street, releasing the gas and switching into second gear. Then third, then fourth. She stayed there. Fast, but not speeding— the dial resting at a steady forty miles per hour.

Her nails dug into the steering wheel, hands shaking and heart pounding. She sped around the turns, her body swinging to the side. Maybe this was why Zahara always drove so recklessly— right now, Leah wanted nothing more than to speed to a steady seventy miles per hour.

Blue and red filled the vehicle. Leah checked her mirror— a police car trailed behind her, sirens blaring to life. Her breath caught in her throat as the automated message broke through the air.

"Pull over."

"Pull over."

"Pull over."

No. *No*! Leah was suddenly very aware of the fentanyl resting in her pocket; the morphine coursing through her veins, so ingrained into her body it was as important as breath. Her needles lay in the back seat, remnants of the drug sloshing in the glass.

She couldn't get caught.

She wouldn't.

Leah punched the gas, her engine whirring up to speed. She released the gas, stomping on the clutch and switching into the fifth and final gear. The car sputtered, adjusting. Leah thrust her foot into the gas, accelerating to eighty miles per hour.

The police car followed, its horn singing behind. The red and blue illuminated her car, flashing through her windows. Leah spun the wheel, taking an unexpected turn.

But her wheels didn't stick. Her car screeched, spinning off of the road. Leah switched into neutral— slamming on the brake. But the car kept spinning, flying into a ditch and stopping just before the long grass.

Leah leaned forward, gasping as she leaned onto the steering wheel. The police car had stopped just before the ditch, lights blinking in red and blue flashes. The car was staring at her— stunned for a moment. As if it wanted the chase to go on.

Leah pressed the clutch, switching the car back into first. She shifted from the gas, but the car scrambled on the mud, eventually tilting backward and sputtering into a stall.

Her fist collided with the steering wheel, the car screeching in frustration. She tried again, the wheels skidding against the mud before the vehicle lurched, stalling a second time.

"*Fuck*!" Leah pushed her foot into the clutch— attempting to reverse. But the same happened. She was met with a stall. Stall. Stall. *Stall.*

The police car moved closer, wobbling off the road and rolling behind Leah. Just before hitting her tailgate, it stopped. There was a crackle and the loud speaker crackled to life.

"Step out of the car, Leah."

Not an automated message this time. A human voice, warped from the electronic but undeniable. Leah got out of her car, tipping back her hood and letting the blue and red light her face.

Savana stepped into the glow, still in her basketball uniform. Her red hair tipped down her shoulders, bleeding into her skin as the red flashed across her body. She folded her arms, confidence blowing off her with the night wind.

"Savana?" Leah breathed. "What are you doing here?"

Savana tilted her head. "What am I doing?" she cackled, the sound lifting into the air and intoxicating the night. "I'm winning."

She said the words so softly— the syllables blending into the night. It was so natural for her— stating her cruelty in the sweetest tone.

"It took me a while, but I think I finally figured it out." Savana grinned, drumming her fingers against her car.

Leah's lips curled into a scowl. "Figured what out?"

"You." Savana said, the warmth of her breath turning to mist in the cold. "I thought I could destroy you through jealousy, and when that didn't work I tried to demoralize you." She stepped forward. "But God, Leah. You only got angrier, faster, *better*. And then I thought— when was the only time I ever saw Leah Taven broken? And it hit me!"

Leah stepped back. "Ezra…"

Savana grinned. "When I left you, all those times I turned my back I heard your screams— your *wails*." Her voice was like syrup, dripping from her mouth and burning the floor below her. "And then I realized; for you, this game wasn't about winning. It wasn't about beating me or Swan. It was about love. Toxic, fleeting, ever so sweet *love*."

"And?" Leah spat. "That's why you do it too, isn't it? Because of your father, because he hurts you?"

Savana snorted. "Well *obviously*!" she extended her hand to Leah's shoulder, brushing a finger along her collarbone. "But it wasn't him doing it. No, it was always you. Because every time I failed, every time my shot rattled from the rim, I was compared to you. He wanted me to be *you*."

Leah stepped back, her foot slipping on the mud. Savana just smiled— that same stupid grin she'd had her entire life.

"I heard it, you know." Savana said. "Heard that story he told you— about Viren. About what happened to him— his peculiar predicament. Finding Viren's email wasn't hard; and of course I was already quite knowledgeable about Ezra. I only had to ask Viren to pin the blame on you— and well, he didn't take much convincing. Like for most people, Leah, you didn't leave a favorable impression."

"Viren is an *awful* person." Leah drawled. "And you willingly conspired with him—"

"Oh please," Savana shrugged. "I did nothing more than you. If you really thought he was so awful, you would've turned in that hard drive as soon as you found it."

Leah swallowed. How? How did she know this much? *How on earth* did Savana corner her in such a God awful position?

"I heard him leave you, you know." Savana trailed her hand along Leah's car, circling her like prey. "Only muffles at first, but then—" she chuckled. "Well, you have a tendency to scream very loud, Leah."

The anger pumped into her veins before she could stop it. The fire propelled her forward, and suddenly, Zahara's voice was back whispering orders in her ear.

Kill her.

Kill her.

Kill her.

Leah lunged for Savana's torso, only for her enemy to dodge. Savana laughed, her cackle filling the empty air. Leah turned, going for her face— but Savana spun away, pushing Leah forward and into the mud.

"You should be glad your little girl left." She jeered. "Because if you thought what I did to Ezra was bad—" she knelt next to Leah, lips brushing against her ear. "You should've seen my plan for Trisha."

Leah spun around, propelling her knee into Savana's stomach. She stumbled back, recovering much too quickly. "I beat you!" Leah spat. "I scored the third shot and I won our game. It's over!"

"Oh," Savana cackled, strands of red hair hanging over her face. "This is so far from over, Leah. Because you were playing a bigger game than I ever realized. For you it wasn't just the ball and the court— oh no, there was a third component."

Leah's breath caught in her throat.

"Valania Frank sells several drugs, right?" Savana regained her posture, brushing the strands from her face. "Specializes in opiates, if I'm not mistaken. So which one are you on?"

Leah swallowed.

"No no, don't tell me." Savana grinned. "Let me guess; oxycodone, opium, codeine?"

She looked up, as if trying to find the answer in the stars. Leah watched her every move, like she was a snake ready to pounce. But when her enemy's gaze shifted back, there was only a grin.

"Oh, I'm all through." Savana chuckled. "Tell me, what was it? You might as well give me this grace. After all, my father will find the answer in your blood in just a few minutes."

The air around her suddenly got very thick. "What?"

"That's right!" Savana clasped her hands together. "We're almost to the fun part! But for now, I want to finish my story. I knew there was some supplement that you were taking, I just didn't know to what scale. But when I read about Valania in my father's police records, I knew. I just *knew*. So I followed you home— silently. And soon enough—" Savana flashed a smirk. "You confirmed my suspicion. I made an anonymous tip to the police, and soon my father had men raiding the place— but *you*, oh you Leah Taven, somehow got away."

She tilted her head. "And now there's nowhere to run. No where to hide and no one to save you." Savana stepped closer. "My father could have you jailed for all you've done— a permanent stain on a once shining stone. But—" Savana pressed her tongue to her teeth. "But I want to offer you a separate solution. A small *mercy*."

"What do you want, Savana?" Leah snapped.

Savana's smile stretched— her fire burning red in her gaze. "An ultimatum, Leah. It's either I call the cops now and you go to prison—" she tapped Leah's nose. "Or you quit. Don't play basketball in college, don't even play next year. Cut ties with everyone connected to the game and concede that I am so much *better* than you."

Leah froze. She couldn't. *She couldn't*. All that work, all the moments Gael had— had… Everything would be lost. Her relationships, her goals; everything she had worked for every moment of every day of her life. The abuse, the sacrifice, the morphine, the *pain*.

All gone. All for nothing.

And Savana would win. *Savana*, who left. *Savana*, who demoralized her at every turn. *Savana*, who hurt Ezra to every extent. *Savana*, who was going to do much worse to Trisha.

Something in her changed in that moment. Her goals shifted, her fire burned with a greater rage. It wasn't about winning, it was never about winning. And now victory was no longer on her mind. Leah didn't care if she was loved anymore— no, that ship had long sailed. Care was pointless. Now, her only goal was to make sure Savana *lost*.

She turned, sprinting towards her car. This time, Savana didn't chase her; instead laughing in that sugary condescension.

"You can't drive away, Leah." Savana hummed. "You've already tried that, remember?"

Leah didn't respond. She stuffed the syringe in her pocket, the glass clinking against the vial of fentanyl. Her blows came fast— she wasn't in control anymore. Her rage and drug had consumed her, and now all essence of humanity had evaporated. The weapon was firing— poison shooting with the bullets; and now there was no controlling the casualties.

She knocked Savana to the ground, Leah looming over her. She pinned her wrists to the mud— halting her enemy's movement.

"Are you going to beat me?" Savana cackled. "Come now Leah, you're just making it easier for the prosecution."

But Leah wasn't going to beat her. No, Savana would be left with no bruises. Instead, she withdrew the drug from her pocket, filling the syringe with practiced perfection. She held the death with purpose, pressing the tip to Savana's neck.

"Morphine," Leah breathed. "That's what I was taking, morphine."

Savana snorted. "Your plan is to get me high? Oh Leah, you really have lost it."

"Oh," Leah grinned, running her tongue along her teeth. "You must be mistaken. This— oh *this* isn't morphine." Savana's eyes widened. "It's fentanyl. A hundred times stronger than anything I've ever taken. And a dose this size—" Leah dug the needle deeper into Savana's neck. "It will kill you in minutes."

The flame in Savana's gaze extinguished— icy horror flooding through her face. Her breath quickened as the revelation hit. And then she started to beg.

"Leah—" Savana gasped. "Leah no, you can't—"

She tightened her grip on the fentanyl.

"Oh, no Leah—" tears began to trail down Savana's cheeks. "*Please*! I don't — I don't—"

Leah tilted her head. Savana had been many things to her. A teammate, a friend— her brilliant enemy. Their relationship coursed through the waves of life for years— souring day by day. But just as the court was under their feet and the net hung over their head, one thing about them would never change.

Savana Afren would always and forever be an *opponent*.

So Leah stabbed the fentanyl into her neck.

THE TRAGIC LEGACY OF SAVANA AFREN

Leah embraced Savana as she died.

She pulled her close, resting her enemy's head on her shoulder as the drug seized control. The fentanyl took Savana's breath— at first it was erratic; the heaves for air attempting to get past the wall of death. But then the rise of her chest fell and her breath became shallow, and then negligible. Her life was replaced with a low, strained rattle.

Leah hummed her mother's lullaby while humanity drained from Savana. It wasn't loud; it wasn't overpowering. The syllables of her song synchronized with the strain of Savana's last breath.

When Savana went completely limp, Leah knew she was gone. Her dark brown skin had turned a murky ashen. The fire completely extinguished from her features and now her eyes held a terrified daze in death. Savana Afren would forever be left in fear.

With two fingers, Leah closed her eyes. She held them there until they stayed, and Savana entered her eternal sleep.

The entire overdose took two minutes. Two minutes of watching her die. After that, Leah got to work.

She dug her fingers under Savana's bandages, revealing just a peak of her forearms. Cuts and scars lingered over her skin— some new, some old, all horizontal. Done in such neat, organized lines— so intentional in her crutch.

Next, Leah opened Savana's fingers, placing the fentanyl syringe in her grasp. The vial was placed beside her, all contents pouring into the ground. The perfect picture of a suicide.

Leah arranged the cars next. She managed to haul hers out of the ditch and park it right behind Savana's. The needles that lived in her car were smashed — her heel grinding the glass to a fine powder. She discarded her drugs in the tall grass: so deep only a bird would find them. Then, she grabbed Savana's phone, unlocking it with her gray, ashen face and fabricated a story.

She typed the messages quickly— first from Savana's phone; vague threats of death and depressing notions. Then from her own, begging her not to die— pleading with her to keep her life.

Come to the cornfield. Right next to the highway.

Savana please! You have to think this through. Don't do it!

Don't try to stop me.

The final peace of her plan was herself. A tear stained face, a horrified expression. A girl who'd lost her closest friend. And when the tears started tumbling down her face, they weren't a facade. Her pain and grief were all too real.

"Nine-one-one what's your emergency?"

"My friend—" Leah gasped. "I think she might've killed herself. She texted me to meet her at the cornfield and when I got there—"

"Ma'am," the corresponder's voice was laced with tranquility. "I'm sending cars as we speak. Is your friend breathing?"

"No—" Leah choked. "Her skin's the color of ash. She has a vial of something in her hand, and— and a needle. I don't know what she took—"

"Emergency services will be there in under five minutes."

The phone beeped and the line died. Five minutes. Five minutes to say her condolences. Leah drifted to Savana's body. She was long gone; her chest hadn't held breath for minutes.

Leah knelt down, brushing Savana's hair behind her ear. She brushed her lips over her forehead— she was still warm, the remnants of life still clinging fruitlessly to her body.

"Forgive me," Leah murmured. "When the cold has grasped us both."

She took Savana in her arms, cradling her figure against her chest. The tears weren't forced— they weren't fake. They never were. The grief splattered on her enemy's face; as if the drops would somehow reverse what had just happened.

Leah barely noticed the police pull up to the scene. The red and blue lights reflected off Savana's skin. It didn't make her look anymore alive, didn't make the death evaporate from her body. She simply reflected the colors— no more inanimate than when her breath had halted.

Soon the hands were there, pulling her way from Savana's body. Her teammate's red hair disappeared behind a flock of officers— piecing together the perfect scene Leah had constructed

"The chief's daughter…"

"—overdose—"

"—self harm scars—"

"—fentanyl—"

"—she killed herself—"

Someone must've phoned Savana's father, because he arrived shortly. He cradled his daughter in his arms, loud sobs echoing around the cornfield. It was so perfect; such a tragic picture of father-daughter love.

But it was fake. So fake. That man didn't care— not about Savana at least. The only loss he suffered was the loss of a weapon who he called a daughter. A narcissist putting on an act— forever in performance of any emotion.

Someone gave Leah a blanket. She held it over her shoulders— watching as they put a tarp over Savana's corpse. At one point, a police officer tried to talk to her. But Leah didn't respond; she couldn't. She couldn't take her eyes off her teammate.

Ezra showed up. Leah didn't know how or why, but he was there. He didn't say anything, didn't come near the scene. But he was there— watching as they carried Savana's body away.

Him and Leah caught each other's gaze. They held still for a moment, a tragic history flickering between them. Ezra's gaze was unreadable— emotions crossed his face momentarily before fading into the dark. He knew what she'd done. Leah was sure of it. He always knew everything.

Ezra Soren was so smart— a genius among imbeciles. But at the same time, he was so unbelievably stupid. Just as his past had given him strength, it made him so unbelievably weak. So resilient to pain, but so, so susceptible to the aches that came close to home.

Leah was his home. They had gotten too close to each other and it was only destiny that the universe had to rip them away. Both were too broken— too shattered and too similar to love each other. There was no way— love was a spoil neither of them were granted.

But he held his tongue. She didn't know why; couldn't comprehend it. Perhaps it was for the sake of their old relationship. Or maybe he simply didn't want to lose another daughter.

Ezra drove away without a word, and Leah was left in the darkness. The police officers roamed the area, moving on from Savana's death to other things. Leah supposed a teenage suicide wasn't too big in the scope of things.

She caught Val's name. She had gotten away— of course she had. Val always got away. She was too smart to be caught, too brilliant to accept defeat, and too cynical to ever stop her dirty business.

Maybe she'd go to Stanford, back to Zahara. More likely she'd flee across the country, taking her assistance with her. It wasn't like she could be here anymore— the city had betrayed her, and now it would crumble without her help.

"Hey," a female officer placed a hand on her thigh. Leah staggered back, fear jolting her back to reality. The cop's hands shot up in an attempt to look non-threatening. Leah didn't buy it. "Let's get you home."

Leah scowled. "I can drive myself."

"Sweetheart—" the officer pinched her lips, pity contorting her face. "You're in shock. We can't let you drive."

Leah moved away from her, hands curling into fists. "Unless one of you can drive a manual, then I suppose I'm giving myself a ride."

The officer smiled— so light and fragile like a larger one may break Leah. "My colleague can do it. We can't let you go alone, sweetie."

Leah didn't respond. She slumped from the car trunk, shrugging off the blanket. Her car was ice cold— colder than it had ever been. Her entire world had been covered in an icy haze; her life had frozen over.

The drive home was silent. Leah spent it with her head on the window, looking out into the dark landscape. She had been alone her entire life— always fending for herself. But there were always people around her: people she thought she knew. Now, they were all gone.

Swan had quit. She was out there somewhere— oblivious to almost everything. Ezra hated her, and even if he didn't their relationship was too broken— shattered beyond recognition. And Savana—

Her enemy, her opponent. And yet the only one Leah had ever understood. They were parallels— one in the same. Each ready to sacrifice anything for their goals.

But there was one key difference. Savana was willing to hurt people. The scope of love had been beaten from her long ago, leaving her incapable of caring for anyone. Savana couldn't love at all.

And Leah loved too much. She was so scared of abandonment that she sacrificed everything— *everything* for those she cared about. Her body, her mind, her soul. Just like Zahara said she would. Except it didn't do any good. They all left anyway.

Maybe she should've just taken Savana's path; not let anyone into her heart. Maybe then she'd be the one laying in a morgue, finally gone from the cruelty of the world.

Leah sighed, pressing her knees to her chest. A tear drifted from her eye, trailing down her cheek and splattering on the floor. Gone. Like everyone she'd ever cared for. Gone like the tragic legacy of Savana Afren.

JUST A GAME

The next few weeks went by in a blur of withdrawals. Leah crawled her way to school, nausea slowly wrapping its shivering hands around her. The panic started only at night, then bled into the day and embraced her in its cold grasp. Then the aches came. And then the depression. And soon, she could barely move to get up in the morning.

But she did. Slowly— every day. She kept her grades just above an A minus, only enough to keep her GPA at a four point five. Just enough excellence to get her into Stanford, then she could rest.

She drove home fast— part of her hoping that another car would swerve and kill her. It would be a quick death: painless if she was lucky. But none ever did. She supposed the world finally decided to grant her some luck.

After she parked she would saunter into her room, lay on the floor, and close her eyes. The pain was always worse then— when all the demons towered over her. Remnants of Gael, Viren, Trisha, Ezra, *Savana*. They were always there— but not in company. Simply there, judging her, scolding her, torturing her.

And for once, Leah couldn't find the energy to care.

School ended on a warm Friday; kids yelping in joy at the summer ahead of them. Leah spent her summer break in her room, staring at the ceiling. Zahara was her only companion, whispering in her silky smooth tone. Leah couldn't understand what she was saying anymore. Honestly, she didn't care.

Savana was there too. But she wasn't a hallucination; she was a memory. A checklist of everything Leah had left to do. Her words— forever ingrained into her mind until Leah met the grave.

If you really thought he was so awful, you would've turned in that hard drive as soon as you found it.

And Leah did. She didn't go to the school this time; or the education board. No, she learned from Ezra's mistakes and took it right to the police. Hard, indisputable evidence.

She left it on the stairs of the station, hiding in the bushes until an officer picked it up. There was no trace of herself or Ezra on the tape— nothing that could possibly cause either of them any more pain.

Viren was arrested at one of the few high school practices Leah attended. The cops tackled him to the ground with a cruel ferocity— they had definitely watched the tape.

The freshman watched in horror as their coach was led out of the gym. Some of them started crying. Leah couldn't help but roll her eyes. She had found that tape as a freshman and she herself had gotten Viren begging for her mercy.

God, how this game had hardened her.

Ezra didn't testify, but he was at the trial. Leah knew he was— she had no proof, but she just knew. He had to watch Viren get charged with twenty three rape sentences. He had to see for himself that his abuser was finally going away.

Viren would die in jail. It wasn't a life sentence, but everyone knew he would die. Cellmates would kill him after they found out what he'd done to children. Even compared to murderous criminals, Viren was the cruelest type of man.

Savana's funeral was a week after she died. Leah made a point to be there— to appear mournful. It was dismissed easily as a suicide— her father adding to the case by pointing out her self harm addiction. The man knew, he always knew. But the cutting helped her play. Of course he didn't care.

They buried her in a dress. A blue one with sleeves and a turtle neck. Her blood hair was tied into a tight bun and her ashen face was caked with makeup.

That wasn't Savana. That was never Savana. Savana Afren was strong, unruly, and ever so broken. They hid her scars with her clothing, hid her rage with those colors, and hid her tragedy with the mask of makeup. Leah didn't know who was laying in that coffin, but it wasn't her enemy.

College admissions rolled around with Leah's senior year. Much to her counselor's disgust, she only applied to one university. Stanford. She sent her grades, her essays, and most importantly the videos of her playing. All a mask. The result that showed so little of the pain.

Every day that passed without the morphine was a new day of pain. Some moments Leah could barely walk. At first she tried to get herself to school— tried to function for just a few more months. But after a few weeks of unbearable nausea and sickness, she gave up.

She had already applied to college, already had all her grades submitted. There was no need to try anymore. She had already destroyed her body, mind and soul. And for the first time ever, this game couldn't take anything else from her.

Ezra's message lit up her phone one Friday night. For a moment, hope flickered into Leah's heart. But then she remembered— remembered exactly why she was laying on the floor. Remembered why her body was eating her from the inside out and remembered that Ezra didn't care about her anymore.

Game tonight. It's important. Be there.

Leah lifted herself off the floor, panic surging into her chest. She gasped, collapsing back onto the floor as shots of pain cascaded through her body. Tears fell down her face as she scrambled against the wall, chest rising and falling with the unforeseen terror.

She didn't know why it was there or why it came to bother her. But she knew it wouldn't leave. It never left, ever. It was the only thing that accompanied her; the only thing that would never abandon her.

With trembling hands, she grasped her desk, hauling herself to her feet. Her legs were fragile beneath her, as if they may shatter at any moment.

She leaned against the table, tears splattering onto the wood. Her hair tumbled down her back, falling over her shoulders and spilling onto the table. A breath breached her lips— quickly morphing into a choked sob.

"Agh!" she slammed her fist against the desk, the room trembling in response. "Fucking *work*!"

She reached for the blade lingering on the desk, grasping the hilt between her knuckles. The consideration of self harm had flashed through her mind briefly before, but she couldn't find the energy to grasp the knife. But now— now she needed the pain: the physical blood would distract her from the hurt boiling in her mind.

The metal was cold against her wrist. The blade cut smoothly, blood rising with a light sting.

It wasn't morphine, nor was it any other drug. But it would work. *She* needed to work. Just one last time, for everyone. One last performance.

~~~

Leah arrived at the game in a daze. She moved like a ghost, drifting past her teammates and sitting on the bench. No one moved to talk to her, no one bothered. But they all stared.

Stared at the girl who watched Savana die. They all thought it was a suicide —that's the police report at least. Unless Ezra had said anything different, that's what they believed. They always believed everything.
~~~

Ezra didn't make eye contact with her. Leah didn't try to look at him. They were too separate now— and barely a string of hasty respect lingered between them.

When the buzzer went off; the team drifted into warm ups. First shooting, then dribbling, then free throws. No one talked to each other, and if they did, Leah didn't notice.

She focused on the ball spinning in her hands, the way her shot finished in a perfect, crisp follow through. Each tiny detail of this game was practiced ten thousand times over.

And for what? All this pain and sacrifice for a college acceptance letter? No, that wasn't it. That was never it. She did it for the love— always for the love. The first thing she ever told Zahara was that she wanted someone to be proud of her.

Only then did she remember what her mentor said. God, how stupid she was. There was never a promise of love— never care. If anything, her tragedy was decided as soon as she became Zahara's protégé.

A hero or a villain, a martyr or a demon, Leah Taven, you will be known.

Oh, what a curse it was to be known.

The whistle blew. Ezra beckoned the team to his bench, clipboard at the ready. But Leah stayed, lingering beneath the basket.

"Leah!" Ezra called. "What are you doing?"

She was looking at the game. Really looking at it. For the first time in life, she noticed all its angles and fine lines. The way the net waved in the light breeze. How the wood reflected the ceiling. The paint, perfectly arched in the three point line.

Through all its victories and failures— all the imperfections and high expectations. All the pain and sacrifices for this court, and Leah was just realizing the truth.

She had sold herself to wood and paint. This game— the game she gave her life too— was really *just a game*.

Leah pulled her jersey above her head and off her body. She held it in front of her for a moment, weaving the cloth through her fingers. The number seven stared back at her. Zahara's number. Zahara's legacy. Their tragic legacy.

She let the jersey slip through her fingers, allowing it to fall to the floor. Then she turned away, walking out of the gym and leaving everything she ever was behind.

THE TRAGIC LEGACY OF LEAH TAVEN

After that game, Leah retreated back into her room. She lay on the ground, let her braids unravel, and closed her eyes. There was no eating or sleeping— those were virtually impossible. She just sat there waiting— the withdrawals eating her from the inside.

Her life ran in front of her, replaying every moment. The days with her mom— the ones she could barely recall. But she remembered her mother's scent— whiskey with a touch of lemon grass. It wasn't pleasant at all, but it was hers, and every time Leah hugged her, she felt like she was home.

Until she hugged her for the last time. When those drugs ate her alive. And then it was just her and Gael. All that love and comfort extinguished from her life forever.

He didn't even make an effort to try and raise her. His grief destroyed him— and it was Leah's job to make sure pain didn't swallow them both.

Serena met her then. It was recess in elementary school. She had pointed out Leah's eyebags, and suddenly, Leah had broken down crying. Best friends forever, she promised. Serena said she'd always be there for her.

And Leah supposed she hadn't broken her word yet. But she would, or she would get hurt. Everyone who got too close got hurt. The poison didn't discriminate.

Then there was Zahara— and the work. She really thought it would make her valuable; make her *lovable*. But really, it just proved to people that they could use her. That she was expendable— a shiny new weapon that ran until it faltered.

And then she found a way to stop her mistakes— to keep the weapon firing for eternity. And at that moment, she didn't care about the price. Because it meant that maybe, if she became good enough, she could be loved.

And for a short moment, maybe she was. Maybe Ezra did care about her, before all of it went to shit. Maybe he meant it when he said he'd never hurt her. Until her poison seeped into him too and dissolved any hope of the relationship.

But Trisha. Oh, *Trisha*. Her kid; her talented, amazing kid. The stray gunshot — the one that ran away on Leah's order.

She would make it. Leah was sure of it; smart and talented and running on Leah's final word to her. She would get away, live a long life, change the world.

And maybe, when she was higher than the clouds, she'd remember the girl who used to drive her to practice.

But both of them left. The two people she'd do anything for, and they abandoned her. Due to one vile, beautiful person.

Savana Afren. Her enemy and friend. Her only parallel— the girl who thought the same way she did. The girl who would do *anything* for success.

And Leah killed her. Not for victory. Not for love. For revenge. Against everyone she had ever hurt.

"Leah?" a knock followed the call. It wasn't Gael's voice— but softer. The door creaked open, revealing Serena peaking through the crack.

Leah rolled to the side, curling up on the floor. "Go away."

There was a brush of air. Serena knelt down next to her, placing her hand on Leah's side. She didn't have enough energy to remove it.

They didn't talk for a long time. Serena brushed her hair behind her ear, running a finger along the long strand. Leah pressed her knees to her chest, repulsed at the touch.

"Why haven't you given up on me yet?"

Her voice was so small— barely breaching the quiet. But Serena stopped stroking her hair, hand hovering over the floor.

"What?" Serena breathed. But she had heard her. Leah knew she had. She didn't answer, simply shrugging into a tighter ball.

Serena sat back, crossing her arms over her chest. "I haven't given up because I love you Leah." Her eyes widened. "Because through all you've done, through all you've been through, you're still that girl I used to gossip with before games. You're still the girl that rode the bench with me in middle school. You're still my *best friend.*" A sob cracked her voice. "And I still want you to be okay."

Leah sat up. It took a considerable amount of effort, the pain cascading through her body like fireworks. She propped herself against the wall, hair pooling around her.

"I'm not going to be okay, Serena." Leah looked down. "It's not possible."

"Yes it is!" Serena grasped her shoulders, a smile showing through her tears. "It is! You can come live with me; forget all about this awful charade. You can get better." Her hand moved to Leah's cheek. "*Please.*"

"No," Leah brushed off her hand. "I'm too far gone."

"We can get a doctor to help with the withdrawals." Serena said. "Patient confidentiality. We'll get you a therapist— you can file for emancipation. No one will bother you anymore. Leah I promise—"

Leah shook her head, putting up a hand. "Savana…"

"Oh," Serena's gaze softened. "I heard. You found her body. God, I'm so sorry." She flung herself around Leah. "But the suicide wasn't your fault—"

"It wasn't a suicide."

Serena released her. "What?"

"Savana didn't kill herself." Leah murmured.

A glance of confusion flickered over Serena's features before compassion rushed back. "It doesn't matter how she died. It doesn't matter what the circumstances were. It's not your fault and I can't imagine the pain you must be feeling—"

"Stop treating me like a victim!" Leah's shriek rang through the walls. Serena flinched away. "I am not *helpless*!"

"Leah I never said you were—"

"You wanna know what went down that night?" Leah drawled. "You wanna know what *really* happened to Savana Afren?" she leaned forward, her voice barely above a whisper. "*I killed her.*"

Serena took a shaky breath, tears filling her eyes. "No—" she swallowed. "Leah please—"

"Savana sabotaged every aspect of the game, punched me when I tried to make it right and told Ezra's rapist where he lived." Leah seethed. "So when she pulled me over on the side of the highway and threatened to put me in prison for illegal opiate use I pinned her down and pushed a full syringe of fentanyl into her neck." A tear leaked down her face. "I faked the texts, the story— fuck even the drug bottle in her hand. No one suspected a thing. But you wanna know the real truth? *I murdered Savana Afren.*"

Serena backed against the door, tears splattering from her chin and onto the floor. "No," she shook her head. "No, no. Please, Leah. Tell me you're lying."

Leah stayed silent, the fire lighting up her body for a final time. "You better get as far away from me as possible—" she breathed. "Before you're poisoned too."

A world of grief flickered across Serena's face. A final droplet slipped from her eye, splashing on the floor. Without saying a word, she rushed out the door, slamming it behind her.

It was for the best. This way Leah's poison could be confined to herself.

A light buzz echoed around the room. Leah picked up her phone, tapping on the notification.

Stanford. An acceptance to the school and the team. Leah read through the email once before taking a screen shot. With as much fake enthusiasm as she could gather, she posted the picture to Instagram.

The views piled up— people she barely knew commenting half-hearted congratulations. Was this the love she had fought so hard for?

Leah closed her phone, setting it on the ground. She placed her hands on the desk, hauling herself to her feet.

For a moment, she just looked. Looked at her room— the place she had her entire life to decorate: to make her own. But it was plain. Clothes littered the floor, the walls were blank, and a fine coat of dust fell on her desk.

Rooms were supposed to display someone's personality— someone's pride. But Leah's medals were stuffed carelessly into her desk drawers and the only hint that someone lived behind these walls was a picture.

Leah and her mom. She must've been around three— holding a basketball between her small hands. Her mother stood behind her, a bright smile painting her face. They both looked so happy: so full of life.

It was ironic now.

Leah wished her mother had died. If she had died, then she wouldn't have voluntarily abandoned her. But no— Leah still remembered that final click of the door, her blood curdling scream that followed.

"You'll be okay," her mother had leaned down, brushing a strand of hair from Leah's eyes. "I've left you enough to be okay."

"Mommy no!" Leah had sobbed. "*Please* don't leave. *I love you*!"

She hadn't responded— simply left. Gotten on a bus with all her drugs and left. Gael tried to find her once before. But she made it abundantly clear she loved her crutch more than her daughter.

Leah took the picture, raising it above her head and slamming it on the ground. The glass shattered— shards covering her floor.

"No..." a tear leaked from Leah's eye. Her knees buckled and she collapsed. "No no no no *no*!"

Her hands moved to her ears, covering them as Zahara's voice radiated around the room. She pressed her head against the floor, shards digging into her skin. The rivulets sank from her gaze, landing on the wood.

"I'm sorry Mom." Leah choked. "I'm sorry I poisoned you— I'm sorry I made you leave—"

She turned onto her back, long hair spreading throughout the glass. A scream ripped from her throat, echoing around the walls. The pain seeped from her pores— so much her body couldn't contain it anymore.

Her hands found her phone on the floor. With shaking hands, she tapped her mentor's contact. It rang three times before she picked up. And when her voice came over the speaker, Leah couldn't tell if she wanted to laugh or cry.

"Leah?" Zahara's voice was so kind: kinder than Leah ever allowed her memory to be. "Congratulations! I saw your post—"

"Does it get better?" Leah asked— her voice small.

There was a pause. "What?"

"You were right, Zahara." Leah murmured. "It takes everything and a bit. Your body, your soul, your mind. And I've made it." She took a breath. "Tell me it gets better."

"Leah," Zahara almost laughed. "I'm not sure I understand."

"I want it to go away." Leah sobbed. "I want— I want the withdrawals and abandonment and *pain* to go away. Please, Zahara. Does it ever go away?"

"Leah…" panic edged Zahara's tone. "What are you going to do—"

"*Tell me*!" Leah screeched. "Zahara *please*! Tell me it's worth it!"

Silence again. A choked cry came from the other end of the phone. "Leah please. Do I need to call the police? Are you okay—"

"*Zahara*." Leah's voice was stone cold. "I need you to tell me. Are you still on the opium? Are you still so exhausted you may pass out? Are you loved yet?"

Zahara swallowed. Her quiet was long— filling up the air with only the crackle of her sobs. Finally, she said something. "I can't answer that."

Leah nodded: a tear fell down her cheek. She set the phone down, replacing it with a shard of glass.

"No no *no*!" Zahara shrieked. "No Leah *please*! You can't—"

But Leah wasn't listening anymore. Zahara's voice faded into the background as she closed her eyes, tears trickling down her face. She smiled as the glass touched her throat.

She understood then. Understood everything. This story wasn't about her: nor Savana or Zahara. They weren't enemies or opponents, they were parallels. All the same, forced to fight for an inkling of love. And that fight had destroyed them: all of them.

It wasn't Leah's tragedy. It wasn't Savana's. It wasn't Zahara's. The tragic legacy touched them all. Their tragic legacy. Our Tragic Legacy.

Leah squeezed her eyes shut, a gentle smile curving her lips. *Hold your resiliency, Ezra. Never stop running, Trisha. Keep your hyperbolic warnings, Zahara. Don't get poisoned, Serena*. She dug the glass into her skin, blood seeping from the edge. *I'm coming, Savana.*

With a smooth, steady hand, Leah slid the glass across her throat.

AUTHOR'S NOTE

Knowledge, they say, is power.

And I completely agree. However the ability to learn and be educated has many other effects, especially on the widespread scale. Knowing your surroundings, rights and the difference between critique and abuse can greatly impact one's safety and life experiences. However, lack of such information can lead to naivety and blindly accepting maltreatment— especially if such ignorance is on such a wide scale.

That being said, when I wrote *Our Tragic Legacy*,I had three goals in mind. One— to create a dark, emotional sports tragedy that every current or former athlete could relate to in some way. Two— to spread valid information about abuse, doping and mental illness in sports. And three— to push for more studies and articles on athlete safety as a whole.

1.) Correlation between research and storyline.

To create a story containing all elements of the mental struggle in athletics, I focused on four main themes: abuse done by parents, abuse done by coaches, doping and mental illness.

Parental abuse: possibly the least researched out of the previously listed five categories is parental maltreatment. Leah's experience with Gael is primarily based on the few athletes who have dared to speak up about their childhood. This includes Christian McCaffrey, who spoke up about how his father "would ground him if he was 'jersey tackled' during games when he was seven or eight years old," in an article by Joshua Rogers. I also drew from Gretchen Kerr's "Neglect in Children's Sport" when referencing Leah's early years and experiences with her father.

Coach's abuse: repeatedly shown in studies to be the most common abuser in sports, coaches are frequently found guilty of sexual, psychological, physical and emotional abuse. I embodied this statistic with the character Viren— making him physically, emotionally and psychologically abuse Leah by tugging her hair, pushing her and hollering at her in front of people. He also physically and sexually abused Ezra through means of rape and sexual exploitation. Sylvie Parent's study "Sexual Violence Experienced in the Sport Context by a Representative Sample of Quebec Adolescents" finds that "0.5% of adolescents experienced sexual abuse involving a coach. When considering adolescents who experienced sexual abuse in their lifetime (10.2%), it appears that 5.3% of them were victims of sexual abuse by a coach."

Doping: Both Leah and Zahara doped opioids— I chose this drug because of its addictive and harmful tendencies but also because the article "Opioid Use in Athletes: A Systematic Review" says that "Opioid use among professional athletes at any given time, as reported in 2 different studies, ranged from 4.4% to 4.7%, while opioid use over a National Football League career was 52%. High school athletes had lifetime opioid use rates of 28% to 46%." (Ekhtiari, et al) These drugs also have awful withdrawal symptoms, ranging from nausea to personality disorders (Listos, et al), which brings me to my next subject.

Mental illness: this category stems from the previous subjects, but mental health problems are not exclusive to having these experiences. However, due to complex abandonment issues and a morphine addiction, Leah displays symptoms of silent borderline personality disorder, such as splitting and possessing a favorite person. Additionally, due to the abuse she experienced because of Gael and Viren, she experiences emotional flashbacks and low self esteem along with other symptoms of Complex Post Traumatic Stress Disorder. Savana, while also expressing narcissistic tendencies, also engages in self harm. Studies show that "60% of athletes… experienced psychological abuse: of those 60%, 24% suffered an eating disorder while 18% engaged in self harm." (Willson, et al).

2. Under reporting and the acceptance of abuse.

My second goal with writing Our Tragic Legacy was to spread information and awareness about sports abuse— but why does that need to be done? While research has been done to shed light on the harmful effects of behavior in sports, most of the studies require the consent of all parties involved— this includes coaches, parents, and other people who may be the perpetrators of wrong doing. Don't get me wrong; when it comes to these studies consent is 100% a good thing. However this filters the data pool because the parents, coaches, etcetera who know that what they're doing is morally wrong don't consent to the study. Therefore, the most reliable data produced about sports abuse has to come from athletes who were/are victims of it. This brings me to under reporting— which is a massive problem in sport. According to Erin Willson and Gretchen Kerr in their study "Prevalence of Maltreatment Among Current and Former National Team Athletes—" "Of those current and retired athletes who experienced abuse, bullying or discrimination, only 15% reported their experiences." Along with that, an athlete interviewed in the study said "Knowing we can be replaced and our careers are on the line, you are regularly forced to ignore issues or maltreatment out of fear. I have witnessed blackmail, intimidation, favouritism, experienced verbal and mental abuse personally. We are silenced or put down if you ask questions. I am fearful that after I speak out, I will be punished." The culture, power structure and normalities in the sports world not only hide abuse by making it acceptable, but punishes athletes for speaking out about such abuse.

3. My solution.

To get a reliable study and resources for more information on this topic, we need athletes to report their experience. However, with the under reporting problem, the results will be skewed and minimalized. Therefore, the source of the problem lies within the sports culture that is accepting of this kind of abuse. In order to get accurate reporting and information, athletes have to be aware of what abuse is and that it still exists in sport. Excessive screaming, pushing, using unhealthy amounts exercise as punishment and/or restricting food or water are all examples of abuse that would not be acceptable in a school or home setting. But in sport, those are normalized to the point of acceptance. Abuse needs to be talked about in the sport setting and athletes need to know what is and isn't okay— therefore having the knowledge, power and confidence to report and create meaningful and long lasting change in the sports world.

www.ingramcontent.com/pod-product-compliance
Lightning Source LLC
LaVergne TN
LVHW071124140526
838852LV00038B/462
* 9 7 9 8 9 9 1 0 2 9 3 5 3 *